MAREN MOORE

*To the man who taught me fear before love and taught me everything **not** to be…*

Your legacy ends here.

note from maren

It took me almost seven months to write this book. There were a few reasons for that but mostly because this story is deeply, profoundly personal to me.

At some points, it was very hard to write, but it was also cathartic and healed me in ways that I never anticipated.

I hope that you too can find love, healing and understanding within these pages. There is **always** a brighter day ahead.

All my love,
Maren

content warning

In my books you can always rely on having ample sugar and spice. My hope is that my stories are light, feel-good, swoony and fun.

The Bad Boy Rule delivers on all the usual Maren Moore banter, heart, and spice, but it does also deal with some topics that some may find triggering.

Content warnings can be found below. I value your mental health and well-being, but please note these might be considered spoilers for parts of the story.

<u>Content Warnings</u>
- Emotional and Physical Abuse by a Parent (mostly off page)
- Drug and Alcohol Abuse of a Secondary Character
- Toxic Familial Relationships
- Chronic Illness of a Child (briefly mentioned, very minor secondary character)

Content Warning

- Fighting/Physical Violence (on page)

playlist

Iris- MGK & Julia Wolff
how could u love somebody like me?- Artemas
Tattoos- Artemas
Cut my hair- Tate McRae
You Were a Dream- Artemas
Casual- Chappell Roan
Good girl- Artemas
Siren sounds- Tate McRae
Wet dreams- Artemas
Daylight- Taylor Swift
Lonely- MGK
I still say goodnight- Tate McRae
Fade Into You- Mazzy Star
Bow- Slowed Reyn Hartley
Zombie- YUNGBLUD
I Was Made For Lovin' You- YUNGBLUD
Family Line- Conan Gray
Sabotage- Bebe Rexha

To listen to the full playlist click here.

chapter one
SAINT

"GOD, you are such a *motherfucker*, Saint Devereaux."

Apparently, this is only a revelation to the naked blonde standing in front of me, who's still wiping my cum off her face.

She knew exactly what this was, or what it wasn't. It's not my fault she didn't listen when I told her.

It's simple.

I don't do sleepovers, I don't kiss, I don't cuddle.

I'm not the guy who's going to tell you everything you wanna hear, the one you take home to your parents or tell all your girlfriends about.

I'm the guy who fucks you better than you've ever been fucked.

I'm the guy you'll think about months later when you're taking it missionary from a finance bro that lasts three minutes and couldn't make you come even if his *trust fund* depended on it.

I leave a lasting impression, and it's in the shape of my cock.

That's the one and only promise you'll get from me. "Damn," I tut as I slide off her bed onto the furry pink rug on the dorm room floor. "That's the thanks I get for making you come two, no... *three* times?"

I swipe my T-shirt off the floor and drag it over my head. Everything in this room is so goddamn pink that it's giving me a headache, so the sooner I can get out of here, the better.

"You literally just came on my face, and now you're... leaving. Just like that?" she mumbles with a furrowed brow.

If I wasn't an asshole and I hadn't told her the score before sticking my dick in her, I might feel bad.

But unfortunately for her, I *am*, in fact, an asshole, and I *am*, in fact, leaving.

I quickly drag my sweatpants up my hips, grab my phone off the nightstand along with my keys before shoving them in my pocket, then turning back to her. "Just like that. I thought you understood what this was. Sorry that you didn't. Was fun though, yeah?"

Tossing her a smirk and taking one last look at her perky, full tits that undoubtedly are what got me into this shit in the first place, I brush past her toward the door.

"I should have listened to everything they said about you." Her words are thrown at me, dripping with venom, like they're meant to wound, but they fall flat.

Because I don't give a fuck what she or anyone thinks about me, and I never have.

I jerk my gaze back over my shoulder at her, the corner of my lip curving into a half grin, half sneer that makes her eyes burn even brighter with anger. "Yeah, probably should have. But whatever they said? I'm so much fucking worse."

I don't wait for her to respond before wrenching the door open and slipping outside. The second that I shut it behind me, there's a loud thud of something heavy slamming against it and a high-pitched screech from the other side.

Yeah, I've gotta chill with the hookups for a while because as much as I love getting my dick sucked, this shit has been a headache, and I've got enough headache-worthy shit in my life as it is.

And then some.

Speaking of headaches, I pull my phone out of my pocket, glancing down at the screen and seeing the time.

Goddamnit.

Now I'm going to be late, and I can't be late.

I can't afford to.

♥ ♥ ♥

It takes thirty minutes to get through campus traffic to the other side of town, and I'm late as fuck. I pull my bike into the last open bay of Tommy's Garage and cut the engine.

Generally, I'd leave it parked outside, but I know better. Growing up here, I learned quickly that this isn't the part of NOLA where you leave your shit outside at night and expect it to still be there in the morning.

So, when I work late at the shop, I park it inside with me so I can keep an eye on it because outside of hockey, my bike is what I'm most proud of.

A '53 Indian that I found with Tommy in a junkyard one day when I was fourteen.

He wanted to pull old parts for a rebuild he was working on, and since I was working at the shop that day, he let me tag along.

The bike wasn't shit to look at back then, an old heap of rusted metal, a battered relic from a time that no longer existed.

But I saw past the rust and mangled, wrecked pieces of metal. I saw the potential. I saw what it used to be and knew that I wanted to be the one to bring it back to its former glory.

I used every penny I had saved to buy it as it was, and I spent the next four years restoring and rebuilding it until it was no longer a shell of its former self but something I was proud as fuck of.

I learned everything I could from Tommy and the other guys so that I could save money on labor and do the work myself. I didn't have two pennies to rub together back then, so it was either that or I wasn't ever going to restore it.

Yeah, it might not be the fastest bike, but it's a fucking classic.

Timeless.

They don't make machines like this anymore.

This bike is the one thing in the world that's *mine*. The one thing my father can't fucking touch, and good thing because everything he touches turns to shit. Like a disease, infecting everything he comes in contact with.

"You're late," Tommy grunts without looking up from the Mustang transmission he's bent over. His voice is gravelly from the two packs a day he's smoked since he was younger than me.

I've got no idea how old he actually is, but if I had to guess, he's somewhere in his late sixties and still working at the shop daily, putting in more hours than most guys half his age.

He probably won't quit coming in until he's dead.

His dad opened this shop when he was a kid and named it after him so when he was too old to take care of it, it could be passed down to him. Only the legacy will end with Tommy because he's got no biological children of his own.

Just a few guys working here that give him more shit than his own kids ever would.

"Yeah, sorry," I mutter as I grab my old, grease-stained jumpsuit off the hook near the office and step into the legs.

I hate being late, and it's not something that happens often, especially for… extracurricular activities. I just lost track of time, and that's on me.

Finally, he looks up from the transmission and catches my gaze. The skin on his face is weathered, like it's been left in the sun for too long, and there's a thick streak of grease over his brow, smeared into a nearly perfect line.

"Thought we weren't going to make it a habit?" His brushy gray brow arches.

He's referring to last week when I was an hour late because I was dealing with shit at home, and I didn't want to leave Mom, but of course, he doesn't know that's the reason behind it.

I don't tell anyone the personal shit in my life, but if I did, it would be Tommy. He's an observant old fuck, and truthfully probably one of the only people in the world outside of Ma who gives a shit about me.

"We're not. Sorry, old man, won't happen again."

He hums but doesn't respond, instead looks back down at the socket connected to the transmission and continues working. He's never been a man of many words, but when he does speak? You listen.

"You should head to bed. I've got this. It's late." I walk over to the Mustang, pulling out the black bandana that I left in the pocket of my jumpsuit during my last shift and tying it at my nape to keep my hair out of my face.

It's too fucking long, but I haven't had the time or the extra money to worry about getting it cut. I've thought about buzzing it all off a hundred times with how hot it's been this summer but just haven't gotten around to it.

"Don't tell me what to do, boy," he grunts but still sets the wrench down on the engine and straightens. His back isn't what it used to be, and when he spends hours bent over the inside of a car, he's even more of a dick because he's hurting and would never admit it to any of us.

Pride's a funny thing.

"I'm not, but if you do everything, then what's left for

me to do?" I ask, my shoulder lifting in a shrug, playing it off. "I need the work."

I'm not lying; I need the money. Even if my dad somehow manages to keep this job for longer than a month, it's inevitable he'll do something to fuck it, get fired, and everything I've saved will go to making sure rent is paid.

Which isn't as much as I want right now.

"Yeah, yeah, I know. How's your ma doing?" His gaze finds mine as he reaches for his rag, cleaning up some of the oil from his hands. "She doing okay?"

"She's good."

Even though he doesn't really know the full extent of the shit that's going on, I think he suspects, and this is his way of asking without really asking.

He's likely suspected since the day I stumbled into the shop at fourteen with two black eyes and a busted lip, asking for a job when I didn't know the first fucking thing about cars.

It's probably the reason that he allows me to work the schedule I do, primarily at night, unless it's during the off-season and I don't have any classes scheduled.

Any work he doesn't get done with the guys during the day is what I handle at night.

We've made it work, and I like it this way.

The quiet.

The solace I get from the chaos at home.

And one day, I'll find a way to repay Tommy for doing this for me.

For offering me a place to sleep in the apartment above

the shop whenever I need. For never asking questions that I don't want to answer and probably never will.

He's given me so much over the last six years, and I'm not sure if he really even realizes. He's saved my life more than once.

Tommy nods, his sharp eyes crinkling in the corners. "That's good. Had a few cars come in earlier, hoping to get 'em out by the end of this week if we can. Damn electric car with a battery issue. Fucking shocker."

He hates electric cars, and if he didn't need the business, he'd probably turn them away at the door. Says America was better when it was muscle and not electric bullshit.

"Got it. I'll get it done. See you tomorrow," I respond, lifting my fingers in a salute.

For a second, he rocks back and forth on the balls of his feet, hesitating like he might say more, but after a beat, he nods, muttering a goodbye.

Thankfully, it only takes me a few hours to work my way through the cars, so I make it home just after 2:00 a.m.

I'm so fucking tired that I nearly fell asleep driving home, and I desperately need to catch up on sleep. I'm just gonna take a quick shower, scarf down some food, and hit the sack in the next thirty minutes, which means I should be able to get roughly six hours of sleep before my business economics class.

Now that classes have started again, I've got to cut back my hours at Tommy's. Hockey season is about to start, so between managing to keep my grades passing and the grueling practice, conditioning, and games schedule, I'll barely have time to sleep, let alone pick up any shifts.

I'm just going to have to rely on my savings to get me by.

Get *us* by.

Dropping my bag by the front door, I quietly kick off my shoes. My gaze bounces around the living room, landing on Ma curled up on the couch, sound asleep.

She looks so serene that it makes a space somewhere in my chest begin to ache. I wish that her life was easier and that she could have the peace she deserves.

But she never will. Not when she stays in this house with him.

I've tried to convince her to leave, begged her more times than I can count to let me find us both an apartment, but she refuses. She says that he's her husband and that she's not going to leave him, even when it's rough, that they made vows and she can't abandon them.

Like him trying to beat the shit out of her is a *rough spot*.

That's why I still live at home and not on campus in the dorms. Because I'm not leaving her here with him.

I can't. I'm fucking terrified of the thought of not being here to protect her.

There aren't many things that make me weak. Not when I've spent a lifetime building a wall around anything that could hurt me.

But Ma?

She's the softest spot I have.

I'd burn down the world for her.

Starting with *my father*, if that's what it took.

chapter two

LENNON

THERE IS ABSOLUTELY *nothing* I hate more than being late.

And of course, of all of the times for me to be late, it's now.

My type A personality is to blame, but after waiting months for this day to come, I don't want to lose any precious time.

Blowing out a frustrated sigh, I hike my bag higher on my shoulder with one hand and push through the doors to the rink with my other.

Crisp, bitter air hits my cheeks, a welcome reprieve from the hot, sticky air outside. I can't believe that it's been a whole entire year since I've been to a rink. A year since I've felt the ice beneath my skates.

It feels like much longer. Especially when you've spent over half your life doing what you love, only to have it ripped away in the blink of an eye.

God, I can't even imagine the coronary my father

would have if he found out I was doing this. I can practically see the crimson shade of his face and that vein in his neck that bulges when he gets angry.

But... he's not going to find out. I'm keeping this one secret all to myself, where it's safe and unable to be stolen.

For the first time in my life, I'm doing something for *me*.

And honestly, it feels... liberating. It's the first taste of true freedom I've had in longer than I can remember.

As I suck in the fresh air around me, a smile pulls at my lips despite the onslaught of nerves grouping in my stomach.

I know that it's more than likely I'll never skate competitively again. That my days of competing are probably over. It's been a year since I've been on the ice, and my body is no longer in the shape that it used to be. Not only that, but I no longer have a coach to rely on or expertly choreographed routines, and I've missed too much competition time. But regardless of whether or not I'll ever compete again, I just want to skate. Even if it's just for an hour twice a week. I want to be on the ice, where I've always felt at peace.

An excited shiver racks my spine, my fingers tightening around the strap of my bag as I come to a halt inside the entrance of the practice rink on campus. It's my first time at this rink, and while it's not as state-of-the-art as the arena where the hockey games are held, it's more than enough for what I need.

Especially because it's free. And I'm in absolutely no

position to be picky about something that I'm getting for free, not when it finally gets me back on the ice.

When my father forced me to quit competing my freshman year at OU, he decided that he would no longer pay for my coaching or rink rental because he thought skating was a waste of time, a distraction from me focusing on my studies and from becoming the perfect trophy wife that he raised me to be.

It was never *my* decision to quit, and a part of me has never been able to forgive him for taking something so important away from me. He took something that was a lifeline for me, and it became yet another thing he could control me with.

Little did he know, he fueled a fire of resentment inside of me that's only begun to burn brighter in the last few months.

I set my bag on the metal bleachers and pull out my skates, the same ones that I've had since high school, and quickly put them on, lacing them tight. It feels like second nature putting them on, something I've done a thousand times before, only now it feels like I'm reclaiming a part of me that was stolen.

That's what my father never understood. That figure skating was more than just a hobby for me, more than something I just did for fun.

Skating was my emotional outlet.

A way to deal with my anxiety when it felt like I was suffocating, where I felt like I could be myself, where I felt free and happy, and when he took it away, it felt like there was a fundamental piece of me that was ripped away with it.

One that I've been living without ever since.

Suddenly, something hits the glass in front of me, shattering my thoughts with a loud, resounding thump, and I jump, startled by the intrusion.

I've been so lost in my head that I didn't even realize that I'm not alone.

The sound of grunting and the echo of blades pinging against the ice has my gaze snapping to the figure surging across the ice.

Wait... Why *is* there anyone else here? This is supposed to be my *private* ice time.

I slowly step forward until my front is flush against the boards and narrow my eyes to get a better look.

The first thing I notice is the scuffed black hockey stick in his hand.

A hockey player.

Whoever he is, he's tall with thick, broad shoulders, hair dripping with sweat, so dark that it appears black, plastered against his face. For a moment, I'm frozen as I watch him sprint from one side of the rink to the other. It seems almost impossible for someone that large to skate that quickly.

A few seconds later, he comes to a sudden stop, slinging ice up as his chest heaves, reaching for a black water bottle that's sitting along the top of the boards. I watch as he squirts a stream of water into his mouth with a large gloved hand and then douses his face before slamming the bottle back down onto the edge. He turns back to the ice, skates to the red line in the center, and starts quickly stepping over each foot in a repetitive motion. Like a drill of some sort.

I clear my throat, plaster on a bright smile, and call out, "Hi!"

But he doesn't stop, continuing to move across the ice in rhythmic motions, stepping one foot over another.

Maybe he didn't hear me.

"Hi!" I say again, louder this time, stepping out onto the ice in a slow glide. There's a slight tremble in my legs, mostly in anticipation of finally being back on the ice. I skate closer until I'm almost at the space where he's practicing. "Um… Hello?" My words come out a bit louder than intended, my greeting crassly bouncing off the walls of the rink, causing my cheeks to heat when he whips around, dark eyes landing on me.

His brow arches. "Heard you the first time."

"Okay, well, uh… hi. Sorry to interrupt, but I think maybe there's been some type of mix-up? This is supposed to be my scheduled ice time. *Private* ice time that I booked months ago."

Unhurriedly, he skates closer to where I'm standing but says nothing, just stares down at me with an annoyed expression. His brows are furrowed, lips pulled into a slight scowl. As if my stopping him from whatever he was doing was the biggest inconvenience he's had to experience today.

Now that he's closer, with only a few inches of ice separating us, I can make out his full features. Without skates, he must still be well over six feet, easily towering over my short five foot two. His tousled hair is drenched from sweat and water, the unruly strands nearly falling in his eyes as he peers down at me.

His eyes are deep brown, nearly the same shade as his hair, and appear almost black with how intensely he's narrowing them. High cheekbones, sharp jawline with a dust of fresh facial hair.

He's built like most hockey players, broad and powerful, only he seems more... intense.

Reaching for the hem of his black hoodie, he lifts it to wipe away the sweat trailing down his face, revealing a set of contoured abs and a small trail of hair leading into the waistband of his sweatpants. The sleeve of his hoodie bunches just enough to reveal a splash of dark ink circling his wrist that trails up and disappears beneath the fabric.

I realize that I'm staring at this point, so I quickly drag my eyes back to meet his, slowly shifting from one foot to the other.

Get it together, Lennon. It's not the first time I've been around an attractive hockey player. I've been at a rink nearly my entire life, and I've learned that most, if not all... are *exactly* the same.

Cocky. Arrogant. Complete womanizers.

Not to stereotype anyone, but just my personal experience.

His brow arches. "Private ice time, huh? Obviously not, since it's mine."

My mouth falls open slightly at his bored and dismissive tone.

Ummm, alright. That's rude.

I blow out a small exhale and paste on a fake smile, the same one I've practiced for the majority of my life. I am a Rousseau, after all, which means that I've perfected the art of poised and put together, even when I feel anything but. "I think there must have been a scheduling error of some kind because this is the time I chose based on my availability."

For a moment, silence meets what I've said as his gaze travels down my body in an unhurried perusal, like he's actually only now seeing me for the first time. When his eyes drop to the white athletic skirt and tights covering my legs, the corner of his mouth tugs up into a smirk that seems entirely condescending and patronizing without even speaking.

His gaze lifts back to mine. "I'm not giving up my ice time, *princess*. No matter how much your parents probably paid for you to have it."

What?

"Excuse me?" I mutter in disbelief. "You don't even *know* me."

The dark pools of his eyes move down to my skates, where he nods. "Expensive skates? Diamond ring on your finger? Don't have to."

My gaze drops to my feet, then back up to meet his cocky smirk as I cross my arms over my chest.

Not that I need to explain anything about myself, but I've had these skates for years, since I last competed. I can't even really be upset with him judging me when I'm guilty of doing the very same thing about him a few minutes ago. Except I had the decorum to do it internally and not to his face.

"My parents didn't pay for anything, not that it matters. I have every right to be here just as much as anyone else does. Just as much as *you* do."

The arrogant expression on his face dims slightly, and he skates even closer, closer than what would be socially acceptable, but for some reason, I stay rooted in place, unwilling to back down and give him exactly what he's expecting.

"Still... not... leaving." His words are low and heavy, his brow arching as he says them.

"Neither am I." I lift my chin. "Seems like we're sharing the ice, then, doesn't it?"

What I should do is grab my phone and call Summer, the coordinator for the rink. She'll probably be able to get this fixed in no time, but now I'm staying here solely on principle. Just to show this jerk that he can't bully people into submission.

That cocky smirk returns, his gaze dropping to my lips, then languidly returning to meet mine. "Not big on sharing."

I match his smile with a saccharine one of my own. "You should probably work on that. Better late than never." Skating backward, I leave him on the other side of the red line and wave my hand toward the divide. "You stay on your side, and I'll stay on mine. Easy."

"Fine." His tone is clipped.

Now, I'm just being petty, but he doesn't get to have the last word. "*Perfect.*"

I can practically see his eyes roll from here before he

turns and skates back to the pucks on his side, then slaps one with his stick, sending it down the ice.

Turning my back to him, I skate to the other side of the rink, doing a few slow circles to get warmed up. I'm hoping that it'll be like riding a bike, getting back into training and practicing.

Although today, I won't be doing anything but reacquainting myself with the movements. Easing myself back into it.

I have a habit of jumping all in when it comes to anything that I'm excited about, so I have to mentally tell myself that I'm out of shape, that I haven't been on the ice in a year and I can't come out the gate doing the same thing I once was able to without injuring myself.

Even if I want nothing more than to show up this jerk, who is absolutely the reason for my distraction today.

It's impossible to ignore his hulking presence as I skate, but eventually, the hour is up, and we're both making our way toward the exit.

Before I step off the ice, I turn toward him.

He skids to a stop in front of me, purposefully slinging up a spray of ice in my direction.

"Oh my—" I yelp as it covers my front, clinging to my face, the front of my shirt, skirt, and legs. I blink up at him, disbelief momentarily stealing my words, before wiping away the melting ice from my face and flinging it.

Oh, this… *dick.*

"Are you freaking kidding me?"

His lips roll together as if he's trying to stifle a laugh, and for a second, I'm worried that my restraints have snapped, and I just might take him out with the blade of my skate.

"Whoops." Clearly, he's not sorry, judging by the smile on his face.

If looks could kill… Well, then he might be the reason I end up on a true crime podcast.

Asshole.

I inhale a breath that's meant to calm me but only seems to make me more annoyed when I feel the cold ice seeping through the fabric on my chest to where I can even feel the bitter bite through my sports bra.

He brushes past me off the ice, nearly checking me with his shoulder, and I whip around. "Oh, don't worry, *I'll* reach out to Summer and figure out what's going on. Please don't stress yourself about it. You're a dick, you know that?"

A beat passes before he turns back to face me, amusement or something much like it dancing in his eyes. "Yeah, that's what I'm told."

I'm contemplating taking my skate off and chucking it at him when his eyes travel down to my chest, and his lip curves into a grin. "Might want to get out of those wet clothes. It's cold in here."

My eyes widen, and I glance down, realizing that my nipples are hard and pebbling beneath my top, and immediately cross my arms over my chest with a scandalized gasp.

Jesus, this just keeps getting worse and worse and worse. I'm so beyond ready to leave and hopefully, with any luck, never have to see this dick again.

I steel my jaw before asking, "What's your name? So I can be sure to tell Summer that I'd rather choke and die than ever share the ice with you again."

Without turning, he calls over his shoulder, "Saint. Devereaux. She'll know exactly who I am."

"Oh? Nice to meet you, *Satan*. I'm Lennon. Rousseau. Hopefully, you'll forget it before you make it out of the building."

Even though he's got his back turned, I lift my middle finger to send him off.

chapter three

LENNON

THE ENTIRE WALK HOME, I replayed the last two hours in my head, and by the time I get to my apartment fifteen minutes later, I'm even more annoyed than I was at the rink.

I've never met someone so… rude and condescending. Completely unprovoked.

Like seriously, who does this guy think he is?

I slam the front door shut behind me and drop my pink quilted skating bag down onto the floor with a loud sigh, toeing off my tennis shoes by the welcome mat.

"Maisie, you home?" I call out for my best friend as I make my way down the hallway.

When I walk through her bedroom door, passing through the strings of brightly colored beads that hang from the top of the frame, I spot her on her latest thrifting find—a vintage, oversized velvet reading chair that looks like it's straight out of the seventies. She's lying on her back with her head dangling over the edge, her wavy blonde hair cascading beneath her like a waterfall as she holds a worn paperback above her face. She almost had a heart attack when we found it at one of our favorite antique places in the French Quarter.

I'm not surprised in the least to find her here, sprawled out on a chair, book in hand. If there's one thing about Mais, no matter where she is, she's likely got a romance novel within arm's reach. Almost always a paperback because she refuses to read on an e-reader or an iPad, saying that there's absolutely nothing that could ever replace the feel or the smell of old pages.

One of the things that we both wholeheartedly agree on.

"Ah… *Fabio's Revenge*. That's a new one. Sounds suspenseful," I say, eying the yellowed, worn pages of the book with the bodice-ripper cover featuring a half-naked guy clutching a girl in a torn ball gown.

She tosses the book down beside her on the art deco–printed chair and flips over to her stomach with a wide grin, waggling her pale blonde brows suggestively. "I found this used bookstore outside of campus when I stopped in between my creative writing class, and there was a whole *box* of these, Len. Literally a gold mine."

As many things as we have in common, there are twice as many things that we are complete opposites about. And I think that's exactly what makes our friendship work. It's always been easy with her, and in the fifteen years that we've been friends, I feel like there's no one who knows and understands me the way that she does.

Maisie has always been my safe place to land. She's the

one who keeps all my secrets and is honest even when it hurts. She tells me when I'm wrong and would defend me with her dying breath, even if I was wrong. We've always had each other's backs, and now that we're at OU and roommates, I can't imagine what my college experience would be like if I didn't have my best friend with me.

Certainly less exciting.

Suddenly, her brow pinches tight. "What's going on? You look… annoyed."

See? Uncanny ability to read me like a book. Almost two decades of friendship will do that to you.

Sighing, I flop down onto her bed and peer up at the ceiling she's covered in retro floral wallpaper. "Probably because I just met the biggest asshole ever at the ice rink."

I hear rustling, and then she's bounding onto the bed and flopping down next to me, propping her head up on her arm. "What happened?"

"God, you should've been there, Mais," I say, sitting up from the mattress and crossing my legs. "I showed up to the rink for my ice time, which is supposed to be mine for an hour, and there was a guy there. Which, I thought, was no big deal. Clearly, there had just been a mix-up. Except he was the biggest prick ever and rude to me for absolutely zero reason. I mean, a grade A asshole. Seriously. But then again… he was a hockey player, so I can't say I'm entirely surprised. "

"Did you get his name?"

My shoulder lifts in a shrug when I think back to our parting words. "Saint? Devereaux? Satan is more fitting, therefore I'm only referring to him by that from here on out. I don't think I could've handled another second around him before I ended up in a jail cell."

It's not as if he was exactly conversational when he was too busy being an ass.

When Maisie's breath audibly hitches on his name, my brows lift in confusion.

"Shut up. Shut up. Shut *up*," she nearly screams, her eyes widening. "*Saint Devereaux?*"

The space between my brows furrows in confusion. "I guess? He is absolutely not any sai—"

"Wait," she cuts me off. When she sits up abruptly, I'm even more confused by the expression on her face. "Six foot four, dark brown hair, broody eyes, bad attitude, right?"

I nod, and she continues. "Oh my God. You're telling me that you've never heard of Saint Devereaux?"

"Nope." The *p* in my response pops as I shake my head. "Can you tell me why you're freaking out right now?"

"He is literally a legend at OU, Len. I mean, he's a dick, but still," Maisie says, eyes widened.

Hmm. Now I'm intrigued. The only thing I learned about this guy was that he's an ass with a capital *A*.

If we're basing anything off a first impression, I'm good with never having a second.

"This is the most exciting thing to happen to me all year," she squeaks. "*Of course* you'd end up face-to-face with the biggest playboy on campus, who's notorious for leaving a trail of broken hearts. There's literally a rumor that he's slept with the entire cheerleading team. Like... every single one of them. Multiple... at once."

I do the math on that in my head and scrunch my nose. If that's true, he's got to be exhausted. I don't even get a word in because Maisie continues rattling off. "Ugh, he's ungodly hot. You'd have to be blind not to notice that, Len, come on."

Sure, he's... attractive.

But... he's also way more of a jerk than he is hot, so it completely cancels out.

Trust me when I say I've had enough experience with one egotistical, womanizing asshole to last a lifetime.

Gross.

"Yes, well, honestly, I was trying not to knock him out with his own hockey stick, so I was a little preoccupied." I snort.

"That's fair. But you're the minority. Girls throw every ounce of self-control out the window and toss themselves at him on, like, a daily basis."

My brows are knitted tightly together as I peer over at Maisie. My best friend is the furthest thing from the rumor mill to ever exist, so I'm starting to wonder how she even knows about this guy. "How is he such a player if he's that much of a dick? I can't imagine anyone wanting... that."

"Dunno. But a girl from my creative writing class was talking about him the other day, that he slept with a girl and then just said thanks and then walked out. He didn't even put his shirt on before he left. He walked all the way down sorority row shirtless, with everyone looking at him.

I mean, obviously, no one cares if he's broody if he has good di—"

I reach out, slapping my hand over her mouth to cut her off, my eyes wide. "Okay, can we not objectify the jerk that I met earlier today? Seriously, I do not want to think about him any more than I have to."

The sound of Maisie's giggles floats past my hand, and I pull it away with a laugh as she says, "Fine. Skating with him should be lots of fun…"

Uh, yeah, right.

"Mais, he was a total prick. Trust me when I say there is absolutely not a 'fun' bone in that asshole's body. Honestly, I never want to have to see him again, and if I do, it'll be far too soon. Today was *more* than enough. I'm going to call Summer first thing tomorrow morning, and I know that she'll get this all straightened out. Then I can pretend this entire thing never even happened."

For a beat, she stares at me, rolling her bottom lip between her teeth as she bites back a knowing grin.

Seriously, she can think whatever she wants, but there's not going to be a repeat of today. It was a one and done, and I plan on never having to subject myself to that torture.

Ever. Again.

chapter four
SAINT

UNLIKE A LOT of the guys on the team, I'm a morning person. It's always been that way.

Comes with the territory of pretty much working a full-time job since I was in high school in order to keep a roof over my head and food on the table. If I didn't do it, I wouldn't eat. Providing for his wife and kid is something that my dad should've been doing, but he was too fucked-up to do anything other than try to drink himself to death.

And even though most of us have been doing this for years now, my teammates still waste their time bitching and complaining about having to be up at 5:00 a.m. for a practice skate.

It didn't make a difference to me.

When everything started imploding and going to shit in my life, I turned to the one and only thing I had: hockey.

It's been my escape for as long as I can remember. It saved me. It gives me an outlet, a way to get out every ounce of my aggression without getting into trouble that I already can't afford.

I've been obsessed with the game since I picked up a stick for the first time when I was seven and learned early on the more I pour into it, the better off I'll be.

I once heard this saying in a class back in high school that you are a product of your environment. Meaning that if you were raised by fuckups, then nine times out of ten, you're going to become the very same fuckup.

It's statistics.

But if nothing else, I'm a stubborn motherfucker, and I refuse to let that happen, if not for myself, then for my mom. Because she deserves at least one good thing in her life, and I want to make her proud.

I know that she loves me, but my mother is a victim. She's fallen prey to my father's narcissistic, brainwashing bullshit and abuse. That's what motivates me, pushes me harder, to be the best and accept nothing less.

Her.

My plan has always been to get drafted by the NHL, and then I can put her in a nice house in a safe neighborhood that's not falling apart. Get her anything she needs or wants without blinking or having to think twice about where the money will have to come from. So I can take her the fuck away from my father and make sure she's safe, cared for, *happy*. Until then, I put my head down and keep the tunnel vision.

Besides, I would never give my father the satisfaction of ending up like him.

And that's why whenever I'm exhausted and weary, I remind myself of that very thing.

How no matter what hand I'm dealt, I'm going to be more than just the poor kid from the wrong side of the tracks with a shitty life and an even shittier father. More than the kid who had to pay for dinner in quarters or had to take secondhand hockey gear because it was all he could get. But mostly how much I *can* never fucking be like him.

Sticking the end of the hockey tape in between my teeth, I work on wrapping the end of my stick, shifting it back and forth in my hand to make sure it's taped correctly.

"Hoooooooly shit," a voice sounds from beside me as my teammate Bennett Legros flops down onto the bench, dropping his hockey bag on the floor next to him. "I have to tell you what the hell happened to me this weekend. You're not even going to believe it."

Let's be real, my tolerance for people in general is pretty fucking low. Never been much for small talk. I can barely tolerate my teammates, and that's really because I have no other choice.

But if there was anyone I could *almost* call a friend, I guess it would be the dramatic, cocky, and completely unaware-of-personal-space goalie sitting beside me.

We've been playing hockey together for the last two years, and the fucker just has a special talent for weaseling himself in, so I couldn't get rid of him if I tried.

Trust me, I've tried. Until I was blue in the face, but apparently, "fuck off" in Bennett language is "love me forever."

"Yeah, something tells me I'm going to believe it if it has anything to do with you," I grunt my retort, glancing back at my stick and pretending that I didn't spend the last five minutes taping it just so I can cut this conversation short.

"Listen, dude, honest to God, I accidentally found a dead body." His voice is exasperated, but there's a hint of awe in his tone like it's the most exciting thing that's happened to him all month.

"You know I actually do believe that, Legros, because whenever there is *shit*, you're not far behind."

"What can I say? It follows me around," he mutters, unzipping his bag and pulling out his water bottle. He might annoy the shit out of me the majority of the time, but he's one of the best goalies I think I've ever seen.

As long as I've been playing hockey, I've learned one thing: goalies are a whole different breed, and Bennett is no exception.

He starts to suit up for practice and shakes his head. "It was wild. The one time I decided to go off campus and go to Bourbon like a fucking tourist, and there's a dead dude in the middle of the street. It was traumatic, to say the least. Fuck, I think I might still be a little drunk."

"Well, you were on Bourbon Street, so I'm not really sure what you expected."

Shrugging, he rakes a hand through his hair. "I mean, I went there for a good time and… a hand grenade because you know that's my shit, not the coroner on the literal corner."

I roll my eyes, and he just smirks, a shit-eating grin that

reveals teeth that are far too perfect for a dude that plays hockey, but he's like me and never takes off his mouth guard. "Surprisingly, though, finding a dead body is not the talk of the campus. *You* are."

"Enlighten me. Why am I the topic of conversation this week?" I sigh.

"Everybody's talking about your little stroll"—he waves his fingers through the air—"down sorority row in nothing but underwear. Jesus, dude, can you leave a little for the rest of us?"

Figured that would probably happen, but whatever. People are always going to talk; who gives a shit if it's about me or something else. What they waste their time on is not my concern.

If I cared what people thought about me, I wouldn't have time to worry about anything else in my life.

So what... I like to fuck and blow off steam. Sometimes I walk down sorority row in my boxer briefs because a girl kicked me out when I reminded her that it was a one-night thing.

I don't drink. I don't do drugs. And I don't stick my dick in the same girl twice.

I've got it down to a science.

A few of our teammates begin to filter into the locker room ahead of practice, offering us a nod and not much more. They already know I'm not much for conversation off the ice. I might be an asshole, but I'm an asshole who's damn good at hockey.

That's all I'm here to do. I'm not here to make friends. I'm not here to do anything but pave my way to the NHL.

That's it.

That's all it boils down to.

The rest is just a distraction, and I can't *afford* distractions.

That's why I signed up for extra ice time. Because I needed some extra time to work on improving my agility on the ice and conditioning, my stick-handling speed. Failure isn't in my vocabulary, so that means that I have to push myself to the limit.

My position for the Hellcats is left winger, which means I spend a lot of time battling for pucks, intimidating the other team, causing them to fuck up so they draw a penalty and we can have an extra guy on the ice. Unofficially, my title is the enforcer, the one who pushes them to the limit and makes them snap.

But what a lot of people don't understand is that unlike the NHL and a lot of minor leagues, there's absolutely no fighting in college hockey. The NCAA does not fuck around with fighting on the ice, point-blank. You fight? You're thrown out of the game, and then you're not useful to your team at all. So as much as I like to get my aggression out on the ice, check the fuck out of guys, talk shit to them, back them into a corner, I do it without hitting anyone. But off the ice? That is a different story.

You'd think after all the fights that me and my old man have gotten into that I wouldn't want anything to do with it, but maybe... I just like a little touch of violence sometimes. Call it daddy issues, call me depraved or whatever the fuck you want, but it doesn't make it any less true. At least I'm self-aware.

I set my stick down beside me and work on lacing up my skates while Bennett is prattling off about his night on Bourbon when it hits me.

Who better to pump for information than the guy who knows everybody's business on this entire campus?

Don't ask me how, but he somehow manages to be more involved with the drama than half the girls I know.

Turning to look at him, I lift a brow. "What do you know about a Rousseau? Lennon?"

Legros blows out a whistle, shaking his head. "Oh, *Lennon Rousseau.* I'm surprised you don't know who she is."

I shrug. "Should I?"

At first, I *didn't* recognize who she was when I saw her stomping onto the ice, her face set in polite determination, words dripping with a saccharine sweetness that I could practically taste even from across the ice.

Even when she yelled her name as I was walking away, it still didn't fully hit me.

Rousseau's a fairly common last name in New Orleans, but then I realized where I knew her from. That article in the *Gazette*. The one where I saw her standing, poised and proper, next to her piece-of-shit father, looking every bit the pet that I would expect her to be. The article painted her family as the perfect Stepford family, complete with a white picket fence, but I knew better. I knew there was more than what they wanted the world to see.

Because it didn't divulge any of Rousseau's transgressions, the ones I'm all too familiar with.

The realization slammed into me like a truck, causing

me to replay our interaction over and over in my head. I suddenly hated that my very first thought about her was how hot she was and imagining that sassy little mouth in a hundred different ways involving my dick now that I knew who she was.

Yet the girl with the fiery red hair and a mouth to match plagued my thoughts the entire weekend, whether I wanted her to or not.

So yeah, I know who Lennon Rousseau is. But I'm not going to be telling Bennett that because I want to learn whatever I can about her. What the newspaper and social media *didn't* say. That's the shit I need to know.

"Everyone knows who she is. She's little miss perfect. On the dean's list, the honor society, president of the Social Club bullshit. Volunteers at charities and shit. Doesn't party or do anything remotely fun." He leans closer as he says, "Dude, if you're thinking about trying to hit that… think again. She's off-limits even to *you*, the mighty Saint Devereaux. "

That can't be true because I'm fairly certain there's not a single girl on this campus who's insusceptible to my charm.

I arch my brow. "Off-limits?"

He nods, his lips twitching. "Yeah, so rumor is she has some kind of pact to stay a virgin until she gets married or something. It's like this unspoken thing that everyone knows about. Got a whole-ass promise ring and all. Heard it from a couple guys who tried to hook up with her. So if you're looking for an easy hookup, she's not it, man."

A virginity pact?

This whole thing just got a lot more interesting.

Alright, Lennon Rousseau, you have my attention.

chapter five
LENNON

WHEN FRIDAY FINALLY ROLLS AROUND, I'm dreading it. Something I never thought I'd say.

Is it possible to loathe someone you've met once and only spoken a handful of sentences to?

I'm fairly sure the answer to that is yes, because the last thing I want to do is willingly spend any length of time around Saint Devereaux, yet due to the joke that is currently my life, it looks like that for the foreseeable future, I have no other choice.

Turns out, there *has* been a mix-up with our ice time, and there is no additional time available.

Nothing.

Nada.

Zilch.

Despite nearly begging Summer for quite literally *anything* else. I was willing to take whatever scraps she would give me if it meant that I wouldn't have to be around him again.

But as sympathetic as she was for the mistake on her part, she didn't have anywhere for either of us to go.

So, my only option? Share the time slot with the devil himself or... lose it.

And I *can't* let that happen.

If I don't use the rink at school, then that means that, once again, I'm going to have to give up skating. That feels cruel to think about when I've only just gotten it back. I can't afford private ice time at a club rink, especially because this is something I have to keep from my parents, and dumping likely a thousand dollars a month into anything is going to flag them, without a doubt.

The majority of this week was spent trying to come up with a plan, something, *anything*, as a solution to what I didn't even think was going to be a problem that has turned into a much larger one in a very small span of time.

And I came up with exactly... nothing.

It looks like I'm just going to have to suck it up and deal with it. Honestly, my plan is to ignore him entirely and focus on what I came to the rink for—training.

I've spent too long letting the things I want take a back burner to the plans my parents have laid out for me.

They've dictated every aspect of my life for as long as I can remember.

What I wear, the friends I hang around with, the plans for my future, my extracurricular activities, the classes I take... even who I dated.

And now that the veil has been lifted, I see just how much control they had and how little I did.

It's never about *my* hopes, *my* dreams, *my* ambitions. So getting back on the ice is the next step in reclaiming *me*.

I can't even imagine what's going to happen when I tell them that I'm going to be stepping down as the president of the Social Club, New Orleans's highly esteemed club comparable to the Junior League. A leadership role they've been preparing me for since I was practically in diapers, the perfect stepping stone and resume builder for a future New Orleans socialite… and trophy wife. The more I think about my parents' lives being my future, the more sick to my stomach I feel. The truth is, I'm not sure what I even want my future to look like. I just know that it isn't being my father's puppet on a string.

My phone chimes, the sound pulling me out of my thoughts. The screen is lit up, unopened notifications and the time glaring back at me.

Shit.

If I don't leave now, then I'm going to be late, and I refuse to be late after last week.

Grabbing my skating bag off the floor, I toss it on my shoulder and head out the door to the rink.

I hate that I'm no longer looking forward to today. That asshole Saint, better known as *Satan* as he should've been named, is tainting something that I've been so excited for. I've been counting down the days until I could be back on the ice, and now I've got a sinking feeling in the pit of my stomach, and it is entirely his fault.

The whole walk to the rink, I give myself a pep talk, reminding myself that I'm lucky to be here, and I should be grateful that I have the time, even if I have to share it with someone who makes me want to commit a crime.

I'm going to focus on the plan that I put together to achieve my goals, and the rest is white noise.

No distractions.

When I finally get to the entrance of the rink, I take a deep, hopefully calming breath as I wrench the door open and step inside, glancing down at my watch.

I'm actually a few minutes early. And the best part?

Inside is blissfully *silent*.

Which means that I've managed to make it here before he did.

My lip curves into a grin as I make my way over to the bleachers and set my bag down, open it, and pull out my skates. It doesn't take me long to get them on and laced tightly. I unzip the fitted jacket I wore over my top and set it next to my bag so I can stretch.

Standing, I walk to the boards and lift one leg to rest my skate on top, folding forward to make sure my hamstrings are properly stretched. They're always so tight, it helps me to spend extra time working them out. The last thing I want is to get injured because I didn't take enough time to stretch.

"Come to watch me practice?" a deep, gravelly voice sounds from somewhere behind me. "Cute. You didn't strike me as a bunny, but then again… "

A surprised gasp escapes the back of my throat as I drop my leg and whip around so quickly that my head momentarily spins.

My gaze narrows when I see Saint leaning against the

boards, wearing a cocky grin, elbow propped along the top, staring at me.

God, I hate him.

I barely know him, and yet I hate every single thing I've learned about him.

I cross my arms over my chest, squaring my shoulders. "Trust me, the less time I have to spend being graced by your presence, the better."

"Ah, now, that's rude. Not what I expected out of OU's *golden girl*."

"Well, we've already established that you don't know me, so you know what they say about assuming. Makes an ass out of you… Seems like it's a habit for you? I guess just another one of your sparkling personality traits."

His grin widens, and it momentarily catches me off guard, disarming the confidence I've been clinging to. I swallow hard, ignoring the flutter in my stomach.

The OU hockey hoodie he's wearing is old, the letters on the front faded and peeling, as if he's washed it a thousand times. It stretches across his chest, the worn material curved around the muscles of his biceps.

Much like last time, he's wearing a pair of loose sweatpants, his hockey bag resting casually on his shoulders. But today, his hair isn't wet; it's floppy and falling into his eyes, and there's a thick, dark shadow of a beard along his jaw, traveling down the slope of his neck.

It would probably look unkempt on someone else, but on him, it just fits the rugged, sharp-around-the-edges vibe. His sharp, intense eyes hold mine as if he's trying to get a read on me, the same way I'm glaring back at him.

Fine. *Maaaaaybe* I can see why he's got girls throwing themselves at his feet.

He's... hot.

Completely objectively speaking.

But I'm pretty sure I've heard somewhere that Satan was the most attractive, charming angel there was when he fell from the heavens, so this checks.

"Reputation *is* important," he replies smugly. "You'd know, right? Ms. Perfect, 4.0, valedictorian, Social Club socialite. I'm in the presence of Orleans royalty."

"Ah, asking around about me? That's cute that I left such a big impression."

For a beat, he's quiet, and my smirk widens, splitting my face with a victorious smile.

I'm surprised when he says, "Yeah, let's go with that."

My brow lifts. "Whatever. Look, there's no other ice time. We either share it, or we lose it, so as badly as I don't want to have to be around you for *any* length of time, there's no other choice. I'm not giving up my time, and I'm sure you aren't either, so we suck it up and deal with it. Just like last week"—I wave my hand toward the red line in the middle of the ice—"you stay on your side, and I'll stay on mine. Got it?"

chapter six
SAINT

"YEAH, GOLDEN GIRL, I *GOT IT.*" I lift two fingers to my forehead and give her a salute, tossing her a shit-eating smile that has her glaring even harder at me. Her pink, pillowy lips are pursed into an annoyed scowl as she throws daggers at me with piercing emerald eyes, arms crossed over her chest, chin lifted in defiance.

She finally rolls her eyes and lifts her middle finger toward me before she skates off.

Damn.

That ass.

I run my tongue over my teeth, shaking my head at the thought.

Lennon Rousseau has surprised me, and that takes a lot.

I've always been good at reading people.

I'm the quiet one who sits back and observes rather than engages, and if I had a superpower or some shit, it would be knowing exactly who someone is the moment they open their mouth. I've usually got someone all figured out from the jump, but this girl?

This girl... she's a fucking spitfire. She doesn't back down, doesn't take my shit lying down, and that's the part that surprises me.

I expected her to never show up again after how much of a dick I was to her last time, but instead, she doubled down. I spend the majority of my time on the ice intimidating grown-ass men into fucking up, but this fun-sized little redhead wasn't even fazed. I would almost respect it if she wasn't the daughter of the man I hate.

Which is exactly why I haven't been able to stop thinking about her and what led me to ultimately asking Legros about her the other day at practice. And looking up articles on the internet, searching for her socials, even though I don't have any myself.

She's right, she did leave an impression, and apparently, my new obsession is finding out everything I could about both her and her asshole of a father.

I've spent the last eight years of my life thinking about how I could ever inflict the same amount of pain on Edward Rousseau as he has on my family.

It's one of the only things I felt like I had left when my life was falling apart... my hatred.

I held on to it like a raft on a sinking ship.

Her father's always deserved whatever fucked-up karma was headed his way. I just never thought that it would be in the form of me.

Until now.

It seemed almost too perfect for this, for *her*, to just fall into my lap like this.

It's like the universe was presenting the perfect opportunity to me, wrapped with a bow on top. And I'd be a fucking fool not to take it.

What better way to get revenge on the man who ruined my life, who fucked up any good I ever had, who fucked up my family's reputation than to give him a taste of his very own medicine.

What would it look like if I took Edward Rousseau's precious, untouched good girl and dirtied her up?

The idea began with the first little granule of information—*her name*—and has since morphed into something else entirely.

I'm going to ruin her the very same way her father ruined my family.

Every bit of information I learn from this point forward, I'm planning to weaponize and use against OU's golden girl to get the revenge I deserve. Granted, I know she's not just going to stumble over to this side of the tracks for a guy like me, so I know I'm going to have to put in work, probably be slightly less of an asshole, but that's a sacrifice I'm willing to make.

Although something tells me she likes going toe to toe with me, even if she doesn't realize it yet, or if she does, she'd rather bite off her tongue than admit it.

Looking over, my gaze moves back to where she's skating in slow, measured circles on the opposite side of the ice, looking every bit the rich, spoiled daddy's girl.

Her long red hair is low on her nape in a tight braid

that hangs down her back. Her light pink, pleated skirt falls mid-thigh, leaving her pale, creamy legs on display and the fitted lavender bodysuit is molded around her ample curves.

Golden Girl might be my key to revenge, but I'd have to be blind not to notice how hot she is.

I turn my back toward her and start warming up, skating from one side of the ice to the line and back in short, quick sprints that get my heart rate up.

Each time I do a lap, I sneak a glance out of the corner of my eye, the same way she is, because our eyes keep connecting, and she quickly turns away when she realizes I've caught her staring.

I move to the net and line up pucks so I can work on my slap shot. I'm the best winger on the team, and it's going to stay that way. There's a frustrated sigh from behind me, so I turn and see Lennon attempting to do some type of twirl that I won't even begin to name, but she falls. Judging by the amount of powdered ice currently covering her skirt, legs, and ass, it's not the first time.

"Ouch. Need some help?" I call out from across the ice.

Her head whips to where I'm standing, leaning against my stick, her eyes turning hard as they burn holes into me. "No, but thank you for asking. I'm sure it pained you to do so."

My lips curl at the edges. I should probably leave well enough alone, at least for now. But fucking with her is the most fun I've had in a while, so nah. Fuck that.

I skate toward her, crossing her metaphorical and figurative line drawn in the middle of the ice, coming to a slow stop in front of her.

"You know, it looks like you might be out of practice. Sure it's safe for you to be trying shit like that?" My tone is condescending, hitting something that makes her body go taut. I feel the corner of my lip tugging as I try and fight the urge to grin but fail.

It's too much fun watching her expression turn murderous and her eyes narrowing into slits.

Up this close, I notice how flushed she is, a bloom of red on her cheeks from exertion. There's a small bead of sweat hanging on her skin just above her plump lips, which are currently pursed into a tight scowl. "Did you miss the part where I said you stay on your side of the ice, and I'll stay on mine? Or is your hearing as bad as your personality?"

Apparently, she saves all of her hatred for me because Bennett said that everyone loves her, that she's kind and nice to *everyone*.

Even fucking better.

I can deal with hatred. Actually, I prefer it.

"Nah, I did. I just chose to ignore it." I skate a slow circle around her, letting my gaze linger on her hips before I stop in front of her, closer this time. Her throat bobs as she lifts her chin and squares her shoulders like she's preparing for battle. "Real bad at authority. Following directions. *Especially* from spoiled little rich girls."

There's an audible gasp that slips past her lips, eyes glinting with animosity that, I'm not going to lie... turns me the fuck on.

"I'd rather be a spoiled rich girl than an asshole with a grudge against the world because of his mommy issues."

My brow arches. She's got teeth, sharper than I expected and not far off but not quite there yet.

"What's with all the hostility? I'm just trying to be a gentleman."

Scoffing, she crosses her arms over her chest. "Yeah, and I'm the president of your fan club. Look, we have less than an hour. Can you go back over there"—she waves her hand dismissively—"and chase your little puck around so we can stop wasting time? Unlike you, I actually *need* to be here."

"Oh, I know, I can tell."

I swear, I can see fucking steam radiating off her, and my crooked smile only seems to make it worse.

"You're such a dick," she says through clenched teeth. "As if you could do any better. Anyone can pick up a stick and hit a puck into a stupid net."

"Yeah?"

She nods with a cheeky smile, glaring at me. "Yep. It's not like it's rocket science. Stick… puck… net."

I step closer. "Prove it."

"W-what?"

I've caught her off guard by calling her bluff.

Reaching into the front of my hoodie pocket, I pull out a puck and drop it onto the ice between us. "Put your money where your mouth is. If it's so easy to get the puck into the net, do it. Get it by me."

chapter seven
LENNON

HE'S GOADING ME. Pushing me until I snap, and I'm falling right into it before I can even stop myself. "Fine."

Just when I thought that I couldn't hate Saint Devereaux any more than I already do, he does something stupid like *open his mouth*, and inevitably, I hate him more.

It's like he has this incessant, effortless way of getting under my skin and driving me to the point of insanity without saying very much at all.

It's enough.

In just the few times that I've been around him, he's managed to get a reaction out of me more than anyone ever has. And I have absolutely no idea why. Why I'm so easy to rile when in his presence. Why I feel like a different person, one who just reacts without thinking the second he starts in.

It's absolutely infuriating.

Maisie wasn't wrong. Facts are facts—he is very… easy to look at.

But he's such a dick that I can't even stand to share the same air as him for the one hour, twice a week, that we're forced to.

Truly, I don't know how I'm going to manage this for the rest of the semester, let alone the year.

I know I shouldn't let him bother me as much as I do, but every single time I give myself a pep talk and tell myself that I'm not going to let him provoke me, it still manages to happen.

I'm a ticking time bomb when it comes to him, and he just so happens to be the only one with the match.

God, Lennon, what are you doing?

You literally just told him that you didn't have time to waste, and here you are, agreeing to some stupid childish thing he's said simply to provoke you, all because you can't bear to let him have the pleasure of winning.

Without another word, he turns, then skates back toward the empty net on his side of the rink. And against my better judgment, I follow behind him. It's impossible not to notice how easily he moves across the ice.

Graceful, almost, in a way that you wouldn't normally expect a hockey player to be. They're agile and powerful but not generally so... fluid.

Once he's in front of the net, he turns to face me. His gaze holds mine as he taps his stick along the ice in rapid succession once, twice, three times.

My brow furrows. "Uh, what was that?"

"What do you mean what was that?"

"I mean that... *stick* thing that you just did where you tapped it on the ice three times."

Saint shrugs. "Superstition. Now…" He uses the end of his stick to send the puck flying toward me, where it glides to a stop against the blade of my skate. "Let's up the ante. If you get a puck past me, I'll stay on my side of the ice, and I won't say a word to you."

I cross my arms over my chest, cocking an eyebrow. "Oh, it's *that* easy to shut you up? Get a single measly puck by you?"

"Easy as that." He chuckles lowly, the sound entirely too… hot.

"Right. And what happens if *you* win?"

"If I win, you tell me why you're trying so hard to get back to skating."

The scoff tumbles past my lips before I even realize it. "I'm not telling you that."

"Why? Did I hit a soft spot?"

"No, because it's none of your business," I retort, clenching my teeth together, my jaw tensing at the question that I'm not ready to answer. "How do you even know that I haven't been figure skating?"

His deep, raspy laugh floats through the air, the sound echoing around as it bounces off the boards. "Because I've played hockey my entire life—I know someone who's comfortable on the ice versus someone who's not. Clearly, you've done it before. Just seems like you're out of practice. And if I win, I want to know *why*."

"Why do you even care?"

He doesn't immediately respond, the silence hanging heavily between us, and I think he might actually not even answer my question. Finally, he says, "I don't know. Call me curious."

"Whatever, fine. I'll agree to your stupid bet. Let's just get this over with," I huff, rolling my eyes.

"I've got an extra stick over there in the penalty box," he responds with a nod toward the box at the side of the rink that I have no doubt he is very well acquainted with. I was going to ask him why he would just carry extra sticks around, and then I realize that I've seen them snap a hundred times, so it's probably good to have a backup.

I didn't even think I was going to speak to him at all today, at least not if I could help it, and I certainly didn't expect him to ask any questions about me or my life. I honestly never thought I'd have *any* kind of conversation with him outside of us being rude to each other. So, I'm slightly taken aback as I make my way over to the penalty box, pushing through the low door and grabbing the well-used hockey stick that's leaned against the boards.

Once I skate back to where he's standing, he nods his head. "Back up some."

I've lost track of how many times I've rolled my eyes at this point. Like a few feet is truly going to make the difference. "Really? Are you intimidated by me hitting a little, tiny *puck* at you?"

"Nah, but if we're going to do this, we're going to do it fair. It's so easy, remember? It's not rocket science." His voice is mocking as his lips curve into a cocky, full-of-himself grin. "Time to prove it, Golden Girl."

Ugh. I *loathe* him.

chapter eight
SAINT

EVERY TIME I call her Golden Girl, the more mad she gets, and admittedly, that only makes me want to do it *more*.

See just how pissed off I can get her, taunting her until that good girl facade drops.

Piece by piece.

I like seeing the fire blazing bright in her eyes, and the second I got a glimpse… I wanted more.

That's why we're facing off in front of the net right now, even though there's not a chance in fucking hell she's getting that puck by me in her frilly, short little skirt and leotard.

Not even if it's slightly distracting with the way it's seated around her curves.

No shot.

"Let's go. What are you waiting for?" I arch my brow as I bend my knees deeper in a squat above the ice.

"Unless you're scared? We can always call it like it is. You forf—"

"Shut up," she cuts me off. "I'm just thinking of my strategy. *Do not* rush me, Devereaux."

My lip twitches. "Well, can you strategize a little quicker? Some of us have other things to do than play with a spoiled princess all day."

I soak up every bit of the indignant look on her face. I'm fucked-up, but I never claimed to be anything else.

I think there's a technical term for it, but I'm too busy staring at her pretty little lips, which are twisted into a scowl, to think of it.

"You know, I find it hard to believe that you are *this* much of an asshole," she says, shooting daggers across the ice at me with her eyes.

"Believe it. Actually, give me a little more time, and you'll see I'm even more of an asshole than you thought. Now, shoot. The. Damn. Puck."

Chin raised, she cuts a final look at me before squaring her shoulders and swinging the stick. It's almost as tall as she is because my stick is fit for me, and I'm almost six five with skates on.

The puck lands directly between my legs, which I block by turning my foot to the side and letting the puck rebound off the blade of my skate, barely moving at all.

"Shit." The low curse floats between us, and I smirk, cocking a brow. "Don't move from that stupid net. That was just... a bad shot."

Mhmmmm.

"It's so easy. Stick... puck... net." I slap the puck back

to her with a flick of my wrist. "Right?" Her eyes narrow into slits, and I grin, dropping back down into a defensive position, hips bent, eyes holding hers.

I could do this all day, blindfolded, with my hands tied behind my back, with her standing about three feet closer, but I actually do have somewhere to be, and our hour of allotted ice time is almost up.

Time flies when you're busy talking shit to the vapid, spoiled little princess who thinks that she's better than everyone.

I might not know Lennon Rousseau, *really* know her outside of the things I've learned about her and her family, but I know exactly the kind of girl she was before she ever opened her mouth.

I'm judging the fuck out of a book by its cover.

Again, she slaps at the puck, and it flies toward me, pinging noisily off the steel of the net before sliding back toward her across the ice.

"Ugh." She groans and drops her head back on her shoulders, staring up at the ceiling.

I'm about to go in, running my mouth just to piss her off, when suddenly, she slips and loses her footing, falling backward and hitting the ice, *hard*, with a pained groan, the hockey stick clattering to the ground beside her.

Shit.

I sprint toward her, closing the short distance between us in a few strides. "You okay?"

She pushes up into a sitting position and pulls her knee to her chest, rubbing her ankle, her lips twisted in pain.

"I... I think I tweaked my ankle." Her voice breaks as she pulls her bottom lip between her teeth.

Fuck, is she going to cry? I have no fucking clue what to do with that.

Sure, yeah, I'm a dick, but I don't want her to get hurt. I'm not a sadist.

Reaching up, I drag a hand through my hair. "Do you want me to... carry you? Off the ice?"

"No, I'll be fine. Can you just help me up?" Her lip quivers, and I nod.

I tuck my stick under my arm, and her palm curves around my forearm as I help her up. For a second, her leg seems to tremble when she tries to put any pressure on it, her nose scrunching in pain. "Ouch."

"Okay, just let me carr—"

In the blink of an eye, she's snatching my stick from under my arm, checking my shoulder as she skates toward the puck, then slaps it directly into the net.

"Yesssss." Lennon throws her arms in the air like she just scored the game-winning goal, a cheeky, shit-eating grin turning her pink lips up in the corners. "Take that, Devereaux! Sucks to be a loser."

That sneaky little shit.

Her ankle wasn't fucking hurt at all—she was playing me like a goddamn fool, and I fell for it.

Motherfucker.

If I wasn't so annoyed that she did so, I'd be slightly impressed. Clearly, she should be in the theatre or whatever the hell it's called with that performance.

"Can't win if you're cheating, Golden Girl. Which is the

only fucking way you were getting that puck by me." I shrug as I slowly skate over, stopping in front of her.

The balls of her cheeks are flushed red, and her piercing jade eyes are dancing with mirth instead of burning bright with her usual hatred.

Honestly, I can't decide which one is hotter.

"You didn't say anything but, and I quote, 'You can't get the puck by me,' and wouldn't you look… I did. It's sitting right there in the net." She gestures behind us. "Might want to choose your words more carefully next time. Oh, wait… that's right, you can't say a word to me now."

Yeah, and maybe I'll go back on my promise just to piss her off.

My lips quirk as I fight back a grin.

Maybe she isn't as mindless as I thought.

"Nice knowing you, Satan. I would say have a good day, but I really hope you don't."

With that, she drops the stick at my feet and skates off toward the exit, with me watching her hips sway the entire fucking way.

chapter nine
LENNON

A CAGE IS *STILL* A CAGE, regardless of how brightly the bars gleam.

And lately, the bars surrounding me seem to be closing in, leaving no space to breathe. Each inhale is a pained reminder that every move I make is on display for the world to see and whisper words of judgment about.

I've spent my entire life trying to be the perfect daughter. To never make mistakes. To only be someone that my parents could be proud of, in all aspects.

Bleeding myself dry to be the perfect puppet for everyone to admire.

Turns out being perfect is fucking exhausting.

Somewhere along the way, resentment planted roots, deep and twisty, in my heart and bloomed into something else entirely.

Something that has me desperate to break the lock on my cage. To be free from everything I hate about my life.

"Would you like a glass of champagne, Miss

Rousseau?" The waitress's soft voice beside me jolts me from my thoughts. I glance over to see a large silver platter resting on her splayed hand, full of ornate glasses filled to the brim with bubbling Dom Perignon.

Pasting on a bright smile that I know won't reach my eyes, I shake my head and politely decline. "No, thank you."

"Of course. Enjoy your evening." With a slight nod, she turns on her heel, leaving me with my thoughts once again.

Although I could never admit it out loud, I hate these events almost as much as I hate the people attending them.

They're an opulent show of wealth and power that always has me feeling slightly dirty when I leave.

My gaze roams around the room packed full of people my father invited to tonight's charity gala in hopes that they'll donate, largely, to the cause.

The grand ballroom where tonight's dinner is being held is lavish in the old-money kind of way. The walls are painted a deep crimson that appears almost black and are lined with expensive oil-painted art framed in ornate gold. The floors are original hardwood that's been kept polished and pristine, dating back to when it was first built. A large crystal chandelier is suspended in the center of the room along the vaulted ceiling, the intricate pieces catching the dim light and sparkling. The scent of champagne and cigar smoke hangs in the air, draping over everything inside of the room.

It's every bit of what you'd expect when hosting some of the wealthiest people in the state.

And I want nothing more than to leave and go back to the confines of my apartment, where I don't have to play the perfect, dutiful daughter.

I'd even rather be facing off with Saint Devereaux for the second time today rather than be here, and that is saying a lot since I loathe him with every fiber of my being.

How ironic that tonight is supposed to be about raising money and awareness for charity, yet it feels like a fashion show where the wealthy are trying to outshine each other.

Everyone's dressed to perfection in designer gowns and custom-tailored tuxedos, the wives dripping with Harry Winston diamonds, Cartier gold around their necks, Oscar De La Renta ball gowns cinched around their waists.

Outfits that likely cost more than the donation they'll pledge tonight.

Eying the amount of money in this room causes the thin strand of pearls that my parents gifted me for my fourteenth birthday to suddenly feel heavy and constricting around my neck.

Usually, when I attend these events for my father, I spend the majority of the time watching the clock and counting down the minutes until I'm free to leave. And tonight is no different.

The last hour has dragged by even more than usual, the minute hand on the large grandfather clock on the wall seeming to tick by at an unnaturally slow pace, one that has my feet aching from these heels. Nearly as much as my face hurts from the fake smile I've worn the entire night.

God, I want out of here.

No, I *need* to get out of here before I scream.

I search for the exit to slip away to the bathroom, hopefully unnoticed, when I spot it across the room, the floor stretching so much farther than my feet can possibly carry me in these heels.

Everyone knows that you have to break in Louboutins, but when my mother presented this entire outfit for me earlier today, I knew that I couldn't say no. Not unless I wanted to see disappointment in her bright green eyes, which are almost a mirror to my own.

My heels click along the hardwood in a low echo, even over the sound of light classical music by the pianist in the back of the room, and I put on another fake smile, mumbling apologies as I push through the crowds toward the exit. When I finally get to the bathroom at the end of the hallway, opening the door and slipping inside, relief floods me in a wave.

It's completely empty. The silence is a welcome reprieve.

A shaky exhale jumps past my lips as I walk over to the large mirror on the bathroom wall and peer into it, gaze roving over my reflection staring back.

The pale yellow Valentino draped silk gown is exactly the type of dress that my mother loves to dress me in, and admittedly, one that I would've chosen myself, given the chance. Its hem kisses the floor, the cowl neckline showing a modest hint of my chest, the waist cinched with a dainty gold clasp. Although it's classic and beautiful, wearing it makes me feel like a shiny show pony trapped by my parents' whim. Each step is choreographed, every breath measured. Captive in their relentless, never-ending parade.

My long, red hair is curled in soft, flowy waves down to my waist, with a small pearl clip pinning one side just behind my ear, showing off the pink sapphire earrings my parents gifted me when I was a freshman in high school.

Sighing, I brush my fingers through my hair and take one last, final look at my reflection, soaking up the few remaining seconds of quiet. Seconds I know I'll undoubtedly wish for the moment I'm back out there.

I truly don't know how much longer I can keep doing this until I break.

Until I lose even more of myself than I already have.

Swallowing, I swing the door open and step back into the bustle of people, instantly regretting that I didn't accept the offer of champagne.

Maybe tonight would've been slightly more tolerable.

Suddenly, I feel a hand curving around my elbow, and my father appears in front of me. "Oh, Lennon, there you are, sweetheart. There's someone here to see you." The creases of his black tux are starched to perfection, his smile wide, causing the corners of his eyes to wrinkle slightly.

The person who steps out from behind him makes my stomach dip, and unease races down my spine. A giant lump settles at the base of my throat, and for a second, panic seizes my chest so intensely that it feels like I can't actually breathe.

No. What is he doing here? I haven't seen him since… since he cheated on me.

"Sweetheart, I know that you and Chandler had a slight *disagreement* in the past, but he cares about you, and he's willing to look past the… rough spot. To give your relationship a second chance."

My jaw falls open.

I shouldn't be as shocked as I am that he's done this, but then again, I never expected him to be so completely… *heartless*.

I met Chandler for the first time at an event our parents forced us to attend. Our fathers do business together, and we bonded over our common dislike of having to be dragged along to the events.

At first, we struck an easy friendship that was the result of our social circles spinning around each other.

But then in high school, that friendship turned into something… more.

Chandler Masters was every girl's dream.

Senior.

Captain of the soccer team.

Insanely hot with tousled blond hair, a bright, blinding smile, and charm that could disarm anyone.

From the moment that he gave me the attention I was craving, he had me eating out of the palm of his hand. I was young and stupidly thought I was in love.

A deadly combination when it came to a guy like him. I fell hard and fast, not caring how hard it would hurt when I finally hit the bottom. Naivety will do that to you. Make you feel invincible when you have no idea what's coming next, only the high of the feeling you can't get enough of.

"Lennon, stop being silly. Talk to me." Chandler's voice pulls me from my thoughts, the timbre more whiny than I remember. He reaches for me, brushing his fingers along my arm, and I physically recoil, my stomach blanching. "Don't be like this, baby. It's gone on long enough."

"Do not touch me. Don't you dare put your hands on me," I hiss, completely disgusted by the smug, arrogant smile on his lips.

Disgusted by *him*.

God, he actually thinks that I would fall for this? That I would allow him to touch me after everything he's done?

Looking back, I hate the girl I became when I was with Chandler. The one who shrunk herself to fit the box he placed me in, the same box my father wanted me in. The one where I let all of my dreams and ambitions take a back seat to what they wanted. I wasn't Lennon anymore; I was Chandler Masters's girlfriend.

Our parents were over the moon, and we soon realized they had been playing matchmaker for years, unbeknownst to us.

I was shaping up to be the perfect trophy wife, exactly what they expected out of me. I stopped hanging out with my friends and only hung out with him and his friends. I cared more about his hobbies, what he wanted to spend our weekends together doing, the restaurants we went to, the events he attended. Everything was his choice. His decision.

Him expecting that out of me should have been the first red flag, but unfortunately, getting my heart shattered into a thousand pieces when I caught him having sex with a girl from my friend group without even having the sheer decency to stop when I walked in on them was the only red flag I ever saw. Until it was too late.

And when I cried and confronted him, brokenhearted and betrayed, he admitted that he was tired of me not sleeping with him. So he simply found it somewhere else.

My entire life, I was raised to hold on to that piece of me until marriage, a gift to my husband, something only he should cherish.

Now I know how utterly fucking ridiculous and archaic that notion was, along with the promise ring my parents gave me, and the ideology of saving myself for *this*.

For a "good guy" like Chandler, who tossed me aside like trash, who disrespected me, cheated on me, had no regard for my feelings.

That was what I was saving myself for, and at that moment, I knew I was done saving myself for anyone.

After the breakup, everything slowly started to unravel, thread by thread. I questioned my entire outlook on relationships. The road to hell was paved with guys like Chandler.

The kind that seem utterly perfect, but beyond that mask, they're a poison.

As badly as it hurt, it opened my eyes. The clues had all been there. And the more I looked around, the more I saw that my father's world was full of men just like Chandler.

And I have no intention of dating anyone like that ever again.

Despite the music and people around us, the words carry, and my father steps closer, palm curving around my forearm tightly, "You are *not* going to make a scene, Lennon. This is neither the time nor the place to do so."

I gather any and all courage I have, simmering to a fiery hot boil inside of me, feeding off the anger coursing through my veins as I rip my arm free, stepping back from both of them. "Apparently, it is since you brought him here... knowing. How could you do this to me?" I somehow choke the words out, even though I feel the bitter sting of tears gathering in my eyes. "He *cheated* on me, Dad. You know what he did! You know that I walked in on him having sex with my friend, without an ounce of remorse."

When I told my parents what happened, my mom at least apologized for what I went through, but my father? He chuckled and said that sometimes we look past a person's missteps for the greater good.

That our families' alliance would pay off more than I could ever understand.

An alliance.

That's what he was concerned with. His image. His reputation.

His business.

Clearly, that hasn't changed. I can't wait to hear his reasoning behind suddenly shoving Chandler into my face again. I'm waiting on bated fucking breath.

"Lennon..." My father sighs raggedly, as if I'm the issue in this entire scenario. "Please, enough of the dramatics. We've discussed this, and Chandler would like to speak privately with you about this and apologize for his misstep."

A humorless chuckle spills from my lips at the same moment the first tear falls, wetting my cheeks. I quickly reach up and brush it away. "A misstep is forgetting my *birthday*, not sleeping with my friend."

Chandler opens his mouth to speak, but I shake my head, lifting my hand to stop him before he can say anything at all.

I don't care to hear another word out of his mouth ever again, and I thought I had made that abundantly clear when I threw everything I owned of his in his front yard and told him that.

"There's nothing you could ever say or do to change the fact that you used and disrespected me. In case you've suddenly forgotten what's happened… Fuck you, Chandler. Do you understand now? This is never happening again, despite my father's disregard for your cheating, lying bullshit."

I turn back to the man I'm beginning to learn is nothing like I thought he was.

"I could expect something like this from him"—I gesture to Chandler—"but you? I've never been more disappointed in you in my life."

My father has completely ignored my feelings, my wants, my needs for whatever suits him.

And I am so done.

I'm beyond done.

Parading the man who cheated on me in front of my face and demanding a reconciliation despite his infidelity is apparently my breaking point.

This isn't who I am. This isn't the life that I want.

I'm very well aware of the privilege that I have when it comes to schooling, housing, and all of the things that my parents have supported and provided for me, and I am grateful for them. It's just those things come at a cost, and I'm done paying the price for my parents' love.

No one should have to feel like they're suffocating.

No one should have to feel so... alone standing in a room full of people with all eyes on them.

No one should feel caged in a life they don't want.

And I've done it for so long. I've fallen in line and done everything I've been told because as suffocated as I've felt, I hate feeling the weight of my parents' expectations.

I want to make them proud, to be everything they wish for, but I'm exhausted and weary.

I can't do this anymore.

I won't.

chapter ten
LENNON

I REFUSED to let myself cry in front of either of them, to give them more power than they already have over me, but the second I stumble out of the Uber in front of my apartment, the tears fall hot, heavy, and wet on my cheeks, my chest heaving with small sobs.

My hand's shaking so badly I can hardly get the key into the lock.

Somehow, I manage to unlock it and step inside, throwing my purse on the foyer table, not caring where it actually lands.

"Oh, you're home, good. You can help me wax my bikini li—" Maisie stops short as she appears in front of me, her words dying on her tongue when she sees me. Undoubtedly, there's mascara running down my cheeks, my eyes red and puffy from crying. "Len, what's wrong? Are you okay?"

She rushes over, gathering me into her arms without hesitation, where I crumple, crying into her chest. Her fingers stroke my hair, and for the first time tonight, I feel safe to break.

To let go of everything I've been carrying that feels like the weight of the entire world.

It doesn't take me long to recount what happened, my watery words trailing off into sobs, until I'm completely empty. There's nothing left to cry.

My hurt begins to morph into anger, the disbelief wearing off with it.

The betrayal by Chandler feels like nothing compared to my father's, and it hurts. It enrages me in a slightly unhinged way that I don't feel the least bit guilty over.

"The audacity. The only thing Chandler has is freaking audacity..." Maisie says when I'm done, shaking her head. We're sitting on the hardwood in the hallway side by side, my head lying against her shoulder. "I bet you he had a little dick too."

I laugh. "If it's in comparison to his ego, then yes, absolutely. There's no way there's room for both." Sitting up, I pull my knees to my chest and wrap my arms around them, resting my cheek on top.

"I'm sorry, Lenn. Chandler's a complete asshole, but your father bringing him there is unbelievable. I'm sorry that you had to go through that. He never deserved you then, and he sure as hell doesn't deserve you now."

She's right, and I know that. I've never questioned the decision to walk away from him because it is and always was the right choice.

I just wish that my father cared more about me, his

daughter, instead of how I represent him. I'm not a shiny trophy for anyone, especially not a guy like Chandler.

And I wish that Chandler would get the point. Move on and leave me alone. He fucked up my life enough to come back and try to do it all over again.

My gaze moves to the pink gemstone on my finger.

After everything that happened with him after my senior year, I decided to rebrand the promise ring that my parents got me. Instead of throwing it out along with the stupid promise I made to my parents, myself, and the man I would marry one day, I've used it as a way to take a step toward reclaiming pieces of myself.

My body. My choices.

If I wanted to hold on to my virginity until I'm a hundred and die an old spinster without ever giving it away, then it would be my decision, and no one would make it for me.

From that moment on, I made a promise to *myself*.

That when the time came, I would give my virginity to whomever I felt ready to without consequence.

No one would control me by guilt or archaic expectations.

I took the ring to a jeweler and had the phrase "*De meo arbitrio*" inscribed inside of it in Latin, which means "from my will."

Fuck the patriarchy and their arbitrary roles that women should play.

I'm going to play by my own rules.

A realization ripples through me, an idea forming somewhere in the depth of my anger and hurt.

"Mais..." I start, swinging my gaze to her. "You know my father wants so badly for me to be a perfect, dutiful wife, hanging on the arm of a man who doesn't love or respect me because it *looks* good for him. He doesn't care that I have my own hopes and dreams, my own goals. He doesn't care that I would be in a loveless marriage with a man who can't keep his dick in his pants. All for appearances."

"Right, because he's a superficial dick," she says.

"He chose someone perfect, in his eyes, at least. Influential family, good gene pool, a trust fund. He chose the epitome of the 'good guy'..." I trail off, chewing my lip until a smile tugs at my lips. "So what if I choose the exact opposite?"

"What do you mean?" Maisie asks, brow furrowing.

My knees drop, and I sit up, turning toward her. "I mean... from this point forward, fuck the good guy. The one with the perfect mask in place. Look where that got me. Cheated on. Heartbroken. Used. I'm going after the type of guy my father would hate. Not only because it'll send him completely over the edge, and I can't wait to see it, but because the bad boys? They're the safe bet. They don't want wives. They don't care about anything but having fun, no strings attached." I shake my head. "Me telling Chandler to fuck off and throwing his shit in his front yard was clearly not enough to send a strong enough message that I'm done with him, but moving on with a guy that's his polar opposite, and a guy out of my father's nightmares... sure as hell would."

Maisie perks up, her blue eyes widening while a smile takes over her face. "Okay, okay, okay. I'm listening."

"Imagine if I brought the absolute *worst* guy I could find on my arm to an event, paraded him in front of my father and all his colleagues. He would have a heart attack on sight."

She laughs, the sound echoing throughout the hall, causing me to laugh too. "Yeah, I'd pay money to see you walk in with someone like your new 'skating partner.' Can you even imagine his face if you rode up on Saint's motorcycle in a freaking Chanel gown?"

My nose scrunches.

"First of all, he is absolutely *not* my skating partner, and second, well, that would require us to survive in each other's presence for longer than an hour. We can't stand each other."

"Len… wait," Maisie squeaks. "What if you actually *did* though?"

I scoff. "Okay, this went a little haywire. Let's rein it back in. It would never work. He's an arrogant, self-centered, intolerable asshole who has the manner—"

Suddenly, her hands are on my forearms, and she's shaking me, cutting me off. "Lennon, listen to me right now. This is the perfect idea. Saint Devereaux is *the* bad boy of Orleans U. He's covered in tattoos, always has a black eye or busted lips from getting into fights. He drives a freakin' motorcycle and is a hockey enforcer with a horrid reputation. If you brought him around your dad, he would actually keel over and die. I can't even think of anyone more perfect than him."

Okay, well, she's right about one thing: he is absolutely an asshole and the definition of a cliché bad boy. It's a little ridiculous, if I'm honest. Maybe that's why he acts like that. It fits his whole broody, fuck-the-world vibe.

The reason I want to strangle him with my bare hands, and I'm not even a violent person.

Well, unless it comes to him.

"Maisie, we hate each other, like… wholeheartedly cannot stand to be in the same room together."

Her shoulder lifts. "And? You don't have to like each other for him to be your pretend boyfriend to piss off your father. I mean, he's also not that bad to look at. There are worse guys to dangle around like a boy toy, for sure."

I chew my lip contemplatively. God, this sounds insane, but also…

I'm considering it. Aren't I? I'm actually entertaining this. She's right, he *isn't* bad to look at… and if I could harness his assholeness for good, it would actually help that he's horrible.

But how? How would I get him to agree to that, with his obvious hostility, even if it was just fake?

Oh.

OH.

"He wouldn't just help me to be nice because he's not. But I could offer him my ice time for next semester. Summer said that since technically I signed up first, I get first dibs for next semester… which I'm not even sure he's aware of yet. I could give it up to him, if he agrees."

Maise's eyes widen as her lips quirk in excitement. "Yes. Oh my God, this is kismet. It's perfect, Len."

"It's *crazy*," I correct her.

Maybe just crazy enough to actually work.

"Yeah, maybe so, but you know what else is crazy?"

"What?"

"Your father when he thinks you're riding more than Saint's motorcycle." She giggles loudly, biting at her bottom lip.

I blanch, reaching out and pushing her shoulder. "You're ridiculous. He is stupidly hot though. I'll give him that."

"Yeah, he is, but on a serious note, if you do this, there has to be a rule." Her gaze is serious as she peers over at me. "The one and only rule: don't fall for the bad boy. Under any circumstance, do not let yourself get caught up in all of his charm. It's a trap, and if you think being hurt by a trust fund fuckboy hurts… imagine having to see Saint around campus, flaunting his prospects in your face. Unbearable. He's clearly good at winning people over because girls fall for it all the time. Don't be that girl, Len."

"Trust me, the last thing I have to worry about is falling for Saint Devereaux. Hell will freeze over before I catch any kind of feelings for its *ruler*."

chapter eleven
SAINT

I PROBABLY SHOULDN'T BE LOOKING FORWARD to stepping back on the ice with the princess herself as much as I am, but I'd be lying if I said that my dick wasn't already half-mast at the prospect of seeing just how far I can push her in the next sixty minutes.

I walk into the rink and stop in front of the boards, dropping my hockey bag onto the bleachers. She's already on the ice, attempting a series of twirls that have the short, bright yellow skirt she's wearing lifting, revealing the delectable curves of her ass.

I take a front-row seat as I pull out my skates and lace them up, watching her move across the ice like she's performing only for me.

If she didn't drive me fucking crazy, I'd entertain the idea of sinking my teeth into her plump little cheeks before I fisted them both in my hands and spread her open, watching how wet she gets from hating me.

Something tells me that Golden Girl would never

be able to handle my special kind of *tastes*, but then again, picturing her on her knees with my cock stretching her throat feels a lot like Christmas morning. Who would've thought that prim and proper princess with a stick up her ass and not one for pleasure would have the ability to make my dick hard, but here we are.

A warm, wet hole is a warm, wet hole no matter who it belongs to, apparently.

I watch as she eats shit a handful of times while attempting some type of move that clearly is so far out of reach she's going to actually break her ankle, for real this time.

She must feel me staring at her because she stops abruptly, the blade of her skate kicking up ice as she comes to a halt.

"Oh, look who's here."

Smirking, I grab a handful of pucks from my bag, then get my stick from beside me and step out onto the ice. "Miss me?"

"In your dreams," she retorts, words heavily laced with disdain.

"Mmm. The funny thing is…" I skate over to where she's toeing the centerline of the ice and lean forward, dipping my head so close that I could count the freckles that are dusted across her nose and cheeks. "You're right. You're in a lot of my dreams, Golden Girl. Wanna hear about 'em?"

Her breath catches, and her mouth falls open, eyes widened as she stares up at me. "You're *much* nicer in them, especially when you're bent over with your lips wrapped around my di—"

"Oh my God, you're *disgusting*. Shut up."

The sheer look of shock coating her face has satisfaction rippling through me.

I simply smirk and tap my stick along the ice, "Thought I wasn't supposed to talk to you. What happened to that? Can't help yourself?"

She rolls her eyes as she crosses her arms over her chest, and I unabashedly let my gaze drop to the swell of her creamy tits that pushes against the leotard she's wearing before lifting my eyes back to her. "God, I hate you. Have I mentioned that?"

"Once or twice. There's that saying though. A thin line between hate and wanting to fu—"

"That is not even how it goes. You're just being crude to get a rise out of me."

I shrug. "I think it's working though, yeah?"

"I can't believe I'm doing this." Her words are muttered as if she's talking to herself. She shakes her head. "I have something to ask you. Do you think you can table the whole asshole thing for a second?"

"Doubtful, but proceed," I retort, leaning against the top of my stick.

She tugs the bottom of her lip between her teeth. "I have a... proposition. For... you."

My brow arches. What could Golden Girl possibly need from *me*?

After a brief moment of silence, she finally spills, a rush

of words tumbling out of her lips so quickly I barely catch them. "I need you to date me."

A deep rumble of a laugh vibrates out of me and echoes around the rink, causing her lips to pull tight into a scowl, the expression on her face remaining serious.

"Oh, wait, you're serious?"

"Yes, I'm serious, you dick." She huffs, reaching up to finger the ends of her long, auburn curls. "Not like actually date me, but… Look, you are exactly the type of guy my father would *hate*. You're crass, rude, arrogant, and covered in tattoos. Not to mention, you drive that death-trap thing out there."

"Are you supposed to be convincing me with that speech? Because you're doing a real shit job at it," I deadpan.

"I'm saying I need you to *fake* date me. To just go to some events as my date, let me parade you around my father so he'll believe that I've fallen for a delinquent, cliché bad boy, and so that he'll wake up and realize I'm not the prodigy trophy wife that he's been grooming me to be."

This is the most insane shit anyone has ever said to me, which is already saying a hell of a lot, and I'm slightly impressed that she had the balls to do it in the first place.

I don't date. I don't even *fuck* the same girl twice. I don't sleep over, and I sure as shit don't play the doting boyfriend.

Before I can even respond, she's continuing. "Summer said I have first dibs on the ice next semester. If you do it, then I'll give it to you, no question. All yours. And you won't ever have to deal with me again."

That sweetens the pot some, but... what Princess doesn't realize is I don't even need her ice time to agree to this because the in I needed to get with her father and exact the revenge I deserve?

It's her.

She just played right into my waiting hands, and she has absolutely no fucking clue.

Ever since talking to Bennett, I've been mulling it over. Trying to think about how I could use this, her, to my advantage, and it seems like fate has decided for me.

Here's Rousseau's daughter on a silver fucking platter. The perfect little innocent virgin, ripe for me to corrupt. And once I do, I'll make sure he knows all about it. Knows that because of his fucked up decisions I fucked with his daughter. But in order to do that, I'd have to get closer to her. To seduce her. Hard to do when she spends all of her time hating me.

She's just given me the perfect excuse to get closer to her. To dirty her up, and when I do...I'll make sure he knows that it was Devereaux who seduced and used his daughter.

He fucked with my family, so I'm going to ruin his.

chapter twelve

LENNON

"DO I look like the kind of guy who '*dates*'?" Saint says haughtily, lips curled at the edges in a cocky smirk.

Of course he neither looks nor seems like the kind of guy who takes a girl out to a nice dinner. He absolutely seems like the kind of guy who would have *you* for dinner instead.

A shiver dances down my spine at the thought, and he arches a brow.

"No, but that's exactly what I'm banking on. You're an asshole, and you have the manners of a farm animal, and that is precisely what will send my father careening over the edge."

For a second, he says nothing, and I shift from one skate to the other, an awkward, heavy silence hanging in the air between us and making me feel even more ridiculous for asking this.

I knew it was crazy and completely ludicrous, but still, I—

"Fighting is my favorite foreplay, Golden Girl. Just so you know. Keep insulting me. It makes my dick hard." His deep, raspy voice rips me from my thoughts, dousing me in figurative ice-cold water.

A visceral reaction that I'm not in control of. Goose bumps dust my flesh, and my heart seems to slip out of rhythm at the carnal, velvety seduction in his words.

God, he's crass and beyond inappropriate, and for some reason... my body responded to it.

"What? Is that too much for you? Didn't you *just* say you wanted an untrained asshole?"

I open my mouth to speak, then snap it shut.

That *is* what I said, but his inability to behave like a normal person seems to still surprise me despite the time I've spent in his presence.

"Yes, when we're surrounded by the rich and high society of New Orleans and not *alone*."

"Yeah, well, where's the fun in that?" He chuckles, skating closer, crossing the proverbial and literal line that separates us on the ice. "So you want me to be your boy toy? The spoiled, rich princess leaving her million-dollar mansion and slumming it with trailer trash? Daddy doesn't want you all dirtied up by a guy like me. Hmm?"

Lifting my chin, I run my tongue across the front of my teeth and lift a brow. "Whatever you want to call it, the outcome is the same. I never thought I'd be making deals with the devil, but desperate times and all of that..."

"And you couldn't think of *anything* else to piss daddy dearest off other than me?"

"Why doesn't matter. It's none of your business," I retort, narrowing my eyes at him. He's the most infuriating person I've ever met in my *life*.

"It is my business when you want to *use* me, Golden Girl. I'm more than just a hot body with a big dick. I have feelings too, you know?" He feigns hurt like he actually does have feelings, which we both know is bullshit.

My eyelashes kiss the top of my eyelids because I roll my eyes that hard as I let out a defeated sigh. "You know what? This is never going to work. I knew better than to ask you, so how about we forget I ever said anything and go back to ignoring each other. Okay? Great." When I turn and start to skate back to the other side of the rink, his fingers wrap around my forearm.

"Wait."

Slowly, I turn back toward him with a look that could most likely kill.

Saint licks his lips, running his tongue along his bottom lip, and for the first time, I notice the faint cut along the corner, still slightly raised and red. "Say that I agreed to be your glorified arm candy. *Hypothetically*. What exactly does that mean? What would I have to do? My schedule is packed. Regular season is starting, and I can't just parade around town with you at your beck and call."

"I never said that you'd be at my beck and call. Don't be dramatic."

He snorts. "I think we both know which one of us has got the flair for dramatics here. Remember your Oscar-worthy performance the other day?"

"If you agreed to this, then I would just need you to attend a few events with me, maybe a dinner or two. Just enough to convince my parents that I'm head over heels for you. Which is going to be nearly impossible as it is, but as long as I can keep myself from murdering you, then we can pull it off. The quicker, the better."

chapter thirteen
SAINT

SHE'S EXACTLY right about that. The quicker I can get in, the better. That's the thing about poison... even the smallest dose can be lethal. It may spread slowly, damaging everything in its path, but in the end, it does exactly what's intended.

Destroy.

And I'm going to poison the Rousseau family drop by drop.

"I'll do it."

Her mouth falls open as her eyes widen in shock. "*Really?*"

I shrug, not wanting to seem overly eager to ruin her life. "Yep. I want the ice time—why not? I can pretend to be your boy toy for a few weeks if it means in exchange, I get peace and quiet."

She's eying me warily as if she can't quite believe that I'm actually agreeing to what she's proposing, and if what she was offering wasn't as inciting as it is, then there would be no fucking way I'd agree to voluntarily spend more time with her. But the payoff is well worth a few bullshit events.

She stares up at me, brows arched, moving a palm to curve around her hip. "You're really going to do it? You know it has to be fairly believable in order to fool my parents."

There are worse ways to spend my time than rubbing elbows with rich fucks and more than likely getting a free meal out of it. Hard to come by for a guy like me. Not that she needs to know that.

"Never had a problem convincing anyone I'm an asshole, Golden Girl."

"That's not what I mean, and you know it."

I smirk, lifting a shoulder. "If anything, you should be worried about you. You look like you've sucked a fart anytime you're within three feet of me. Kinda hard to convince people that we're together when you look like that."

Her eyes narrow before she rolls them. "Sorry, it's exhausting being in your presence."

"Yeah, I hear that a lot. Specifically, after you spend the night bouncing on my co—"

Abruptly, she reaches out, slapping a hand over my mouth, surprising us both by cutting me off. Her fingers are soft and warm, slightly clammy pressed against my lips.

My lips part, and I nip at her finger, causing her to yelp, cutting her eyes at me.

As quickly as she placed them there, she snatches her

hand back toward her, falling to her side like she's been burned.

"I've heard more about your... dick than I have ever cared to learn, so please, can you stop?" Her throat bobs, swallowing hard. When I grin, arching a brow, she just rolls her eyes. A shitty comeback is on the tip of my tongue, but she beats me to it. "As much as I need your crude, broody assholeness in my favor when it comes to them, I also need you to not be over-the-top to the point that my parents think I'm dropping out of college and having a shotgun wedding."

I shiver at the thought.

Me? Married?

Absolutely the fuck not.

I mean... I'm all for the deflowering part, so I guess I could get on board.

"I can practically read your mind right now. Stop it."

"You said it, not me," I grunt. "Get your mind out of the gutter, Golden Girl. Now, what else? I've got shit to do."

"Ah, that's right, can't keep your fan club waiting."

I nod as I pass my stick back and forth between my hands. "Hard work, but someone's gotta do it. I take my responsibilities very seriously." My lips curl into a crooked smile, flashing teeth.

I couldn't bite the smile back if I tried, seeing her cheeks flush a delicious red and her head shake. I love riling her, pissing her off, getting a response out of her. It makes my fucking blood rush. It's effortless.

Turning, I start skating away, and her voice comes from

behind me. "We should probably exchange numbers so I have a way to contact you outside of the rink."

Slowly, I turn. "Give me yours and I'll text you later."

"How are you going to remember it if you don't have your phone?" she asks warily.

I tap my temple and watch her roll her eyes as she prattles the number off.

I'm sure she probably thinks that I'm nothing but a dumb athlete, but she'd be surprised as fuck to know I have a 3.5 GPA. It's part of the reason I'm even able to attend Orleans University because I'm on a scholarship. If I weren't, then hockey wouldn't be enough.

"See you soon, Golden Girl."

"Unfortunate for me, Satan."

♥ ♥ ♥

After stopping at Tommy's once leaving the rink to pick up a part for my bike, I pull into the driveway of my house after dark. I'm exhausted from practice, class, and skating all in one day, but I've still got an assload of homework to work on and turn in before midnight.

The lights are on inside, dim and warm, shining through the windows of the old, run-down trailer I've grown up in. When I was younger, I was embarrassed to live here. In a metal tin can that probably should've been condemned years ago.

It wasn't always in *this* shitty of a condition. It was

never a mansion in Beverly Hills, but it at least used to look livable. Lately, it's looking more and more dilapidated with each passing day. I keep the lawn cut and the trash taken out, but I don't have the time or resources to keep it up.

It needs a new porch, a new roof, a fresh coat of paint, and a pressure wash. Maybe on my next day off, whenever the hell that will be, I can at least do the pressure wash so it doesn't look so much like a fucking trap house.

I lock my bike up, pocketing the keys in my sweatpants pockets and haul myself and all of my shit through the front door, immediately assaulted by the overwhelming stench of stale beer and sweat.

Not that it's surprising. The one and only thing my father is good at is being a drunk fuckup.

"Shut the door behind you, boy. You're letting out all the fucking cold air," he grunts from the recliner in front of the TV, his voice heavy, words slightly slurring.

I roll my eyes, slamming it behind me. I don't even glance at him as I walk by because I already know exactly what I'll find—him in an old, stained shirt that smells as bad as he does, a pair of boxers he probably hasn't changed in days, with a twenty-four-ounce can of beer clutched in his meaty hand, watching the same reruns of *WWE* on the TV.

I've thought about this a hundred times, maybe even a thousand times in the last ten years. How if I didn't hate him as much as I did, I would almost feel bad for him. For his pathetic, disgusting existence that's been reduced to this—drinking himself to death in front of a busted-ass TV in a piece-of-shit trailer. That's his life. That's the only future he'll ever have, and it's just... sad.

But he chose this life. He makes that decision every morning he wakes up, and I hate him for every day that my mom and I have been subjected to his selfish decisions. For making us suffer because he's a weak and dumb motherfucker that gets drunk and tries to use either of us as a punching bag for his anger.

He used to beat the shit out of me when I was younger. Back when I was smaller than him, but now... most of the time, he knows better. Unless he's shit-faced and not thinking at all.

I never hit him back. I never engage in the bullshit because I know that if I did... I'm not sure I would be able to stop. Not when it all comes pouring out of me. The years of pent-up rage, hurt, fucking disappointment. I don't know if I'm a good enough person to not let that anger take over.

I'll never become him. Even if it fucking kills me. Even if sometimes walking away is the hardest thing I've ever had to do when he gets drunk and tries to put his hands on my mom.

Those are the nights that I see red. That I feel out of control.

The nights that I feel like maybe I *am* becoming him, and panic seizes my chest.

"Saint?" My gaze swings to Mom, who appears at the end of the darkened hallway, her thin brown robe wrapped tightly around her. I hate how the old fabric is draped over her shoulders, swallowing her, a combination of stress and not taking care of herself the way she should because she's taking care of my father instead.

"Hey, Ma." I open my bedroom door and set my bags down on the floor, turning back to her. "Sorry I'm late. Had to stop by Tommy's to pick something up."

"Don't be sorry. I just wanted to wait up for you to make sure that you got home okay. You know I always worry about you on that bike. I left you a plate of red beans in the microwave," she says as I wrap an arm around her shoulders and pull her to me, resting my chin on the top of her head. She feels so small and delicate in my arms, and it makes something deep and dark in my heart twist.

"Thanks, Ma. You okay? How was your day?" I pull back and look down at her, taking in the dark bags beneath her eyes and the lines wrinkled near the corners, exhaustion evident on her face.

Her eyes are the same dark chocolate shade as mine, the one thing that I got from her.

Ma used to be different. Happier, lighter, even though I was so young I can hardly remember those days. The days before everything went to shit and my life wasn't as fucked-up as it is now.

Back when Ma used to smile and laugh. I miss her laugh.

If there's any good inside me… it's because of her and only her.

We wouldn't even have this piece-of-shit trailer if it wasn't for her and the hours that I pull at Tommy's when I can, but honestly, even then, we're barely scraping by.

Most nights, it's beans and whatever I can grab on campus for next to nothing. It's not my house that embarrasses me anymore; I stopped giving a shit about that long ago. I knew better than to ever invite friends over. If someone ever picked me up during high school, then I'd have them pick me up at the grocery store down the street.

I hated being embarrassed by where I lived and where I came from.

Turns out it's not the house or the fact that my family's poor that's the embarrassing part. It's the fact that my father is an alcoholic asshole.

I could strangle that motherfucker with my bare hands and not feel an ounce of emotion.

Maybe in a different life, I could've been a good guy, but with my father's blood running through my veins, I've always been doomed.

"I've told you a hundred times, I'm fine, Ma. I'm too stubborn to die." I grin, trying to lighten the mood. "Thank you for dinner. I'm starving."

She nods, and her eyes soften as she peers up at me. "Welcome, honey. Your…" She trails off, glancing down the hallway to where my father sits. "Your dad's in a mood tonight. Best steer clear, okay?"

Yeah, I have no plans to deal with his shit tonight, so I'm grabbing my dinner and staying in my room till tomorrow with the door locked.

After hugging Ma good night and grabbing my shit, I walk through the living room, fighting the urge to kick over the recliner that my father's passed out in, drunk or high or probably a mixture of both.

He doesn't stir as I pass, a deep snore pushing past his lips. As fucked-up as it is, I'd rather deal with this version of him than the one where he's just getting started or using his fists as a way to take out his anger. Starting shit with me for no reason.

The hallway that leads to my bedroom is lined with jagged, fist-sized holes. A constant reminder that my life will never be normal. Not until I get out of this place.

It wasn't always like this.

At least the few memories I have of before. We were never rich, we didn't have much. Secondhand shit, but at least my father wasn't a drunk and addicted to pain pills.

That's what I can thank Edward Rousseau for.

He's the catalyst that set my fucked-up life into motion.

If it wasn't for him, my dad never would've fallen from that scaffold. He never would've gotten addicted to the pain pills the doctor prescribed him, and he wouldn't have added alcohol into it. Abuse.

None of that would have ever happened if Rousseau had taken responsibility for his company's negligence. Instead, he falsified those accident reports, claiming my dad was already an addict and high on the job, and *that's* why he fell.

All because he didn't want his fucking company to be seen in a bad light or to shell out money to compensate his employee for a faulty fucking tie-off that the safety foreman should have checked.

My father wrongfully lost his job, and suddenly, everything happened at once. We had a mountain of medical bills that no one could afford. He couldn't work because he was hurt, and he was denied unemployment since he technically "quit" his job.

On top of it all, he was addicted to the pain pills the doctor prescribed to help him.

None of it should have happened. Except it did.

And the millionaire got the easy way out while we've been living a fucking nightmare.

Now, it's his turn.

chapter fourteen

LENNON

"YOU'RE LATE," I say through clenched teeth the moment he pulls up on that death trap he calls transportation and cuts the engine.

To no surprise, he's not wearing a helmet because that wouldn't fit the cliché bad boy image he's got going on.

Danger, living on the edge, might end up splattered on the pavement... oooh, ah.

Rolling my eyes, I cross my arms over my chest, completely and utterly annoyed that I've been waiting out here for almost twenty minutes when we *just* texted about this last night and he confirmed our plans. It's early September in southern Louisiana, and I'm nearly drowning in my own sweat from the humidity, and I'm feeling slightly emotionally unstable after the conversation I had with my dad this morning.

It was the first time we've spoken since the night of the gala with Chandler, and he truly has no grasp on understanding why I'm beyond upset at him. If anything, he blames me for "making a scene" and embarrassing him in front of his friends and colleagues. Hearing that out of his mouth instead of an apology only made me that much more angry, frustrated... and most of all *hurt*.

I almost felt a sliver of guilt for skating in secret behind their backs, but after talking to him today, I only feel like it's one step toward gaining back everything he's taken from me.

"This might surprise you, but my schedule doesn't revolve around *you*, Golden Girl. I had practice, and I barely had time to shower before coming all the way over here," he grunts as he swings his leg over his bike and shoves his keys into the pocket of his athletic shorts. Now that he mentioned a shower, I see his dark, unruly hair is still wet and curling at the ends around his nape, and it looks like he hasn't shaved since the last time I saw him, a dusting of hair covering his chiseled jaw.

Not that I allow myself more than a second to look because... No. I am not going there.

This is strictly a mutually beneficial business arrangement.

"Well, my schedule also does not revolve around *you*, Satan. You're like thirty minutes late," I retort.

"I'm here, aren't I? You know, I'm starting to think you've got a degrading kink or something with how much you like to talk shit to me. Does it get you hot?" he asks, a lopsided grin pulling at his full lips.

I haven't a single clue why, but his crass words cause my pulse to race.

I push down the strange feeling swirling in my

stomach and scoff. "You wish. Seems like something you'd be into."

His shoulder lifts. "I'm into a lot of things. None of which you could handle."

Like… what? I want to ask, even though I shouldn't care.

I hate him and literally everything about him. I do not need to know what kind of depraved, kinky things he's into.

"Mmmm, Golden Girl's blushing." My gaze snaps to him and off the tight contour of his bicep beneath the black T-shirt he's wearing. "I think I'm onto something. Miss prim and proper likes it dirty, doesn't she?"

Ignoring the rapid patter in my chest, I turn toward the tailor shop and swallow hard. I can hear him chuckling behind me, and it makes me consider turning back just to throttle him.

He's so smug… and arrogant. Infuriating.

"Don't worry, I won't tell." The rough, low timbre of his voice sounds next to my neck, where he dips his head, lips almost brushing against my ear. I can feel the heat of his breath caressing the shell of my ear, and I nearly shiver. It takes every ounce of control in my body to stop the visceral reaction. "Your secret is safe with me."

Something tells me that nothing is safe when it comes to Saint Devereaux and that I should remember that no matter what.

"Are you done yet?" I mutter, my voice slightly shaky.

A beat passes between us, heavy and thick with something expectant, before he reaches past me, wraps his large hand around the handle of the door, and starts to open it. "Ladies first."

His hand finds the small of my back, a gesture that I would think to be gentlemanlike if I didn't know who he was. Still, it causes my stomach to dance in a foreign way.

Once we step inside the custom tailor, I have a hard time focusing, my gaze locking on Saint as he looks around the modern store with light gray walls, marble tables, and luxurious gold fixtures. There's a large chandelier with hundreds of crystals gleaming brightly in the center of the room.

"Fancy," he grunts, running the pad of his finger along the soft fabric lining the tables.

It's not the first time I've been in Bordeaux's. They've been in New Orleans for nearly a century, providing custom tailoring for the people who can afford the ridiculous price tag. Which is exactly why I brought Saint here in the first place. I've purchased things from here in the past for other events, and if my dad sees the charge on my account, he won't think twice about it.

He just won't know *what* I'm buying… or for whom.

A tuxedo fit for a king. It just so happens to be the king of *hell*.

"Miss Rousseau, hello! Welcome in." Leo, the tailor I called this morning to make our appointment with, greets us, his blue eyes warm and welcoming as he glances between Saint and me. "And you must be Mr. Devereaux? Pleased to meet you."

He extends his hand toward Saint, who glances down

at it, then back up, arching a brow but making no move to return the gesture.

I quickly step in, pasting on a bright smile. "Yes, uh, we're in a bit of a hurry today, Leo, sorry!"

Leo nods enthusiastically, wrinkles forming in the corners of his eyes. "Absolutely no problem. I'll just pull a few of the most popular colors and fabrics this season and be back in just a moment."

Once he walks away, I narrow my eyes at Saint and scowl. "Can you not be so rude? Jesus."

"Just keeping up appearances. Asshole, remember? Gotta keep up the act." I hate that stupid smirk that turns his lips up, showing the slight dimple in his cheek.

"Yeah, no acting necessary," I retort. "You being an asshole comes naturally."

He chuckles as he walks over and stops in front of me. I can see the slight golden ring that circles his dark irises, like molten honey, and he opens his mouth like he may say something but just shakes his head instead.

I put distance between us, looking around at the various bow ties in glass cases scattered along the wall.

A few minutes later, Leo returns, fabrics laid over his arms to present to Saint.

Who clearly doesn't know or care about what he wears to the event, so I make a choice for him, hoping that it's the right one.

Once Leo disappears once again to the back to prepare for the fitting, Saint turns toward me. "So what's the plan? You're just going to dress me up in a monkey suit and parade me around until daddy loses his mind?"

"A *monkey suit*?" I sputter, "That is a two-thousand-dollar Saint Laurent."

"Do you think I give a shit about that?" he deadpans, expression flat, and I sigh.

Yet another reminder that he and I… we exist in two very different worlds, and I'm not really sure whether that's a good or bad thing anymore.

"I don't know exactly what the plan is yet, but yeah, it does require you to dress up and go to a black-tie event. That's why we're here. Obviously, I'm not here by choice. They have a dress code, so for you to even walk through the door, you have to look the part."

Saint smirks. "And you don't think daddy dearest is going to grill either of us the first chance he gets when you spring this on him? Like how all of a sudden, you're fucking with a guy like me?"

My stomach drops. Shit.

He's right… and I've been so caught up in trying to figure out the particulars of this entire stupid arrangement to even *think* about that.

"Just wanna make sure I'm prepared for whatever shit's coming my way."

I nod. "I mean, he *could* ask questions. Unlikely, but he might. He's mostly concerned with how it looks for him, not what's actually happening in my life, so the image alone of the two of us 'together' should be enough. I guess if he asks, just go with the truth. We met at school."

It's not the full truth, but it's the closest thing to it.

Technically, we *did* meet at school.

"I can tell him how you fell for me the second you stepped on the ic—"

"No," I blurt, cutting him off, my spine straightening. When his brow arches, I blow out a dejected sigh. "I… He doesn't know. That I'm skating again, so please do not bring that up at any point, ever. I'm serious, Saint. Please."

I want to piss my dad off and make him understand that I am never, under absolutely zero circumstances, ever getting back together with Chandler, but I don't want to completely ruin our relationship for the rest of eternity by him finding out that I've been lying and keeping this from him. And I definitely don't want to give him the opportunity to find a way to somehow shut it down again. It's just another tear in the already unraveling relationship.

"Golden Girl's got secrets. Who would've thought," he mumbles, gaze snapping to Leo as he walks back into the room with a dress shirt draped over his arms.

"Sorry to interrupt. Please try this on, and we can check and see how it fits, especially the arm length." Leo passes the fabric to Saint and promptly leaves, clearly picking up on the vibes that he gives off.

My jaw nearly hits the floor as I watch Saint reach for the neck of his T-shirt and pull it over his head, dropping it onto the chair beside him.

I knew he was in shape—he's a hockey player, so that's to be expected—but holy… shit.

He looks like he was carved by a renowned sculptor, molded from the most exquisite marble, with rows and rows of abs and an Adonis belt that tapers into the shorts slung low on his hips.

For the very first time, I worry about what I have *actually* gotten myself into.

chapter fifteen
SAINT

SHE LOOKS like a deer caught in headlights.

Her eyes, a blue-green mixture like the depths of the ocean just as it turns deep, widened. Rosy, plump lips parted, a bright red flush coating her cheeks as she stares at me like I've stripped fucking naked in front of her rather than just taken my shirt off.

If I'm not mistaken, which I rarely am not, there's a look of heat mixed with shock.

Jesus, this is going to be entirely too much fucking fun. Maybe the most fun I've ever had in my life with someone, and that's saying a lot since I spend the majority of my free time between a girl's thighs, tits… or mouth. I'm not picky.

Golden Girl wanted an asshole, a bad boy to let her daddy think she's playing on the wrong side of the tracks, and she found exactly what she was looking for.

"You know, it's not polite to stare," I murmur, my gaze slipping over her delicate features, watching as the realization of being caught hits her, and she stiffens.

She can try and hide it all she wants, but I affect her no matter how much she may hate it and try to act the opposite.

Her eyes fall to the floor, looking at every other thing in the room but me as she smooths her palms over the blue jean shorts she's wearing.

"Not staring."

Chuckling, I slowly slip my arms into the sleeves but leave the shirt hanging open, unbuttoned. "If I'd known the only way to get you to be quiet was to take off my clothes, I would've gladly done it before now."

She rolls her eyes, but I can see the corner of her lip curving even as she attempts to stop it. "Do you take *anything* at all seriously? Ever?"

I shrug, "Rarely."

"Shocking."

Slowly, almost wolfishly, I walk over to where she's sitting in the large, oversized leather chair, watching as her throat bobs and her lips part slightly, eyes widening with each step I take toward her.

I stop when I'm right in front of her, peering down at her doe-like eyes. I bend, flattening my palms along the arms of the chair, and dip my head. "You know, I've been thinking…"

"Also shocking," she retorts snarkily, but her words are breathy, and she's not fooling me, not in the least, not the way she's trying to fool herself.

The sweet, innocent virgin until she probably dies is attracted to the guy that she can't stand.

And I bet she fucking hates herself for it.

My lips twitch as I lean even closer, until I hear her breath hitch. Raising my finger, I bring it to her pale, creamy skin and ghost the rough pad of it along her collarbone, watching as her eyes squeeze shut like it'll somehow make me disappear too.

"You want me to play like I'm your boyfriend, yet I can't even get close to you without your cheeks blazing. How do you think you're going to fool anyone when a simple *touch* makes you respond like this?"

I drag my finger languidly, the barest of touches, down the center of her chest and almost make it to the shallow space between her tits before she reaches up, her fingers curling around mine to stop me from going any further. Smirking, I lift my eyes to hers. "See what I mean, Golden Girl? Can't be your boyfriend if you act like a Catholic schoolgirl the moment I touch you."

Even with her pupils dilating, she tries to deny what's painfully obvious to us both: her attraction to me.

Her green eyes roll. "Sorry that your proximity makes me physically ill."

I chuckle. "Who are you trying to convince... me or *yourself*?"

I can feel the rapid thrum of her heartbeat beneath my finger as she stutters, "I-I... No convincing necessary. How about we worry about that when it becomes a problem? As of right now, I'm not entirely convinced we are going to be able to make it *to* the fundraiser."

Just as I open my mouth to tell her that if we don't, it'll be because of her and not me, I feel my phone vibrating in my pocket. Straightening, I fish it out of my pocket, my brow pinching when I see Mom's name on the screen.

She never calls me during the day.

"Hello?" I answer, bringing the phone to my ear.

"Saint, I just got home from work, and there's a note... A note on the door, and I don't know what to do. I-I'm scared. I don't kno—" The words break as she speaks. She's panicked, strained in a way that has terror wrapping around my throat and cutting off my oxygen. "Can you please come home?"

"I'll be right there. It's okay. Whatever it is, it's okay," I say roughly, trying to reassure her, although I'm not even sure what's happening.

My gaze flicks to Lennon where she's staring at me with wide eyes, concern evident in their depths.

The moment I press End and shove my phone into my slacks, she's rising from the chair. "Is everything okay? You look wor—"

"I'm fine. I have to go," I mutter, shoving the shirt down my arms, one sleeve at a time, as I move across the room toward the dressing room.

"But we're not done—" she starts, and I cut her off again before she can continue her sentence.

"I said I have to fucking go, Lennon."

There's no remorse in my words, in the way that I snap at her. I can't even fucking think straight after that phone call.

Her mouth slams shut, her expression darkening, and finally, she nods.

Without another word, I turn and walk toward the exit.

♥ ♥ ♥

NOTICE TO VACATE

The letter my mom holds in her shaking hands is a fucking eviction letter. We are over a month behind on rent, and we have two weeks to come up with the money, or we'll be homeless.

Fucking homeless.

I take the letter from her, reading it again and again until the words bleed together.

"I-I don't know how he found it, Saint. I hid it in my closet in an old shoebox," Mom whispers quietly, her eyes red-rimmed and puffy from crying. I could fucking kill him.

I'm so pissed right now that I don't trust myself to even speak.

Not that I'm surprised. This is exactly the type of shit that I would expect from my fuckup of a father, but it doesn't make me any less mad.

I clench the paper in my hand, balling it in my fist as I attempt to suck in a breath when my anger threatens to boil over.

How fucking selfish and careless could you be? This is exactly why I told Mom I could take over and make sure things were paid from my bank account, but she was afraid that he would lose it. There's nothing more she hates than seeing him angry, especially when he tries to take it out on me.

She didn't care if she took the brunt of his anger, but never me.

Even though I could take him, could handle anything that motherfucker threw my way.

Yet... she still won't leave. No matter how many times I've begged on my knees, pleaded for her to leave with me. It's always the same excuses, the same shit every single time.

He can't live without me. How will he take care of himself? He'll drink himself to death.

Yeah, well, maybe that's for the fucking best.

I sigh, dragging my palm down my face as I swallow. What the hell are we going to do?

It's the same question I've been asking myself since she handed me the notice. I'm fucking terrified, but I can't show that. I have to be strong for her, no matter what. Just like I've always been.

"We'll figure it out, Ma. Let me handle it," I say, swinging my gaze to hers.

A tear slips down her cheeks, and my heart feels like it's going to fucking shrivel up and die in my chest. I hate seeing her cry, seeing yet another thing my father has done to hurt her.

Despite the fact that she stays after everything he's done and everything he's put her through, at the core of it, she's a victim.

I know that. And it breaks my goddamn heart. Whatever's left of it.

"I'm sorry, Saint. This is my fault. I-I… I should've…" she whispers with a sniffle, using the sleeve of her cardigan to brush away her tears.

"It's not your fault, Ma. You know it's hi—" I stop myself, exhaling. It doesn't help, cussing him into the ground, because she'll never see it.

My father stole all of our rent money from the back of her closet and probably blew it on pills and booze, and still… she'll make an excuse for him.

"Just… I'll take care of it. We have two weeks, and I'll handle it. You don't worry about it, okay?" I loop an arm around her shoulders and pull her to me, where she buries her face into the front of my shirt, sniffling. Even though I'm pissed, so goddamn angry I could put my fist through a wall, I push it down.

So it can't control me. So *he* can't control me.

Right now, I know that she's safe, here with me. I don't know how I'm going to pull it together or what the fuck I'm going to do, but all that matters is that she's safe, right here, right now.

That's what I'm holding on to.

Right now.

Even if it fucking kills me in the process.

chapter sixteen
LENNON

MY STOMACH IS DANCING with nerves as I pace the sidewalk in front of Commander's Palace, my small pearl clutch tucked under my arm and the short train of my vintage Chanel dress swishing with each step.

If Saint's late to this stupid event, I'm going to murder him. Which is unfortunate that after all of the times I've been tempted to, it's all going to end here.

He promised he wouldn't be late, and I'm the very last person waiting outside of the event aside from security, who are currently eying me like they might have to escort me off the premises.

The undeniable roar of his motorcycle echoes down the road, and my chest sags in a flood of relief.

Thank God.

Him actually being on time might be the one and *only* thing that goes right tonight.

I'm already preparing for the absolute worst, hence my anxiety being through the roof despite wearing this insanely gorgeous dress and having my makeup professionally done, which usually always makes nights like this slightly more bearable.

There's no rational reason for my pulse to skitter so rapidly as I watch Saint pull up to the valet stand on his motorcycle, sleek, black, and gleaming beneath the sun that's setting behind the clouds.

It definitely has nothing to do with the way that he looks in the custom Saint Laurent tux, tattoos crawling up his throat and painting his skin in a way that nearly feels unholy. The dark ink peeks out from beneath his cuffs as he reaches for the key and cuts the engine, the fabric of his sleeves tightening around his biceps.

My mouth isn't dry because of him, right? No, it's simply because of my nerves.

I've never been a great liar, even to myself.

Saint Devereaux is the forbidden fruit. The very thing that tempted Eve in the garden, and I wonder, would he be as deadly as I imagine?

His dark, molten gaze connects with mine as he swings a leg off his bike and stands at full height, handing the keys to the valet attendant.

I allow myself only a few seconds to look, imagining that he's not the asshole I know him to be, and then I'm going right back to hating him.

He makes it disgustingly easy to dislike him, but that doesn't mean that I can't acknowledge the very unfortunate fact that he's hot. Ungodly hot.

With his dark hair falling in his eyes from the slick-backed style he has tonight, the dark stubble shadowing his sharp jaw, and black ink peeking out wherever his tanned skin shows, he looks more like a mafia man out of one of Maisie's stupid romance novels than he does a hockey player.

And honestly, I'm not sure which version is worse.

The tux fits him as if it was made for him and not simply tailored to fit. He has the kind of body that fills out a three-piece suit in a way that should be a sin.

I'm still staring when he finally turns my way, his eyes finding mine and catching me in the act of shamelessly drinking him in.

Shit.

His lips tilt into a cocky smirk, and he lifts a brow as he shoves his hands into the pockets of his pants and saunters toward me.

I steel my spine, sucking in a trembling breath while lifting my chin, hoping that my nerves aren't written on my face.

"Golden Girl." His voice is a low, rough, decadent timbre that unleashes a foreign feeling in the pit of my stomach, and I push it down, along with the shiver that threatens to rack my spine.

I swallow roughly. "Satan."

His lips twitch. "Nice dress." I feel his eyes everywhere as they travel down the length of my body in an unhurried perusal. Each place his gaze touches feels hot, like my skin would burn if I brought my fingers to it.

I'm obviously having a mental breakdown after all the stress leading up to tonight.

That's the only reason I'm feeling so flustered and on edge right now.

Clearing my throat, I glance up at him. "Thanks. You… clean up nice."

"Nice? Sunday school clothes are nice. There's nothing nice about me, remember? I look hot as fuck in this monkey suit." He brings a hand to his chest, fingers splayed over his heart, clutching it as if he's wounded. "It's okay to admit it. I won't tell anyone the bad boy from the slums turns you on."

And there it is.

The cocky, self-assured ego so big it barely fits into whatever room he's walked into.

"Your lack of humility never ceases to surprise me. You'd think that I'd be used to the stuff that comes out of your mouth by now, but yet, here we are," I retort with an eye roll before dragging my gaze to the entrance of the restaurant. "Are you ready? We're going to be late, and there is nothing my father hates more than me being late."

His snark is immediate, his stupid grin spreading into a shit-eating smile. "What's that saying about apples never falling far…"

My elbow connects with his ribs, and despite my sudden violence, he simply chuckles like I've tickled him, then turns and starts walking toward the entrance.

I catch him with my fingers curling around his thick bicep, halting him. "Wait."

"I thought you said we're going to be late?"

Licking my lips, I blow out an exhale, dropping my hand away from him when I realize that I'm still touching his arm. "I need you to take this seriously if we're going to sell this."

Slowly, he steps forward until he's so close that the smell of his bodywash, fresh pine and cedar, surrounds me. "And what makes you think that I'm not taking being your *fake* boyfriend seriously, Golden Girl?" His lips curl around the edges, dark eyes heating until I swear they're simmering in the depths before he dips his head down to my ear. A wave of goose bumps scatters along my skin when his warm breath caresses the shell of my ear, and I hate that my body reacts to him when my mind wants anything but. "I'm completely dedicated to playing my part, but the question is, are *you*?"

Driving his point home, he rubs the tip of his nose down the length of my neck, the ghost of a touch, and my heart feels like it might burst free from my rib cage and fall between us at our feet.

My God.

How am I going to pull this off when every time he's near, I have heart palpitations just from the filthy things that leave his mouth? Add in proximity that makes my pulse pound, and I feel light-headed, nearly swaying on my four-inch Valentino heels.

"We're going to be late," I murmur, my words breathy, barely decipherable. It feels like they don't even belong to me, my voice no longer my own.

"Then you better get ready to put on an Oscar-worthy performance, Golden Girl."

chapter seventeen
SAINT

I FEEL like a wolf in sheep's clothing walking into this party. Gala, fucking fundraiser, whatever they're calling it.

Like I'm stepping into a world I don't belong to and never will. A world that I fucking hate. These rich people flaunting their money and fancy fucking outfits, trying to hide the fact that deep down, they're all as fucked-up as the rest of us. They're just masking it with materialistic shit.

"Okay," Lennon mutters, seemingly more to herself than me, sucking in a breath so deep her chest moves with it. Her gaze swings to a waiter who's passing in front of us with a platter of champagne glasses, and her eyes light up as she stops him, quickly swiping a glass off the tray. Obviously, drinking age doesn't apply to said rich people. "Gonna need this. Want one?"

"Nah, I'm good. Not much of a drinker."

I couldn't tell her that I'd rather drown myself than

drink a drop of alcohol. The result of having an alcoholic drug addict for a father. I would never touch that shit.

She nods, staying silent as she brings the glass to her plump, red-painted lips and takes a large sip.

I have a pretty good idea of what to expect out of tonight's charade, but the one thing I didn't expect?

Her in that goddamn dress. Black satin molded to every inch of her curves that's making my mouth fucking water. I almost swallowed my tongue the moment I saw her, heat ripping through me when my gaze found the long slit that traveled up her thigh and the red fuck-me heels on her feet that gave her a good extra five inches. She's still tiny compared to me, head barely reaching my chest, but fuck, her legs go on for days in this dress.

But I wasn't going to admit that she almost knocked me on my ass tonight. Instead, I opted for "nice dress," even though I had a litany of other things going through my head.

Like how my dick was hardening behind these stupid pants at the thought of tossing those legs over my shoulders and making her dig those heels into my back until I bled while I devoured her.

Not exactly the kind of thing you lead with instead of hello.

"Shit. There he is," she mutters with her eyes wide. I follow her gaze across the room to the *he* in question and see her father. The resemblance between them is uncanny. Same auburn hair, high cheekbones, striking green eyes. He's dressed like he's going to the fucking Oscars or some shit, and not just some rich asshole without a moral compass and more money than sense.

I feel her stiffen slightly beside me as she steels her spine, straightening like a warrior preparing for battle, and I do the same.

Not for the reason she'll think, but because I'm finally meeting the man I've spent nearly my entire life hating with every fiber of my being.

Pent-up rage bubbles hotly beneath the surface of my skin, threatening to boil over as I stare at him, laughing without a care in the fucking world. Surrounded by his rich friends, wearing his expensive fucking suit and watch, living a life that he doesn't deserve because of the people he's stepped on to get there.

I flex my fist by my side, curling and uncurling my fingers when they begin to ache.

I want to wrap my hands around his fucking throat and squeeze until that rage is gone, but I push it down, burying it deep beneath the surface, keeping the mask on my face firmly in place. I have to play the long game.

I have to see this through until the very end because if I don't, then it'll all be for nothing.

A shrill bolt of excitement rolls down my spine at the fact that I'm finally going to come face-to-face with the motherfucker who's responsible for the fucked-up mess that's been my life.

I'm finally going to look him in the eye, shake his hand that's covered in the metaphorical blood of my family... all while he has no idea that I'm about to blow up his entire fucking life.

That I'm going to fuck his daughter, taking her precious little virtue, and he's got to live with the fact that a trashy piece of shit like me is the one that dirtied her up.

He'll never see it coming until it's too late. Until I've dirtied her all up and ruined her.

Edward Rousseau is going to pay for what he's done, one way or another.

"Looks like we're up," I mutter quietly.

Her gaze whips to mine, and I smirk as I reach between us and grab her free hand, the one not currently clutching the champagne glass so tightly I'm worried she might actually break it, and lace my fingers in hers.

Her palm is warm and slightly clammy, a sign that she's nervous as fuck about tonight. Even more than she wants to let on to me.

It's a conundrum. How she's parading me around as her fake boyfriend to piss off her dad, to stick it to him, yet clearly cares what he thinks. For someone who tries so hard to pretend she doesn't give a shit when it comes to him, her body betrays her.

It's the one thing I can't figure out, the one thing I can't put my finger on.

Why?

Why the sudden rebellion when it's obvious she's never done a thing wrong in her entire fucking life.

What changed? What pushed her to using me as her way of getting back at her father?

Her eyes move down to where our hands are clasped together, and I watch her throat bob as she swallows roughly.

"Just… follow my lead," she finally says before turning up her glass and draining the last of her champagne in one swallow, then placing it onto a nearby table. Her exhale is unsteady as she blows out a breath, then begins to drag me through the crowded room.

I can feel how nervous she is, and it makes me wonder if she knows who her father *really* is… would she still feel the same way about him? Would she still care about what he thinks, knowing all of the fucked-up shit he's gone to lengths to hide from her?

Something tells me… no, she wouldn't.

And I can't wait to see it all fucking fall apart.

A few of the people we pass lift their glasses and speak to Lennon as we pass, but she doesn't falter, continuing on a straight path to the other side of the room.

This is her element, somewhere I'm sure she's been a thousand times before now, but somehow, it still feels like she doesn't fit. Not all the way. Not the way the others do.

And that surprises me. Maybe she's just as much a wolf in sheep's clothing as I am… or maybe Lennon Rousseau is something that I've yet to even discover.

We stop a few feet from her father, who hasn't noticed his daughter is even standing in front of him, lost in conversation with a tall guy wearing a fucking overcoat like some type of English lord.

I feel her hand trembling in mine, her nerves ramping up, so I step closer, dipping my head to her ear. "Exactly how much of an asshole do you want me to be? Just so we're clear?"

Jade-green pools meet mine. "Oh, you know… just be your *normal* self."

Yeah, she has no fucking clue.

I nod just as her father glances up and sees her for the first time, his eyes widening slightly before his well-practiced mask drops back in place. He bends slightly, whispering something in the ear of the blonde standing beside him, who I assume is Lennon's mother. She glances up, eyes flicking between us as she nods, pasting on a smile that feels as fake as she looks.

Showtime, Golden Girl.

"Lennon, sweetheart, I'm so glad you were able to make it," he says, walking up and reaching for her, placing an arm around her shoulder.

It feels… forced from the outside looking in. She looks stiff and honestly pretty fucking uncomfortable, and my head goes back to *why*?

Hmmm. Maybe this shit with her father is a lot messier than I thought.

"Hi."

Her mother steps forward to pull her into a hug, wearing an emerald gown, heavy diamonds adorning her neck and wrists. She presses her lips to each of Lennon's cheeks, keeping her hands along her arms as she steps back to admire her. "You look absolutely beautiful, darling. I love this dress on you. Very classic."

Lennon smiles politely. "Thank you."

Finally, her mother glances over at me, her smile dimming slightly. "And… who's this?"

Her throat bobs before she looks up at me, then back at her parents. "This is Saint. My…"

"*Boyfriend*," I finish for her with a smirk.

Her mother looks almost as surprised as her husband, but she never loses her perfectly poised smile. Clearly, she's well versed in keeping up appearances, but then again, I can see past the bullshit. The little things, the sharp intake of breath, the slight twitch of her smile, the way she swallows roughly.

I know better than anyone about not letting the world see what's beneath the mask.

I stick my hand out for her father to shake, and his gaze drops down, slowly flicking over the dark ink on the top of my hand.

I wish I could take my phone out and snap a picture of his face. Like he's smelling shit, nose scrunched slightly, crinkling on the top as his lips are pulled tight in a combination of a smile and a grimace.

"*Boyfriend?*" he mutters, ignoring my outstretched hand altogether.

"It's fairly new, but I couldn't wait any longer for you and Mom to meet him," Lennon says before looking up at me. I give her a wink, ready to amp up the assholeness because I'm dying to see that vein in his neck to poke out even more. Damn, he's already turning a violent shade of red. He might want to get his blood pressure checked.

Mission accomplished, Golden Girl, and I haven't even said anything offensive… *yet*.

This is far too fucking easy.

To be fair, though, I don't blame him for not wanting

someone like me with his prim and proper princess. Which will make it all the more fun when I finally do.

"You know what they say... when you know, you know. And trust me, I knew. Right, baby?" I murmur before dipping my head and pressing my lips to the space right below her ear. She shivers against me, and then she tightens her hand in mine, squeezing my fingers until they feel like they're going to break off.

A warning.

Too bad I don't give a fuck about warnings. Exactly why she chose me for this shtick in the first place.

Damn, though, for someone so tiny, the girl is surprisingly strong.

Her mother lets out a choked sound, and we both glance up at her. She's got her hand pressed against her mouth, and she clears her throat quietly, another smile slipped into place. "Well, it's so lovely to meet you, Saint. We're delighted you could be here tonight. This is an event that's very near and dear to Edward's heart. He loves this foundation and tries to make this the top fundraising event of the year."

My gaze shifts to Lennon's father, and my stomach churns. Yeah, he's an outstanding fucking citizen alright. Donating to charity, taking pictures with the lowly people who work for him. Too bad the world doesn't know that he's a lying piece of shit who would do anything, step on anyone, to keep this lifestyle up.

Edward smiles, and it doesn't meet his eyes. "Yes, absolutely. We should probably head to our table. The auction should begin right after dinner is served."

"Perfect. Could you give us just a minute?" Lennon asks. "We'll be right there."

Her mother's nose bunches in obvious disgust at us being alone. "Uh... of course, sweetheart."

They glance between us for another moment before disappearing into the crowd.

I can feel Lennon's entire body sag the second they're out of view, putting a stop to the performance. She untangles our fingers, taking a step away from me and glaring up at me with a fiery stare.

"What the hell, Saint?" she hisses, glancing around to make sure no one heard her. "What was that?"

My brow lifts. "What was... what?"

Her eyes narrow. "The touching. That... *kiss*."

I almost laugh out loud. She has no fucking clue what she's signed herself up for. *Oh, you poor, sheltered, innocent girl.* It's almost a crime to be the one she chose for this. I step closer until I feel the front of her pressed against me, drinking in the surprised, sharp intake of breath as she peers up at me. "Just playing my part. You want to convince them or not?"

"Of course I want to. You're here, aren't you? That doesn't mean you have to..."

"To what? Kiss you here?" I bring my fingers to her neck, ghosting them along the spot where my lips were just minutes ago. She shivers beneath my touch, her piercing green eyes widening. "Don't forget, Golden Girl, that you're *mine* to kiss... touch... whatever I want. Even if it's just for show."

chapter eighteen
LENNON

MY FACE IS BURNING as I sink down into the chair at the dinner table, the flush creeping down my neck and disappearing beneath the front of my dress. Every cell in my body feels like it's on fire, and it has nothing to do with the temperature in the room and everything to do with the far too tempting hockey player next to me.

I am so beyond in over my head. *I'm his to "kiss and touch."* What the *hell* was that, and why does it make my stomach dip just replaying the gravelly tone of his words?

Clearly, that champagne went straight to my head. I shouldn't have drunk it on an empty stomach, and I absolutely should not be thinking about the way his lips felt as they brushed against my ea—

"Lennon?" My father's voice stirs me from my thoughts, and my face feels even hotter.

I clear my throat as I look up, gaze darting to Saint, who's grinning like he's just won something, then to my parents, who look slightly concerned still.

"Yes? Sorry, I was…" Saint kissing me in different places besides just behind my ear? Guilty. "Uh, just thinking about the test I have in my finance class."

I'm going to crawl under this table any minute now.

"I was asking how the two of you met?" Mom asks as she swirls the red wine in her glass around slightly, wearing a knowing expression.

Shit.

I knew they'd ask questions, and I told Saint to go with the truth, but my mind is suddenly blanking, and I'm starting to panic until I feel his hand on the top of my thigh beneath the table. It's warm and oddly… reassuring, even though I'm not sure if that's what he meant it to be.

I suck in a deep breath, quickly gathering myself. He squeezes my thigh, and I fight the urge to press my legs together.

"We met at school," I finally say, my words coming out in a rush. I reach beneath the table and try to pull his hand from my leg, but his fingers tighten.

No need to crawl beneath the table when I'm going to spontaneously combust. Why is my body being such a traitorous bitch when I hate this man?

I don't understand.

Mom smiles. "Are you also majoring in business, Saint?"

I look over at him, praying that he doesn't say something inherently ridiculous, which is the majority of what comes out of his mouth. "Nah. General studies. Just need to keep my grades passing so I can stay on the hockey team. I'm a left winger."

"Oh, I see. I guess I'm just trying to figure out how the two of you... crossed paths?" She laughs airily. "Are your parents OU alumni?"

For a second, he's quiet, something dark passing over his face, but it's gone as quickly as it came.

"They're not. I'm the only one in my family to go to college. First one out of the trailer park." He chuckles, and Mom's eyes widen. She looks over at my father with a cut of her eyes, nostrils slightly flaring.

Damn, he's good.

"Ah, what an unlikely pairing between the two of you." Her smile is strained as she lays down the backhanded insult.

What she really is saying is why am I with a hockey player, with no trust fund, no Roth IRA, no prestigious family name... no future.

At least not the one she and my father have been priming me for.

"Yeah, but this chemistry between us is just too fuc—" Saint starts, only to be interrupted by a flurry of waitstaff sweeping into the room, carrying the first course of the night. Plates of steaming steak, topped with garlic butter and greens, alongside roasted vegetables and fingerling potatoes.

Saved by the bell.

Relief floods me, my shoulders sagging. As much as it pains me to admit, Saint was right. We should've probably prepared better for this.

We somehow make it through the first course unscathed. Although my parents ask way too many questions that we manage to answer without the whole charade blowing up in our faces. It's surprisingly easy to lie to them. Something I've never done before.

Until recently.

I pretend to know the guy sitting next to me, and the truth is, the only things I know about him are ones that drive me insane.

Like the way his fingers are currently trailing up the exposed skin of my thigh through the slit in my dress, dancing along my heated flesh until my nipples tighten.

My heart is racing as I look over at him, expecting his gaze to be on my parents, the party, his food.

Anywhere but… me.

His eyes are on *me*. The dark flare of hunger burning in the depths takes me by surprise and sends my pulse skittering, making me breathless.

God, what the *fuck* is happening right now?

I would clench my thighs together to stifle the persistent throb forming between them, but I can't because then he'll know exactly what he's doing to me.

I hardly touch the rest of my food because I'm too focused on not reacting to Saint's fingers dancing across my thigh.

I have absolutely no idea how I'm going to survive the rest of *tonight*, much less the entirety of this arrangement. Ironically, it's not because I'm going to murder him, although the jury is still out on that. No, it's because the one thing I wasn't expecting was for him to be attracted to me at all and for it to be mutual.

He's the last guy I should ever go for. Brooding bad boy couldn't be further from my type, yet... I can't deny it.

Maybe this attraction has existed since I met him, but only now with the sudden proximity, I'm painfully aware of the fact.

Even if I hate him.

This is why Maisie made the one and only rule... Don't fall for the bad boy.

Bad boys are for fun only.

"Lennon, your mother and I need to make our rounds and speak with a few of the backers before the auction starts. Are you two planning on staying?" Dad asks from across the table, his eyes shining with disapproval as they bounce between Saint and me. He wouldn't say it out loud because he's far too proper for that, but I can tell that he hates this. The fact that I'm "dating" Saint and that I've brought him here tonight.

"No, I actually think we're going to head out. Saint has an early practice tomorrow, and I need to keep studying for my finance test."

None of that is true, but I think we've tested our luck enough times tonight.

I lift the napkin from my lap and set it onto the plate of barely eaten food, then turn to Saint. "I'm okay with heading out if you are?"

His eyes twinkle. "Of course, baby. I parked my bike out front."

"*Bike?*" Mom blanches.

"Oh... I drive a vintage Indian classic motorcycle. I restored it myself at the auto shop I work at," Saint says, his grin proud. "But don't worry, my girl has her very own helmet. Safety first."

He pats me gently on the top of my head, like I'm a cute little toddler.

My stomach lurches. My God, I might actually be responsible for my parents keeling over in the middle of this damn fundraiser.

Wait, I didn't even know he had a job. I wonder if that's real or just part of the ruse?

Honestly, he's so good at this I can't tell the difference. I make a mental note to ask him about it later as I watch Mom's eyes widening in near panic, and Dad, well... he looks like he's going to drop the "everything's fine" facade any second now if the crimson shade of his face is any indication.

I think we've dropped one too many things on them tonight, and their decorum is fading.

"It's totally fine. He drives very slowly," I say with a bright smile, my voice an octave higher.

"Yep. *Very* slow, and Lennon knows how to ride. She's a natural," Saint says with a wink as he rises from his chair and offers me his hand. My cheeks are flaming, and I think I might swallow my tongue, but still, I slip my slightly clammy palm in his, and he helps me out of my chair.

"It was a *pleasure* to meet you both. I'm sure we'll be seeing each other again soon," he drawls lazily.

I feel his arm slip around my waist, and I lean into him slightly as I offer my parents a smile. "I'll check in sometime this week?"

A beat passes, the silence strained and tense as Mom

nods. "Yes, that sounds good. I'll call you about the upcoming fundraising gala." Her eyes flick toward Saint, nostrils flaring beneath a brittle smile that's so thin and forced I'm sure even he sees through it. "It was... lovely to meet you, Saint."

He says nothing, just smirks, and it feels like a taunt more than anything.

I know that it's probably terrible of me to feel this way, but seeing the hard look on both of their faces is worth every single second of stress orchestrating this has cost me.

Hopefully, my father gets the picture. That I'm not going to be with Chandler. *Ever* again.

Without another word, Saint pulls me away from the table and my parents toward the exit.

"Oh God, that was..." I breathe when we walk outside of the restaurant, the hot, humid September air sticking to every inch of my skin. "*Incredible*. Did you see their faces? They totally believed it."

Saint chuckles roughly from beside me. He's got his hands shoved into his pants pockets, and the jacket he took off the second we walked outside is thrown over one arm, the sleeves of his button-down rolled up his elbows, showcasing the dark ink bled onto his skin.

I've never seen it this close up before, and the art is actually really beautiful. It's black and white, classically timeless. The large rose covering his hand has wilted petals, falling away from the flower like it's dying, and I want to ask him more about them, but if I did, he'd probably give me a bullshit answer.

"And the motorcycle part? That was the nail in the

coffin. I thought he was going to flip the table." I laugh, admittedly having a slight pep in my step.

Take that, Chandler, and your stupid, lying, cheating dick.

I actually haven't told Saint about that part of this yet, but we're still on a strictly need-to-know basis.

Hence me not asking personal questions about his art and what it means.

"Good job, Golden Girl. You're slightly less of a kiss-ass than I thought you were."

I halt mid-step, whipping to look at him. "I am *not* a kiss-ass. That's rude."

"I call it like I see it, and you are absolutely a kiss-ass. Tell me one thing you've ever done that wasn't something someone else told you to do."

Easy. "Skating."

Saint shakes his head. "Nah, besides that."

I chew the inside of my lip as I think, but ultimately, what *have* I ever done that was just for me?

I hate that he's so easily honed in on it without even trying, uncovering one of my insecurities.

Rolling my eyes, I continue walking toward the rideshare parking lot. "I'm not having this conversation with you."

His laugh sounds behind me. "Yeah, because you can't even answer that. Life would be so much more freeing if you stopped giving a shit what people thought, Golden Girl. It's great not having to answer to anyone but yourself. You should try it."

Yeah, well, not everyone has that luxury.

chapter nineteen

Saint

"THIS IS IT. Our last practice before opening night. You've worked your asses off the last couple of months, and I'm a hundred percent confident that you're ready to play the best season of your lives. For a lot of you, they'll have scouts in the stands, assessing you, watching you work independently and how you work as a *team*. This is when you show them the type of player that you are," Coach Taylor says, glancing around the locker room at all of his players.

He's a damn good coach, and I'm lucky to have had him as mine for the last two, almost three seasons. He's the type of guy that leads by example, and because of that, we respect the shit out of him.

Not to mention, he's a retired goalie for the Blackhawks and is one of the best coaches in the NCAA.

"Our first game is against Shreveport, and you all know how important this game is. It's going to set the precedent for the entire season, so let's show up and show them exactly who the hellcats are."

A series of whoops and whistles ring out around the room, and even I can't help but grin.

The energy is already charged off the fucking charts, and it's not even game day yet.

"Get suited up, and I'll see you on the ice," Coach says before turning and walking out of the locker room.

I turn to my locker to grab my gloves but first check the notifications on my phone.

I'm surprised as fuck when I see a text from Golden Girl on the screen. It's been a few days since the fundraiser event, and it's been oddly quiet. She didn't show up to our ice time on Tuesday. Part of me wanted to text her and ask her if she'd had enough of our little game, but I figured if that was the case, she'd already be texting me.

Nah, sweet, innocent little Lennon has a fire, and she's not backing down. She's not folding.

And there's also the fact that I shouldn't be worried about what she's doing in the first place. It shouldn't be something that even crosses my mind, yet it has, more times than I can count since I last saw her.

Obviously, because if she... I dunno, got hit by a car or something, then my revenge plan would go down the drain, so I'm going with morbid curiosity.

Lennon: Are you free in... two weeks? I have another event that I need you to come to.
Saint: Depends.
Lennon: On what?
Saint: Do I have to wear that fucking tie?

Lennon: Well, it's a fundraising gala for my father's company, so yes, the tie isn't optional.

Saint: I'm out.

Lennon: Can you not be a pain in my ass for like five seconds? What happened to a deal is a deal??

Saint: Maybe I changed my mind.

I'm bullshitting her just to get her worked up, my favorite extracurricular activity. Well, besides fucking. I might be a dick, but I keep my word.

Lennon: Please do not make me kill you. I don't think I'll survive prison.

Saint: Nah, you're way too high maintenance. Plus, that orange jumpsuit is going to make you look like a fucking traffic cone with your hair.

Lennon: You're such a dick.

*Saint: *shrug emoji* yet... you're still here.*

Lennon: Not by choice. Can you make the event or not? I have to get to class.

Saint: Ask me nicely, and I'll be your arm candy, Golden Girl.

Bouncing dots appear on the screen, then disappear before reappearing again.

Clearly, she's typing something, then deleting, and I can't stop the shit-eating grin on my lips.

Lennon: Will you come to the charity gala, Saint? I will forever be in your debt oh great one.

Saint: You're missing one important thing.

I can just imagine her face right now, cheeks flushed, eyes blazing, smoke nearly coming out of her ears as she plots a thousand ways to off me.

Fuck, I'm getting a hard-on in full uniform right now.
Lennon: What is that?
Saint: Please.
Lennon: God, I hate you so much.
Saint: Remember that saying about hate and lust...
Lennon: I wouldn't sleep with you if you were the last person on earth so that is complete bullshit.
Saint: Mmmm. That's a bet I'd fucking love to take, Golden Girl.
Lennon: *eye roll emoji* Will you PLEASE come to the charity gala.
Saint: I dunno. I'll think about it.

Tossing my phone onto the shelf in my locker, I grab my stick before adjusting my dick in my pants.

"Who the hell are you texting grinning like that, Devereaux?" Bennett asks from behind me. When I turn to face him, he's pulling on his goalie suit, wearing a smirk that mirrors mine.

Another one of my teammates, our center, Tyler walks by, slapping me on the ass with the end of his stick. I reach for him, ready to shove mine up his, when he jumps out of reach, waggling his thick, dark brows. "Yeah, Devereaux, who's flavor of the week? She got a friend?"

"Fuck off. Both of you," I mutter, narrowing my eyes at both of them. "Whoever I'm fucking, or not fucking, is none of your business."

"C'mon, man, throw a dog a bone. Give us the deets," Tyler says as he sits down next to Bennett to lace up his skates.

"You're a fucking dog alright."

He just smirks, elbowing Bennett in the ribs, which I know he barely fucking feels due to the obscene amount of padding he's wearing. "I get as much ass as Bennett over here."

These fucking clowns.

I don't give a shit about who's fucking whom.

Look, I don't get into anyone's personal life, and I'm sure as shit not getting involved in that. What he chooses to do with his dick is his business.

"Shut the fuck up, Gravois," Bennett growls, shoving him so hard he tumbles off the bench to the floor, laughing so hard there might be a puddle of piss beneath him when he gets up. "For fuck's sake, why is everyone so worried about my sex life."

I shake my head as I make my way to the door, trying to ignore the dipshits I call teammates.

"Yo, wait, Devereaux," Tyler calls. I turn to look back at him, brow arched. "You wanna go out for beers with us after practice? One last hurrah before the season starts."

No one on the team knows about my home life, including Coach, and that's how it's going to stay. It's bad enough that people in high school knew that I was piss-poor, always having secondhand hockey gear, shoes, clothes. Whatever I could get my hands on.

Now, I don't give a fuck, not the way I used to, but I still don't want people to look at me with pity. I've worked my ass off to be here, and the last thing I want is for my teammates to think any differently of me.

Most of the guys already know I'm not a drinker, just by picking it up during the times I have reluctantly agreed to go out with them. I'm not a big party person in general. Never been one for bars, or clubs, or generally anywhere there's a lot of people in a tight space.

I feel trapped in situations like that, like the walls are closing in around me.

It's not like I'm a very social person to begin with.

"Nah, I have some shit to take care of after practice. Thanks though," I say, gaze swinging to Bennett as I give him a nod.

"C'mon, let's hit the ice," Bennett says to Tyler and me, brushing past us toward the locker room exit.

Say less.

chapter twenty
SAINT

"DAMNIT, would you look at that... on time tonight." Tommy whistles when I roll my bike into the open garage bay door at six thirty on the dot. "Must be my lucky night. Gonna buy me a lottery ticket when I leave here."

I kick the stand out, propping it up as I turn to him with a smirk. "That would require you to actually leave, you know, old man?"

He waves an oil-smudged hand through the air at me, but I see the corners of his mouth curling beneath his long gray beard. "Who you callin' old, boy? Remember who signs your paychecks, yeah?"

With class, hockey, the... *arrangement* with Golden Girl, it's been a while since I've been at Tommy's, and I've missed the familiarity of the shop, the smells, the comfort of a place that's become like a home to me. I even missed the old man.

I wouldn't admit it out loud, but it's the truth.

"Yeah, yeah. What do you need me working on

tonight?" I ask as I grab my jumpsuit and bandana. I quickly suit up and walk over to where he's sitting on his signature stool, the leather busted from hell and back on the seat that he refuses to part with.

That's the thing about old men... they're stuck in their ways. Nearly all of them.

"Got a couple oil changes, alternator replacement. Few things here and there," he mutters, gaze moving up and down me. His bushy brows pinch together. "You getting enough sleep? Eating good? Lookin' a little scrawny."

I grin.

Yeah, right. I'm in the best physical shape of my life, despite the fact that I am, in fact, not getting enough sleep, but with everything I've got going on, it's a miracle I get to sleep at all.

When I told Tyler earlier at practice that I had something to take care of, I meant work so I can somehow attempt to keep us from being evicted and fucking homeless.

"I think that's just your bad eyes. You been wearing your reading glasses?" I shoot back, ducking when he throws an old rag at me.

"You know damn good and well I don't need those things. I can see just fine. It's those damn little bitty words—they just seem to get smaller and smaller the longer I stare at the stupid paper."

I roll my lips together to bite back a chuckle.

"Whatever you say, old man." My palm curves around his shoulder when I brush by, giving it a squeeze.

I always said if I ever went pro, ever got a contract that

paid money that I've only ever dreamed of, that I'd set Tommy up for life. Try to repay him in some way for everything he's done for me since I was a kid.

He saw potential in me when there was none to see. Yet somehow, he did. He believed in me and gave me something I'd never had before.

A dream. Hope for the future.

I grew up in a broken home, and when you grow up like that, you don't have big dreams. Growing up, all I ever wanted was a house that no one could take away and a safe place to land.

But Tommy gave me something to look forward to. He gave me this shop and a family within the walls.

"When's your first game? Me and Burl are going to be there."

Grabbing the new oil filters from the shelf, I walk back over to him. "Friday. 7:00 p.m. You know I always leave tickets at the will call for you."

He nods, affection flitting in his eyes.

It's crazy to think that my entire college career is almost over, and my father hasn't attended one of my hockey games. Not a *single* fucking game. Yet Tommy makes every game that he can, without me ever asking.

It's his way of showing me that he's proud, and it means so fucking much to me. Everything.

"Hey, I wanted to ask... if you have some extra hours or things around the shop that you need done, I can pick up a few extra shifts this week and next."

He cocks a brow. "You've got class and hockey. Why are you trying to take on more hours?"

I shrug, holding back the full truth. "Just could use the extra money."

For a beat, he's quiet, staring at me with a look of concern in his eyes.

Even though I trust Tommy more than anyone else in my life besides Ma, I still don't want to burden him with my shit. I never have, and I'm not going to start now.

I'll figure it out. Just like I always have.

"You know if you need something, all you have to do is ask. No questions," he finally says, words a quiet murmur.

"Yeah, Tommy, I know. I just need a bit of extra cash. Everything's good." I swallow down the wedge at the base of my throat, pushing the words out. I hate lying to him, more than anything. But my father and our fucked-up mess is just that—mine to handle. "C'mon, let's get to work, old man."

One day, I'll be able to repay him, somehow, someway, but until then, I'll give him everything I have to give.

chapter twenty-one
LENNON

I HAVE a tendency to push myself to whatever limit there is... mental, physical, emotional... whenever I feel like I'm failing.

Which is the result of spending your entire life thinking that failure isn't ever an option.

I hate the thought of falling short in, well... *anything*.

My brain just isn't wired that way. Especially when it comes to academics and figure skating.

"Damnit," I groan painfully, my hands splayed on the ice beside me, my ass already feeling the brunt of my failed attempts at the double toe that I've been attempting for the last thirty minutes.

How is it possible that I've spent almost my entire life skating, but a single year off has completely derailed all the years of work and progress?

Or at least that's the way it feels right now, seeing as I'm spending more time flat on the ice instead of skating on it.

I can't even land a simple jump, one I've been doing for years.

I'm frustrated to the point of tears, hot and stinging behind my eyes, a bitter reminder of what the last year has been like.

I'm angry at my father for being the one to take it all away from me and at myself for *allowing* him to. For putting my parents' wants and needs, their dreams, over my own.

Exhaling, I slowly push myself up off the ice and stand, ignoring the slight tremor in my legs as I straighten my spine and prepare to do it all over again.

"Correct me if I'm wrong, but aren't you supposed to be *upright* when figure skating?" The unfortunately familiar, deep voice that haunts my dreams, I mean nightmares, comes from behind me.

Of course he would make his grand appearance *now*.

When I'm on the verge of tears, and my ass and legs are black and blue from all the times I've eaten shit today.

I slowly turn, finding him leaning casually against the boards, arms crossed over his broad chest, wearing a faded Hellcats Hoodie and gray sweatpants that I do not allow myself to stare at for more than a single second. His dark hair is pushed into the backward hat he's wearing, the first time I've ever seen him wear one, and I loathe how stupidly hot he looks in it.

Instead of choosing violence, I choose to ignore him. I'm already in a bad enough mood, and his presence is going to undoubtedly make it worse.

Especially with how good he looks in those stupid sweatpants and that stupid hat.

I lift my hand, giving him the middle finger with the most saccharine, smart-ass smile that I can manage, which only makes him chuckle.

That stupid, gravelly sound that I feel directly between my legs. It only makes me dislike him more.

I hate that my body reacts to him and that I feel so... out of control when he's around.

"Mmmm. She's feisty today," he chides. "Careful, Golden Girl. You know how much I love when you get an attitude."

Still ignoring him.

Turning, giving him my back, I exhale, trying to focus on the jump that I'm going to land, even if I have Satan as an audience.

I skate in the opposite direction, use a three-turn to get into position, and glide into my jump, punching my toe pick into the ice and twisting into another single loop. A single is easy; it's the double that I can't seem to stick to save my life.

I try for another, this time going for the double rotation, but I end up falling flat on my ass yet again.

Goddamnit.

I hit the ground hard, my tailbone stinging from all the previous times I've fallen.

"Damn, I know that one hurt. You good?" he says from behind me.

Squeezing my eyes shut, I ignore him, not letting him

get the rise he so desperately wants out of me. It's a game to him, but I'm not in the mood to play today.

All I want is to land this fucking jump. That's it.

I try again, and again, and again, this time landing so hard that my tailbone feels like it's cracking against the ice, a low, pained groan tumbling past my lips.

Fresh tears spring free, a mixture of frustration and the pain in every part of my body from the beating that I've put myself through today.

I hate this feeling. I hate it so fucking much.

God, I'm probably doing this for nothing because I'll never be able to do what I used to. This is one of my easiest jumps, and I can't even do it.

A second later, Saint appears in front of me, crouching down on his skates. "What the fuck are you doing? You're going to hurt yourself."

I keep my eyes down because the last thing I want is for him to see the tears wetting my cheeks, instead pretending to dust off some ice from the front of my skirt. "I'm fine. Why does it even matter? Shouldn't you be over on your side playing with your little puck?"

A beat of silence unfolds between us, and I squeeze my eyes shut when I can't hold the tears back, the dam of frustration and disappointment in myself breaking free.

When I finally lift my face to him, I see his jaw tense, dark, stormy gaze boring into me as it drags over my puffy, swollen eyes. "I'm the one that's going to have to peel you off the ice when you snap your fucking ankle or break your tailbone, that's why it matters. You're crying, for fuck's sake."

Yeah, and you're the last person I want to be around when I do, I want to say, but I roll my lips together, trying to keep more tears from falling.

"I'm fine." My words are whispered as I tear my gaze away.

"Obviously, you're not when you're punishing yourself like this. Why?" he says gruffly, voice full of reproach.

My throat feels tight as I push down a swallow, the frustration and emotion I've been feeling all day overwhelming me.

"God, I don't know, okay?" The words tumble out before I even think. I reach up and brush the tears away. "I just want to land this stupid fucking jump, one that I used to be able to do effortlessly, and I can't seem to do anything anymore."

He sighs. "What are you training for? Why is this jump so important that you're willing to hurt yourself, Golden Girl?"

His tone is soft, lacking the normal patronizing tone. For once, the nickname doesn't feel like a jab, but it doesn't make the question any easier to answer.

The truth is, I don't know *why* I'm pushing myself this hard, why I'm striving so hard to be perfect.

Maybe because everything else in my life feels so out of control lately. Maybe because this is the one thing that's mine, that I'm reclaiming, that I refuse to let anyone take from me ever again.

The only thing I *can* control.

I hate feeling so raw and exposed in front of anyone else, especially Saint.

I hate that I'm failing at the thing I love the most and that it brings to the surface the fact that I've let my parents control my life this badly, that I gave up my passion because I was too blind to see it.

I hate that all of this goes hand in hand, and it makes me see things for what they really are. And it suddenly feels like too much, like I'm caving under the weight of it all.

"I'm not training. For anything," I finally say, my voice low, holding his stare. Part of me feels terrified being vulnerable with him, while the other part of me feels relieved saying this out loud to someone besides myself. "I… I just want to prove to myself that I can still do it. To reclaim my passion after it was taken from me. I used to be able to land these jumps in my sleep and even more challenging ones. And now it's like I've never put on a pair of skates before. I hate it. I hate feeling this way. Maybe I should just admit to myself that I don't have what it takes anymore. Give up while I'm ahead."

For a second, he's quiet, silence hanging between us until it feels like it might choke us both before he speaks. "Okay, so get up."

My brows pinch together in confusion, and he stands to full height so I have to tilt my head to look up at him. "You're not fucking giving up. That's the easy way out. If you've done it before, then you can do it again. So get off your pretty little ass and prove to yourself that you can still do it."

For a brief moment, I'm stunned into silence. Holy shit, apparently, this is the leader of hell's version of a *pep talk*.

Even so, I suck in a breath and push off the ice, standing. He's not wrong.

"You can do it, but you have to get out of your head, or you're going to end up really fucking injuring yourself, and that move or any move is going to be completely off the table. It's the mental that's the problem. Take a breath, recenter, and then do it again without you shit-talking yourself while you're trying to accomplish it," Saint says matter-of-factly, unbothered.

If I hadn't spent the last couple of weeks getting to know him, against my will or not, I'd think it to be true, but I see the flare of something in his eyes. Something that feels a lot like concern.

"Are you... *worried* about me, Saint?" I taunt, skating closer. "That's not very *cliché* bad boy of you."

His lip tugs upward.

Unsurprisingly, he doubles down. In a heartbeat, he's in front of me, toe to toe, so close that I worry he might actually hear the erratic pulsing of my heart.

He leans closer, gaze dropping to my lips before he murmurs, "Nah, just pretty inconvenient if you break a limb during *my* ice time."

chapter twenty-two

SAINT

LENNON GRINS, her rosy lips spreading wide and revealing a perfect row of teeth. "Mmm... well, I do love inconveniencing you."

"Quit stalling," I huff, nodding toward the ice. "Let's go. You can talk shit once you land that jump."

There are a lot of things about the last few minutes that I should immediately put a stop to. Like that I was, in fact, worried about her because she was going to fucking kill herself.

I keep telling myself it's just because I couldn't take the tears, but it's bullshit.

The truth is I didn't want to see her get hurt, especially not from punishing herself. I recognized in her the same thing that I do to myself, pushing my body until it's ready to break to escape whatever fucking demon of the day I'm running from. Fucked-up recognizes fucked-up.

That's the truth, and I'm never admitting it again, not even to myself.

Second of all, I should be practicing. Running drills. Working on my endurance. Shooting pucks.

But no, instead, I'm watching Golden Girl twirl around in her pink, frilly fucking skirt because I can't stop. Because as much as I goad her, as much shit as I talk to get a rise out of her, she's fucking incredible. She glides across the ice with an air of effortlessness that I'm so envious of I'm burning from the inside out.

A body like mine could never, but her small frame is graceful and lithe.

I don't know shit about figure skating, but what I do know is how it feels to hit the ice repeatedly. The shit fucking hurts. It leaves you black and blue, every muscle in your body screaming for relief.

I watch as she tries again… and eats shit.

"Goddamnit," she groans, peeling herself off the ice, her face tight and full of frustration.

"Again."

Her throat bobs as she stares over at me, a beat passing like she's questioning herself whether she's actually going to quit or not.

Then she exhales, nodding.

Good girl.

It takes her three tries, painful ones to watch, but finally…

"Holy shit. I-I fucking did it!" she says between pants, her cheeks red from exertion. "I actually did it. I mean, my landing was shit, but I did it."

I roll my lips together. "Not going to say I told you so, but I to—"

She launches forward, slapping her hand over my lips, silencing me. "I don't need to hear your 'told you so,' ass." Her lips are curved in a small smile. "But... thank you, for your weird pep talk and, you know, not being worried."

Since I can't say anything with her hand on my mouth, I shrug.

She didn't know that I have ulterior motives mixed with some shit I'm not even attempting to unpack.

Finally, she drops her hand but doesn't step back, and I use the opportunity to drag my gaze from her eyes to the light freckles along the bridge of her nose and cheeks, then dropping to her full pink lips.

Those fucking lips.

I haven't stopped thinking about them, painted in that bloodred lipstick she wore at the fundraiser, wrapped around my cock, dreaming about me fucking her throat until she swallows my cum down.

I continue the perusal, not giving a single shit that she's tracking my gaze, watching as I drink her in.

My gaze drifts down the delicate slope of her neck to the front of that purple leotard that's practically painted on her body, curved around her small but full tits, the kind that would be the most perfect fit for my hands.

Lower and lower.

Down to the flare of her waist, where her athletic skirt hugs her hips tightly, stopping at the creamy, pale skin of her upper thighs.

She's fit but still soft in all of the places I want to kiss, drag my tongue along and find out if the same freckles are scattered where no one can see.

Lennon Rousseau is every fantasy I've ever had come to life.

It's a shame since she's only meant to be a pawn in a game that's far bigger than her. But that just means I'm going to enjoy every second I get until I finally win.

She might be the enemy, at least in namesake, but my dick clearly isn't on board with that.

I drag my eyes back to her face when she mumbles, "What are you staring at?" Her words are breathy, light, as if they escaped before she could think better of it.

The air has shifted around us, thick tension seeping into my lungs with each breath I drag in, and I have no doubt that she feels it too.

It's palpable.

"You."

Her throat bobs as she swallows, lips parting slightly, staring up at me with those wide, innocent eyes.

The perfect prey made for a predator to devour with sharp teeth.

And that predator is me.

I'll be her villain. I'm the big, bad wolf, and the only thing I'm hungry for is the taste of sweet little Lennon.

"*Why* are you staring at me?"

"Sure you want me to answer that?" I ask, reaching out to ghost the pads of my fingertips along the top of her thighs, just below where her skirt ends. Her breath hitches at the contact, and my eyes never leave hers, holding her stare, watching as her pupils dilate.

It's different this time. Me touching her.

I'm not doing it because of an audience, because of our

arrangement. And she's fighting herself, *hating* herself for how badly she wants to give in to her attraction to me.

She doesn't have to say it out loud for me to know that it's true. I can read her like a fucking book, with my eyes closed if I had to.

Her body betrays her in ways that her mouth never would.

I trail my fingers higher, a slow inch, and then another, testing the waters.

Just how far would Golden Girl let me go?

My palm curves around the back of her thigh while my thumb sweeps a slow path along her skin. Her soft, *untouched* skin.

"Y-yes," she stutters. "That's why I asked."

My lips twitch. She still hasn't stepped back or moved my hand. I drag my palm up the back of her thigh, until it rests along the curve of her ass beneath her skirt.

It dawns on me that our hour is almost up, and the next person scheduled could walk in at any time and find us like this.

Her nearly flush against my front, cheeks burning red, my hand underneath her skirt.

They'd have no idea what they were witnessing. Sure, it's something seemingly innocent, but what they can't see is the line that's being crossed and the white flag being waved.

Surrender.

It's one step closer to getting what I want, no fuck that, what I *deserve*.

My revenge.

Even if that means that she's the casualty in it all.

My fingers press into her thigh as I tighten my grip, my other hand finding the curve of her waist to haul her flush against me as I lower my lips to her ear. "I'm staring because you look good enough to fucking eat, and all I can think about is laying you down right here on this ice, flipping up that little fucking skirt, and seeing just how good your sweet little pussy tastes."

chapter twenty-three
LENNON

I'VE SPENT an embarrassing amount of time over the last twenty-four hours replaying every single moment of… whatever the hell happened between Saint and me during our ice time.

I've tried to stop thinking of it, about *him*. I should be pretending that it never even happened at all, but I haven't been able to stop.

For a girl who's never even had an orgasm, not from lack of trying, I felt like I was going to *burst* just from the way his breath caressed my ear and his fingers dug into the back of my thigh as he held me against him and whispered the filthiest thing I've ever heard.

About *me*.

It was the hottest moment of my life, despite the overshadowing fact that my unfortunate attraction to him is ridiculous. And that he's truly the last guy on the planet I should willingly choose to be attracted to.

Really, it's the only time I can ever recall wanting

someone so fiercely that I *ached*. Throbbed between my thighs until I thought I was going to spontaneously combust.

I never once felt that way with Chandler, nothing even close. Yet another reason that breaking up with him and never looking back was the right choice. Not that I needed another. Him cheating on me was more than enough.

And now, after spending the last day obsessively thinking about Saint, I'm about to see him for the first time since.

In front of my parents.

Surrounded by volunteers at the pediatric hospital, where we're going to spend the day.

I thought the next event I would need him at was the upcoming gala, but with everything going on, apparently, I forgot to write down today's volunteer work in my planner.

Completely unlike me.

I'm generally type A, compulsively organized in every aspect of my life, but lately... my mind has been occupied, hence the last-minute text I fired off to him this morning asking—no, begging—for him to come with me today.

I was shocked when he agreed and said he'd meet me here.

My pulse skitters when I see him sauntering up the sidewalk, and I force myself to take a shaky breath and stop being ridiculous. This is the same guy who has slept his way through every girls' sports roster on campus. The asshole who's crass and rude and selfish.

You don't have to like him to want a repeat of yesterday, the voice in my head says, and I groan inwardly.

This is going to be great. Perfectly fine.

"Golden Girl," he murmurs, coming to a stop in front of me. His full lips quirk when he eyes my braided pigtails, reaching up to twirl the end of my hair around his finger. "*Cute.*"

I roll my eyes at the patronizing tone of his voice. "The kids like them."

A beat passes, the silence stretching between us and making my stomach flip.

I tear my gaze away, the unspoken elephant in the room making us both acutely aware of the awkward tension hanging in the air.

I feel him step closer as my eyes stay on the smooth concrete beneath my feet until his lips brush against the shell of my ear, and I fight the shiver threatening to strike. "Don't worry, Golden Girl. I'm not going to tell anyone how wet you got with my dirty, filthy hands all over you."

My eyes dart to his in panic. "How would you even…"

The words trail off because, like a fool, I stepped right into that.

Shit.

His shit-eating smirk widens, and he arches a brow.

He knows exactly what he's doing, just as he always does. And of course, he has me exactly where he wants me.

Pushing my hands in the back pockets of my jeans, I step back, desperate to create space between us as a turmoil of unwanted feelings storms inside of me.

I hate him. I hate him. I hate him. I repeat the mantra over and over because I obviously need the reminder.

I clear my throat. "Thanks for coming on short notice. Uh... My parents are already inside. It shouldn't be but a couple of hours, and while generally I would encourage your uncouth ways, there are children here, so let's keep it PG."

The space between his brow cinches tight, and he scoffs. "Jesus, Lennon. I'm a big boy. I can handle myself."

"Yeah, well, I need you to be a good boy today."

When he grins, I shake my head. "See?"

"Don't act like an idiot in front of the kids. Act like a dick in front of your parents. Got it," he mutters with a mock salute. "Now, are you ready? I have something to do tonight."

Like... another girl?

God, why am I even *thinking* this right now? It's not even remotely my business what or who he spends his time doing.

"Let's go." I brush past him toward the hospital, trying to refocus before the performance that it feels like neither of us is ready for.

Saint is quiet as we walk through the hallway of the hospital, his hands shoved into the pockets of the dark jeans he's wearing, gaze settled in front of him.

He doesn't say anything until we get to the entrance of the pediatric ward, turning toward me as we stop. "What are we going to be doing?" His head jerks toward the door. "In there."

I shrug. "Whatever the kids want us to. We basically

just hang out with them, color, read, play Barbies. There's a therapy Labrador retriever named Muffin that comes by and sees them every day. Sometimes we do arts and crafts or play a game."

"Yeah, I should probably go ahead and warn you that I'm not great with kids." He pauses. "There's only one thing I hate more than people."

My brow lifts in question.

"*Tiny* people. Ones that ask a thousand fucking questions about why is the sky blue and why you have to breathe air to survive. I'm an only child—I don't know shit about kids except they poop in diapers and cry all the time."

I bite the inside of my cheek to stop from laughing. Saint not great with kids… *shocker*.

"Saint, most of the kids in here aren't babies. They're older toddlers and young kids. Sure, they'll probably ask you a billion questions, but you're not going to have to change any diapers."

"Thank *fuck*," he mutters, rubbing his palm over the back of his neck. "This was not part of the arrangement, Golden Girl. You're lucky I'm ready to get my *peaceful* ice time back, or you'd be here by yourself."

I laugh. "I said thank you once, that's all you get. C'mon, let's go. We're going to be late."

He's still muttering behind me as we push through the doors and head to the volunteer coordinator's office. She goes over the visitation rules, specifically noting to make sure we sanitize before going into the playroom, and once she's done, we walk back out into the hallway.

The first thing I spot is my parents chatting with the hospital president in front of the playroom. As usual, my mom's dressed like she's attending a business conference instead of hanging out with kids all day. She's got on a pair of black slacks and an off-white blouse with a pair of Chanel slingbacks. Her honey-blonde hair is tightly coiffed at the nape of her neck, not a strand out of place. It makes me feel like I'm underdressed in the old pair of blue jeans, OU sweatshirt, and sneakers I'm wearing, which is insane, but that's the effect that Madeline Rousseau has on people.

I've always felt smaller standing beside her, even if she didn't purposefully try to make me feel that way.

"Why does your mom look like she's going to a board meeting? Does your family own this place too?" Saint mutters beside me.

My head shakes. "No. That's just… who she is. Casual to her is leaving the pearls at home."

Both of my parents turn to look at us when Saint snickers, and I suck in a deep, unsteady breath.

Here we go.

Before I can move to walk across the room to where they're standing, I feel Saint's palm sliding along mine as he threads our fingers together, holding my hand tightly.

"What?" he asks when he sees me staring up at him.

"Nothing. Are you ready?"

He nods. "Lead the way, Golden Girl."

chapter twenty-four
SAINT

"HI, MOM. HI, DAD." Lennon greets her parents with a sweet smile, leaning in to hug them both. Much like last time, it looks mechanical. Stiff. Something that's done out of obligation, not actual affection.

The dynamic between them seems different than what I thought after seeing the glowing articles about their perfect family.

"I'm so glad you could make it today, sweetheart," her mother coos before turning her attention to me. "And you brought… Saint. How *lovely*."

I smirk, lifting my hand and waving my fingers.

Lennon steps back into my side, sliding her arms around my waist and peering up at me. "Oh, I hope it's okay that he came today? He needs a few more hours for his community service, and I figured this is the perfect opportunity."

Her father clears his throat. "Sorry, community service for… your resume?"

His face is almost as red as his hair when I look over at him, wearing the cockiest smug grin I can manage. I'm planning on bullshitting my way through her little fib, but she beats me to it.

"Oh, no. He's required to report it to his probation officer."

I bite back the laugh that's threatening to rumble out of me. This fucking girl.

Keeping my expression neutral, I exhale. "Yeah, I'm just thankful that Lennon loves me unconditionally and doesn't judge me for my past mistakes. It seems like they haunt me, always following me around."

Lennon scoffs, pulling my attention to her as she pokes out a lip. "Oh, babe, that's because you got jail tattoos… those kinds of things never go away."

I chuckle.

"Lennon, honey," her dad interrupts the one-upping he is unknowingly witnessing. "I think maybe you should go ahead and go in with the children. Your mother and I need to speak with Dr. Baker for a bit, and we'll be right in. We can… chat more later," he says, eyes finding mine again.

From the second her father clocked me beside her, he's kept his gaze firmly rooted on me, trailing over the tattoos on my arms, down to the old work boots on my feet, silently passing his judgment just based on the way I look, the way I dress.

Deciding that I'm not good enough for his daughter.

And he's not wrong, but he can fuck off with his entitled, holier-than-thou attitude.

Fuck him for his judgment when he's standing in a glass house with more skeletons in the closet than anyone. Difference is that he hides them better than most.

And I'm going to be the one that shatters that fucking house, razing every inch of it to the ground until there's nothing left standing.

"Saint?" A soft voice pulls me out of my head, and I glance down to see Lennon staring up at me. Her brow is pulled tight, a bewildered expression on her face. "Did you hear what I said?"

"Nah, sorry, what?"

She looks slightly confused but repeats it slowly. "I said that we're going to go ahead and go in while my parents are talking to Dr. Baker." She waves her hand toward them as they both walk across the hospital and then disappear out of view.

I nod, opting to remain quiet.

"*Ooookay.* Let's go." Lennon turns on her heel and starts off down the hallway toward the end of the wing. The walls are painted in bright yellows, greens, and blues and are covered in finger-painted pictures that I can't even begin to decipher. Along with the paintings, there are popsicle stick crafts, rainbow-colored construction paper folded flowers, and all of the patient room doors that we pass are decorated in a fall theme.

It's the first time I think I'd ever call a hospital... cheerful.

"It's amazing, isn't it?" she murmurs, following my gaze. "It feels a lot less like a hospital and more like a home away from home."

She's right. It's clear the staff make an effort to make it feel this way for the kids. I've only been to the hospital a few times, and most of them were for hockey. A few because of my dad.

One time, I got in a fight with my father that resulted in me needing stitches. I was probably eleven at the time, and the butterfly bandage I kept trying to close it with wouldn't hold, and blood was getting all over the house. That only pissed him off more.

I was fucking terrified when we got to the hospital, mostly because I was scared of what would happen if I told the truth. He told the nurses it was a puck to the cheek, when in reality, it was his fist that caused it.

He wouldn't even allow Mom to come with us, and we sat in the emergency room, covered in blood for hours that night. I hated it. It was stark white, sterile, and the overwhelming stench of antiseptic hung in my nose for the rest of the night.

At least these kids have the comfort of people who care about them and try to make their time here more bearable, more welcoming.

"If I was a kid, the last place I would want to be is stuck in a hospital. Scared, overwhelmed, away from my home, family, friends." I look over at her, keeping the fact that I was that kid more than once. The scared one who felt alone, even though I was sitting around doctors, nurses, adults who could've helped me if I'd had the courage back then to tell the truth. "It's good that they make them feel more at home."

Her expression softens as the corner of her lip tilts up

into a smile. "Wow, that might be the nicest thing I've ever heard you say."

"Yeah, well, don't get used to it. I do have a reputation to uphold."

"Mhmm."

We stop at a set of double doors at the end of the hallway, and she pushes them open. I'm not sure what I was expecting to find, but a playroom wasn't it. There are a handful of kids scattered across the room, coloring at wooden tables, sitting in miniature chairs made just for them. A couple are sitting on a plush blue bean bag in the corner, reading picture books, and then there's a little girl with a button nose, probably five, maybe six, pushing a small grocery cart full of recycled boxes made into pretend food around the room with an older nurse.

There's even a huge rainbow painted on the wall with a sea of clouds and a pot of gold at the end.

"Are we on a playdate right now, Golden Girl?" I ask, moving my attention to her, smirking when she rolls her eyes and laughs, soft and breathy.

"Sure, if that's what you want to call it. This is where the kids get to hang out and play, which means we get to hang out here with them. C'mon, I'll introduce you to a few of them."

I follow behind her as she crosses the room to a small wooden table where a little boy sits, wearing a plush gray robe. He looks up as we approach, and the smile that transforms his face at the sight of Lennon is almost enough to thaw my black heart.

Almost.

"Lemon!" he cries, knocking his small blue chair backward as he stands and rushes over to her as fast as he can with the small oxygen tank on wheels trailing behind him. She squats down, opening her arms just as he barrels into them, throwing his small arms around her neck, squeezing her tightly.

He's clearly familiar with her, comfortable in a way that I wasn't expecting. I guess she visits the hospital more than I thought she did.

Add it to her list of Golden Girl accolades.

Except this one… I respect the fuck out of her for it.

"Hi, little guy," she murmurs after a second, pulling back to look up at me. "There's someone I want to introduce you to."

The kid looks up at me warily, not entirely standoffish, more cautious than anything.

"This is my friend Saint. He came to hang out with us today." She looks down at him, wearing a grin. "Guess what? He loves to color."

Fuck. Me.

I haven't colored since I was about… five.

"Saint, this is Decker."

I'm in uncharted territory right now. Do I shake his hand? Give him a high five?

"Hey," I finally say, offering a small wave. "Nice to meet you."

Decker simply stares at me, big brown eyes scrutinizing me. Finally, he says, "Why are you so tall?"

A chuckle vibrates out of my chest, and I shrug. "Born this way, I guess."

He nods, pursing his lips. "I was born with a broken heart." Reaching up, he pulls the robe open slightly, showing me the thick, uneven scar that travels down the center of his chest and disappears beneath the fabric.

Shit.

"Well, that's a pretty sick scar. Makes you look really bada—" I snap my mouth closed when I catch myself. "I mean… It makes you look really cool."

Decker grins, his face beaming with pride as he nods. "Yeah, my dad says I'm the coolest kid he knows. Maybe it's true. Sometimes I think he just says it because he has to. He's my dad."

I shake my head. "Nah, you're definitely the coolest kid *I* know."

He's the only kid I know.

Lennon smiles, a smug look on her face, and judging by that, I know she's never going to shut up about this.

What? I feel like shit that this kid's stuck in here. If I'm going to be nice to anyone, it's gonna be him.

"Hey, Decker, why don't you show Saint some of your drawings?" She gestures to the table he just got up from. "I bet he'd love to see them."

Decker looks from her to me, and I nod.

"Okay," he says, grabbing his oxygen tank and wheeling it back over to the table, reclaiming his seat. "These are my superheroes. They save all kids from bad hearts and lungs and brains. They can save *anyone*. That's their superpower."

The coloring sheets in front of him have various superheroes that he's colored, mostly staying in the lines, and he's drawn a few hearts on them.

"Those are cool. Way better than I could ever do," I tell him honestly, watching as he picks up a blue crayon and starts to color in the chest of one of the superheroes.

Lennon leans into me, standing on her tiptoes to whisper in my ear, "My dad just texted and asked me to come talk to him and Mom. Think you'll be okay here for a second by yourself?"

For a second, I panic. I have no fucking clue how to… be around kids like this. I'm winging this shit harder than I've ever done anything in my life.

"It's easy," Decker says, glancing up from his paper. "I could teach you to color in the lines if you want."

I drag my gaze from him back to Lennon, then back to him once more before sighing and dragging a hand through my hair. "Okay, yeah, that sounds cool."

"Be right back. It'll be quick, I promise," Lennon says to both of us but offers me a secret smile and then walks toward the exit.

And that's how I end up squeezing all six foot four of me into that tiny-ass chair, coloring superheroes with a kid who's got a bad heart and scars… just like me.

chapter twenty-five

LENNON

I SHOULD PROBABLY BE SLIGHTLY MORE worried about leaving Saint alone with Decker when he's so... *Saint*, but right now, the dread of the impending conversation with my parents is overshadowing that.

He's an adult, and I think he can handle ten minutes by himself in a playroom with kids and toys.

Well, then again...

"Lennon." I stop mid-step when Dad calls my name, my eyes flitting to him and my mother, who are standing in the wide hallway, solemn expressions on both of their faces. I can practically feel their disappointment from where I'm standing, and it makes my stomach twist, a knot forming in the pit of it.

God, when did things start to feel like this between us? So fucked-up. They're my parents, and I wish that I didn't feel like this, but I do.

I guess it was once the veil began to lift from my eyes,

when I started to see how out of control I've been of my own life, my own choices, my own decisions.

When Dad pushed Chandler on me, knowing the details of what happened between us, that was the final nail in the coffin, the voice in the back of my mind says.

All of those things are the reason that I feel this way, and no matter how badly I wish that it was different... we can't go back to the way things were. I can't just forget or pretend that I'm okay with what they've done.

I love them—they're my parents—but this is my life.

By my own will.

"Hi. I got your text, but, um... I left Saint inside with the kids, so I really don't want to be gone long," I say, my gaze bouncing between them. "Is everything okay?"

His lips twist into a tight scowl at the mention of Saint's name. Neither of them has said a single word yet, but I already know exactly where this conversation is headed.

A sigh pushes past his lips before he looks at Mom, then back at me, arching a thick brow. "What's going on here, sweetheart?"

"What do you mean? I'm here to volu—"

"Lennon. You know that's not what I mean," he cuts me off as Mom reaches out and places her french-manicured fingers along his arm, as if he needs fucking support to have this conversation. "I mean with... this random boy. You've never even mentioned him to me or your mother, and then you just show up at the fundraiser with him riding a damn motorcycle and completely blindsided us. You're not acting like yourself. What's really going on?"

I don't miss a beat, despite the thick lump that's settled in the base of my throat. "Nothing's going on. Saint's my boyfriend, and he's... he's good to me. I care about him."

In a strange way, it feels like the easiest lie I've told in a long time.

Saint may be an asshole and have a litany of other things wrong with his personality, but at least he's honest and true to who he is. He's not pretending to be anything else.

It's refreshing. It's real.

"Oh, honey..." Mom steps forward and reaches up, cradling my face in her hand. I feel the sweep of her thumb gentle on my cheek, a soft caress that makes my heart squeeze. My parents have never been overly affectionate.

Her expression is soft as she says, "I'm sure you do care about him, Lennon. You've always had a thing for strays."

I go taut, my spine straightening like I've been doused with ice-cold water. I don't even manage a word before she continues, driving her point home. "He is not right for you, and right now, you're blinded by... good looks, attention. All the things that a young girl like you craves."

Stepping back, I pull her hand from my face.

I don't want her to touch me.

"Darling," my father says, moving toward me. His green eyes, which are so much like mine, are hard, his gaze disapproving. His hands push deep into the pockets of his pressed slacks. "Your mother is right. Whether you want to see it or not, we're your parents, and we know what's best."

I almost scoff, almost tell him that the only thing he knows is what's best for *him*. What it looks like for *his* reputation.

I wrap my arms around my waist as I shake my head. "You're wrong. You hav—"

"We're not wrong, and the sooner that you realize what's happening, the sooner you will come to your senses," Mom murmurs, lifting her chin slightly as she brushes her hands down the front of her blazer. "We have always known what's best for you. Provided the best for you. Given you anything you've ever desired, Lennon. This boy… he's trash. He's the kind of guy that will get exactly what he wants from you and leave you high and dry."

"Stop," I say, my words carrying loudly down the hallway, my hand lifted between us. "Just stop. I'm not going to stand here and listen to you disrespect him. Disrespect me." I swallow hard as silence stretches between us. This might just be an arrangement between us, but I'm not going to listen to them talk about him this way when he's not here to defend himself. My gaze swings to my father, where I narrow it. "Haven't you done that enough?"

"For Christ's sake, Lennon. I told you Chan—"

"No." I steel my spine, gathering all of the courage I have inside of me. "*No*. I don't want to hear anything about Chandler and the excuses that you continue to make for him. I'm done with this conversation. Saint is my boyfriend, and that's not going to change just because of your disapproval of him. If you haven't already noticed, I'm an adult who's capable of making her own decisions. I choose him."

My stomach is in knots as I spin and walk away despite both of them calling my name and telling me to stop.

I don't stop until I make it back to the playroom, and only then do I let out the exhale I've been holding, giving myself a single moment to feel… all of it.

It's a conundrum. The biggest part of me wants nothing more than to piss off my parents, to show them that I'm going to be my own person, control my own life, no matter the cost. Somewhere along the way, I lost pieces of myself, and now it's up to me to find them. To put them back together. No one is going to do that for me.

And then there's the other part of me that still hates to feel the weight of my parents' disappointment, to be the one causing the disconnect in our family. I hate that I'm not acting like the perfect daughter, doing exactly as I'm told, just as I always have.

It's like all of it is just ingrained in my head, and I can't just stop overnight.

Even though I wish I could. Just not care. Live my life without worrying about anything other than how *I* feel.

Standing at the arched window outside of the playroom, I see Saint and Decker exactly where I left them. I'm not sure what I thought I'd come back to, maybe Saint teaching him how to play beer pong with cups from the pretend kitchen, but my heart does a weird stutter when I see them.

They're still coloring superheroes together. A blue crayon that is comically tiny in Saint's large hand moves across the paper, and Decker's genuine smile is wide and infectious as he watches him.

I feel like I'm watching something private that I shouldn't be seeing, a side of Saint that I honestly wasn't even sure existed until now.

Decker says something, looking up at him with a sweet smile, and Saint nods, a smile of his own spreading his too-handsome face.

It hits me that I've never seen a real smile from him, not like this. I've seen him with shit-eating smirks, cocky grins, crooked smiles after he says something that makes my cheeks feel like they're on fire. But this smile... God, it's blinding, lighting up the room, and I'm transfixed. I can't stop staring. I don't want to take my eyes off him for even a second for fear that I'll miss it.

He nods to whatever Decker asked him, and then suddenly, Decker's tiny little arms fly around him, squeezing him tightly in a hug that makes my chest physically ache.

For a second, Saint is completely frozen.

But then... slowly, he angles his tall, broad body and wraps his arm carefully around Decker, hugging him back. I watch his Adam's apple bob as he swallows, clearly caught off guard.

Probably by the same emotions that I am, and I'm only watching it unfold.

Saint Devereaux, the guy who's closed off, emotionless, who makes it a sport to show the world just how much of an asshole he can be, who runs from anything that gets too close. The guy who has made me question everything about him since the moment I met him. I've wondered time and time again if a heart truly lived beneath his ribs at all.

Now I know it's there, quietly beating, hidden away behind a fortress of impenetrable walls built not to shut the world out but to guard the most vulnerable part of him.

chapter twenty-six
SAINT

"FOR SOMEONE WHO HATES KIDS, you did great with Decker," Lennon murmurs softly from beside me as we walk on the hospital sidewalk toward the parking garage. When she came back into the room after talking to her parents, she was quieter, not as mouthy as she usually is, and I almost asked her if something happened, but I reminded myself that even if it did, it's not my business.

And I don't care.

I'm aware that one of those is a lie, but still, I keep my questions to myself. I've got enough shit going on in my life to start caring about someone who's only supposed to be a means to an end.

My shoulder lifts in a shrug. "He's not so bad. Although he asked me at least twenty questions every five minutes, it was still… fine."

Her lip curves. "Yeah, he's a really great kid. He's positive and uplifting even when the world has never really given him a reason to be."

"You volunteer here a lot? Is that how you got so close to him?"

Lennon nods, rolling her lips together. "I've been volunteering here since I was a sophomore in high school. I met Decker when he was about two? I think. Both of his parents work two jobs, so it's sometimes hard for them to be here when he's here. I try to come at least once, usually twice a month. At first, it was because I needed volunteer hours for the Social Club, but I quickly realized that I loved being here, so even without needing more hours, I come. I come because I love the kids. I love seeing them smile and laugh. It makes me happy to know that even if for just a few minutes, they're getting a reprieve from the heaviness in their lives."

It seems genuine, what she's saying. Even I can tell she cares about Decker just witnessing them together.

"*Very* admirable of you, Golden Girl."

Her eyes roll. "Guess that makes *you* admirable too, then, since you willingly spent your Saturday here."

"Woah, woah, chill." I lift my hands, palm up. "Don't be saying that shit. This was a one-off thing. Part of our arrangement. That's it."

"Mhmm," she hums with a knowing smirk. "Don't worry, your secret is safe with me."

Yeah, something tells me that little miss perfect might have more of those than I do at this point. When we make it to the parking garage, I follow behind her through the entrance to the first level.

I'm not even going to pretend like I didn't watch her

heart-shaped ass sway the entire way. I've got zero fucking shame.

And goddamn, it's an amazing ass.

Perfectly curved and filling out every inch of those jeans. My eyes drag over the dip below her cheeks, the fullness, how fucking ripe she looks.

I'm an ass guy, and Golden Girl has one that I want to sink my teeth into. That's my plan anyway.

Suddenly, she comes to an abrupt stop in front of me, causing me to collide with said amazing ass, and I almost groan when she brushes against my dick.

"Shit, sorry, I didn't even think about calling an Uber. Do you think you could drop me off at my apartment before... whatever it is you have to go do?"

My brow arches. "*You're* gonna get on my bike?"

"Yeah, sure, why not?" she says nonchalantly, as if her riding a fucking motorcycle isn't something that I'd be questioning.

Her.

I bark out a laugh, the sound echoing around us as it bounces off the concrete walls of the parking garage. "Ever ridden on one before?"

Her head shakes. "Nope, but I'm... trying new things."

"Your parents are going to lose their shit," I finally say.

The grin on her lips falters slightly, almost indecipherably, but she quickly recovers. "Exactly. Isn't that part of the plan?"

Touché.

"I can drop you off, but I don't have a helmet," I say as I reach forward, pressing the button for the elevator. I'm on the sixth floor because the garage was packed when I got here this morning.

"It'll be fine. I only live like ten minutes up the road."

I shove my hands into the pockets of my jeans and nod. A comfortable silence settles over us as we wait for the parking garage elevator, which seems to be taking its sweet fucking time. It's old, the entire hospital is, but goddamn.

Lennon pulls out her cell phone from the back pocket of her jeans and starts to scroll her socials, a small smile playing at her lips as she double taps the screen.

I don't even have social media, but if I did, I'd undoubtedly opt for watching her instead.

I like observing her in secret moments like this. When she's unguarded and lost in whatever she's doing. My eyes trace the delicate slope of her nose, which is dusted with freckles despite the makeup she has on to conceal them. I never thought I'd like freckles, but here I am, wanting to count them like a psychopath.

I watch as she rakes her teeth over her plush bottom lip, a soft, sweet giggle bubbling out of her.

Freckles and giggling are new turn-ons for me, go fucking figure.

Finally, fucking finally, the elevator dings, and the doors slide open for us to step inside. Lennon goes in first, and I follow behind her, subtly adjusting my dick, which is semi-hard behind my zipper.

The doors shut, and it feels like all of the air has been sucked out of the small space, a stiff reminder that even in

September, it's still going to be Satan's asscrack in Louisiana.

"Jesus, it's *hot*. Why is there no air-conditioning in here?" she groans, slumping against the wall of the elevator, dropping her head back.

I press the sixth-floor button and stand across from her. "No clue."

When the elevator jolts to life and starts to rise, both of her hands fly out, curling around the railing beside her.

We're only three floors up when suddenly, there's a god-awful noise somewhere above our heads, and it lurches to a screeching stop. The power cuts, leaving us in the dark, aside from the small amount of light that seeps in through the vent at the top that dimly illuminates the inside.

Motherfucker.

"Oh fuck. Fuck, what's happening?" she cries.

I pull my phone out of my pocket and turn the light on, shining it onto the panel. Completely dark. "I don't know. We must have lost power. Fuck, I have no signal. Do you?"

"God, no. I never have signal in here." Her voice trembles. "No, none. My phone's about to die anyway. I've got two percent. I forgot to charge it last night."

I reach for the panel and press the call buttons. Fuck, I try *all* of the buttons, but there's no luck. It's completely dead. When I look over at her, she's breathing heavier, eyes widening when she sees that the whole panel is black. "It's probably just a blackout. It'll come back up soon."

Although I've got no clue if it's actually going to happen, she seems like she's starting to panic, and the last thing I need is her freaking the fuck out in this small-ass elevator when it's so hot I can already feel my balls starting to sweat.

"I hate elevators," she says quietly, sliding down the wall until her ass hits the floor. "And it's so fucking hot."

I nod. "Not a fan of small spaces either."

What I don't mention is that it's because of my piece-of-shit father locking me in the closet when I was a kid.

I wouldn't tell her that anyway, but for some reason, it was on the tip of my tongue.

The heat must be getting to my head already.

I take the wall opposite of her and slide down to the floor, setting my useless-ass phone beside me.

"How long do you think we'll be in here? All night? The buttons aren't w-working…" The panic in her voice is hard to ignore. Her chest rises and falls quickly, *too* quickly. Tears well in her eyes, her voice breaking with each syllable. "What if we're stuck in here all day and no one even knows that we're here and… an—"

"Hey, take a breath. Slow." I scoot closer to her, watching her attempt to do as she's told. Her breathing is shallow and uneven, and I recognize the panic attack happening probably before she does. I've had enough to know it when I see it. It's too hot in here, and her chest is tight. She probably feels like she's suffocating.

Reaching for her, I brush back a piece of her hair that's come free from her braids. "Just breathe with me. In… and out. Slowly."

Her wide, panicked gaze meets mine, but she manages

a small nod, taking a slow, shaky breath, even though I can see her still struggling.

I place my palm over her chest. "Breathe, Lennon. You're going to be okay."

Her eyes drop closed, and her hand finds mine, sliding over the top, and we move together with each breath.

In and out.

In and out.

I don't even realize when we're breathing that my thumb is sweeping slowly along her skin and that we've moved closer together, her nearly in my lap. Like some type of gravitational force that I didn't even notice because I'm so focused on helping her calm down.

After a few minutes, her breathing starts to return to normal, and she opens her eyes, connecting with mine. "T-thank you. I've never... That's never happened to me before. It was scary."

I nod. "I know. It was a panic attack. They're terrifying, and your fear probably triggered it."

My own sometimes present themselves the same way, triggered by my anxiety or anger, but over the years, I've learned ways to cope with them, and they happen less now than when I was a teenager.

"Getting stuck in an elevator was not in my plans for today," she finally mumbles, laughing quietly.

"People *plan* to get stuck in an elevator?" I grin.

The light is low, but I can still make out her face, the upturn of her lips, the flash of white teeth.

Our hands still pressed against the sweat-slicked skin of her chest.

My gaze drops, and she follows it, suddenly dropping her hand and clearing her throat.

I sit back against my wall, and we face each other, neither of us speaking.

I want to tell her that she's not alone and that I've been here more times than I ever want to remember, but I don't. I can't.

She's just a piece of the puzzle, a means to an end, and that's it. Something I'm having to remind myself more often than I'd like.

"We should do something to pass the time." My brow arches, and she scoffs, laughing. "I mean like a *game* or something. Something to take my mind off the fact that we're stuck in this ungodly hot tin box, and we may or may not be rescued anytime soon."

"Yeah? What kind of game."

She shrugs as she reaches up and wipes the sweat off her face, nose scrunching, "I dunno. Twenty questions?"

"Pass." That sounds like my worst nightmare.

"Oooookay, what about… never have I ever?" Her tone is hopeful as she wiggles her fingers in the air.

I lick my lips. "Not sure you'd have a shot in hell on that one, Golden Girl."

"Let's do it, then… unless you're scared?"

A deep laugh vibrates out of me. "Be for real. Okay, alright, yeah, let's play, but fuck putting a finger down. Instead, you take off a piece of clothing."

The pink in her cheeks deepens, the heat already causing her heated skin to be flushed. Her mouth opens, then snaps shut when I lift a brow, silently taunting her.

"I'm not getting naked in an elevator… around you," she stutters.

I lift my shoulder. "Okay, then don't lose."

I can see the war raging behind her eyes, her pupils flaring as she fights herself. Fights her idea of wrong and right.

Until finally, she says, "Fine. Let's do it. But no bitching when it's you that's naked in front of all the hot firefighters that are going to come rescue us."

chapter twenty-seven
LENNON

WELL, that back fired... by a lot.

Strip version of never have I ever? Who even am I right now?

Not going to be the one that backs down, that's who. I can tell by the expression on his face that he never actually expected me to go with it. He thought he could take the easy way out of playing by offering me something I wouldn't take.

Joke's on you, Satan.

Although after today... I'm starting to believe that nickname might not fit him at all, the way that his Golden Girl might no longer fit who I am. Maybe the old me, but the new version doesn't have anything golden about me.

I can still feel his palm pressed against my chest, feel my pulse skittering and my heart thrashing beneath his touch.

It wasn't just a panic attack. It was the proximity, his

touch… so many emotions swirling around in my head in that one single moment.

It was sweet, the way he talked me through it, his voice soft and low. He didn't have to do that, but somehow, he knew exactly what to say, exactly what to do.

I'm sweating in places that I had no clue I could even sweat in, and this might be the most insane thing I've ever done, but fuck it.

"Ladies first," he murmurs as he pushes back the dark, damp hair that sticks to his forehead. The tattoos on his arms seem darker, more pronounced from the sheen of sweat covering them, and I swear there's a flutter between my thighs.

The air around us feels thick with tension. Coupled with the unbearable heat, it feels hard to breathe.

"Never have I ever… driven a motorcycle," I say as I twist the pink heart-shaped ring on my finger around, holding Saint's stare.

His lip tugs up in a smirk before he drags his teeth over his lips and sits up, reaching behind his neck to pull his shirt off. The sweat-drenched fabric falls to the floor next to him, and then his eyes are back on mine, staring me down with an intensity so strong that it feels like I might cave.

It takes everything inside of me not to let my jaw drop.

Holy. Shit.

My wildest, horniest imagination could have *never* conjured up an accurate representation of what this man actually looks like shirtless.

He looks like he must have been carved from stone by the greatest sculptor to have ever lived, each of the muscles in his chest sharp and defined, leading down to rows upon rows of chiseled abs. I watch a bead of sweat travel down the hollow space between his pecs, tracing along each muscle in a languid pace that makes me throb... *everywhere*.

I've gotten a glimpse of those abs before on the ice, but it's nothing compared to seeing the whole picture.

God... he's beautiful. Truly, there's no other word for it.

No other way to describe it. No wonder his ego's this big.

His body was built for hockey. Strong, unyielding, powerful. Conditioned to take hits.

It's the first time that I've seen the amount of ink covering him. It doesn't just stop at the full sleeve on his arm, the top of his hand. It travels in pieces along his chest, along the muscles on his obliques.

"My eyes are up here, Golden Girl," he rasps darkly, the low, seductive sound settling around me.

My gaze whips to his, cataloging the slow, wolfish curve of his lip, and I clear my throat. "Uh... it's your turn."

"Indeed it is."

Grasping the front of my shirt, I attempt to fan myself with the already damp fabric, and it doesn't do much at all, but it's better than nothing.

I'm never going to take air-conditioning for granted ever again.

If we ever make it out of this elevator.

"Never have I ever..." Saint trails off. "Been in a relationship."

Shit. Shit. Shit.

Of course he's never been in a relationship. Commitment probably gives him hives.

Instead of taking my shirt off, I kick off my tennis shoes. "There."

"Do *shoes* count as a piece of clothing?" he asks.

I shrug. "Not sure, but unless you've got a strip *never have I ever* 'official' rule book handy... I guess we're going with it."

He laughs, eyes glinting with amusement. "Fair. Alright, your turn."

I take a second to think carefully about the next one, and then suddenly, it hits me.

"Never have I ever... failed a class."

He doesn't take anything off, his brow quirking. "3.5 GPA, Golden Girl."

"Wow. You can read?"

"Remember when I told you I was more than just incredibly good looks and a big dick? Wasn't lying. *Big* brain too." His dark brows waggle, and I toss my head back, a throaty laugh escaping of its own accord. "Never have I ever... figure skated."

My mouth hangs open. "That's cheating."

His shoulder lifts. "I haven't. I play hockey. Now... do you have that rule book?"

He's... just trying to get me to take off my clothes. He knew exactly what he was doing by choosing that, of all things.

I can feel my fingers trembling as I reach for the hem of

my T-shirt and slowly lift it over my head, my earlier confidence nowhere to be seen when I need it the most.

Once it's off, I set it next to me and swing my gaze back to Saint.

He doesn't even bother to hide the way he looks at me. Unabashedly, his eyes drag torturously slowly down my body to my white lace bra, which is soaked with sweat, and I watch as he licks his lips, swallowing roughly.

God, how is it that I can practically *feel* his eyes on me even when he's on the other side of the elevator? As if his gaze is a physical caress, trailing over every inch of my exposed skin.

The thick muscle of his jaw flexes before he meets my eyes again.

I had no idea eye contact could be so… hot.

So *purposeful*.

Despite the stifling heat and tension surrounding us, a shiver races up my spine, sending a flurry of goose bumps erupting along my skin.

"Never have I ever kissed someone in an elevator." His low, raspy words suck the rest of the air out of the room, specifically from my lungs. "Never have I ever wanted to kiss the girl who's driving me fucking insane with how badly I want my lips on hers in a broken elevator where she looks so goddamn beautiful I feel like I can't even breathe."

He adds the next part as if he needs to make it even more clear to me that *I'm* the girl he kissed… or intends to.

My head feels light with the way he's looking at me. Like I'm the only thing that's going to breathe air back into his lungs. His eyes are hooded and dark, holding mine with rapt intensity.

"That's just because there's no air-conditioning." My words are breathless.

His lips twitch. "No. It's *you*." His palm curves around my ankle, the pad of his thumb sweeping at the small sliver of skin that peeks out from the bottom of my jeans. The barest brush, and yet it feels *monumental*.

Gently, he tugs me a little closer. "Come here, Golden Girl."

I'm frozen in place. This is a line that we've never touched. One that I'm scared to cross for so many reasons, but God, I want to. Even if I shouldn't, even if it's the absolute last thing I should want to do, it doesn't change the fact that I *do*.

Especially after today. Seeing a new side of him. One I didn't even know existed.

"Lennon." God, my name rolling off his lips feels like a sin, and I want to drown in it. *"Come. Here."*

I push down the reasons I should say no, that I should stay on my side of this tiny elevator, and I slowly crawl over to his side, lowering myself to the floor beside him.

Neither of us says anything for seconds that seem to stretch on forever, staring, breathing.

Until he reaches out, palm curving around my neck as he hauls me to him, smashing his lips against mine.

chapter twenty-eight
SAINT

SHE FUCKING *WHIMPERS*.

So soft and goddamn sweet that it shoots straight to my dick, the sound permanently ingrained in my head like a brand, one I won't be forgetting as long as I live.

I don't know soft or sweet. I don't know slow. I don't know gentle or patient.

I'm not that guy.

But as my palm slides along her jaw into the hair at her nape, I touch her as if she'll shatter in my hands. Like she's the most fragile thing I've ever encountered, and I'm afraid I'll be the reason she breaks.

At first, her lips move hesitantly against mine, cautious, even as the war between her mind and her body rages inside of her, but then something *shifts*.

I can feel the moment she surrenders, and nothing has ever felt so utterly victorious in my life.

She fucking *melts*.

I sweep my tongue along the seam of her lips, asking—

no, fucking *begging* for her to let me in, and then her plush lips part, another soft throaty sound ricocheting against my mouth.

Everything about this kiss is desperate, frantic, an eruption of something explosive between us that neither of us had the willpower to deny any longer.

Lennon's fingers tangle in my hair when my tongue slips past her lips and slides against hers. I grip her nape and haul her into my lap, where she settles along my dick, which I'm pretty positive has never been this hard before.

Over a fucking *kiss*.

My palm trails up her back, my fingertips tracing along the notches of her spine, pulling her closer until she's flush against my chest.

It's hot as fuck, our skin slick with sweat and sticking together, but I don't give a shit. I want every inch of her pressed against me while I take her mouth. If I had it my way, I'd have her naked and on my cock in seconds.

I don't even think she realizes she's rocking against my dick, her hips chasing friction to dull the ache between her perfect little thighs.

Thighs that I can't fucking wait to throw over my shoulder and sink my teeth into before I lick her pussy.

I tear my mouth from her lips, tangling my fingers in the hair at her nape and tugging her head back so I can nip at her jaw. My tongue sweeps along her heated skin, tasting the salty twinge of her sweat as I trail a path down her neck.

A throaty hum fills the space around us when I graze my teeth along the soft spot just below her ear before sucking it into my mouth, hoping that it'll leave a mark behind.

It's fucked that I want everyone to know that she's mine, even if it's just part of an arrangement, a plan she's completely unaware of.

It stirs something inside of me, something feral, hungry.

I glide my tongue over the pulse point on her neck that's pounding wildly and grin against her skin when she presses down on my cock, attempting to squeeze her thighs together.

Suddenly, the elevator lurches, the lights flickering before turning back on, prompting Lennon to freeze.

Fuck. Me.

I nearly groan.

Of all goddamn times for this piece of shit to decide to work again, it's when I've got her in my lap, panting while she's writhing on my dick.

I want to pick right back up where we left off, but the spell is broken, and Lennon is sliding off my lap and scooting back to her side of the elevator, back hitting the wall.

Creating distance because it's finally hitting her that she just gave in to her desire.

It won.

Her lips are swollen and red like a ripe strawberry as she stares back at me. She seems to read my mind as she lifts her hand to her mouth and runs her fingers along her bottom lip, stroking the spot where my tongue just was.

I sit there completely still as I watch her, the elevator

slowly coming to a stop at the sixth floor as it should have in the beginning.

I expected her to have lots of *feelings* about what just happened, especially since she's so clearly anti-me in all aspects, but what I *didn't* expect was for her to bolt the second the doors slid open, disappearing into the stairwell.

Well... fuck.

chapter twenty-nine
LENNON

SHIT. *Shit. Shit.*

I keep repeating the same words over and over, but also… yes, yes, yes.

God, that was incredibl…y stupid.

Right. It was totally stupid.

Or… was it? Maybe not?

"Maisie!" I yell as I burst through the front door of our apartment, nearly tripping over the pile of shoes inside.

When I lift my hand in front of me, I note the tremble of my fingers, meaning that an hour later, I'm *still* shaking from what just happened.

I squeeze my fist shut and swallow hard. "Maisie, where *are you*?"

I almost called her in the Uber on the ride here, but I knew this was a conversation that I had to have face-to-face because I am slightly freaking out.

Okay, that is a lie. I am freaking the fuck out.

Full stop.

"What's happening?" Maisie says as she appears in front of me, her blonde hair mussed and sleep still heavy in her eyes. She's wearing an oversized OU Debate Club sweatshirt and fuzzy slippers. "Why are you yel—"

"I... kissed Saint. In an elevator at the hospital after it broke down. For like... a while," I blurt out over the remainder of her question. The words rush out of me, and the moment that they do, I feel just a tad bit lighter.

If I'm going to have a freak-out, Mais and I are having it together. She's part of the reason I'm in this... situation to begin with.

She stares back at me with her mouth agape, eyes widened, no longer half-asleep. "*Holy. Shit.*"

I nod, sucking in a shaky breath as I bring my thumbnail to my lip and chew nervously.

"Okay, but like... what happened? Give me all the details, and don't spare a single juicy moment, or I'm going to punch you in the tit." Her hand curls around my wrist, and she drags me into the living room and onto the couch.

I flop onto the cushion and bury my head in my hands, groaning.

"Mais. God, it was... incredible, and so hot, and absolutely so stupid. I knew better, but I just..."

I feel her tugging my hands from my face, revealing a grin that splits her face, and it's every bit of what I would expect from her. "Couldn't help yourself?"

I shake my head again. "It was an out-of-body experience. I don't even know how it happened. One second, we were playing the strip version of never have I ever, and then I was… in his lap, and he was kissing the ever-living shit out of me."

Maisie squeals, nearly giddy from excitement. "God, I was waiting for this to happen. Seriously, I've been waiting ever since you told me you were going to be forced to share the ice with him. And then, you know, when he became your kind of fake boyfriend-ish in a way, that absolutely sealed the deal. I hate to break it to you, babe, but this was inevitable."

"It was not!" Her brow arches, and I sigh, swallowing hard. "It was the single hottest thing I have ever experienced."

Granted, my experience is next to nothing, but, still.

"Okay, so what's the problem?" she asks.

"The problem?" I blanch, standing up from the couch. I grab the ends of my braids to give me something, anything to help with the anxious excitement coursing through me and start to undo them as I begin to pace. "The problem is that he is quite literally the biggest fuckboy on campus. He's the complete opposite of any guy I'd ever go for. He rides a motorcycle, he has tattoos. God, Mais. So. Many. Tattoos. When he took his shirt off, I actually thought I was going to spontaneously combust when I saw all of his abs, and God, then he had this little trail of sweat that was running between hi—"

A velvety soft throw pillow barrels into my face, and I squeal. "What the hell, Maisie!"

"Focus!" Maisie says through a laugh. "Why is this a bad thing? You're literally just telling me all the reasons why you should have another very hot make-out session in an elevator with Saint."

My brow pinches while my fingers rake through my hair, pulling out the remaining pieces.

"Because, Mais, it's complicated. He's... Saint. He drives me insane ninety-nine percent of the time. The other one percent is reserved for when he's kissing me, apparently. And this is supposed to be just a show to piss off my father, remember?"

She chuckles, pulling her knees up to her chest and resting her chin on the top. "Then don't make it complicated. Look, this is exactly what we talked about when you asked him to fake date you. Bad boys equal fun. No-strings-attached fun that doesn't result in having your heart broken. As long as you follow the rule."

I sit down beside her on the couch and sigh.

"He's not going to be like Chandler, Len. Do you know why?"

My brow lifts in question.

"Because you're not giving him the power to be. Hook up with him, have all the fun you've denied yourself because you were with someone who couldn't have found your clit even if you gave him the chance to." Her nose wrinkles as she shivers. "Sorry, I almost just gagged a little."

A laugh slips out of me as she continues. "It doesn't have to be complicated, and it doesn't have to be anything other than fun if that's what you want. *If* that's what you want. If not, you can just pretend it never happened, and he'll just be dreaming about what he's missing for the rest of his life."

When she sees me twisting the promise ring on my finger she adds, "Remember what that ring has become for you? It's about *you*, Len. Your choices. *Your* life. *Your* body. *You* have the power."

I let the question bounce around in my head. Do I want to have a friends... no, *enemies*-with-benefits thing with Saint? Can it really be uncomplicated and *just* fun?

Really, what I should be asking is... do I want a repeat of what happened today in the elevator?

I don't even really need to think about that because the answer is absolutely yes. It felt so... freeing.

To say fuck it, to stop worrying about the consequences or what's going to happen next and just *be*.

To shut my brain off and just live in the moment.

Finally, I say, "You make it sound so easy."

Maisie grins and lifts her shoulder in a shrug. "You can make it whatever you want, babe. That's the glorious part of hooking up with no strings attached. Easy."

Something tells me that nothing would ever be easy with Saint. He's too intense, too magnetic in the way that draws every bit of the air out of a room when he walks in.

My strong dislike for him clearly has not suppressed my desire in any way, or I wouldn't even be questioning it.

"Do whatever makes you happy, Len. But know this: *orgasms* make you happy, and I know without a shadow of a doubt that man would make you come." She giggles, rolling her lips together.

Yeah, I have no doubt either, if today was any indication.

Chewing the corner of my lip, I blow out a breath. "Am I really going to do this?"

"I dunno... are you?"

Finally, I nod, a shrill of excitement burning through me.

Holy shit.

I'm *really* going to do this.

I'm going to hook up with the devil himself.

chapter thirty

SAINT

BENNETT LEGROS ADDS SAINT DEVEREAUX TO BOY GANG CHAT.

SAINT DEVEREAUX HAS LEFT THE CHAT.

BENNETT LEGROS ADDS SAINT DEVEREAUX TO BOY GANG CHAT.

Bennett Legros: Let us love you, goddamnit

> Saint: Stop adding me to this shit Legros. I see enough of you fucks on the ice.

Tyler Gravois: He's right which is scary, but… let us looooove you Devereaux. Come play COD with us.

SAINT DEVEREAUX HAS LEFT THE CHAT.

TYLER GRAVOIS ADDS SAINT DEVEREAUX TO BOY GANG CHAT.

Bennett Legros: We're not giving up. You're going to be part of our boy gang.

> Saint: Did you... just refer to yourselves as a... BOY gang?

> Bennett Legros: It is, ain't it?

> Bennett: You're in right?

> Bennett: Saint?

> Tyler: Sigh.

I'M SHOVING my phone into the front pocket of my hoodie when I hear the heavy doors of the rink slam shut behind me.

Right on time, Golden Girl.

It's been three days since the elevator, and it's been radio silence. Not that we have a habit of texting when it's not necessary, but I'd be lying if I said I didn't think about texting her after that kiss.

Ultimately, I decided not to because 1) it would be weird if I checked in on her.

Who the fuck am *I*, checking in?

And 2) I know her well enough to know that she's as skittish as a stray, sometimes feral cat, and pushing her too far isn't going to get me what I want.

I might not know everything about her, but I *do* know that.

So, I'm going to leave the ball in her court, and I'm not saying shit about it.

Not a fucking word.

We'll play the longest cat-and-mouse game in history if that's what it takes because I'm patient enough to wait it out. Especially when I know just how sweet the payoff will be.

I slap a puck into the net, then pick up another with the end of my stick and flick it up, catching it on the end. I toss it up a few times before snapping it into the net with the rest.

I hear the smooth glide of her blades when she hits the ice, and I slowly turn, my gaze sliding to her. My fingers tighten on my stick as I tamp down the groan.

Fuck, she looks good.

Another frilly little fucking skirt that gives just enough of a glimpse of her creamy thighs to have my mouth watering.

I swear she wears this shit solely to torture me. It's even worse now that I've touched her, felt all of those soft, lush curves beneath my hands. Now I know what I'm missing.

As if she feels my eyes on her, she lifts her gaze but quickly drops it to the ice, tucking her long hair behind her ear. Even from halfway across the ice, I can still see her cheeks blazing.

Yeah, remember every fucking second of my hands on you. Fuck knows *I* haven't stop thinking about it since it happened.

That's exactly the reason she's blushing like a schoolgirl the second she sees me.

I skate to the center line, the one she's banished me behind. "Golden Girl."

She looks up, crossing her arms over her chest. "*Satan.*"

I smirk, then turn and skate back to the net, scooping all the pucks out so I can work on more shots.

There's a thick silence that lingers around the rink, with only the sound of me steadily slapping pucks into the net.

It's so quiet that I almost think she's left until I hear her let out an exaggerated huff.

"That's it?" I hear from behind me. "No shit talking? No goading me until I'm ready to snap?"

Slowly, I swivel toward her, brow arched. "You *did* tell me to stay on my side of the ice, yeah? Just following directions like a good boy." Her eyes widen in surprise. Guess that wasn't the answer she was expecting. "Unless there's something *you* wanna talk about?"

"Nope. All good."

Bullshit.

Tossing her a smirk, I give her a salute and turn to the net yet again, going back to my drills. I make a point not to glance over at her a single time. But I feel her eyes on me, can practically feel how badly she wants me to bring up what happened, but I won't.

The hour passes quickly after I finally push out all of the distraction and lock in, and by the time I'm done, I'm fucking drenched, and my muscles are screaming.

I've got work tonight, another shift I picked up so I can somehow pay the rent. Even though I'm exhausted and need to catch up on sleep, there's no other choice.

A few more shifts should take care of it, but fuck, they're dragging on.

Hopping off the ice, I sink down onto the bench and quickly take off my skates, tossing them into my bag.

Since I need to head straight to Tommy's from the rink,

I gotta take a quick shower in the locker room because I smell pretty fucking foul.

There have been more times than I can count that I've opted for a shower at the rink instead of going home, avoiding my father at all costs. Sometimes it feels like I live out of a bag between the school, the rink, and Tommy's.

I push through the doors and head for the shower stall, hanging my hockey bag on the hook before shedding my sweat-soaked clothes and stepping beneath the freezing spray.

The quick equivalent of an ice bath.

I should probably roll my hips and quads because they're already hurting, but I'll have to do it after work, maybe before I finally crawl my exhausted ass into bed.

After washing my hair and body, I turn the water off and grab a towel from the cabinet, quickly drying off.

With the towel knotted around my waist, I walk back out into the locker room, my hair still dripping from the shower, when the door suddenly flies open, and Lennon breezes in.

"You're not attracted to me," she blurts, hands on her hips, eyes dropping to the towel before she hitches a breath and drags her gaze back to mine.

My brow arches. "You asking or telling me? Unclear."

"I mean… Are you *not* attracted to me? I-…is that why you're pretending that Saturday didn't happen?"

"Who said I'm pretending it didn't happen?" I lean back against the counter in front of the mirrors, curling my fingers around the edge as I stare back at her.

"You haven't brought it up at all, and you're not being your normal asshole self."

I chuckle darkly, satisfaction rippling through me. I fucking knew it.

"Yeah, and neither did you."

For a second, she's quiet. Her mouth opens, then snaps shut before she says, "Well... now I am."

I push off the counter and prowl toward her, stopping when I'm towering above her tiny frame. "Now you are." I dip my head to her ear. "Do you need a reminder about how hard I was beneath your hot little pussy? Does that answer your question about whether I'm *attracted* to you?"

She has no goddamn clue about all the filthy, disgusting shit I want to do to her body.

How out of my fucking mind that one small, very innocent by my standards moment has driven me in the last three days.

I pull back and look down at her, cataloging the way a rough swallow slides down her delicate throat, how her lips part, the way those bright green eyes flare like wildfire.

"God, I can't even *think* when you're around." She takes a step back and then another and another until she's colliding with the wall behind her. "Stay over there."

Am I going to listen? Probably not.

I smirk. "Why are you here, Golden Girl?"

"I... It was our ice time."

I shake my head as I pin her with a *get fucking real* stare. We both know exactly why she's here, but I want to hear it out of those pretty little lips. "You know that's not what I'm asking."

For a moment, she hesitates, chewing the corner of her lip as her eyes bounce between mine.

And then she answers so quietly I barely hear the words I've been waiting for.

"I want to do it again."

"Gonna need you to be more specific. Do *what* again?"

Her eyes roll. "Hook up. We're already doing this… whatever we're doing to piss off my parents. Why not at least have fun while we're doing it? It would make the fact that I'm stuck around you *slightly* more tolerable."

"Oh?" I murmur, biting back a grin.

Lennon shrugs noncommittally, feigning a nonchalance that I see all the way the fuck through. She's fidgeting with the hem of her skirt, tapping her foot against the tile as she adds, "I mean, if you want to. If not, no big deal. Actually, you know what, this was stupid. Forget I even brought it up."

When she turns to leave, I push off the counter and close the distance between us, crowding her back against the locker room wall, causing a surprised burst of air to fly past her lips. I flatten my palm along the wall behind her and use my other finger to tip her chin up. "If you wanted my dick, all you had to do was ask."

chapter thirty-one
LENNON

"WHY DO you have to ruin *everything* with your mouth?" I groan as I reach up and splay my palms along his chest to push him away from me, but I don't get very far because he captures my wrist, circling it with his massive hand and keeping it there.

I'm all too aware that he's naked from the waist up, his broad chest hard and unyielding beneath me, his skin warm and still slightly damp from his shower.

That tiny, flimsy towel knotted at his waist is the only thing keeping him from being fully naked while he's nearly flush against me.

I suck in a staggering breath, willing my heart to calm as it pounds wildly in my chest.

God, what am I even doing right now?

I've thought the same thing a hundred times since I made the decision to come here.

His chuckle dusts my lips, unfortunately forcing me to squeeze my thighs together because my body is a traitor, and the dull throb between them is only intensifying with each passing second.

How is it possible that he's this much of a dick, and yet somehow, I *still* want him to do the dirtiest things to me?

"You haven't even begun to see the things I can do with my mouth."

Oh my God.

Before I can even form a rational thought to respond, he adds, "But if you ask nicely, maybe I'll show you."

I can *feel* every syllable as he speaks directly in my clit, pulsing in a type of desperate anticipation that I've never experienced before.

Throbbing in sync with my heartbeat.

The furthest I've ever gone was with Chandler, and that was… not very far. Over-the-clothes rubbing that was honestly uncomfortable and not at all memorable.

But here I am, ready to throw myself at a guy that I dislike. *Strongly.*

I somehow manage to clear the fog surrounding my brain for a single moment of clarity. "O-okay." My voice breaks slightly, a combination of want and a heavy dose of nerves. I twirl my ring around my finger as I add, "But no sex. I'm… It's off the table."

His thick brow arches, the smooth space between them furrowing. "But… everything else is on it?"

I nod. "I'm… inexperienced."

"Yeah? Me too." The corner of his lip pulls up in a smug smirk, and I roll my eyes.

I'm fairly certain he's written the book on casual hookups.

"Shut up. I'm serious. I'm... a virgin. And I haven't really done anything... at all. But I'm okay with everything *but* sex. I'm just not ready for that yet."

After a pause, he nods, his gaze dropping to my lips when I press them together, and only then do I realize that I'm still touching him, my palms still pressed against his hard, naked chest.

"I can't give you gentle and sweet. Not built like th—"

"I don't want that. Just because I'm inexperienced doesn't mean I need to be handled like I'm going to break. I know how to ask for what I want. I think you know that by now."

I see surprise cross his face before it morphs, changes right before my eyes into something... hungry, a dark expression passing over his face.

With that look, I expect him to kiss me or touch me... something, but instead, he drops his hand from the wall and turns, walking away, the defined muscles along his back rippling with each step.

What?

I'm just about to ask if he's already changed his mind when he saunters over to the bench and sinks down, arms stretching wide along the back of it like a king taking his throne.

He spreads his legs and plants his feet, eyes pinning me with a look that compels me.

With a jerk of his head, he calls me to him without saying a single word.

Those dark, stormy irises of his eyes seem to burn as

they slowly travel down my body, tracking each step I take toward him.

Despite the tremble in my legs, I continue across the locker room until I stop directly in front of where he sits.

He hasn't even touched me, and yet my body feels like it's on *fire*. Untamed flames lick every inch of my skin.

Anticipation coils tight inside of me, pent-up need, desperation for more of what I felt the last time we were together.

Like an addiction that only *he* can feed.

I can hardly remain still while waiting for him to move.

Speak.

Do something.

Anything.

Finally, when my heart feels like it's going to launch out of my chest, he leans forward and slides his big, rough palms along the back of my thighs until they're curved just beneath where my skirt ends. Torturously slow, he inches them higher, disappearing beneath the fabric and causing my breath to hitch, all while holding my eyes so intensely that I nearly cave from the weight of it.

His thumbs sweep along the bare skin on the back of my thighs, dangerously close to the spot where my ass curves.

I fight back the urge to shiver.

In one swift motion, he lifts me and places me in his lap, my legs falling open to fit around his hips, his mouth hovering over mine.

It feels like an eternity passes as I wait, and he remains rooted in place.

"Are you going to kiss me or not, Satan?"

His lip twitches as he leans forward and gently drags his nose along mine, lips ghosting so close that I can almost taste them, but still... he doesn't kiss me.

God, the teasing, hands everywhere but where I'm aching for him... It's maddening.

I'm burning up.

Then he lunges, his mouth colliding with mine and stealing the breath from my lungs. My hands fly to his hair, fingers tangling in the inky strands. He teases the seam of my lips, not asking, commanding me to open for him, and obediently, I do. He swallows down every whimper, every moan, stroking my tongue as his hands find my ass, sliding higher and higher along my back until he's pulling me flush with every hard inch of him.

My nipples are pebbled and taut, pressing almost painfully against my sports bra. Every brush against the fabric feels like it's the catalyst for a detonation inside of me.

Saint tears his mouth from mine and leans back, chest slightly heaving. "Take it off." His eyes drop to my shirt.

God, did he feel them through my shirt?

"Now, Lennon."

I sit back slightly, reaching for the hem of my cropped top and slowly dragging it over my head, tossing it somewhere behind me. I've never been particularly self-conscious about my body, but under his molten stare, my confidence slightly falters.

That is until I watch his throat bob as a rough swallow

slides down it, and then his eyes move down to my chest, flaring. His tongue darts out, and he licks his lips.

Jesus, having a guy look at you like... *that*.

It makes me feel powerful.

And now, I'm even more thankful that I wore my favorite bra today, bloodred lace that clearly he's a fan of. Red always makes me look good since it's such a stark contrast against my pale skin.

"I want you to use me to make yourself come." His low, guttural words send sparks coursing through my veins.

I pause for a moment because I'm not entirely sure how to admit this without dying of embarrassment. Warmth creeps up my cheeks, and his brows cinch together when he notices.

Exhaling, I let the words escape out with it. "I... don't know how."

"What do you mean?"

"I mean that I don't know how to make myself come... because I've never *had* an orgasm."

I feel his entire body stiffen slightly, almost indecipherably, but it's there. Something dark passes over his face, silence stretching around us until I can't even take another second.

"God, say *something*."

Finally, he speaks. "With someone else or... ever?"

"Ever," I say. "I mean, I have tried by myself, but..." I trail off, wishing for the floor to suddenly open up and swallow me whole. I glance down at my lap, then feel his finger tipping my chin up, forcing my gaze back to him. "I just can't. It just doesn't happen. I'm pretty sure I'm just one of those girls who just... can't."

"Bullshit."

Before I can even ask what that's supposed to mean, he leans forward and slides his hand into my hair, palm curving around my nape, and pulls my mouth down to meet his, stealing the words altogether.

He sucks my tongue, kissing me like I'm the last breath he'll have on this earth, until I'm a panting, writhing mess.

"Just like that," he murmurs when he pulls his mouth away, staring down at me. I've been so caught up in the kiss that I didn't even realize that I've been rocking myself back and forth, chasing friction over his erection.

Heat ripples through me when I feel how hard he is beneath me. My God... he's huge.

Why am I not at all surprised that the man is walking around with that in his pants?

I roll my bottom lip between my teeth, pulling it into my mouth.

The fabric of my leotard is thin, leaving not much of a barrier between us with him still only in the flimsy towel, so each time my hips rock, I feel the head of his dick rubbing against my swollen clit.

God, it feels so good.

Saint feels so fucking good.

I hate it at the very same time that I'm feral over it.

The strangest combination, and still, I'm chasing the high as a result of it.

Saint's hooded gaze moves over my face as if he's cataloging every movement, every breath, and I'm not sure what's hotter... using him or the way he's *watching* as I do.

chapter thirty-two

SAINT

"OH—GOD. *GOD*," Lennon chants, voice breaking as her hips move faster, finding the perfect rhythm that has my dick fucking weeping.

I'm ready to bust, and I haven't even touched her yet.

Haven't *seen* what's beneath that fucking skirt that I'm obsessed with.

If I yanked that little scrap of fabric to the side, I know that I'd find her dripping, pink, and glistening, her little clit peeking out and begging to be sucked and flicked by my tongue.

My fingers tighten around the back of the bench, the wood creaking and groaning beneath the force, desperation snaking down my spine and taking hold.

Fuck, I want to sink inside of her and lose myself.

Suddenly, her body pulls taut as she stills, her blown pupils flicking down between us. "*Saint.*"

I follow her gaze and see that my towel has fallen open,

freeing my cock, a thick bead of precum glistening on the slit.

Lennon's lips fall open. "Is that... Is it..." Her words trail off, and I chuckle.

"Is my cock pierced? Yeah, Golden Girl. It is."

Her eyes widen as her gaze travels slowly along my length, pausing on the silver barbell pierced through the underside, right below the ridge of my head.

I watch as she swallows thickly, observing with hesitant curiosity and interest.

My hands move to her hips, gripping tightly as I slowly drag her forward until the wet, warm heat of her pussy is settled along the base of my cock, causing us to both hiss.

"If you ever want to find out how good it'll feel inside of you, let me know," I whisper before sealing my mouth over hers, sweeping my tongue through her parted lips, and swallowing down her sweet little whimper.

There's a possessive place inside of me that's preening with the fact that I'll be taking all of her firsts. That no motherfucker on this planet will have them.

It's fucking mine.

She's fucking mine.

Even if it's only temporary, even if she's not mine to keep. Even if this is all just strategy.

The pads of my fingers dig into the soft flesh of her hips as I rock her back and forth along my cock. Unhurried, controlled movements that have her swollen clit dragging across every inch of me.

I'm taking my time, in no fucking hurry for this to be

over. I'll stay here all goddamn day if it means watching her come for the first time.

"God, it feels…" she breathes, eyes dropping shut as her head falls back, and she moves faster, her nails biting into my shoulder, creating tiny half crescents along my skin. "It feels so good. I-I want you to come too. With me."

Motherfucker.

Her words are a breathless whisper, her chest rising and falling in rapid succession, and I can't look away.

I can't stop watching her.

Lifting my hand from her hip, her green, molten eyes find mine, and I hold open my palm in front of her. "Spit."

Her pupils darken, turning hazy and unfocused as she pulls her bottom lip between her teeth.

And like the good girl I fucking *knew* she would be, she listens, spitting into my hand while her eyes never leave mine, making my balls pull tight.

Fuuuuuck. Yes.

My throat works as I palm the head of my cock, coating it with her spit before pumping roughly.

I'm teetering on the edge, the edges of my restraint fraying with the desperate need to touch her.

To lick her, fuck her, take everything she has to give.

I slant my lips over hers and pull her back over my cock, feeling the lips of her pussy slide around me, my blunt head rutting against her clit even through the thin material covering her.

A breathless cry sounds against my mouth, her fingers flying to my hair and tugging hard as she rotates, writhing, my hips flexing to meet her movements.

Tearing her lips free, she buries her face into the crook of my neck and moans unabashedly, just as far gone as I am.

"I think…" Her lips move against my skin as she whispers, "I'm going to…"

My grip on her hip tightens when arousal yanks at the base of my spine, my balls tightening as I get ready to paint her with my cum.

"Come for me." My voice is so low and rough that it sounds like sandpaper, the words clawing their way out of my throat. "Be my Golden Girl and come on my cock."

Blinding bolts of pleasure shoot through me as she does exactly as she's told, hips squirming as she falls apart.

Her entire body pulls tight, muscles taut, fingers tangled in my hair and tugging hard as pleasure swells inside of her, the orgasm she was so sure she couldn't have hitting her like a tidal wave.

Fuck, I wish I could see her face as she comes, but her face is buried in my neck, her teeth raking along my skin as she clings to me.

I can feel every part of her trembling, her thighs shaking as she rides it out, and I can't hold back any longer.

My head falls back as I come, coating us both, painting a messy portrait along her stomach, thighs, pussy, so fucking much that it drips onto my stomach, pooling along the cut of my abs.

I'm pretty sure I've never come this much in my life, and it's because of this girl and my feral fucking hunger for her.

Lennon's shuddering breath ghosts my skin, both of us sticky with sweat, unmoving after... whatever the fuck that just was.

Seconds tick by, slowly turning into minutes as she catches her breath, limp and sated, draped on top of me.

"Should have done that sooner. I might hate you a little less now," she murmurs, sitting up. "I mean... a tiny, *tiny* bit less."

I chuckle. "Yeah? Bet so. Think about that the next time you get an attitude."

Her lips tilt into a slightly shy smile. "Pretty sure that attitude is what you like best about me, so..."

"Nah... that would be your pussy."

She scoffs, reaching out to push my shoulder. "Dick."

Then her gaze drops between us to where we're both covered in my cum, something carnal surging in my chest at the obscene sight.

"That was unexpectedly hot," she says, rolling her lips together, her expression one of satisfaction.

Yeah, well, me coming all over myself after dry humping was not what I thought would be happening today, but she's right. It was surprisingly fucking hot.

"I can't believe I... you know."

"Came on my cock," I finish her sentence. "I told you that was bullshit. You just needed to get out of your head and be patient with yourself. You didn't need me for it to happen."

She nods as she hums and looks down between us, her curious gaze dropping once more to the cum on her pussy.

My brow arches.

Reaching down, I drag my thumb along the front of the wet fabric at her seam, causing her breath to hitch as I gather some cum on the pad of my finger and slowly bring it to her lips. She doesn't even hesitate as her lips part, and I slide it into her mouth.

"Look at the mess you made, Golden Girl," I rasp, feeling her swirl her tongue around the pad of my thumb, tasting my cum. "Bet you never thought being bad would taste so good, did you?"

chapter thirty-three
SAINT

"I'M HERE, OLD MAN," I call out as I throw my leg over my bike and start to roll it into the garage bay at Tommy's. My third shift this week, and it's only Wednesday, and fuck, I'm tired but one step closer to getting the rent money.

As much as I don't mind being here with him, I'm ready for a single night off so I can sleep all fucking night instead of the four hours max I've been getting.

I've got my bike halfway into the garage when I hear a soft giggle, a sound that has me stopping short. What the hell?

I turn to the source and see none other than the girl I've been thinking about over and over again for the last twenty-four hours.

What the fuck?

"*Golden Girl?*"

The sound of my voice startles her, and she jumps,

nearly dropping the lug wrench in her hand that is as big as her fucking arm. Her long hair falls in deep waves around her waist, shining beneath the fluorescent light of the garage, and because I'm losing my goddamn mind, the first thought I have is how soft it was when I slid my fingers through it when she came on my dick and then swallowed my cum.

Yeah, I'm fucking sick.

All I've been thinking about is Lennon and her magical pussy, which has taken over my every waking thought.

There are streaks of grease on her cheek, chest, and hands, and it's a stark contrast compared to the pink, girly shirt and cutoff, blue jean shorts she's wearing.

"Saint?" she murmurs. "W-what are you doing here?"

I arch a brow. "Working?"

"You work *here*?" Disbelief laces each syllable.

Yeah, I'm just as surprised as you are.

My gaze moves to Tommy, who's grinning like a fool beside her, his thick, bushy brows waggling as he leans against a sleek black Range Rover.

"Appears so."

Her cheeks tinge pink, and she nods. "Oh, right. Uh, well... I had a flat tire, and the tow truck brought me here. Tommy's the only one who had my tire in stock this late in the afternoon. He's so kind to have stayed this late to help me." She looks beside her and gives him a dazzling smile that even I somehow feel the effects from all the way over here.

"Aw, darlin', it's nothing. I didn't have anything better

to do anyway." He responds in the softest tone I think I've ever heard him use in all of the years that I've known him.

Lennon's smile widens. "It means so much to me." Her gaze finds mine again, and I nod, then push my bike the rest of the way into the bay and kick the stand down.

"Been teaching her how to change a tire," Tommy says when I walk over to them, my jumpsuit in my hands. "I told her every young lady needs to know how to change a tire."

A deep laugh almost bursts out of me at the thought of Golden Girl changing a fucking tire in her frilly little skating skirt.

Now, that's a sight I'd pay to see.

I turn to her, noting the proud expression and triumphant smile pulling her rosy lips. "*You're* going to change a tire?"

"You say it like I *can't* change one. Tommy just taught me how." Her brow arches.

"Might break a nail."

She cuts her eyes at me, and I smirk, offering her a shrug. I'm mostly teasing, but I'm not far off. I can't see the pretty little princess getting a speck of dirt on her, but then the last thing I ever expected was to walk into Tommy's and find her standing here, grease smeared all over her.

"Don't be a judgy ass." Her chin lifts, and she crosses her arms over her chest, still clutching that lug wrench in her tiny fist.

Tommy chuckles beside her, nodding. "She's right. Leave her alone, boy. Now, come on, Lennon. Let me finish showing you how to tighten the nuts back on once you get this tire on."

Giving me one last silent glare, she turns back to her car and listens as he begins to run through the instructions.

I step into my jumpsuit, never taking my eyes off them, silently observing the scene before me.

She might be only five foot two and tiny, but she uses every bit of her strength to pull on the lugs and then looks to Tommy for approval. When he nods, she squeals, "Yes! I knew I could do this."

"Your daddy never taught you how to change a tire?" he asks.

For a second, she's quiet, the smile on her face dimming before she quickly recovers. "Uh... no. He's a businessman and has a really hectic schedule. Honestly, I'm not sure if he can even change one himself. He probably has someone to do it for him. Plus, we're not... our relationship's kind of complicated."

That sounds about fucking right. Entitled fuck.

Tommy shakes his head, shoving his hands into the pockets of his suit as he nods. "Well, now ya know, darlin'. And listen, if you ever run into trouble again, you know who to call. Tommy's will always take care of you."

"Thank you, Tommy. I hope you know how grateful I am." She hands the lug wrench back to him and swipes the front of her palms onto the front of her shorts, removing some of the grease. "I'm going to bring you some of my favorite strawberry beignets as a thank-you, and I am not taking no for an answer. They're from the bakery up the road, Ever After, and they are to *die* for."

He chuckles. "I think I can handle that, darlin'. Thank you. But this old man is going to head to bed now. It's a little too much past my bedtime. I'm sure Saint here can handle the rest, right, my boy?"

I nod.

Lennon turns to him, throwing her arms around his neck in a hug, and he laughs, gently giving her back a few pats before she untangles herself.

Watching the two of them together, Tommy's quiet reverence and care for the girl he's only just met, and her... kindness and warmth shining in her eyes, it causes something strange to stir in my chest.

Something foreign I wasn't expecting.

Something I can't even really put my finger on.

Tommy shoots me a wink and strides towards me, dipping his head to my ear so only I can hear, "She's a good one, boy. You better take care of her."

"We're no—" I start, but he brushes past me, calling out, "Night, y'all."

Damn old man.

The stairs groan and creak as he climbs them, and once he reaches the top, the apartment door shuts, and a heavy silence settles between us.

My gaze stays rooted on her, part of me wanting to kiss the fuck out of her, the other part wanting the private, quiet solace of what Tommy's is for me back.

Now that she's here, I'm not sure it'll ever be the same once she's gone.

Would the familiar smell of gasoline and oil be replaced with the scent of her? Warm vanilla and honey that's so sweet it makes my mouth water whenever I catch a whiff.

"I swear, I had no idea that you worked here," she says, one of us finally breaking the tension.

It's not uncomfortable. It's just… different.

I shrug as I reach up and plow a hand through my hair. "There's no place better than Tommy's."

"Yeah, I see why." She smiles, soft and sweet. "Have you… worked here long?"

"Since I was a kid. Fourteen or so." I'm surprised by my honesty, but the answer comes out of me without thinking, naturally. I grab some of my tools from the nearby bench and walk over to the older Ford next to her, placing them on the metal frame beneath the hood.

She watches me quietly, observing.

"If my tire's done, um, I can get going. I know you probably have a lot of work to do, and I've already disrupted your evening."

The corner of my mouth twitches, and I hold my stare. "Or you could stay."

I don't know why I offered or what the hell I'm thinking in the first place, but having her here while I work isn't the *worst* thing.

Might pass the time faster.

Or maybe I say it because I just want her to be here. The revelation of that washes over me in a wave of unexpectedness.

"Or I could stay," she murmurs.

I toss her a grin and grab my tools, then sit on the creeper.

Her hands flatten on the hood of her car, and she lifts herself, plopping down on top. She's so damn short her feet dangle, and it's... cute.

Fuck, I gotta get under this car.

Before I say or do some shit that I'm going to regret tomorrow.

I lie back on the creeper, using my feet to propel me beneath the car, and get to work.

chapter thirty-four

LENNON

"BULLSHIT." Saint's low, gravelly voice is slightly muffled coming from beneath the car he's working on. The sound of metal clanging together fills the air around us, but I haven't the slightest idea of what he's *actually* doing under there.

I can only see the bottom half of him, thick, powerful hockey thighs covered in the faded blue coveralls that are covered in old grease stains. Thighs that I shamelessly rode until I had my first orgasm.

God, do not start thinking about orgasms here, I tell myself, biting back the grin by biting the inside corner of my lip.

"I'm serious." I place the pizza box onto the hood of my car and do my best to push down the dirty thoughts that were just infiltrating my mind. "Jesus, my stomach is growling so loud I can't believe you can't hear it."

Suddenly, he slides out from beneath the car, stormy eyes finding me. I notice the smallest smudge of dirt on his cheek that almost matches the short stubble along his jaw.

I watch as he sets the tools he was working with down beside him, then pushes off the contraption beneath him and stands, coming to full height.

"You're telling me that you've lived in NOLA your entire life and been at OU for almost two years, and you've never had a pizza burrito from Jack's? No fucking way."

"I am." I exhale a laugh. "But... if you're done calling me a liar, then I guess I'll finally be able to."

My stomach shouldn't dip when he flashes me an ultra-rare smile, but God, does it.

It might be the fact that I'm starving to death, but I'm pretty sure it's just the Devereaux effect.

That's apparently a thing. That I'm clearly falling victim to.

He swipes the large pizza box off my hood and saunters toward the exit, calling back over his shoulder, "You coming or what? If not, I'm eating both of 'em."

As if. I'd wrestle him to the ground and steal it before that happened. I'm past hungry; I'm hangry, and he does not want those problems.

I'm practically power walking to keep up with his strides, following behind him as he walks outside of the garage and over to an old vintage truck that's covered in patches of rust and peeling paint. It's... seen better days, but it's also really cool.

"This is Betty." Saint lowers the tailgate and places the box onto the back. "Tommy's one and only love. 1957 GMC that he's been saying at least once a day since I was fourteen that he's going to get around to restoring."

I run my finger over the peeling blue paint along the

tailgate, trying to imagine what it might look like if it ever was restored, and also wondering if Tommy will ever get around to doing it. "I bet it was amazing back in its prime."

"Here," Saint murmurs from beside me, voice suddenly low near my ear. I glance up at him just as his large palms slide along my waist, gripping my hips and effortlessly lifting me onto the tailgate.

Like I weigh absolutely nothing at all.

"Thank you," I squeak, suddenly nervous at the contact. His *proximity*.

I think there's a part of me that's still trying to wrap my head around the fact that this is even happening. The hooking up, the talking that doesn't end up in bickering.

Being *here* with him at all.

"Wasn't sure if your short little legs could make it up here," Saint teases with a smart-ass smile.

I roll my eyes. "Shut up."

The truck takes a sudden dip when Saint's large frame slides onto the tailgate beside me and reaches for the box, pulling out the pizza burrito.

"Alright. This is about to change your whole fucking life. Get ready."

I take it from him, resisting the urge to roll my eyes again at the dramatics, something that he has a flair for despite the broody, asshole vibe he exudes.

At least that's what I think until I take my first bite, the warm, savory marinara sauce flooding my tongue, along with spicy pepperoni and so. Much. Cheese.

"Oh my Gooood," I groan. My eyes slam shut as I chew

slowly, savoring every second of the bite. "This is swooooo gwwoood," I say around a mouthful, which is hardly ladylike, but truly, I'm having an out-of-body experience. "*Howyyyy. Shit.*"

Saint laughs. "I told you. Now, tell me I was right. C'mon."

My eyes crack open, and I narrow them, shaking my head.

He reaches for the burrito and snatches it from my hand in a single breath, holding it above my head. Damnit, his arms are so freaking long there's no way I'm getting it.

"Say it."

I throw daggers at him with my eyes as he brings it to his mouth and takes a huge, ridiculous bite out of it, groaning loudly.

"Ew. Saint, what the hell? God, that's worse than double-dipping!" I screech, attempting to snatch it back.

There's a brief pause, and then his laugh spills out, the sound curling around me and causing my lower belly to tighten.

That stupid, delicious sound.

"Pretty sure we're past that, yeah?" he rasps. "Or did I just dream about you sucking my *cum* off my fingers?"

I reach out, slapping a hand over his mouth, my face burning with embarrassment. I'm fairly certain I'll never get used to his filthy mouth… nor the way it makes me throb.

I feel his teeth nip teasingly at my palm, followed by the slow swipe of his tongue, and I drop my hand away, laughing as I wrinkle my nose. "You're ridiculous. You know that?"

All he does is smirk.

And *I* use the opportunity to steal my burrito back. "Fine. Maybe... you were right."

He sucks his teeth. "Damn, I know that had to taste bitter."

As much as I feel like throttling him the majority of the time, the back-and-forth between us feels different today. Less vitriolic and more playful? I just haven't quite figured out why yet.

Instead of answering, I take another bite and peer up at the inky, star-scattered sky above us.

I can't even remember the last time I sat outside and watched the stars. My life has been a constant go, go, go for so long it sometimes feels like I never take a full breath, never stopping to enjoy moments like these.

There's never been time. Between my parents constantly adding obligation after obligation to my plate, my classes and extracurriculars, serving on the board for the Social Club, volunteering, skating—before it was taken away—there's never really been a moment to just... be.

"You got quiet," Saint murmurs beside me, and I look over at him, "What are you thinking about?"

I look back up, my gaze moving over the stars until I find what I think might be the Big Dipper. "Just kind of realizing that it's been a long time since I've done this."

"Eat pizza in the back of a classic truck?"

Laughing, I shake my head. "Yes, I only do this like twice a year, max. It's a tragedy." When I feel his shoulders shake with a silent chuckle, I add, "I mean, look at the stars, the quiet… all of it, I guess."

A beat of silence hangs between us. It's comfortable, easy.

Which surprises me.

"Earlier, what you said about your dad… he the reason you push yourself the way you do when you skate?" he asks.

The question catches me off guard, not at all something I would expect him to be curious about, or honestly even care about, but clearly, this is new, unexplored territory between us.

I swallow, pushing down the sudden bout of emotion lumping at the base of my throat.

"That's a complicated question, with an…" I trail off, trying to find the right words. "Even more complicated answer."

His eyes darken as he nods. "I know a thing or two about complicated."

"No is the simple answer, but also… yes. I think that I probably push myself the way I do *because* of the level of perfection he expects from me. And lately… I'm realizing how unrealistic and unattainable that standard is. But that doesn't make his expectation any less." I pause before adding, "Honestly? Being perfect is fucking exhausting."

This wound is still fresh and raw, now split open and exposed for him to see.

Being vulnerable, no matter how little, is still terrifying.

"And you know what the worst part is?"

His brow lifts. "What?"

"I was complacent in my own suffering. I've spent so long being the dutiful, perfect daughter who always does as she's told that I didn't even realize how out of control I've been of my own life. I didn't even realize anything was wrong." Emotion pulls my chest tight, a humorless laugh escaping from my parted lips.

Saint's quiet as he listens to me talk, not pushing or asking questions or making stupid small talk to make me feel better, just… listening. It's comforting.

"I think my breaking point was when he blindsided me with my ex-boyfriend, Chandler, at a fundraiser. We broke up freshman year because he cheated on me with one of my friends. I walked in on him having sex with her, and he wasn't even sorry. Was only upset that he got caught."

"Fucking piece of shit," he grunts.

I nod. "Yeah, and the most fucked-up part was that my father knew that happened. I told him what Chandler did to me, how he hurt me and disrespected me, and yet he still brought him back around, all but demanding we get back together. Insisting that I 'forgive' Chandler's misstep. I told him that forgetting to buy me a birthday present was a misstep, not fucking one of my friends."

He chuckles, a broad grin overtaking his too-handsome face. "Thatta girl. Should've kicked him in the dick."

"Which one?"

"Both."

"It was just eye-opening, painfully so. I don't care about Chandler in the slightest, and now that I look back, I'm glad that it happened so I didn't end up with a guy who didn't value or love me. But my father is a different story. He's supposed to love and *protect* me, but it feels like all he cares about is how I fit into his agenda. It was like the final nail in the coffin for all of the things I had already been unhappy with. It just really hurts to realize your parents might not care about your own happiness because they're too focused on how you can help theirs. So I guess now I'm just trying to take back my life, but it's hard, you know? He's still my dad."

I can't believe I just word vomited all my family trauma on him.

But honestly, it feels good to get it off my chest, to stop holding it all inside.

Outside of Maisie... I've never told anyone else.

I just never thought that person would be Saint Devereaux.

"That's the long answer. The short answer is... I guess I've just got daddy issues," I add with a laugh that feels a little scratchy, trying to turn the mood a little less heavy.

I'm sure the very last thing he wants to hear about is the shit with my father when most of the time I try my hardest not to even think about it myself.

That's the cruel thing about awareness. Once it hits, you can never go back to the way it was before.

There's only before and after.

Taking another bite of my burrito, I reach past him and set what's left in the open box. "What about you? Are you close with your parents?"

I feel his body pull taut beside me as he reaches up and drags a hand through his hair, pushing it back from his face. It's longer now, floppy and falling in his eyes, so dark that it seems to cast a shadow.

"Complicated question, complicated answer," he finally murmurs. His voice has gone rough, and I feel the shift in him, the way that he's tense and on edge, shutting down, reinforcing that wall he's so expertly constructed.

"You don't have to tell me, Saint. I know how hard it is to be vulnerable, and I know how much it sucks," I say softly.

Silence meets what I say, and I wouldn't expect anything less from him.

Except he breaks the silence with a deep, shaky exhale. "My old man's a piece of shit. A waste of space that makes my life fucking difficult just by breathing."

The sharp edge to his voice is mixed with something a lot like… anguish. His brows are cinched tight, jaw tense and working as he grits his teeth together, eyes blazing with a tortured pain.

"Looks like we've both got daddy issues, Golden Girl."

My gaze drops to his hand that rests on the tailgate beside mine, and I brush my pinky against his, holding those dark, intense eyes that are a window into all of the things he tries to bury.

Except I see him more clearly than I ever have before, and it's both terrifying and overwhelming.

I see the Saint who colored superheroes with a sick little boy in a hospital simply because he asked him to.

I see the Saint who works his ass off every week on the ice just to be the best he can be.

I see the Saint who gives his rare, real laugh when he's ribbing the old mechanic he clearly loves and respects.

I see the version of him that he hides from the world, and I want to reach out and hold on to it.

Savor it.

Lifting my hand, I gently place it over his, and we stay that way, silence stretching between us, neither of us speaking or even moving.

Just… existing in the quiet.

Breathing beneath a starlit sky on the back of an old, rusted truck in an auto shop parking lot.

Until he turns his hand over and threads his fingers tightly through mine, holding on like he's afraid to let go.

chapter thirty-five
SAINT

GOLDEN GIRL: I blame you for my pizza burrito addiction.

GOLDEN GIRL: I can't stop thinking about it.

> SAINT: And here I thought you were going to say you couldn't stop thinking about the locker room. Guess I need to step my game up.

GOLDEN GIRL: That was... memorable. Just not as much as that delicious burrito.

> SAINT: We'll see about that, Golden Girl

GOLDEN GIRL: 😇 See you later Satan

GRABBING my hoodie off my desk chair, I pull it over

my head and shove my phone in the front pocket, then grab my hockey bag before walking out of my bedroom.

It's rare that I get to come home between class and the rink, but there wasn't an option today. I had to drop off the rent check to our landlord before tomorrow's deadline, which means heading all the way back to campus.

At least it's paid, and it's one less thing for me to fucking worry about.

Now that it's done, I can take the next few nights off and catch up on homework and sleep.

Dread, heavy like weighted lead in my stomach, sinks when I step into the hallway and hear my father yelling, the words slurred and thick with drunken rage.

Motherfucker.

It's fucking four o'clock on a Tuesday, but the last thing I am is surprised.

Just a normal midday afternoon in this fucking household.

Usually, he's throwing shit at the TV because of whatever hockey or baseball game he's losing his ass on after betting money he didn't have to begin with.

That or he's misplaced the remote or run out of beer.

I can read his moods most of the time from the moment I walk into a room.

Some days, he gets in a few shitty digs when I walk by but leaves it at that, taking out his anger on whatever else is in his path.

And then there are days like today, where Ma and I are the only thing he's willing to use as a punching bag.

When I walk into the kitchen, I find him cornering her

against the cabinets as he yells in her face, spittle flying everywhere, hand raised like he's going to slap her.

I see red. I don't even think; I just move.

In a single breath, my hockey bag hits the floor, and I'm barreling over to him, my fingers curling around the T-shirt at his nape, yanking him backward, and throwing him onto the linoleum floor. "Don't fucking touch her."

Ma's broken sob reverberates around the small, shitty kitchen around us, and I swallow, pushing down the rage that's bubbling inside of me. For her sake and nothing else.

I fucking hate this. That this is our reality, that she has to live like this, and that I have to feel like I'm becoming him just to protect her.

And myself.

"Don't you tell me what the fuck to do in my house," he mutters, pushing himself off the floor.

Looking at him now, I hardly even recognize the man he's become. There aren't many good memories I have of him, even before the "accident." He was always cold and never affectionate when I was a child, but now, he's a shell of a man.

His long, salt-and-pepper hair is greasy and unkempt, eyes dull and glassy, black bags beneath them making him look sickly.

He's going to drink himself to death.

And the fucked-up part of me, the part I bury deep down because even as much of an asshole as I am, I'm ashamed that sometimes, I wish he would.

I can smell the stench of whiskey permeating off him as

if it's escaping through his pores when he steps closer, narrowing his lifeless eyes.

"How about you get the fuck out of here, Saint."

Ma whimpers behind me, and he looks past me, nostrils flaring, "Shut the fuck up, boy. All you do is baby him. The boy's a grown man, and he's got to learn how to start acting like it."

I snort. "Yeah, you're right about that. Just so you know, I paid the fucking rent so you'll still have a place to sit on your ass and take up space."

His hands hit my chest, and he shoves me hard. Only I barely even feel his sloppy, drunken attempt because I'm not the thirteen-year-old kid he can beat around anymore.

I've got three inches, forty pounds of muscle, and a sober fucking head on him.

"Saint, please, just… just go to practice. Everything's going to be okay," Ma whispers as her small hand curves around my bicep.

My jaw feels like it might pop from how hard I'm grinding my teeth together.

I hate this, and I fucking hate him.

"Listen to your mother," he sneers, eyes glinting with pure hatred. "Go play your little game. Leave. I don't want you here."

He's baiting me, trying to get me to react, just like always.

And I'm not doing it.

Stepping closer, I lean in. "Don't fucking touch her. Leave her the fuck alone, do you hear me?"

I don't bother listening to his slurred response. Instead,

I turn to her, "If he touches you, call the cops, Ma. Promise me."

She hesitates, eyes darting to him, then back, but she nods. "Go. He'll calm down once I make dinner, get food in his stomach. It was just a little disagreement."

It's the same thing she always says.

He'll change, he'll get sober, he's not going to hurt me. He doesn't mean to. He loves both of us.

The same excuses, the same lies. Over and over. So many times that I think she truly believes it.

She's a victim of his physical and mental abuse, just as much as, if not more than, I am.

And it breaks my fucking heart.

"I love you, Saint," she whispers.

"I love you too, Ma. Always."

We can't keep living like this. Something has to change, not only for my sake but for hers.

chapter thirty-six
LENNON

GLANCING AT THE DOOR, I sigh and continue skating another slow circle around the rink, chewing my lip nervously.

Where is he?

We were just texting an hour before ice time, making plans for after, and now thirty minutes have already passed, and he still hasn't shown.

He's never this late, and I probably shouldn't be, but... I'm a little worried.

Which means that I'm not focused, and I'm not even going to attempt to work on toe loops when my head isn't in it.

I'm realizing just how much my mental state affects my ability, and I do not need a repeat of the last time. I had bruises all over my ass and thighs after trying too hard when I was not in the right headspace.

Suddenly, the doors fling open, and Saint storms through. They shut heavily behind him, and he walks directly to the bench, slamming his hockey bag onto it so hard that I jump.

Something's wrong.

Something's happened between our conversation earlier and now because this is an angry, volatile version of Saint.

His shoulders are tense, the muscles in his jaw flexing as he drops down onto the bench and wrenches his bag open, pulling out his skates.

Never looking up at me.

"Saint?" I say softly. "What's wrong?"

I never thought that I'd know him, certainly not this way, but after the weeks we've spent together, I think I do.

As much as he's allowed me to, at least.

And I know that right now, he's a live wire of something that could potentially burn us both.

I skate closer, my hands finding the top of the boards and curling around the edge as I watch him lace up his skates, each choppy pull harder than the next.

My mind is going in a thousand different directions, a hundred scenarios racing through at breakneck speed, and it's causing my stomach to tighten into a knot.

I'm not even *supposed* to care about him.

About anything he's going through.

About him at *all*.

And I can lie and tell myself that I don't, but there's always a moment of truth in a lie.

I push the rink door open and step off the ice despite not having my guards because I have to go to him. I need to see that he's okay, even if he pushes me away.

Stopping in front of him, I watch him hang his head between his knees and hear the long, ragged sigh that spills past his lips.

Then he looks up at me, his eyes flaring with anger. "I'm fine, Lennon. Go back on the ice." His words are cold and dismissive, and even though I know it's his way of protecting himself, of keeping his walls high, it still slightly stings.

"No," I say, shaking my head and stepping closer until I'm standing between his parted thighs, my knees hitting the bench. "I'm not. You don't have to tell me what happened, or anything at all, but I'm not leaving. I have the right to be here just as much as you do."

The same thing I said to him weeks ago, but now, it means something different because *we feel* different.

He can push me away if that's what he needs, but it doesn't mean that I'm going anywhere.

The muscle in his jaw tics as his eyes bounce between mine. "Whatever."

I lift my chin and slowly slip into his lap, sliding my arms around his shoulders and threading my fingers together at his nape. After a beat, his strong arm hooks around my waist as I move my hands to his jaw and sweep my thumb along the stubble.

"Tell me what you need." My words are soft, barely above a whisper.

"Fuck, Lennon." His curse is low and gravelly, and it causes heat to pool in my lower belly. "I can't. I can't touch you right now. I'm... I'm so fucking angry that I want to put my fist through a wall. I don't want to hurt you." He swallows, trying to look away, but my hand grips his jaw, confidence I didn't even know I possessed bubbling inside of me.

"You're not going to hurt me."

He shakes his head. "You don't know me, Lennon. I'm my father's fucking son."

"I do know you," I murmur. "I know that you're angry right now, and there's so much adrenaline pumping through your veins that it feels like you're burning up."

A beat passes between us, and then he nods, pupils darkening.

"So... let me make it better, Saint." I'm trembling as I slide out of his lap and drop to my knees between his legs, peering up at him. "Use *me*."

I'm shaking because I don't know what I'm doing, but I know that I want this.

I want to take whatever he's struggling with away, even if it's just for a moment, and make him feel as good as he made me feel the other day.

It's obvious that he's not good with sitting in his feelings and that he communicates best with touch, not words.

And if physical touch is what he needs to take his mind off all of this, then I want to do that for him.

"You have no idea what you're asking for, Golden Girl. Not a fucking clue," he says roughly, grasping my chin between his fingers. The rough pad of his thumb sweeps along my bottom lip, pulling it down, his eyes blazing intensely.

Hunger flicks in the depths, dark and unhinged.

"Then *show me*."

chapter thirty-seven
SAINT

LENNON PERCHED on her knees between my thighs, staring up at me with those wide, innocent eyes, telling me to *use her* should feel like a dream.

This is exactly where I wanted her—on her knees, willing to do whatever I ask of her. Taking all that she has to give and weaponizing it.

That was always supposed to be the plan.

But right now, it doesn't feel at all like I expected it to, despite it being exactly what I wanted.

The revenge I've been so desperate for doesn't feel as important the way that it used to.

The way I want her right now doesn't have shit to do with a plan, this fucked-up vendetta, and I'm not sure what the fuck to make of that. Honestly, I have no idea what's the truth and what's the lie anymore. Lines are blurring. It's unnerving because I *should* be using her just like she asked, but for whatever reason, I just can't bring myself to do it.

The girl on her knees for me isn't the spoiled, vapid little daddy's girl that I thought she was.

In fact, she's nothing like I thought she was, nothing like the assumptions I drew.

And right now, she doesn't feel like revenge.

All I know is that I don't want to just *take* from her anymore. I want to give just as much as I take, give as much as she's willing to give me. And that scares the fuck out of me.

But I'm too fucking worked up to unpack any of that right now.

My skin feels like it's buzzing, an electric current coursing through my veins, a combination of heady arousal and fueled adrenaline. All I can focus on is *her*.

"I'm not going to break," she whispers, looking up at me through thick lashes.

Her beauty siphons the breath from my lungs.

Her hands move to the front of my thighs, palms slowly trailing up until her fingers delve into the waistband of my sweatpants. "Teach me. Show me how to make you feel good." The words are low, hesitant yet eager, and they make my dick thicken.

My Golden Girl.

Eager to please *me*.

An opportunity that should have me yanking my pants down, showing her exactly what to do with those plump little lips.

But all I want right now is for her to sit on my face, to drown me in her pussy until I can't breathe. There's nothing more in the fucking world that would make me feel better than to finally get to taste her come on my tongue, feel her squeezing my fingers like the greedy girl I know she'll be.

I'm a patient man, but right now, I'm all out of patience.

"Up," I rasp, reaching down to pull her up off her knees, and then I drop to mine, looking up at her, holding her eyes as I start to unlace her skates.

Can't have her impaling me with a fucking blade when I lick her pussy.

She wants to make me feel good, but all I want is to make *her* feel good.

Once I get both of her skates off, I stand to face her. Her brow is furrowed in confusion as I sink down to the bench behind me, pulling her with me.

"I thought… This was going to be for you. I—"

I shake my head, pressing the pad of my thumb to her lips and dragging it unhurriedly along the bottom one. "As much as I want you to put my cock down your throat… the only thing that's going to make me feel better right now is making *you* feel good."

Lately, I feel like someone completely different when I'm with Lennon, the opposite of who I am, but I tamp the thought down, saving it for later when she's not in my lap and I'm not asking to taste her, to touch her.

"Do you trust me to make you feel good?" My voice is hoarse with need, with intention. I'm desperate to forget everything about my fucked-up life, my piece-of-shit father, the fucking awful situation that I feel trapped in, and all I want to do is lose myself in her.

The rest I'll figure out later.

There's no hesitation in the nod of her head, and part of me hates that there isn't.

That I've been harboring this plan that she has no idea about, and she's willingly *trusting* me with her body.

Without a second thought.

I turn and lay her on the bench beside me. Her long red hair fans out beneath her like a halo, cascading down the sides. Fuck, seeing her spread out beneath me like this has a deep groan sounding in the back of my throat. Lennon's eyes are heavy-lidded, flickering with hunger, never backing down from the intensity of my stare. Her cheeks are a warm, pink contrast to her creamy, pale skin, her full lips parted.

She looks like a goddess.

And I feel un-fucking-worthy.

The air crackles around us as I slowly slide my palms along the soft skin of her thighs, her breath hitching and ghosting along my lips as I hover over her.

I don't just want to taste her, touch her… I want to watch as she falls apart for me. I want to commit it to memory, every goddamn inch, every breath, every second of her pleasure.

My lips crash against hers, and I kiss her like she's the salvation to my ruin. Her hands fly to my T-shirt, fisting in the fabric as she tries to pull me closer, her tongue pushing past my lips and tangling with mine.

It's hot as fuck, desperate, frantic, as if we can't move fast enough.

But if anything, I want to slow it down, savor every single second.

I tear my mouth away and trail my lips down her jaw, tongue dragging along her neck, tasting her as I rake my teeth over the sensitive skin, forging a fiery path down to her chest, where I plant kisses along her collarbone, then the hollow space between her tits that peeks out from beneath the leotard painted on her.

My nose drags along the taut, pebbled peak of her nipple, and a soft, sweet whimper falls from her lips.

So responsive.

Her legs fall open as I make my way down her stomach, pressing my lips in a path lower until I'm at that little fucking skirt.

The one I clearly have some sick, kinky obsession with.

I'm finally going to flip it up and do what I've been fantasizing about since the first day she stepped on the ice, even if I didn't want to admit it to myself then.

I settle between her thighs, looking up her body to hold her gaze, never letting my eyes leave hers.

Intentional eye contact that speaks without words.

Her teeth rake over her bottom lip, drawing it into her mouth as my fingers curve around her thighs, pushing them open even wider, bringing my nose to her spandex-covered slit.

Suddenly, I feel her fingers tugging on my hair, and I lift my head.

"I'm... nervous," she whispers. "What if I don't taste..." She blushes as her words trail off, but I know exactly what she's trying to say.

"There's not a chance in fucking hell that I'm not going to want to drown in you, Golden Girl." To drive the point home, I drag my nose along her pussy, inhaling. "Trust me. I'm about to come in my pants just *smelling* you."

Not a lie, my dick is currently weeping in my pants.

Her lips roll together as she bites back a smile, her limbs loosening as she drops her head back onto the bench.

"Relax, and let me show you how much I like this. How much I want every drop of cum on my tongue. I want to still be tasting you for days, Lennon."

My fingers deftly unsnap the leotard covering her, slowly sliding it open, revealing the sweetest, most perfect pussy I've ever seen.

Motherfucker.

I plant my lips against her thigh and groan, the sound vibrating through us both.

I knew she'd be perfect.

Pink and glistening, the hood of her clit peeking out, completely bare aside from the smallest little strip of hair above.

When I look up at her, brow arched, a cocky smirk curving my lips, her cheeks are flaming. "I wanted to be prepared. Just in case."

Yeah, I fucking bet so.

"The prettiest pussy I've ever seen," I rasp. Unable to wait another goddamn second, I lean forward and flatten my tongue, swiping it through her slit in a long, slow, unhurried lick that has her back bowing from the bench, fingers flying to my hair, tugging roughly at the strands.

"Oh my God," she pants. "That feels… Oh my *God*."

Her thighs slam shut, bracketing my ears when I flick her clit with the tip of my tongue, and I chuckle against her. I can feel her legs trembling, quaking with each lash against her clit.

I planned to ease her into it, to take my time, but a feral fucking beast roars inside of me, and I can't do slow and sweet.

I'm ravenous, a dark hunger raging inside of me that I've never felt before.

I part her open with my thumbs and suck her clit into my mouth, alternating pressure in hard sucks that have her writhing, tearing at my hair, moaning so loud it echoes off the walls of the rink, making me crazy with possessive satisfaction.

"Mmmm. So fucking wet and messy," I drawl, lapping at her as I slip my arm beneath her thigh, hooking it over the top of it, and splaying my hand along her belly, holding her in place.

I circle her entrance with my middle finger, stretching her slightly, and she whimpers, "Please."

Though I'm not sure she even really knows what she's begging for. Whatever it is, I want to give it to her.

"Greedy girl. You want my fingers in your pretty little pussy, stretching you open the way I would with my cock?"

Her response is a strangled breath and a clench of her pussy that, fuck... I can actually see. She clenches around nothing, and for whatever reason, it's the sexiest thing I've ever seen.

"My Golden Girl wants to be filled. No, she *needs* to be

filled, doesn't she?" I slowly sink the tip of my finger inside of her, and her pussy sucks me in deeper.

Fucking Christ... she's so tight, so wet, so fucking perfect that I'm trying not to come in my goddamn pants. My cock is so hard it hurts, my hips flexing against the bench in the desperate need to be inside of her.

She shudders when I curve my finger and gently stroke her G-spot, legs tightening around my head, a ragged whimper tearing out of her. "Saint..."

The way she breathes my name drives me to the brink of fucking insanity, and I eat her like a man possessed, adding another finger. She's so tight that even with how drenched she is, there's resistance.

"Are you going to be my good girl and come for me? Yeah?"

I can feel her tightening, clamping down on my fingers as she teeters on the edge, and I pull back, only slightly so I can catalog it, the pure ecstasy on her face, eyes squeezed shut, shamelessly chasing the pleasure I'm giving her.

Watching her makes me desperate to taste her again. My lips close around her clit, sucking hard as I stroke her G-spot.

The sound of my fingers filling her, driving into her tight cunt over and over, makes an erotic echo around us.

"Give it to me, baby, *now*." The rough, hoarse command seemingly pushes her over the edge. She doesn't just fall; she fucking explodes, squeezing the fuck out of my fingers as she arches higher, belly and thighs quivering from the intensity of her orgasm.

And fuck, she soaks my face, her cum dripping down

my chin as I lap at her, trying to catch every drop that she gives me.

Her hips rock as she rides it out, never letting her tight grip on my hair go, holding me in place.

I lick her through it, slower, more gentle when she becomes too sensitive until she finally melts into the bench behind her, sated and sleepy.

Only then do I slide my fingers from her and sit up, intentionally catching her gaze. "So fucking sweet." I bring my fingers to my mouth and suck them clean.

She watches with stunned surprise, like she can't actually believe that I'm doing something so obscenely dirty in front of her… Like I didn't just *devour* her pussy.

"Never doubt how much I love tasting you, ever again." I use the back of my hand to wipe away the remnants of her from my face.

"I was supposed to be making *you* feel good. Not me," she whispers, her expression slightly shy after what we just did.

Leaning down, I hover my mouth over hers, my hand bracketing her throat, lips curved into a smirk. "Making you come is *exactly* what I needed, Golden Girl."

She has no idea how much losing myself in her, even for just a while, took everything away.

The shit with my father is now the last thing on my mind. Instead, she's front and center, taking up all the space there is, and it feels… substantial, in ways I don't even fucking understand.

But I think I'm beginning to.

chapter thirty-eight
LENNON

HEAVY RAIN PATTERS noisily against my bedroom window as the storm outside rages on like it has for the entirety of the day. The sky has opened up, relentlessly dumping water over New Orleans in a torrential pour during the first hurricane of the season.

The storm's been brewing in the gulf for days, now finally passing over us and flooding the streets like a river. Wind howls and whips outside, bending the branches of the heavy oak trees until they groan and crack from the pressure. Angry thunder rolls, causing the walls of my apartment to tremble.

Unlike a lot of people, I love hurricanes. I love the dark, thick clouds that roll in, the deep rumble of rolling thunder, lightning that electrifies the sky.

They always bring a sense of peace to wash over me.

Sighing, I turn and look over at the glowing numbers of the clock on my nightstand.

It's late, and I should have gone to sleep hours ago, but

I've been too restless, tossing and turning, kicking the covers off, reaching for my phone more times than I even want to admit.

I want to text him, but I also don't want to seem clingy because I'm not.

It's just... it feels like there's been a fire ignited inside of me, and I'm impatient for the next stolen moment with the man I'm supposed to hate.

It's funny how things happen. How life has a way of unfolding in the way that it's supposed to and not the way you thought it would.

Just a couple of weeks ago, I couldn't stand to be in the same room with him, and now I'm anxiously waiting for the next time that I am.

A sudden boom of thunder claps just outside the window, rattling the pane, followed by a bright flash of lightning that has my heart ratcheting in my chest.

Shit, that scared me.

I reach for my phone, but I stop short when there's another loud rumble that sounds like thunder, except... not outside the window.

My brow pinches.

Then I hear it again, heavy pounding, and I realize it's not thunder at all... it's the front door.

Maisie's at her parents' for the weekend, and I have no idea who would be pounding on my door in the middle of the night during a *hurricane*.

I toss the duvet off and quickly walk to the front door, peering through the peephole. It's hard to see anything at all with the rain blowing sideways under the dim light of the porch, but I can make out a silhouette.

I'm wrenching the door open in a single breath, my heart pounding wildly when I see *Saint* standing in front of me, staring down at the porch beneath his feet.

He's drenched from the rain, his clothes completely soaked through, dark hair plastered to his face, droplets of rain tracing a path down his body.

He doesn't move. He doesn't speak. He stands there, rooted in place, shoulders rising and falling as he breathes roughly.

In and out.

In and out.

In and out.

Until he lifts his head and looks up at me, his dark brown eyes full of so much pain and anguish that it makes my chest physically ache.

Oh my God.

My hand flies to my mouth to stop the noise that threatens to burst free, trapping it in the back of my throat.

He's *hurt*.

His bottom lip is split open and still seeping red. The skin around his right eye is bruised, black and purple and blue, almost completely swollen shut. The cut on his cheekbone is raised and angry, like the skin was pried open, caked with dried blood.

My throat moves as a rough swallow courses down it, and because I can't stop myself, I go to him, colliding against his hard, wet body, throwing my arms around his waist and holding him tightly against me.

He still hasn't said a single word.

I bury my face into his chest, squeezing my eyes shut. I'm not sure what to say, and even if I did, I think... this says more than words would ever be able to.

So I just hold on as tightly as I can. Until my arms ache.

Until his arms finally slip around me, and he holds on to me like he's drowning and I'm the life raft.

Until I can feel his big body trembling against me.

Whether from emotion or the chill of the rain, I'm not sure, but we can't stay outside in this any longer.

"Saint, you're freezing. We have to go in," I say, pulling back to look up at him. When he flicks his gaze to me, his eyes are distant, hazy, and I hate it.

I hate that whatever's happened... it's left wounds that aren't just the ones I can see.

They're inside too, and I've never felt more helpless.

I reach for his hand, threading our fingers together and gently pulling him back into my apartment.

Neither of us speaks as I squeeze his hand, not letting go as I lead him to my bedroom and shut the door behind us. I turn on the lamp next to the bed, bathing the room in a soft, warm glow, and the sight of him steals every breath from my lungs.

It's even worse than I thought. His eyes are red-rimmed and puffy, and I know that whatever's happened, he's been crying.

God, my heart is aching.

He's freezing and hurt, and he looks so completely broken that hot tears prick behind my lids. I close the distance between us and slip my hands beneath the black

T-shirt plastered to him, slowly pulling it up. He tugs it over his head and hisses, face pulling tight, wincing like the movement hurt him.

That's when I notice the large bruise that travels along his side and trails over his rib cage.

"Saint," I whisper. "Do you need to go to the hospital? I'm… I'm worried."

His head shakes.

I want to argue and tell him that he needs to be looked at, but I know that he's not going to go.

Of all the places he could've gone, maybe that he *should've* gone… he came here.

To *me*.

Overwhelmed with emotion, I tenderly press my lips onto his battered and bruised skin, gently kissing every wound I can see, one at a time, each one causing my heart to ache more painfully than the last.

I wish that I could take it all away, but I know that I can't, so for now… I'm going to do what I can.

And that's being here for him.

My feet carry me over to the bed, and I drop down onto the edge of the mattress, leaving whatever happens next up to him.

I know him. I know how hard it is for him to show the fragile, vulnerable parts of himself, to show his hard-fought emotions.

And I also know he's battling something right now that is breaking him, and it's hard to witness.

Part of me expects him to stay rooted in place, unmoving, but he doesn't.

He crosses the distance between us, his chest heaving as he steps between my legs, his eyes searching mine. He smells like fresh rain and spearmint. Of familiarity and comfort.

Slowly, he sinks down to his knees. His arms slip around my waist, his big body draping over my lap as he buries his face into my stomach.

I swallow hard as I bring my fingers to his nape and gently stroke his hair, tracing my finger along his jaw, hoping that my touch helps in some way. "You don't have to tell me. You don't have to say anything at all if you don't want to, but I'm here. Okay? I'm here, Saint, and I'm not going anywhere."

His ragged breath dances along the sliver of bare skin of my stomach beneath my shirt, his arms tightening around my waist in a hold that feels like something is threatening to wrench him away and drag him under.

It makes emotion swell painfully beneath my chest.

This isn't the same man that I met all those weeks ago. The one who pushes everyone away because it's the only way to protect the delicate parts of him, who puts on a front to show the world that he's emotionless, cold, detached.

The man who has shut the entire world out but is letting *me* in.

He's trusting me to anchor him in whatever he's battling, trusting me to hold on to these broken and bare, jagged pieces of him, no matter how fragile they may be.

It's a declaration without words.

This is a version of Saint that I'm unfamiliar with, but it feels like *somehow*, I've known him all along.

I trail my finger along his jaw and gently lift his chin.

My chest starts to feel tight when I see the pain in his eyes, a raw, heartbreakingly vulnerable sea of dark that makes emotion snake up the inside of my throat. "Why did you come here, Saint?"

"I didn't know where else to go." It's a whisper, his voice rough and uneven as he pauses, holding my gaze. "You're the only thing in my life that feels right anymore."

chapter thirty-nine
SAINT

I FEEL... numb.

Hollow.

Inside and out.

The pain from tonight barely even registers. I push it down, push it out of my head before I cave under the weight of it all, submitting to the demons I've been battling for too long.

This moment's all I get. Because weakness is a luxury that I will never be able to afford. I'm all my mom has, and that means that I have to be strong for *her*, even when I'm falling apart inside.

Like tonight.

Lennon's eyes soften as she tenderly strokes my face, cradling my jaw in her palm, using her other hand to comb her fingers through my hair.

She's gentle and tender, and I had no fucking clue just how badly I needed this.

It feels weak to admit, but fuck, I'm *exhausted*. My

bones are weary.

How much it helps to just... rest.

I lean into her, my eyes dropping shut for a beat as I try to wrap my head around how the hell shit got so bad, so fast. How out of control it spiraled in a matter of minutes.

"My dad got arrested tonight. He's in jail. And..." I swallow roughly. "I hope he fucking rots in there."

I feel her stiffen beneath me, her breath stuttering. "Did he do this to you?"

I nod. My arms tighten around her, my thumb sweeping along the sliver of bare skin below the hem of her cropped shirt, more for me than for her.

"I didn't fight back," I finally say.

The chaos of tonight comes flooding back, and it feels hard to breathe.

The officers. The flashing lights. Ma's sobs as they cuffed him and put him in the back of the cop car.

It doesn't even feel real, yet beneath all of the other fucked-up things I'm feeling, there's a sense of... relief.

Relief that I shouldn't feel guilty for, but I do.

Looking up at her again, I shove down a swallow. "I should've known that the other day was just the start of it. That day at the rink... he was the reason I was so angry, so out of control. I was so fucking angry that, yet again, he was drunk and high in the middle of the day, and if I hadn't walked in, he probably would've hit my mom."

"Saint," she whispers brokenly, her words laced with compassion.

It's the first time I've ever told *anyone*.

My whole fucking life, I've endured the pain and abuse

from him because I didn't want to be the reason my mother's heart broke, and tonight only proved that it was the wrong choice. I should've spoken up sooner.

Maybe I would've saved us both years of heartache and pain.

As I speak, she holds me tighter, and it grounds me. Makes it more bearable to spill the darkest, most fucked-up part of me. "Him being fucked-up is nothing new. It's a daily occurrence. I don't know what set him off today... why he lost it. He broke the kitchen table, destroyed anything he could get his hands on, and then slapped my mom across the face. In front of me." The thought makes me so fucking mad that I'm shaking, rage piercing through my chest. "I should've stepped in sooner. I shouldn't have even let it get that far, but I know how much it hurts my mom to see us fight, and most of the time, when I intervene when he's pissed like this... it just makes shit worse. I didn't know he would turn around and slap her like that, or I would've..." I trail off when the image of him hitting Ma flits into my mind again, sending cold, deadly rage surging inside of me. "I could've fucking killed him, Lennon. If it wasn't for my mom, I probably would've been in the cop car. Not him. When I pulled him off her, she put herself between us. She defended him when I was just trying to *protect* her. I saw the utter defeat and resignation in her eyes, and it nearly fucking broke me, Lennon."

Now that I've started, letting all of it pour out of me so I don't suffocate, I feel like I can't stop. A dam breaking after suffering a decade of abuse at the hands of the man who was supposed to teach me, guide me, *love* me.

I've spent years, fucking *years*, harboring anger and hate inside of me, placing the blame on anyone but the person who deserved it the most.

Him.

This vendetta… this revenge that I have against her father, one that implicated her in something she never had fuck all to do with, it's fucked-up.

I realized that tonight as I came here. When she was the one I craved when at my lowest.

Lennon's become the only safe space I've ever had in my life. She's trusted me, listened to me, *seen* me for who I am.

She's the only person who's witnessed all the ugly, broken, fucked-up parts of me and stayed anyway. And she didn't just stay; she pulled me closer.

As my entire fucking life was imploding around me, all I wanted was *her.* If I were going to break, I wanted it to be with her, wanted her to pick up the jagged pieces.

It terrifies me. I'm scared out of my mind to let her in.

But I'm even more scared to let her slip through my fingers by pushing her away. By ignoring my instincts that scream I need her.

"And then he just started on me. He pushed me against the corner of the cabinet, and that's where I fucked my ribs up. Ma begged me not to hit him back, so I kept trying to fend him off without fighting him, which is the only reason he ended up getting any hits in on me. I couldn't stand to let him hurt her any more, so I just let him lash out at me. I just fucking let him, Lennon." My voice wavers, and I hate it. I hate feeling so raw and exposed, but I don't stop. I can't. "I could've stopped him, truly hurt him without even trying, but I didn't. For *her*. It's always for her."

"Saint…" she whispers, curling her small body around me. I feel her lips press against my hair, and I exhale the breath I was holding, so lost in thought that I didn't even notice my lungs burning and my ribs screaming. "I'm so sorry. I'm so fucking sorry."

I'm sorry too.

But not for my father finally getting what he's deserved all along. I'm sorry that in my fucked-upness, I dragged her into this. That I was planning on using her to try and fix the shit broken in my head, and I thought the way I could do that was by seeing her father pay for what he did.

He still deserves to, but she doesn't.

Fuck.

So many things are flitting through my head that it feels like it's going to explode.

"Is your mom okay?"

I nod against her. "Yeah. The EMT looked her over and said it would be a nasty bruise, but she'll be okay. I stayed with her for hours after she fell asleep. Lennon, she wouldn't even press charges. Even after he beat the shit out of me and hit her, she still wouldn't press charges against him, but I did. I had to do what she couldn't. To protect her."

"It's hard to understand what she's going through, Saint, I know, but if this has been happening for years, your mother is a victim of abuse, and it's hard to break that cycle."

She's only saying what I already know, but it still feels impossible to wrap my head around.

I just want her to be safe and away from him, and it feels like the only way that will ever happen, her leaving him, is if she's in a casket. Because she won't go on her own.

Ice floods through my veins. The thought of losing my mom, to him, even at all, makes my vision dance, black spots dancing behind my eyes, sends my heart plummeting into my stomach.

I suck in a breath, trying to breathe through my nose, trying to ward off the panic attack I can feel starting to tighten my chest.

"I'm here," she murmurs into my hair. "It's okay, Saint. It's going to be okay."

I focus on her fingers creating circles on my back, her soft movements, on breathing one breath at a time.

In and out.

In and out.

In and out.

I don't know if it's going to be okay, but Lennon gives me hope that it will be. Somehow, someway, it's going to be okay.

"I walked all the way here. I wasn't even thinking, I just stormed off," I finally say, my voice heavy with emotion, low and gruff. "I couldn't sit there any longer, surrounded by the shit he destroyed. I had to get out. Ma was asleep, so I left her a note on the counter, and then I just took off. I didn't even know where I was going at first. I just knew that I had to get out of there and try to clear my head, to process what had happened. And then... I just ended up here. I think I was always going to come to you; I just didn't realize it until I was halfway here. I needed you, Lennon. Fuck... I just needed to see you, to touch you. I knew I'd be okay if I could just get to you."

I'm shit at words, at emotions, at opening myself up and being vulnerable, and I'm sure she knows that more than anyone, but I'm trying.

Even if it all ends up for nothing, I won't regret her. I won't regret *this*.

Somewhere along the way, this stopped being about revenge. The feelings that I have for her are confusing and scary as fuck, but I know now they're not going away. If anything, they get stronger with every moment like this, where she sees me and holds on tighter.

She sees me at my worst, and it doesn't scare her away.

Lifting my head, I look at her as she whispers, "I won't let go, Saint. I promise."

There's finality in her words, and it hits me directly in the chest.

Swallowing roughly, I nod.

"Will you stay here with me tonight?" she asks, eyes bouncing between mine as she stares down at me.

It's something I've never done before. I've never slept over with a girl.

But I've also never been this way with anyone before, not like I am with Lennon.

"Yeah. I'm going to need a shower... all of my clothes are still wet."

Lennon nods. "Of course. I can throw your stuff in the

dryer while you're in the shower. It might be done by the time you get out."

My balls have started to shrivel up from being in wet pants with the AC at full blast, so I rise to my feet, straightening my spine as I tower over her.

I wish I could somehow express what tonight has meant to me. How thankful I am for her just… being here. Accepting me for what I am. Not judging my fucked-up life.

Words don't feel like enough. They never do when I'm trying to express how I feel, but I'm going to try anyway. I'm going to try for *her*.

I grasp her chin between my fingers and dip my head, pressing my lips softly against hers, unhurried and gentle in a way I've never been.

Her eyes are hazy when I pull back to look at her. "Thank you."

My mind's racing, a hundred different thoughts at once, things I should say, words stuck in my throat, but that one being the most important. "For all of it. Thank you."

chapter forty
LENNON

I HAVEN'T MOVED since Saint disappeared into my bathroom, rooted into place on the edge of the mattress, trying to let everything that I'd just learned sink in.

I'm not sure I'm even fully breathing right now.

There's a physical ache in my chest beneath my rib cage, and I reach up, rubbing at the spot as if it's going to take that pain away.

It's nothing, not even in the same realm of the pain and heartache that Saint's experienced, and that... *guts* me.

I'm struggling to keep the tears at bay when I replay his words in my head. He's been struggling in silence for so long, bearing the weight of this with no one to hold *him*.

But that ends here. Because I'm going to be the one who is strong for him when he feels like he has no one else. In whatever capacity that is, whatever label it needs to hold.

It doesn't even truly matter because I'm going to be here, no matter what.

The bathroom door swings open, and steam billows around Saint as he steps out clad in nothing but one of my pink gingham, laced towels.

Shit. I completely forgot to get up and put his clothes in the dryer.

But also… him wearing that pink towel that's comically small compared to his massive, broad frame has a giggle floating out of me. I bring my hands to my lips to cover it, but his eyes darken.

"Is this a fucking hand towel, Golden Girl? Christ." There's a lighter glint shining in his eyes, and it makes me feel better that maybe our talk and a shower have helped to clear his mind some.

"Nope, you're just huge."

Immediately, my cheeks heat when it comes across very differently than I intended, and he smirks. It still doesn't quite meet his eyes, but it's a start.

I spring up from my bed and rush over to him, swiping his clothes from his hands. "I'll just, uh, put this in the dryer, and then you can change once they're done."

He nods, holding tightly to the towel.

I quickly get them into the dryer and then walk back into my room, finding Saint standing near the bulletin board on my wall, fingers moving over a photo of Maisie and me from last year.

It was from the winter formal for the Social Club. My dress was a pale blue silk that made me feel like a princess, white faux fur draped over my shoulders, pale pink earrings my parents had gifted me in my ears.

We had so much fun that day, and looking back at it,

it's a stark reminder about how much has changed. How much *I've* changed.

As much as I thought I loved the person I was then, it's nothing compared to how proud I am of the girl I am now. Even if I'm still a work in progress.

"Winter formal for the Social Club." I stop beside him, tilting my head slightly to look at the prop in my hand from the photo booth. "That's my best friend, Maisie. She's my roommate too, but she's with her parents this weekend."

Saint hums, his attention moving to me. "You look beautiful."

Heat creeps up my throat at the compliment. I like it. Far too much.

"Thanks," I say quietly, tucking a long red strand of my hair behind my ear. "I'm actually stepping down from the Social Club."

"Why?"

"Because I hate it." My nose scrunches at the admission. It's the first time I've said that out loud to anyone. "I hate the responsibility, the crippling pressure, and the constant need to feel like I have to be this perfect person. I hate the frivolity of all the galas and fundraisers and the opulent show of wealth. In the grand scheme of things, I hate that it feels like all eyes are always on me, for things that don't even really matter. "

Sighing, I glance back at the bulletin board, my gaze moving over all of the memories. Pictures, tickets, mementos. Some of them are happy memories, but mostly, all I feel is relief that I'm no longer going to have to fill the shoes that my family has stood in before me.

"Quitting is another one of those *trying to take my life back* things. I actually haven't even told anyone… but you."

It seems to be the theme of tonight, baring ourselves for the other to see.

Saint's quiet for a moment before he speaks. "You are perfect, and if anyone makes you think any differently, then I'll fuck them up."

It's serious yet ridiculous at the same time, and I giggle softly before a yawn hits me. I can't stop it, and my hand travels to my mouth to cover it.

"I almost forgot that it's the middle of the night." Looking back at the clock on my nightstand, I see it's after 3:00 am. "No wonder my eyes feel so heavy."

"I can take the couch."

My brow arches. "Oh? Have you suddenly become a gentleman?"

"Shut up," he growls playfully, fingers pressing into my side. "It's your house, Lennon. Whatever you want is what happens."

Holding his gaze, I take a step back toward my bed, then another, and another until I drop down onto the edge. "And what I want is for you to sleep right here beside me."

His feet stay planted into the floor as he stares back at me, hesitation flickering in the depths of his eyes.

My eyebrow lifts. "You can stay on your side, and I'll stay on mine. Since we're so good at that." The words are playful, unfalteringly confident in a way that only comes from the shift that seems to have happened between us tonight.

Saint cares about me as much as I care about him, and him showing up, him trusting me, after everything he went through today proves that.

I move towards the headboard and slip beneath the covers when he finally, finally moves toward me, still wearing nothing but a towel that barely covers him.

I one hundred percent realize that I am quite literally inviting temptation into my bed, and maybe that's exactly what I want.

But I also just want to be close to him. I don't want him to sleep alone, to deal with all of the heavy solitude anymore.

Saint crawls over the covers and slips beneath them beside me. His feet are so long that they hang out of the bottom. He's so big that there's barely any room left in the bed. The space between us is far smaller than I anticipated.

I switch the lamp off and then roll onto my side, staring over at him.

There's still a hurricane happening outside, so the moon is tucked away behind thick clouds, and the only light in the room is the soft, dim glow of the night-light coming from the bathroom.

My gaze travels the sharp slope of his nose and cheekbones, pausing on his bruised eye, the pang of concern returning. His lips are full, the spot where it's busted even more swollen, and despite having his face battered tonight, he's still the most beautiful man I've ever seen.

He turns to look at me, and my mouth curls into a small smile. "I like this. Having you here."

"Me too."

A comfortable, easy silence sits between us as we look at each other, unmoving, just breathing, drinking the other in. His shoulders slant as he angles more toward me, reaching for a lock of my hair and twirling it absentmindedly around his finger, the motion nearly lulling me to sleep.

If it wasn't for the heat beginning to pool in my lower belly at the proximity, his lips only inches from mine, maybe I could fall asleep.

But right now, I just want him to *touch* me.

Lifting my hand, I wrap my fingers around his wrist and slowly drag his hand to my chest, placing it there.

I watch the column of his throat move with a rough, uneven swallow. "We've never been great at following the rules, have we, Golden Girl," he murmurs, his voice dropping low.

The rule flitting through my brain has nothing to do with the lines on the ice or the side of the bed we said we'd stay on.

Never fall for the bad boy.

The rule was simple.

Easy.

Except somewhere along the way, I think I broke the one and only rule there was.

And I know now there's no going back to the way it was before.

Before Saint Devereaux.

chapter forty-one
SAINT

"I THINK I've realized that I'm not actually a *rule* kind of girl. Not anymore, at least," she says with a grin that I can barely make out in the darkness of her bedroom.

"Ah, finally. Golden Girl is realizing how much more fun it is to break them, yeah? Rebellious little thing. I love it."

I trail my hand down the front of her chest until my palm is curved along the underside of her tit, the thin pink sleep shirt she's wearing not concealing her taut, pebbled nipples whatsoever. They're peeking directly through the fabric, two perfect little points that are begging for my mouth. I sweep my thumb along the peak, and her breath hitches.

I tug the front of her shirt down slightly, inch by inch, revealing her soft, creamy tits that I want to bury my fucking face in.

Heavy and full, but still not too big for her small frame. I cup them in my palms, dragging my thumb along her nipples again, kneading and squeezing them. Fuck, the perfect size for my hands.

Like she was made for me.

I could play with them all night and still never tire of it.

I realize that this is probably not the smartest idea, being naked in her bed, touching her when the little self-control I have is already frayed and busted at the seams. Especially after the rollercoaster of today, but fuck, I can't stop.

When it comes to Lennon, it feels like I'm spinning out of control, and I have no idea what the fuck to do about that.

My eyes hold hers as I slip my hand beneath her shirt and trail it up, dragging the material along, silently asking if I should take it this far.

She nods and lifts up slightly, and I don't think, I just act, pulling her shirt up and over her head, watching as her tits spill free. I dip my head to her chest and press my lips into her skin, down the center of her chest, nipping at the underside of her tit, every place but where she wants me most because she squirms, clenching her thighs together like it's going to take away the throb building inside her.

It won't. The only thing that's going to help that is my fingers, my tongue… or my cock.

"More." A shallow pant spills past her lips as she grabs me by the hair unabashedly, guiding my mouth to her nipple.

My dirty, dirty girl, telling me exactly what the fuck she

wants, and I don't think I've ever been more proud. Or more turned on.

I close my lips around her nipple and suck, flicking the peak with my tongue, rolling the other between my fingers and tugging.

"God, it feels… so good," she says, falling back against the mattress as I hover over her. Somehow in the last few minutes, we've moved, me fitted between her parted thighs, her in only a tiny pair of sleep shorts that cover little to nothing, and me completely naked.

It's dangerous territory. *She's* dangerous, and she doesn't even realize the effect that she has on me.

It's like I'm compelled as I slam my lips against hers, my hands curving around her jaw and holding her in my palm while I kiss her, drinking down the contented little sigh that pushes past her parted lips.

Like this is what she was finally waiting for.

I feel her fingers trailing along my abs, and the muscles contract beneath her touch, my dick hardening between us. Her soft, small fist circles my length, and she squeezes hesitantly, then more assuredly, as she slowly strokes me.

"Fuuuuck, Lennon," I hiss, dropping my forehead to hers, my eyes falling shut as arousal licks at the base of my spine.

Her thumb sweeps along the slit as she gathers the bead of precum on the pad of her finger, spreading around my head. She brushes the sensitive ridge of my head before moving to my piercing, and my hips flex, thrusting into her hand.

It's slow, and explorative, and drives me out of my

goddamn mind. If I wasn't already about to come in her hand like a fucking teenager, I sure as fuck am now.

My fingers curl around her wrist, stopping her before I embarrass the shit out of myself, and slowly, I slide down her body, my tongue tracing a wet path from her pert nipples down the flat plane of her stomach.

I let my gaze travel up her body as I press a soft kiss to the front of her sleep shorts, where they're practically molded to her pussy, the outline making my mouth water.

"I haven't stopped thinking about eating your sweet little cunt since you came on my face at the rink." I nip at the inside of her thigh before making it better with my tongue. "I'm fucking obsessed with it. All I do is think about fucking my tongue into your tight little hole, getting it ready for my fingers, stretching it open wide for me."

Heat flickers in her eyes, the flames licking inside her pupils as she rakes her teeth along her bottom lip. "Saint." Her words are breathless, barely a whisper.

I know when I dip my fingers into her shorts, she'll be deliciously slick and glistening. Her pussy weeps for me when I say filthy shit to her. She loves my dirty mouth.

I hook my fingers into the waistband and drag them down her hips, tossing them to the floor, leaving her completely naked beneath me.

God, this fucking body.

Soft skin, plush curves, rosy pebbled nipples, the most perfect pussy to ever exist.

I'll never get enough.

I'd die before I got enough of her.

"Now, be my good girl and sit on my face," I grunt as I

flop down onto the mattress beside her, pulling her tight little body over me.

Her eyes widen. "W-what? I can't just... *sit* on you."

I chuckle. "Yeah the fuck you can. Now, get up here and let me drown in you, Lennon." I slap her ass with a smirk.

Still, she stays planted in the spot she's straddling my stomach.

And just as I suspected, she's *drenched*. There's already a wet spot on my abs where her pussy's rubbing against my skin.

Fuck, that's hot.

Now I just need her pussy on my mouth.

"Stop arguing with me. Sit on my fucking face, baby." My fingers delve into the flesh of her hips, and I rock her on top of me, dragging her clit back and forth across my abs and showing her just how good I can make her feel by using my body.

A shiver racks her body, and I smirk, watching as goose bumps scatter across her skin.

Finally, she follows directions and slides up my body, where I take over and settle her over my mouth, pussy hovering just where I want her.

"Grab onto the headboard and ride my tongue. Don't stop until I'm soaked."

The rough, filthy command has her snapping into action, and she lowers herself slowly but not nearly close enough.

I curve my palms over the top of her thighs and wrench her the rest of the way down until she's seated on my face.

I start by circling her clit with the tip of my tongue before I seal my lips around it and suck, hard.

The suction must be the perfect pressure because I feel her back bow as she lets out a strangled cry, my name tumbling from her lips a second later in a breathless chant. I dig my fingers into her hips to hold her in place when the pleasure becomes too much and she's running from my tongue.

Not a fucking shot, Golden Girl.

"Yes, yes," she chants, head lolling back onto her shoulders as I fuck her with my tongue, spearing it deep into her tight little hole. I think I'm going to bust just by the way she's clenching around it.

All of her inhibitions and reservations seemingly have gone out the window. She's riding my face, hips rolling faster with each panted breath.

Yeah, baby, just like that. Take what you want.

Seconds later, an orgasm crashes into her, and I feel her spasming against my tongue, flooding my mouth with her cum, a gush of hot liquid that drips past my lips and down my chin.

Fuck yes. That's my girl.

The realization of how possessive and fiercely fucking crazy I feel about her hits me with the same force as her climax.

I want all of her orgasms, all of her whimpers, all of those sweet little sounds she makes.

She moves off my mouth once the aftershocks wear off, but her legs are still trembling as she peers down at me with a soft, slightly shy smile. Her eyes are heavily lidded and her cheeks bright pink from the orgasm.

"You were perfect," I say as I languidly stroke the inside of her thigh with my thumb. "Now you can do it every day, twelve times a day."

"Or…" The word hangs between us as she slides down my body until she's straddling my hips, darkened gaze holding mine as she moves back even further until she's on top of my cock. A shudder runs through me as her hot, still-dripping pussy drags along my bare skin, coating me in her creamy cum.

Oh fuck.

We both let out a breathy sound, a whimper and a groan. Shit, I can't even differentiate the two.

"You could fuck me."

My eyes widen, brow arching, looking at her like she's lost the goddamn plot. Isn't that the *one* thing she took off the table when we started this?

"Lennon…" I start, trying to find the words. This isn't just hooking up; this is something she drew a boundary around. "You said that you weren't ready for that."

Motherfucker, I have to tell her.

I have to come clean about my stupid fucking plan. Even if I have no intentions of following through with it anymore, she deserves to know the truth.

But *how*?

How do I tell her that I started this with her as my intended casualty for a vendetta with her father but that somewhere along the way, I started to have feelings for her. That I abandoned the fucking plan the moment I realized that she's more important than revenge.

That the revenge doesn't even matter if it means I'll have to hurt her.

That she's become the only real friend I have. Outside of Ma, the most important person to me.

That the thought of hurting her makes me physically hurt.

How the fuck do I tell her *any* of that without ruining *everything* that's happening right now? I'm done with my plan; it no longer applies. But I have to tell her, don't I?

She shrugs, brushing my lips with hers. "And now I am."

"Baby, no, I…" I start, ready to admit my entire fucking existence to her in this moment, but her finger moves over my lips, silencing me.

"Don't. You don't need to say anything. For so long, my life, my body, my choices haven't been mine. But this decision is mine, and only I can make it. And I want it to be you. I want you to take my virginity, Saint."

chapter forty-two

LENNON

MY HEART IS THUDDING OBSCENELY hard in my chest as I stare down at the man who I just offered my virginity to. Although I'm not sure if he's even going to agree because he's currently looking at me like I've said something insane.

"Do you not wa—" The sentence dies on my tongue because he sits up, plastering us tightly together as he captures my lips and silences me with a kiss that makes me feel light-headed and breathless.

When he pulls back, his dark eyes are stormy. "Trust me when I say I want you more than I've ever wanted anything in my fucking life. Don't ever doubt the way I want you." He sweeps his thumb along my jaw, where he's holding me. "I just know that you said you weren't ready, and I don't want you to feel like you're pressured to do anything."

I melt just a little bit at the fact that he's worried about my consent and that I might not be thinking clearly. But the truth is, I've never been more sure of anything.

I kept this promise ring on my finger as a reminder to *myself* after everything that I've been through. It's never been about my virginity, not really. It's always been about choice, about reclaiming my decisions. That whoever I have sex with will be because I *wanted* to.

And I'm choosing Saint.

With him, I feel confident, and comfortable, and safe. I feel seen not just for the person I'm trying to be but for the one I've always been. I don't feel like I have to hide who I am.

Even if we're not together, or even if we don't ever move past this moment, I know undoubtedly that he's the one I want to share it with.

"I'm a thousand percent sure. I want it to be you," I say as I lift my chin, the conviction in my tone evident.

A beat passes between us as his eyes search mine, him drinking in the gravity of what I've just said.

Finally, once the silence surrounding us feels too heavy, he nods. "Okay."

"Now, if you're done trying to protect my virtue... can you go back to the growly, dirty-talking man you were like fifteen minutes ago?" I roll my lips together, biting back a giggle when his gaze narrows, and he leans forward, nipping at the sensitive skin on the slope of my shoulder, his teeth sinking in until I whimper. A needy, desperate sound that, for a moment, I'm unsure if it even came from me.

His tongue sweeps across the spot he just bit, and every single nerve ending in my body comes alive all at once.

God, how does he read my body so well? Sometimes it feels like he knows it better than I do. Exactly where to touch, to kiss, to lick that's going to drive me insane with desire.

After the orgasm he just gave me with his tongue, I'm desperate for *more*.

The throb inside of me builds in intensity with each lash of his tongue.

My nipples are puckered tightly, and the sensation of the peaks dragging across his chest feels so good I wonder if I could possibly come that way.

Tearing his mouth free, his breath cascades along my heated skin, sending goose bumps barreling across my flesh.

He plants kisses on every spot his lips can reach, my collarbone, the swell of my breasts, my neck, until I'm nearly panting. "I want you on top, just like this, taking it as slow or fast as you want. I want *you* in control, baby."

"Okay," I murmur, running my hand over his chest, trying to stop the bloom in mine.

He's being thoughtful, and intentional, and it's... adorable.

A word I never thought I would use to describe the man beneath me.

His eyes hold mine for another beat, then two, as if giving me time to change my mind, and when I don't, only giving him a cheeky smile, he reaches between us and fists the base of his cock, giving it a languid pump.

It's unbelievably hot. I make a mental note to ask him to… explore that more later. There are lots of things I want to explore with him.

"Put my cock in you, inch by inch… I want you to take it all," Saint rasps.

My clit pulses in response. I lift on trembling knees, my hands curved around his shoulders, clutching him as I do as I'm told.

He drags his erection through my pussy, coating the blunt head in my arousal and rubbing my clit with it. The pad of his thumb sweeps over his slit, around the piercing that I'm both excited and slightly terrified to know how it will feel when it's inside of me.

My heart is racing with anticipation, heady desire, so many different emotions, but mostly, it just feels right.

"Goddamnit, I almost forgot a condom. You make me so fucking crazy, Golden Girl." He groans, dropping his head back against the headboard. "And I didn't even bring my wallet, which means…"

"You don't have one?"

He nods. "It's all right though. I'll just make you come with my mouth…" He leans in and presses a kiss to the corner of my lips. "My fingers…" Another kiss at the edge of my jaw.

"Let's not use one."

Abruptly, he pulls back, his brows pulling tight. "I've *never* had sex without a condom."

"Yeah, well, coincidentally, neither have I." I grin. "I've got an IUD. It's good for seven years, which means as long as you're good, then… I'm good."

Saint's throat works as he swallows, his palm running over my hair, his eyes bouncing between mine. "I'm good. You sure?"

I capture my bottom lip between my teeth as I wrap my hand around the base of his cock and line it up with my entrance, holding his intense, heated gaze as I slowly sink down until the tip is inside me. "Positive."

It's actually not as painful as I imagined it would be. More of a biting sting that feels hot and sharp as my body stretches to accommodate him.

"Fuuuck, Lennon." He groans raggedly. I'm distracted from the slight discomfort by watching *him*. His nostrils flare, and his jaw tenses as he grits his teeth together.

Clearly trying to hold on to his resolve.

Suddenly, his lips are on mine, crashing into me like he couldn't last another second without it. His tongue slips inside my mouth as he kisses the ever-living shit out of me, making it even harder to breathe as I slowly drop down onto him inch by inch, an agonizingly slow descent that's a mixture of discomfort and fullness that I've never experienced.

"Yeah, that's my good girl," he praises as he grips my hips, steadying me. "You're doing so fucking good taking my cock, baby. Fuck, just look at you."

My gaze drops to where we're joined, his huge, veiny length sliding inside of me.

"Oh God," I groan, my eyes falling shut. "It's just the *tip*, Saint!"

His chuckle is low and gravelly. "You can take it. I

know you can. Show me how much that tight little cunt was made for me, Lennon, made to take my big cock."

God, I *love* this. His filthy, obscene words.

I never knew I would be so turned on by someone saying things like that to me, but every time he does, it makes me so hot, so wet.

I let out a stuttering exhale, sinking farther onto him until I reach the point of resistance, where it feels like he might split me open with said *big cock*. My nails bite into his shoulders, my eyes squeezing shut.

"You would have a stupidly large dick," I mutter, holding myself completely still.

I feel him shake beneath me with a chuckle. "Pretty sure I told you that when you met me."

Cocky as always.

Hot… as always.

"Breathe through it, baby. It'll feel so much better once you're past this. Just focus on me."

I watch him spit into his palm before he brings his fingers to my clit and circles it slowly, applying the perfect amount of pressure, sending a jolt of pleasure shooting through me. "Come on, baby, fuck yourself onto my cock. Take me like the good girl I know you are."

He's talking me through it in the literal sense, and it's exactly what I didn't even know that I needed.

I swallow down my anxiousness and suck in a deep, shaky breath before slowly sinking down fully onto his cock. It hurts for a single breath as he rips through my virginity, but then… it quickly fades, dulls into a throbbing ache inside of me.

I'm fully seated, my clit brushing the short, soft hair at the base of his cock. Saint's hands move gently along my hips, over my back, his lips pressing to my buzzing skin.

"That's it, baby. I'm so proud of you," he says hoarsely. "Fuck, you feel so good, Lennon. So goddamn good squeezing my cock." I can feel him twitching inside me as his hands find my hips, fingers digging into the soft skin of my hips to keep me still, his breathing strained. "Don't move, or I'm going to come. I need a second."

The thought sends a shiver down my spine, and for the first time, I'm realizing... how much I think I'd like that.

Saint's gaze darkens as it moves over my face, the corner of his lips tilting into a sexy grin. "You like that."

It's not a question but a statement.

A hot blush climbs my neck, racing to my cheeks. I'm not sure why I'm suddenly embarrassed about that, maybe because it's so intimate, so erotic. The thought of him coming inside of me turns me on so much.

"Fuck, baby, I can feel you clenching around me. You want me to fill you up? Pump your pussy full of my cum until it's dripping out of you, hm?"

Oh God.

I can feel my pulse between my legs, and I nod, blurting out, "I want... it everywhere. But I really want it inside of me."

"You're going to fucking kill me, Lennon," he grunts.

My hips squirm, desperate to *move*, to chase the flame that tugs at my lower belly.

I lift on my knees until only the tip of his cock is still inside of me before sliding back down, circling my hips, dragging my clit against his pubic bone. The delicious friction sends my toes curling.

There's the smallest remaining twinge of pain, but it's replaced by something different—blinding hot pleasure.

"I need... I need more. Please."

Saint groans, flexing his hips and pushing deeper inside of me. "Fuck, I love hearing you beg for me."

He guides me up and down on his cock, rocking up into me with hard, sharp thrusts that have my head feeling light, my vision turning hazy.

"Don't stop. Don't... Don't stop-p." I'm panting, shallow breaths.

Suddenly, he's flipping us, the movement effortless, never slipping out of me as my back hits the mattress. His rough palm slides along the back of my thigh, and he hitches my leg higher onto his side, burying his cock inside me again to the hilt.

The position is somehow even better. My toes curl, my fingers tangling into the hair at his nape as he captures my lips, swallowing down the shameless, breathless moans that he's tearing out of me.

He thrusts deeper, so deep that I swear he's in my stomach, and rotates his hips.

Pulling back, I moan, "Oh my God. Saint..." Pleasure steals my breath, and I swallow, sucking in air as he pounds into me, hips slapping against my thighs. "I think I'm... I think..."

"Tell me where you want my cum, baby. I need you to tell me right fucking now."

I'm so close, so, so close, I can hardly form a single rational thought.

"On me."

His hips flex, and he hits that spot inside of me that has my eyes rolling shut. Blinding, bright pleasure crescendos inside of me, pulling me under as my climax crashes into me in a torrential wave. My belly quivers, drawing tight as my orgasm ripples through me.

"That's my girl, milking my cock like she was made for me," Saint murmurs, the filthy words hoarse and full of need, only making my orgasm more intense, prolonging it until every muscle in my body is limp. He pulls out of me, and my eyes snap open as he rises to his knees and pumps his fist around his cock, spilling all over my stomach.

His lips are parted, eyes squeezed as he groans, painting me with his cum, thick ropes that pool in my belly button.

God, the sight of him trembling, muscles rippling as he strokes his cock and marks me, is the sexiest thing I've ever witnessed.

When he's finished, his eyes slowly crack open, drinking me in with a satisfied smile. "You look so fucking good covered in me. My messy good girl."

I draw my bottom lip between my teeth as I bring my fingers to the cum on my stomach and drag them through it, watching his gaze darken, pupils flickering with heat when I bring it to my lips. I wrap my lips around my finger and suck it off, something that I know he loves to see.

That's the only reason I'm feeling so brazenly confident to do it.

"Stop tempting me, baby. You're going to be sore, and all I want to do is fuck you again. Next time, I'm going to make sure every goddamn drop stays inside you," he rasps but moves off the bed.

I sit up on my elbows, about to ask him where he's going, but he disappears into the bathroom, and I hear the water running, only for him to return with a washcloth in his hand.

His knee hits the bed, and he moves over me, gently cleaning the mess he left behind off my stomach. I had no expectations about what this experience would be like with Saint. I know that he's not a soft kind of guy, but he surprises me.

He's tender, attentive, and thorough as he cleans me off, then throws the dirty washcloth into the laundry basket.

I reach for the comforter to cover myself, but he pulls it out of my hand with a shake of his head. "Fuck no." He parts my thighs, dropping onto his stomach between them, eyes holding mine. "Now, let me take care of you, baby."

I think I'm going to have heart palpitations. He just took my virginity. There's probably…

"You don't have to do that, Saint. There's probably some, um, blood… from you know," I say, staring down my body at him.

I feel the warm fan of his chuckle against my sensitive flesh. "And? You think I care about that? I'm going to lick my girl's swollen, little pussy until every fucking drop is on my tongue."

Oh.

Well, okay th—

The coherent thought slips away when he does exactly as he says and drags his tongue through my slit, lapping at me until I'm not thinking about the ache any longer. All I'm thinking about is the way he's unabashedly devouring me without any hesitation.

"You know what you taste like, Golden Girl?"

I look down at him, cataloging his hard, possessive stare, mouth hovering over my pussy.

"*Mine.*"

chapter forty-three
SAINT

"SAINT... DON'T. YOU. DARE," Lennon says as she skates backward one measured glide at a time, putting distance between us. "I *mean* it!"

My smirk widens. "Mmm. Do you though?"

Of course she doesn't.

Dropping my hockey stick, I take off toward her, chuckling when she screeches and skates away as fast as she can... which isn't fast enough since I'm a foot taller and my legs are almost as long as her entire body.

So catching my Golden Girl isn't much of a chase at all.

But motherfucker, I'd chase her across the goddamn world if I had to.

"I swear to God, Saint, if you tou—" Her threat is cut short when I grab her waist from behind, replaced by a squeal and a sweet little giggle that makes my dick hard. I pick her up and spin her around, unable to stop my own laugh when she tries her hardest to wiggle out of my hold.

Get real, baby.

I dip my head to her ear, my voice dropping low. "Didn't I tell you what happens when you taunt me? Or… did you *want* me to catch you?"

She turns her head to look up at me, drawing her plump lip between her teeth. "Maybe."

My threat was to spank her ass, and clearly… not a threat at all.

"Oh shit," she says, eyes going widen as she looks past me. "There's someone over there."

I loosen my hold long enough to turn to look, and in that single second, her bratty little ass elbows me in the stomach, obviously not hard enough to make a difference, but it *does* catch me by surprise. My arms drop, and she's gone, her laughter echoing around the rink as she skates away, tossing me her pink-painted middle finger.

Yeah, she's definitely getting her ass spanked, and I can't fucking wait.

It's been like this between us ever since I showed up at her house that night… The night that she gave me her virginity.

Something I don't feel worthy of, but for her, I'll try to be.

It just feels natural, easy with Lennon. Effortless. There's no pressure or expectation.

We fuck, and we fight, and I chase her around the rink until she's breathless.

At night, she's got me watching stupid movies that bore me to tears, but it doesn't matter anyway because it's her I'm watching the entire time, drinking in the fact that she chooses to spend her time with a fuckup like me when she doesn't have to.

And if I thought we couldn't keep our hands off each other before that night, now it's a whole new arena. That night unlocked something, something that neither of us has bothered to deny.

An unexpected connection that's more than just physical.

I don't understand it, and I don't know what it means. I just know that I like who Lennon is, and not just when she's dragging me into her apartment before I can even say hello.

I like *all* of her.

In the past couple of weeks, I've realized that my Golden Girl is *insatiable*.

It takes me all of twenty seconds to catch her for the second time, and she groans, breathless as she turns to face me, slipping her arms around my neck, her plump, pink lips in a pout. "Can't you just *let* me win?"

"Do you know me at all? Not a chance in hell, baby. You think I'm going to give up the chance to turn your pretty little ass pink? Fuck no." My phone buzzes in my pocket, and I know that it's my alarm telling us that ice time is officially over. Guess we'll have to pick up our cat-and-mouse game later.

She sighs when she realizes that it's my alarm. "That went fast. Uh… what's your plan for later?"

I smirk. "Gonna go home and check on my mom, make sure she's good, then not sure. Maybe sleep. I'm exhausted, you know, from all of the work I've been putting in."

Warmth creeps up her cheeks, and I exhale a laugh when she pushes my chest with an eye roll.

"Come over?" she breathes.

"You mean like I have every night since last week?"

Her lip tilts in a cheeky grin. "Obviously."

♥ ♥ ♥

That's how, two hours later, I'm sprawled out in her pink, frilly bed with my feet hanging off the end, with her draped across me.

Still… mostly clothed.

It's a lot like cuddling, and that makes me shiver a little. It's something I've never done with *anyone* before. Pretty sure I never even cuddled with my own mom as a child.

Affection outside of fucking isn't my normal.

But having her on top of me, comfortable, relaxed, chin resting on the top of her hand as she looks at me… I don't know, it feels right.

Maybe it's my new normal.

And maybe I really fucking like it.

The tip of her finger trails softly across the ink on my chest, tracing the outline of the roses. Her long, auburn hair is twisted up in a clip at her nape, her face free of makeup aside from whatever shiny gloss she put on her lips, her long eyelashes kissing her cheeks as she looks down at the tattoos beneath her.

She's staring at the art, and I'm staring at her.

She has no fucking clue that she's art in the purest form, and I'd ink her onto my skin in a heartbeat.

"Did they hurt?"

"Nah, not really," I say, shaking my head, "It's not too bad. I've got a pretty high pain tolerance." Her eyes flick to the fading bruises around my eye, still a reminder of that night. At least there's something good to take from that shitty situation. This—me and her. "There are a few spots that hurt, like my ribs, my elbow, the top of my hand, but it wasn't unbearable. You honestly start to get addicted to the feeling. Probably why I have so many."

She traces the scripted words down my side, her gaze trailing over the letters. "I love them."

I smirk. "Yeah?"

She nods. "So cliché bad boy of you." Her teasing tone earns her a little smack on her ass, and she giggles before her expression turns serious. "I think they fit you, and I love that they mean something. They're stories that you'll always carry with you."

I've told her about most of them, and she's listened intently, like she genuinely cares about why I got them.

When the pads of her fingers move over my chest again, my gaze slides to the ring on her finger. Pink and gold, heart-shaped, dainty... and feels very *her*.

I know it's her purity ring or whatever only from what Bennett said, but she's never mentioned anything about it.

"What's this ring? I never see you take it off. Does it mean something?" I ask.

She's quiet for a moment before she nods, "Yeah, um… it's my promise ring. It's actually kind of embarrassing to talk about, but it used to be a purity ring given to me by my parents."

Her cheeks are tinted pink, and she rolls her lips together, "I know that's really old school and archaic, but it was basically drilled into my head growing up that I was to save myself for marriage. And after some things happened in my life… I decided to repurpose it. It's now a promise to myself to make my own choices with my body, my life. To never let anyone decide those things for me. Not that it really applies any longer, but to give *myself* to whoever I wanted without guilt or consequence."

Carefully she slips it off her finger and tilts it, "I got this phrase inscribed on the inside the day I made the promise to myself to take my life back."

Inside reads *De meo arbitrio*.

"It means, *By thy own will*." She adds before slipping back into place on her finger. "So, yeah."

That wasn't at all what I was expecting her to say, but I'm glad she's giving her father a figurative fuck you. My fingers trace along the slope of her shoulder, a small sliver of bare, creamy skin that peeks out from the old hockey T-shirt of mine that she stole a few days ago. I almost ripped it off her when I saw her in it for the first time. She walked out of the bathroom wearing nothing but that shirt, and it made something primal and possessive swell in my chest.

Mine was all I could think.

The truth is I don't even know if Lennon *is* mine, but what I do know is she's not going to be anyone else's.

Fuck no.

"What do you want to do once you graduate?" I ask.

The question feels random, but fuck, now all I'm thinking about is what's going to happen next, where do we go from here? About what the future is going to hold with *us*.

What's going to happen if she ever finds out about the shit with our dads?

Would she hate him for the shit he's done, or would she hate *me* for blaming her father?

I'm carrying this shit inside my chest. This... guilt. It's an unfamiliar, uncomfortable feeling to experience.

I just don't want to hurt her. "Honestly? I don't know." She winces, like the thought of being unsure of her future is as uncomfortable as the guilt I'm harboring. "I've spent my entire life doing every single thing that I've been told without ever questioning or giving any kind of resistance. I've always done everything that's been expected of me. The dutiful daughter." I watch her throat rock with a hard swallow.

I reach out and grab her hand, threading our fingers together and doing a slow, steady sweep of my thumb along the soft skin of her hand.

I don't know if it's the right thing to do, but it feels like she needs the assurance of my touch. I know this shit with her dad hurts her, even when she tries to throw up armor as thick as mine.

I've realized that Lennon is soft, in all the places that it matters, but especially her heart.

My thumb moves as she speaks. "Until this year, I never had the freedom of planning for a future outside of the one my parents have set for me. I think about it a lot. The fact that my family comes from money... the nicest cars, a seven-bedroom house when it's only ever just been the three of us, designer gowns. I've lived a life of luxury, and I'm privileged to say that. Trust me, I know that." She pauses, blowing out a breath. "But surrounded by all of that... the one luxury I never had was freedom."

The irony isn't lost on me. My Golden Girl... in her golden cage.

"Anyway, until recently, I haven't really had the chance to think about what I *really* want to do. But I think I'd like to work with children? But also incorporate skating into it somehow. Maybe work with underprivileged kids. Open a rink and make it possible for everyone to have the ability to chase their dreams." She smiles then, her eyes lighting up as she mentions it.

I can't imagine anything she'd be better at. She's kind, patient, down-to-earth.

The exact opposite of the girl I thought she was when she walked into the rink that day.

"I think you'd be amazing," I finally say, offering her a small smile. "Do whatever makes you happy, and fuck what anyone thinks about it. That should be your motto from here on out. Be wild, be rebellious. Total fucking anarchy, Lennon. Fuck it."

Her eyes glint with pride. "Hmm. I like it. Maybe I'll start by getting a tattoo of my own."

"Oh yeah?" I drop her hand to haul her up my body until she's fully on top of me, my mouth hovering beneath hers. "What are you going with? A butterfly?" Using the tips of my fingers, I draw one onto the back of her thigh just below where my T-shirt ends, noting the way she melts into me, a shiver racing down her spine. "Hmm. Nah, too basic. What about… a flower?" I make the lines of the flower, trailing up beneath the shirt as I draw the stem. My lips ghost along hers, featherlight, chaste even, yet hunger flicks within the depths of her pretty pale green eyes. "A heart?" Inch by inch, my fingers move higher, all while I watch her, never letting my gaze leave hers. "No, none of those. I've got it."

"What?" Her words tumble out breathlessly, a whisper against my lips.

"A *golden* phoenix. From the ashes, you rise."

chapter forty-four

SAINT

Golden Girl: I'm not saying I miss you, but I am saying I miss your 🌭

Saint: & what did I tell you?

Golden Girl: ...

Saint: If you want my 🌭 all you have to do is ask. You asking, Golden Girl?

Golden Girl: Come to my apartment after ice time? Maybe… we can play hooky tomorrow? Stay in all weekend?

Saint: Let me check my schedule

Golden Girl: You know what, never mind. No more 🐱 👅 for you

Saint: Yeah, okay. You know I'm the only one who can make you come this hard, the only one who's going to make you come period.

Golden Girl: Are you though? Might have to test this "theory"

Saint: 😬 then it's on you when he ends up with two broken arms and can't even make himself come.

Saint: You know how much I love to fight baby, don't try me

Saint: Wear my favorite skirt today

Golden Girl: And since when do I listen to anything you say?

Saint: Since you want my tongue on your pussy

Saint: Be a good girl and listen.

OF COURSE, she listened, wearing a skirt that made my dick instantly hard the moment I laid eyes on her.

That's exactly how we ended up in the penalty box with her completely, deliciously naked.

Her rosy nipples are pebbled tight from the cool air of the rink, and I can't resist leaning down and sucking one into my mouth, letting my teeth rake across the sensitive peak.

She whimpers, and I smile against her heated skin, rolling her nipple back and forth between my teeth.

"Saint, *please*."

Fuck, I love when she begs.

She's spent the better part of the past few days begging. For my fingers, my tongue, my *cock*.

It's as if the moment that we crossed the line, the night that I took her virginity, we've been unable to keep our hands off each other.

We've both learned how she likes when I'm rough with her and when I bring her to the brink of an orgasm, only to pull it away, edging her until she's going out of her mind. She comes so fucking hard after.

I pull my mouth from her nipple, and it makes a *pop* sound that reverberates in the box surrounding us. "Mmm, please *what*, baby?"

"Touch me. I…" She pants. "Make me come. Please."

When she squirms on the bench, my gaze drops to her pussy, already glistening and wet, creamy arousal coating the inside of her thighs.

"Such a good girl asking so nicely. You sure you're good with this?"

Her tongue darts out to wet her lips, and she nods, never hesitating.

I reach for the roll of stick tape that's been pushed into the corner of the box that someone likely left behind and use my other hand to push her wrists together, lifting them above her head.

Pulling the end of the tape free with my teeth, I start to carefully wrap it around her wrists. Not too tight, but tight enough to keep them bound, tight enough to hold her when she's writhing from my tongue being buried in her cunt.

Once I finish, I lean forward and tear the end off with

my teeth and then toss the roll onto the bench behind her. Gently, I prop her against the back glass of the box and haul her ass to the edge of the bench, spreading her thighs open wide.

I sink down to my knees and lift her leg to rest on my shoulder, pressing my lips along the soft, creamy skin of her inner thigh.

Christ, I can smell how wet she is, a mixture of her sweet citrus bodywash and heady arousal that clings to my nose and makes my mouth water.

I part her lips, spreading her open wide, giving me a full view of every inch of her, and I nearly groan.

The most perfect pussy to exist on the goddamn earth sits between her thighs.

One I want to drown in.

"Fuck, baby, look how messy you are. You love me taping you up to where you can't move, can't fucking run from me, don't you?"

I press my thumb against her swollen clit, and her back bows, wrists pulling at the tape around them as I lower my mouth to her cunt and flatten my tongue, dragging it through her folds. I lap at her in slow, controlled licks that I know drive her fucking crazy because she writhes beneath me, hips rocking against my mouth.

I slide two fingers inside of her tight little cunt while I circle her clit with my tongue before sucking it into my mouth. And then I hook my fingers up, stroking the spot inside of her that has her clawing at her restraints.

"Right there... yes, God... Saint, Saint..." Lennon moans as her greedy little hole sucks my fingers in deeper.

I fuck my fingers into her faster, the sound of her pussy an erotic echo filling the room as I pound them into her, each time hitting her G-spot, alternating pressure of my lips sucking her clit.

She's fucking wild, thrashing, trembling, bucking against my mouth. I've never seen her like this, and fuck, it's making me so hard I can't even think straight.

There's got to be a wet spot already on my pants from the amount of precum leaking out of my cock.

I can feel her pussy clamping down on my fingers, tightening as she barrels toward an orgasm, and I don't let up. I eat her like I'll fucking die unless I get her cum on my tongue, continuing the unrelenting pump of my fingers.

The sounds leaving her mouth are feral, fucking unhinged. Strangled whimpers, breathless moans.

"That's it, baby. You're going to come on my face like my good little Golden Girl."

She doesn't just come—she *detonates* like a bomb that's finally reached the end of its fuse. Her legs shake as she clamps them around my head, her ass nearly lifting off the bench as a rush of warm, wet cum soaks my tongue, my face, fuck, my shirt. Everywhere.

Holy fucking shit.

I just made her squirt.

Fuuuck yeah.

"Oh my God," she breathes, finally turning limp once the aftershocks of her climax subside. I look up her body, my gaze moving over her face, the hazy, unfocused look in her eyes, her hair damp and matted against her flushed cheeks.

Only then do I pull my soaked fingers out of her and bring them to my mouth, sucking them clean.

"Was that…" She trails off, her expression turning shy. "Did I…"

I smirk, my chest swelling with possessiveness, "Yeah, baby, you just squirted all over my fucking face, and it was the hottest thing I've *ever* witnessed in my goddamn life."

♥ ♥ ♥

"Fuuuuck," I groan as my head falls back on my shoulders, and my eyes drop shut. "That's it. Just like that, baby, take every fucking inch."

My fingers tighten in Lennon's hair as she slides her mouth lower on my cock, taking me all the way until the head of my cock nudges the back of her throat.

I'm pretty fucking positive I'm dead and this is heaven because there's nothing on the goddamn planet, aside from her pussy, that could ever touch this.

I swallow, forcing myself to lift my head so I can watch her deep-throating me.

She's a fucking mess, but goddamn, she's the most beautiful mess I've ever seen. Cheeks flushed and wet with tears from gagging, mascara running down her face, saliva seeping out around my cock and coating her chin.

The sexiest part about it is this was *her* idea. She wanted to skip our afternoon class, whispering in my ear that she wanted me to teach her how to suck my dick for the first time.

Naturally, I obliged.

She was so fucking eager to suck my cock. Like the good girl she always is, she's perfect at following instructions.

She gags when I flex my hips, hitting the back of her throat, and when I try to pull her off, she shakes her head, holding me by the back of my thighs.

Goddamnit, this girl.

"If you want me to fuck your throat, then open it up, baby. Open up and take me deeper," I mumble, my voice strained with exertion. My balls are tight and throbbing with the need to come. "Tap my thigh if you want me to stop."

She nods, looking up at me through her lashes, those lush green eyes holding mine as I tighten my fingers in her hair and push her mouth down further on my cock, thrusting deep. Her tongue glides along my piercings, and a shiver racks my body, black spots dancing around the corners of my eyes while I struggle to keep them open.

Pleasure threatens to force them closed, but I fight it because I want to watch her taking my cock down her throat.

"Rub your clit, baby. Get your pussy ready for me to fuck it. Make it wet and slippery for me to bury my cock in," I pant, knowing how much she loves when I say filthy shit to her. Thrusting deep once more, I hold her there, feeling her gag around me.

Then she fucking swallows around my head, and my knees almost give out.

Motherfucker.

I hold her still, trying to remember how to even fucking breathe, and then I pull her off. She inhales a shuddering breath before sucking me deep again, and this time, I can't fucking hold off.

"I'm gonna come, baby. Do you want it down your throat?"

Her head moves in a slight nod.

My head falls back, and I groan, the ragged sound tearing out of my chest as I rock my hips, pumping deep and spilling down her throat with slow, erratic spurts.

The floor sways beneath my feet as I struggle to stay upright, coming harder than I ever have in my life.

"Fuuuuck, Lennon, my good fucking girl, letting me fill her throat with my cum. Drink every fucking drop, baby."

chapter forty-five

LENNON

"OH GOD, SAINT... I CAN'T," I whine. *"I can't."*

He chuckles darkly. "Yes you can, baby. Give me another."

My God, how does he have *this* much stamina? It's obscene.

We've spent the entire weekend locked in my bedroom, with him making me come so many times, in so many different positions, I've lost count. I'm sore and achy from exertion but in the most delicious way.

I'm addicted to Saint Devereaux, and I don't think I'll ever get enough.

His stormy gaze drags down my body in an unhurried perusal, watching as I slide my fingers deeper inside my throbbing pussy.

Looking… but not touching.

Because he wants to watch me bring myself to orgasm.

It's so hot and something I never thought I'd feel

comfortable doing, but he makes me feel brazen and confident in a way I've never known.

"Good girl. Rub your greedy little clit. It needs attention, baby," he rasps.

Even though he's not once touched me, I somehow feel his eyes on my body, making my skin burn hotter, making the wave of pleasure crest inside of me.

The second I touch my clit, I fall apart, a powerful climax washing through me. My head lolls back, and his name tumbles breathlessly from my lips over and over.

"Fuck, you're so goddamn beautiful, Lennon. Look at you coming apart for me, coating your fingers in your creamy cum."

I sink into the mattress, unable to move, even as my entire body trembles.

Saint watches me intensely, his gaze slicing through me. When my orgasm finally subsides, I slip my fingers out of me.

He circles my wrist, bringing them to his mouth. "Now, let me taste."

Even after the orgasm, my clit pulses, and I fight the urge to press my thighs together. My slick flesh is still sensitive and overstimulated.

He wraps his lips around my middle finger and ring finger, and he sucks them all the way into his mouth, tongue laving over my sticky fingers until they're clean.

Suddenly, I feel his lips moving over my promise ring, his gaze connecting with mine as he slowly sucks it off, never dropping my eyes.

He spits it into his hand with a cocky, sexy smirk.

"Why did you do that?" I mumble, the sound still throaty from my cries.

"Because it's *mine*, baby. You chose *me*, Lennon, and this is me choosing *you*."

My mouth falls open, silence filling the room.

Oh my fucking God.

This man just... he just *sucked* my promise ring off my finger because he's... because it's *his*?

I'm trying to even wrap my head around that statement, but suddenly, Saint is prowling forward, sealing his mouth over mine, the ring gone, forgotten, possibly never even existed.

The faint taste of me is still lingering on his tongue, and it's so *hot*.

If there is one single thing I have discovered in the past week, it's that there is nothing Saint loves more than to eat me out.

I've heard from other girls how selfish their boyfriends are—how they never want to give and only receive—so I wasn't sure what to expect when it came to this.

But he's spent the majority of the weekend with his head between my legs.

"Need to be inside you, baby. Right now," he murmurs with a desperate, frantic edge against my mouth. "Flip."

The rough command sends a bolt of pleasure charging down my spine.

Obediently, I oblige and flip over onto my stomach. I have no idea how I'll come again, but the heated look he gives me tells me that I shouldn't worry.

His palms curve around my hips, and he hauls my ass

up. Then, I feel the hot bloom of delicious pain when he smacks my ass, the movement making a gush of wetness pool between my thighs.

Jesus Christ.

His strong, powerful body curls over mine, his lips brushing against my ear. "I'm going to fuck you like I hate you, but it's only because I know how hard you'll come, baby."

That should not be as hot as it is.

It shouldn't, but it totally is.

I mumble a string of unintelligible noises as he grips my hips hard, his fingertips digging into the soft places as he drags his thick, hard cock through my soaked lips.

"Face down," he rasps, and I fall forward, pressing my cheek flat against the mattress.

He slaps the head of his cock against my clit, groaning roughly at the sensation, and then he grabs my ass in his hands and spreads me open, cool air hitting my sensitive core.

"Your tight little hole is clenching around nothing, desperate to be filled with my cock, isn't it, greedy girl? Fuck, that's hot."

In a single thrust, he slams inside of me from behind, stealing the breath out of my lungs, my fingers fisting into the sheets below me as he starts to fuck me.

"Oh God," I whine. "I feel so full…"

It's never felt like this, so deep, so impossibly filled with him.

Saint's hips slap against mine in deep, fast, nearly

brutal thrusts, fucking me so hard that I'm slowly being inched up the mattress by the force.

"Your pretty little pussy is stretched tight around me, trying to take all of me. But you were fucking made for me, Lennon. There's no question you were made to be mine."

His hand slips around my thighs, fingers finding my clit and circling in quick motions that match the time of his thrusts.

"Now, come for me, baby," he groans. "Come with me as I pump you full of cum."

It only takes a few more rough swipes of his fingers on my sensitive clit, and I push back against him, an avalanche of pleasure coursing through me as my climax takes me by the throat, robbing me of my breath, making my vision dance behind my eyes.

I hear Saint's long, guttural groan as a flood of warmth fills me, his cum spilling inside me in thick waves. It only prolongs my orgasm, sending a flurry of aftershocks coursing through me. He presses forward as deep as he can possibly go and rotates his hips, balls grinding against my clit like he's trying to wring out every drop from his body.

"Lennon, baby... fuck. *Fuck.*"

Once my heartbeat starts to calm and my body feels like a pile of bones, he slowly pulls out of me, and I collapse onto the mattress, my eyes dropping shut in a moment of sheer bliss and exhaustion piled into one.

The bed dips beneath me, and it hits me that I didn't even feel him leave, but he comes back with a warm, wet rag in his hand, and I peel my eyes open.

Carefully, he spreads my thighs and tenderly drags the warm rag through me, cleaning me. It's one of my favorite things he does, always taking care of me and giving me the quiet attention that I need after an emotionally charged, intense moment like this.

It means more than he probably even knows.

Once he's finished, he lies down beside me on the bed. The room around us is mostly silent, only the sound of cicadas clicking through the window.

I feel his strong arm looping around my waist before he hauls me against him, thumb sweeping across the bare skin of my stomach.

It feels peaceful.

Right… to be in his arms.

And I find myself hoping that *this* never ends.

chapter forty-six

LENNON

I HAVE no idea why I'm suddenly nervous, but my palms are clammy as I smooth down the front of my dress.

Again.

"This feels very relationshippy for someone who claims they're *not* in a relationship," Maisie quips from the chair at my vanity, where she's swiping mascara on her thick, already long lashes in front of the mirror.

I flash her a look, rolling my eyes. "We're… *us*. I don't know, Mais. We haven't put labels on anything. Plus, this is just hanging out together."

"Like… a double date?" she teases as she tosses the mascara onto the vanity. "Who is he bringing? Is he cute? Do I know him?"

"I have no idea. I told him to bring a friend, and he said, '*I don't have friends,*' to which I said, 'There has to be *one* person you'd consider a friend,' and then I realized he's Saint, and conversation is not his strong suit, so I truly have no idea."

Shrugging, I glance back at my reflection in the mirror. I'm not sure if I'm overdressed or underdressed in the bubble-gum-pink minidress I picked out for tonight. It's one of my favorites, with a sweetheart neckline and a fitted bodice that flares out into a soft, feminine skirt that stops mid-thighs. I paired it with a pair of light-colored espadrille wedges that give me a tiny bit of height. Not that it'll make much of a difference next to Saint.

We're *just* going to Jack's. Which is casual and right off campus, so it's always full of college kids.

So it's not like we're going to a five-star Michelin restaurant. It's Jack's.

But... this *is* the first time Saint and I have done anything together publicly and with both of our friends.

That's where the nerves come in. Not even necessarily in a bad way. I'm just unsure of what to expect out of tonight, that's all.

"Okay, let's go. We can't keep your boyf—" Maisie stops, giving me a grin. "I mean... not boyfriend and his not friend waiting. We're going to be late if you keep staring at yourself in the mirror, babe. You look gorg. Now... let's go."

I steal one more quick glance before turning and following her out of my bedroom.

After a quick ride through campus, we find parking along the street outside Jack's. My stomach growls the moment we step inside, the scent of fresh basil and tomato filling my nose. God, I cannot wait for another pizza burrito.

A smile turns my lips, thinking about the last time.

"Oh, there they are," Maisie says, and my gaze travels along hers to see Saint, his hulking, broad body squeezed into a booth in the corner. Sitting across from him is a guy with dark, dirty-blond hair, around the same height and even a similar build.

If I had to guess... one of his teammates.

I feel Saint's eyes on me as I cross the room, and when I lift my gaze, he's smirking, that signature cocky, small tilt to his lips that I'm admittedly a little obsessed with.

I think I might be becoming obsessed with him just in general, if I'm being honest.

"Hi." I smile, sliding in beside him. He dips his head to my ear to where only the two of us can hear and whispers, "Yet another little outfit that I want to flip up and fuck you in."

My eyes widen, nearly popping out of my head at his filthy words. God, it's ridiculous how much of an effect he has on me. I'm clenching my thighs together beneath the table.

Something he's all too aware of.

"Behave," I mumble, pulling a low chuckle out of him. Turning back to Maisie and his friend with my cheeks currently burning as if they're on fire, I make introductions. "Maisie, this is Saint. Saint, this is my best friend, Maisie."

He gives her a nod and a small smile. "Hey. This is Bennett."

"So you *do* have friends?" Maisie smarts as she angles herself toward who I now know is Bennett and extends her hand. He flashes her a bright smile and slides his into hers.

He reminds me of a Ken doll, but the dirty-blond version. Charming smile, broad shoulders, a dimple in his cheeks.

"Guess so," Saint mutters.

Bennett grins. "Don't listen to him. He loves me. He's just afraid of commitment, so he does it secretly."

"I *tolerate* you. Big difference," Saint retorts.

Both Maisie and I are wearing the same smile as we watch the two of them go back and forth.

"You staying in the group chat says otherwise. Just admit it—we're friends, and you love me," Bennett says, and Saint just shakes his head.

"Because you kept adding me five thousand goddamn times. My phone kept going off 24/7."

"Potato... po-tah-to. The point is you stayed," Bennett responds, clearly very proud of that fact.

And honestly? He should be. Saint doesn't make it easy, and I know that firsthand.

I'm glad that Bennett hasn't given up and he's forcing Saint out of his comfort zone. He needs friends. People who show up for him, who show him that he's not unlovable.

It's slightly ironic that Bennett is the golden retriever to Saint's black cat.

Clearly night and day.

Saint doesn't get a reply in, even though I'm sure there's one on the tip of his tongue, because the waitress comes over to take our order. Obviously, we all get pizza burritos.

"Lennon, you and Mais gonna come to one of our

games? We can get you good seats. Perks of being the star goalie," Bennett says before shoving half a breadstick in his mouth in one huge bite.

I steal one off the plate in front of me and shrug, unsure. "Yeah, if he wants me to."

"I'm pretty sure you're the only reason this dude has ever smiled. Literally, *ever*," Bennett deadpans.

Saint snorts beside me, but when I look over to see the shadow of a faint grin tilting the corner of his lips, my stomach does incessant flips.

"I've actually... never been to a hockey game," Maisie says with a shrug. "But I'm down to go to the boy aquarium."

A deep laugh slips out of Bennett, his head shaking. "Boy aquarium? The fuck does that even mean?"

She shrugs. "Glass... with hockey boys inside. A... *fishbowl*? You know what? Never mind." Her laugh is soft, suddenly shy as she drops her gaze and looks down at the empty straw paper on the table.

"I like it, blondie." He grins.

Is my best friend... *flirting* with Bennett?

I turn to look at Saint, and his dark brow is lifted, eyes bouncing between our friends, and I'm fairly certain he's thinking the very same thing.

♥♥♥

"Thanks for coming tonight. I know 'peopling' isn't really your thing," I whisper to Saint as we walk out onto the covered back patio of Jack's, the humid night air blanketing us like a cloak. In most places around the country, it's turning to fall, and though leaves have already started to fall in New Orleans, we're in the middle of hurricane season, and the days are still hot and ungodly humid.

We escaped when Bennett and Maisie get lost in a very intense "discussion" about ocean conservation. He had absolutely no idea what he was getting into by bringing up sea turtles around my tie-dye, Earth-loving best friend.

Saint's shoulder moves in a shrug. "Apparently, *you're* my thing, Golden Girl." His words warm my insides, sending my heart into overdrive as it beats wildly.

"Am I?" I can barely get them out of my mouth because I'm trembling.

He nods. "I don't know what I'm doing, Lennon. And I'm fucking *terrified*. Terrified that I'm going to fuck up the best thing that's ever happened to me, terrified that I'll never be worthy of you no matter how hard I try. But you're in here." His fingers curve around my wrist as he lifts my hand and places it on his chest, directly over his heart. "In so fucking deep."

I try to ignore the heavy swell in my chest as the steady, strong beat of his heart thrums beneath my palm, but it's no use.

"I don't know what it means, and I have no fucking clue where to go from here… I just know that I don't want to be without you. I *can't* be without you, baby." I feel the sting of tears prick behind my eyes when his voice cracks, like it's raw from emotion.

In a single breath, I'm colliding against his hard, unyielding body, my arms flying around his neck and squeezing him to me as I bury my face into his neck. His strong arms wrap around my back as he lifts me and holds me tightly against him, my feet dangling in the air.

"I'm shit with words... expressing how I feel, Lennon. I'm probably saying all the wrong things, but I've never had to communicate any other way than physically," he whispers raggedly against my hair. And I swear I can actually feel my heart fracturing.

The unspoken words hang so heavily in the air I might choke.

His dad's abuse. His inability to commit past a hookup, his reputation on the ice. His hesitation to connect with anyone.

I tighten my arms around him as I press my lips to his neck, desperate to somehow get closer, to speak in the only way that he knows how to. In the way that's comfortable to him. "It's okay, Saint. It's enough for me. *You* are enough for me. I don't need the perfect words; I just need you. However that needs to be, okay? We're just going to be *us*. That's it."

It feels easy to say in the midst of all the complicated because being with Saint *is* effortless.

Falling for him was as easy as breathing. I think I actually started to fall long before I ever realized it. I was filling my lungs with pieces of him this whole time, never once noticing that he was tangling himself inside of me.

"Don't leave me. Please, baby," he whispers, the desperate words so low that I barely hear them, his arms tightening around me as if he's terrified of the thought.

chapter forty-seven
SAINT

THE ONLY THING I'm even remotely going to enjoy about tonight is Lennon in this damn dress.

I'm half-hard behind the zipper of my pants with no sign of going down anytime soon as I watch her smooth down the black velvet fabric clinging to her body.

I nearly swallowed my fucking tongue when I watched her bunch the dress around the top of her thighs, swing her stiletto over the seat, and settle onto the back of my bike like she'd done it a thousand times before.

It was the sexiest thing I've ever seen, and I've been thinking about taking her back home and saying fuck this stupid-ass gala, one that neither of us really wants to attend in the first place. I'd much rather spend my night buried inside of her, making her come until she blacks out and my balls are empty.

Yeah, my imagination is running fucking wild with her in that dress and heels.

It also seems pretty damn fitting that the first time she

rode my bike was while she was wearing some vintage, expensive-ass ball gown on the way to another stupid fucking gala for her father.

A stark contrast to the girl she was when I first met her to who she is now.

"What?" she asks, her eyes widening when she catches me staring. "Is my ass showing?"

I chuckle, stepping closer and wrapping my arm around her waist. I want to kiss the fuck out of her, but I don't want to mess up the makeup that she spent far too long putting on.

She doesn't need any of that shit. She's beautiful either way, but I do love the bright red lips.

I specifically have plans for those later.

"Your ass isn't showing. If it was, I'd have to fight before I even got inside the door, baby." I lower my lips to her ear. "I just can't stop thinking about all of the things I'm going to do to you later while you wear those heels."

There's an audible gasp when her breath hitches, and I pull back, staring down at her. Her green eyes flare behind dark, thick lashes, and her lips tilt into a coy smile.

"You know, it's funny that you say that because I've been thinking about what we could do with this." Her fingers wrap around the black tie on my neck, and she pulls my lips down to hers, sighing when I kiss her.

I have no idea why the fuck she chose me, but I think I might be the luckiest motherfucker on this planet that she did.

When she pulls back, a giggle spills free. "I forgot about the lipstick." She lifts her thumb and drags it along my bottom lip, wiping it away. "I don't think I can get it all off, but it'll be okay."

Yeah, baby, mark me.

I want to say it out loud, but if I do... we might not make it inside at all, despite standing outside the venue for the last fifteen minutes.

"Let's go, Golden Girl. Before I change my mind." I grab her hand, threading my fingers in hers.

We walk through the entrance hand in hand, and I can't stop thinking about how different shit is compared to the last event I attended with her.

How much has changed in such a short period of time.

The girl by my side is who I thought would be perfect for my revenge, but she really ended up being the thing I needed to see the truth.

If it wasn't for her, I'm not sure I ever would have. I've been too blinded by hurt and rage to even consider how fucking stupid and vindictive my plan was. One I know now I could have never followed through on.

The misplaced anger. Projecting my pain onto someone innocent.

My Golden Girl doesn't deserve to answer for her father's misdeeds.

I have no doubt that her father will have his day of judgment. The day he'll pay for all the fucked-up shit he's done, but it won't be from me.

I'm done giving both him and my own father the power to control me. My emotions. My life. I refuse to let the anger and pain they've caused make me *anything* like them.

Fuck that, and fuck them.

"God, I forgot how much I hate being around these people," she whispers when we walk into the ballroom, her fingers tightening in mine. "The only genuine thing in here is their greed."

I nod but remain quiet.

I want these realizations to be her own, not tainted by my own disgust. It's not a secret that I can't fucking stand any of this, but telling her isn't going to help anything.

The arrangement we once had isn't a deal anymore. We might not have put a label on things, but what we're feeling? It's real.

We're real.

That doesn't change the fact that Lennon is still trying to prove something to her father. That she's making her own choices, her own decisions.

And I'm her choice. For real this time. Not fake.

So, the reason I'm here tonight isn't to fuck with her father. I'm here for *her*. To support her. To stand by her side while she does the bravest thing she's ever done. To show her I'm not going anywhere, even if I hate this is the life she used to live.

"I need to go to the bathroom before we go to the table," Lennon says. "Come with me?"

I nod and place a quick kiss onto her hand.

She leads me out of the ballroom, leaving behind the buzz of people talking and glasses clinking as we make our way toward the end of a dim hallway, where there's a restroom sign.

But before we make it there, she stops and turns toward

me abruptly, then pushes me against the wall. Slipping her arms around my neck, she lifts on her toes to press a chaste kiss to the corner of my lips. "I just... needed that. It's been too long."

I laugh against her lips. "Only been a few minutes, baby."

She shrugs coyly. "Too long." Her fingers slip beneath the collar of my shirt, and her brow cinches tightly. "What's this?"

I stay silent as she pulls the thin gold chain out of my shirt, and her mouth forms an *O* as it falls open.

"Saint... why are you *wearing* my promise ring around your neck?"

I watch her roll it between her pink-painted fingers. "Because now I know what it's meant to you. And if it's okay with you, I want to keep it. This has been a reminder to you that you will always have control of your life, and I want to make sure that I always take care of it. Just like I wanna take care of you."

Her eyes blaze, and she leans in, brushing her lips to mine again. "Keep it. I... I think I like seeing it around your neck."

Grinning, I slide my hand up the center of her chest until it brackets her throat. The sight of the dark ink on my hand against her pale skin makes my dick come to life. I shake my head, squeezing her neck gently as I pull her against me. "Fuck, you drive me crazy, Golden Girl. I'm obsessed with you."

"There are worse things to be obsessed with. And I am *pretty* amazing."

I nip at her lips as she giggles. "*Brat.*"

I capture her lips, unable to last another second without tasting her. Her fingers thread into my hair, and my Golden Girl fucking melts.

Her tongue glides along mine like she's attempting to gain the upper hand, but little does she know, she's always had it.

"*Lennon?*" a voice beside us calls out, ruining the moment. We break apart, both of us turning toward the interloper. I feel her stiffen against me, her entire demeanor doing a complete one-eighty in a split second when her gaze lands on the guy standing there.

He's tall but still a few inches shorter than me, with jet-black hair combed back neatly off his face, wearing a tuxedo that makes him look like a jackass.

I don't have a clue who he is, but now I want to know since he's got enough nuts to interrupt me kissing *my* girl with her name on his lips.

"Chandler..." she says, voice tight.

Well, then.

Apparently, this is the stupid fuck who cheated on her. Instinctively, I step closer to her.

His gaze bounces back and forth between us with his lips parted, disbelief written on his face. "What are you doing? Who the hell is this?"

"This is my boyfriend, Saint. Why are you here, Chandler?" Her voice is low, laced with saccharine venom.

"Because my parents asked me to be here. Because your *father* asked me to be here. Why the fuck are you with this guy?" His lip curls in disgust as his eyes dart my way and then back to her.

The mention of her father inviting him makes hot, heady anger unfurl in my veins. That dick just doesn't know how to stop, does he?

Lennon lifts her chin, her small fists curled at her side so tight her knuckles have turned white.

Fuck, baby.

I reach out and grab her hand, gently opening her fist and rubbing my thumb along the crescents indented on her palm from her nails before linking my fingers with hers.

"Why are *you* worried about what I'm doing? I think I was pretty clear when I told you to fuck off the last time."

"Because he's fucking trash. He must be giving you the dick. Funny how *now* you're into fucking when you were locked up like a fucking nun when I tried. You must be dick dumb."

It's supposed to be an insult, but all I do is smirk. His nostrils flare when he sees that it fell flat.

I don't give a single fuck what this fucker says about me. I'm not stepping in unless Lennon asks me to, because right now, she's got this.

I know how important it is to her to have her own voice, to stand up for herself. And unlike these fucks, I'll never try to take that choice from her.

"You're right, it is such a great cock." She licks her lips when she flicks her pretty gaze to me, and I wink. "Sorry, I know it's probably such a foreign concept for you to wrap your little brain around—Giving a girl an orgasm."

I watch the muscle in his jaw turn steely as he grits his teeth together, his face starting to turn red. Mhmmmm. She hit a soft spot.

"You actually fucked him?" A humorless laugh seeps through his lips. "Fuck, Len, what the hell are you doing?"

"That's none of your business, Chandler. You lost that privilege when you cheated on me. When you used me. When you fucked my *friend*. When you had audacity bigger than your little-ass dick to look me in the eye and ask for another chance without even being sorry for what you did."

That's my girl.

I level my gaze, brow arched as she fucking gives it to him, just like he deserves. I bet it feels good too.

Chandler rubs a hand along his mouth before dropping it and laughing again. This time, it sounds a little more maniacal. "You're such a righteous fucking bitch, Lennon."

Oh fuck no.

Now, that I can't allow.

In two short strides, I stop in front of him, closing the distance between us. "I suggest you watch your fucking mouth when you speak to her."

"Oh yeah? And what are you going to do about it, trailer trash?" he snarls.

My lip curls into a menacing smirk. "If you want to find out, then let me know, pretty boy."

The air crackles around us, heated tension stealing all the oxygen from the hallway. He's lost the fucking plot if he thinks that I'm going to stand here and let him disrespect Lennon. He can insult me all day. But her? Not happening.

Suddenly, a hand slips between us, shoving me away from him as her father steps between us. "What is going on?"

I'm quiet, leaving the answer to that question up to the asshole standing across from me.

His jaw works as he contemplates his answer. "Just a friendly little conversation with the degenerate that's been having sex with your daughter."

Lennon's breath hitches at the same time that her father's eyes narrow into slits, landing on me with a hard, lethal look that should feel intimidating. Maybe it would be to someone else, but not me.

Fuck him.

"Is this a joke, Lennon?" her father hisses quietly, leaning into where we're standing, his gaze darting around the room like someone's going to jump out and tell him he's being punked, or worse, overhear such a scandal. "You know how important this gala is. You know how much rides on the donations, yet you're out here making a scene with these two while they're measuring their dicks?"

I snort. Mine's bigger. Obviously.

"Do you even care that *Chandler* is the one who started it? That Chandler is the one who said vile, disrespectful things about me? Do you even care at all?" Her voice wavers, and I hate that they have this effect on her.

It does nothing to quell the simmering rage that has my blood boiling.

"This is not the place, Lennon. I truly do not know why

you've suddenly started to act so childish and obstinate. But this silly little rebellion ends today. This—" He sweeps a hand toward me. "—ends today. I am not going to have it. Walk away and handle this later. Do not cause a bigger scene." His voice is low, authoritative, and for a second, I'm worried she might back down, that she might cower to the narcissistic asshole.

But instead, she squares her shoulders and lifts her chin, jaw tense as she grits her teeth together. I watch, transfixed by her. "Contrary to what you might think, Dad, my life doesn't revolve around you and what you want. I have my own feelings, my own dreams, my own *needs*. Saint is my boyfriend, and if you're making me choose… I'm going to choose him. Every single time. You'll lose me. Is that something you're prepared for?"

"You are my daughter, and you are a *Rousseau*. You *will* behave like a Rousseau, and you will not embarrass our family any further than you already have, Lennon. You will not be traipsing around town with this trash any longer. Do I make myself clear?" His words drip with venom, face bright red with fury. She wanted to hit him where it hurts, and she did exactly that by refusing to play the part.

When he reaches for her arm like he's going to drag her out of the room, I step forward, blocking him. "Don't touch her."

His face goes slack as he stares at me, then behind me at Lennon, before he takes a step closer. "I don't know who the hell you think you are, but this is a matter between my *daughter* and me. I suggest you back the fuck up before I have you thrown out like the trash you are."

A chuckle rumbles from my chest, devoid of all humor. I'm about two seconds from giving security a real fucking reason to throw me out when Lennon steps between us, placing a hand on my chest and pushing me back slightly. "He's right, this isn't the time or the place. I've said everything that I had to say. He's made his choice, and I've made mine."

For a second, he looks like he's going to say something back. Something fucking stupid, if I had to guess, but ultimately, he says nothing.

She's right. He did make a choice, and unsurprisingly, yet again, he hasn't chosen his daughter.

Lennon captures my hand in hers, her fingers tightening in mine as I throw both of them one last look before we start to walk away.

"You know, Lennon..." Chandler mumbles behind us, "If you ever get tired of fucking the *help*, I'll be here. I can fuck you like the dirty, washed-up cock slut you are now. I should've taken what I was owed when I had the fucking chance."

I don't even fucking think as I drop her hand, spinning toward him.

I vaguely hear her calling my name as I storm over to him, vaguely notice her father stepping forward when I make it to him.

And then my fist is flying, my knuckles smashing into Chandler's face so hard that his head whips to the side, and he staggers backward, clutching his nose, which I hope to fucking God I just broke.

Surprisingly, he doesn't go down. He spits a stream of bloodied saliva near my feet and then charges at me, his arms hitting my waist as he tackles me to the ground with a grunt.

It takes nothing to flip him over until I'm straddling his torso, and this time, I hit him harder, my fist connecting with his cheekbone, blood pouring from the split skin.

Hearing him say that shit about the girl I love was too fucking far.

It's not just the shit that he said but how he's treated her, the shit that he's done to hurt her.

Three hits in, my arms are grabbed by someone, and I'm wrenched off him, my chest heaving as they drag me away, leaving him on the floor, covered in blood and groaning.

"Saint, oh my God." Lennon collides against me, her hands moving over my face, my head, my neck as she checks for injuries.

I force my eyes to hers. "I'm good, baby, I'm good. He didn't even get a fucking hit on me."

Because he's a worthless pussy.

Out of my periphery, I see three police officers heading our way, and I exhale slowly. I knew it would happen, but it was well fucking worth it. Her gaze follows mine, and she draws the same conclusion.

When she looks back at me, there are tears welling in her eyes, and I fight against the security guards holding me back because I need to hold her. I need to wipe away the tears.

"Saint, I'm scared. I-I…"

I drop my forehead against hers. "I'll be fine. Don't worry about me, Golden Girl. I'll gladly sit in a jail cell if it means that piece of shit got what he deserves." Fuck, the insinuation in his words about what he should've done to her makes me blind with rage again.

I pull back and press a kiss to her lips before the security guard yanks me away from her, and I feel the cold bite of metal along my wrists as I'm handcuffed and my rights are read.

I don't regret it.

Not a single fucking second.

Lennon follows closely behind the officer as he hauls me toward the exit, but before I let him pull me through the door, I turn to her father, who's just as guilty, if not more, in all of this. "Unlike you, I will *always* put your daughter first. There's nothing in this world I wouldn't do for her. No line I wouldn't cross. One day, she's going to find out about all the fucked-up, disgusting shit you've done to get ahead, and you know who's going to be there when she does? *Me*, motherfucker."

chapter forty-eight
LENNON

IT'S SO cold in this concrete waiting room that my toes have gone numb and are beginning to turn purple in my Louboutins.

Hours have gone by since they booked Saint, and I've spent the majority of them crying so much that I'm fairly certain I have nothing left in me to cry. I tried to scrub the smeared mascara off my cheeks with a wet napkin in the bathroom, but it didn't help much.

My eyes are swollen and puffy, my stomach twisted into a tight knot that has me nauseous. That and the fact that I can't even remember the last time I ate. There are blisters on my feet from pacing the room while wearing stilettos, but I haven't been able to sit still, overcome with worry.

I drop my head into my hands as another wave of tears threatens to spill when I hear the double doors jiggling. My eyes snap to the door, waiting on bated breath.

A second later, it opens, and Saint walks out of it. My entire body sags with relief, and this time, the tears that wet my cheeks aren't like the ones that I've spent all night crying.

"Saint." His name rushes from my lips as I run to him as fast as my feet can carry me on these heels, and I crash into him. My arms slip around his neck, and I squeeze so tightly that I'm actually worried I might hurt him. "I've been so worried. I'm... I've been going out of my mind..." I trail off when my throat gets too tight with emotion.

His hand runs along my hair as he presses his lips to my forehead. "I'm fine, baby. Are you okay?"

I can't help it—a mixture of a sob and a laugh bubbles out of me, and he pulls back to look at me, smoothing back my hair from my face. "Hey, hey, talk to me." His thumbs sweep along my cheeks, brushing away the tears as they fall.

"God, Saint, you just got arrested. You spent half the night in jail, and you're worried about *me*?"

"Fuck yeah I am. I've been losing my goddamn mind sitting in there, not being able to get to you," he whispers. "I'm so—"

"Don't you dare apologize," I cut him off. "No. You have nothing to be sorry for."

For a beat, he's quiet while his eyes search mine.

"Let's get home, okay? I don't fucking want you in this place any longer. I wish you never had to be here in the first place." His jaw tenses as he reaches for my hand and threads our fingers together, and I nod.

Thankfully, it doesn't take long at all to get an Uber, and we pull up at my apartment twenty minutes later.

Saint was quiet the entire ride, his gaze fixed out of the window, uncharacteristically so. Even when we walk inside my apartment and go to my bedroom, he's still lost in thought.

I shut the door behind us and turn to him, watching as he drops down onto the edge of my bed and stares down at the floor.

"What's wrong?" I ask.

He lifts his gaze to mine. "I need to tell you something."

My heart plummets to my stomach at the look in his eyes, the serious tone of his voice.

I nod, pushing down a nervous swallow. "Does it have anything to do with… what you said to my father?" It's been there in the back of my mind since the gala, a gnawing feeling in my gut that I didn't get the full picture, that I was somehow missing pieces that I don't quite understand. Saint knows something about my father.

"Yes."

I wobble on my feet slightly, and he curses, jumping up from the bed, gently grasping my arm. "Just… go sit, okay? Let me help you take these off."

I don't even feel my feet anymore. They're past the point of numb, but still, he guides me to the bed and places me at the edge. Then deftly works to unclasp the thin straps around my ankle and removes my shoes. I wiggle my toes around to bring the feeling back to them.

Saint stands to full height and shoves his hands into the pockets of his pants. The white sleeves of his shirt are rolled to his elbows, and his tattooed, veiny arms are on display, distracting me slightly.

"Lennon." I lift my eyes to his, and he swallows roughly. "I need you to understand something before I tell you what I'm about to tell you, okay?"

When he sees the slight nod of my head, he continues. "The only person in my life I've ever felt any type of love from is my mother, and even then, it's... it's always felt like her love for me has taken a back seat to my father. I realize that sounds fucked-up, and it is, but it also doesn't make it any less true. Sometimes I wonder if I'm even capable of loving someone. How can I when the only love I've ever witnessed is selfish and toxic. Destructive. Painful."

I bite the inside of my lip to stop from crying, but it doesn't help. If anything the sting only makes the tears well faster.

He exhales, and it's a broken, staggering breath like he's expelling the poison from his lungs.

I want to reach for him, but I stay where I am since he's the one who created the distance.

"I'm fucked-up, Lennon. My *heart* is fucked-up."

I shake my head, denying each word, but he just keeps going.

"I'm the product of a fucked-up family. Of an abusive addict father. And I'm terrified that I'll end up just like him." His eyes hold mine so intensely my heart stutters. "I haven't told you the full truth. I purposefully kept it from you, and I'm so fucking sorry, baby."

I don't understand what's happening. What is he talking about?

He pauses, raking a hand through his hair, tugging at the strands. "My dad used to work for Rousseau Enterprises. Your father was his boss."

When he says it, I feel like the floor has fallen out from beneath me. *What?*

"Why didn't you tell me that? I don't understand."

"Because, baby, your father is the man behind all the fucked-up things that happened to mine."

There's a heavy, crippling silence that fills the room, and I suck in a sharp breath that does nothing to make my head feel less light.

"My dad… used to work in maintenance. He was a structural welder, so he repaired any of the metal foundation issues, things like that. He was working on a scaffold a couple stories up, and he was tied off just as he was supposed to be. Safety requirement. But the tie-off failed, and he fell. Fractured his spine, broke a vertebra, herniated disk. He was in the hospital for six months, had another six of intensive physical therapy. That's when he got addicted to the pain pills. That's when everything went to shit, when my entire life blew up."

I lift my hand to my mouth, covering it to stifle the noise. I still don't understand what that has to do with my dad, but I know that it's… it's bad. It's so bad. I can see how much reliving it just to tell the story to me is affecting him. He starts to pace the room, unable to remain still, hardly taking a breath as he talks.

"It wasn't that he just fell and got hurt. Or that he became an addict using something that was supposed to help him. The only way that he would get coverage for the injury was to use workman's comp to file a claim against Rousseau Enterprises. There was no other choice. None. We were drowning in medical debt. So much fucking debt that I'd probably work my entire life and still not be able to pay it off. Probably not even put a dent in it." He stops pacing to flit his eyes to me, rolling his lips together like the next part is the most painful.

I brace myself.

"It could've been simple—so fucking simple that it makes me sick—if your father had done the right thing, but he didn't. He *fought* the claim with all of his expensive, fancy, piece-of-shit lawyers. Lennon…" He trails off, dragging his hand down his face, and holding my gaze. "He fucked up. The safety protocols weren't followed—that's why the tie-off failed in the first place. That's why there wasn't a failsafe in place. That's why nobody even fucking checked it before he got up there. My dad said he overheard the conversation with his superintendent, and when he confronted him, your father called him a liar and accused him of being high. Said he was using before he ever fell. Your father lied about it all, and my dad's claim was denied. The appeal was denied too."

Oh my God.

"Saint…" I start, but he shakes his head, stopping me.

"He almost died, and your father covered it up to

protect his company. To save face. He has all the money in the world, so could've paid it all off, and my dad never would've tried to file the claim, but instead, he ruined our fucking lives, Lennon."

As I take in everything he's saying about my father, the only question I think is: *Is my father even capable of something so greedy and despicable?* And I immediately know the answer. Yes, yes he is.

I rise from my bed and cross the room to him, reaching out to him, but he captures my hand in midair.

"Wait, please." His words are strained, tight. "Just... wait till I tell it all to you, please, baby. You need to know."

There's more?

Nodding, I take my hand back and wrap my arms around myself.

"It's been years. This has been our life for years. My father has never been able to hold down a job since, which only makes his addiction worse. A never-ending cycle of fucked-up that I've never been able to break free from in the last eight years. I didn't even know who to blame. My father for letting addiction take him or your father for being the catalyst of it all. So, I chose *both*. They are both equally guilty for the things they've caused. I've been living with so much anger, so much pent-up rage beneath the surface, sometimes it felt like I was going to combust. I wanted your father to suffer the same way that I have. And when you walked into the rink that day... I thought I finally found a way to make him pay for it."

I don't even need him to hear it because I know.

I know, deep down in my gut, *I know.*

"Me," I whisper.

A stabbing sensation pierces the flesh over my heart as I say it.

Saint reaches forward, and this time, it's me who stops him by stepping back.

I... I can't.

"Baby, listen to me, okay? Please just hear me out. That's all I'm asking for. If you want me to leave and never see me again once I do, I promise I will leave, but I just need you to know the truth." His eyes are pleading, and he looks like he's moments away from his own tears.

"Did you know who I was? That first day at the rink, did you know, Saint?"

He tilts his head, hesitating. "No. I mean... once you told me your last name, I suspected. I put two and two together after that."

My stomach twists, and for a moment, I'm afraid I might be sick. "Tell me."

"It was so fucking stupid, Lennon. So goddamn stupid. I was out of my mind with this vendetta against your father, I thought I could get close to you, fuck around with you and use it as a way to get back at him. To piss him off that his daughter was with a guy like me. *Trash.*"

Oh God. My cheeks are wet with tears as they stream down my face, so hard that my vision starts to blur from the wetness.

"Shit, please don't cry, baby. Please," he begs, reaching for me again, and I step back out of his reach.

"So this was all fake? All of it?"

The thought makes me physically ill. I clutch my stomach with one hand as I swipe away the tears that just won't stop.

"Fuck no," he says, shaking his head. "Did I agree to your whole fake boyfriend thing to try to get closer to you in hopes that it would be the answer to my problems? Yeah. I did. But Lennon, I need you to believe me when I say that it stopped being that for me a long time ago. I didn't give a shit about the revenge, or your father, or *any* of it once I started to care about you. When I started to have real feelings for you, it made me realize how goddamn stupid I'd been, trying to use you to get back at him. You are innocent and had nothing to do with it, but in my head, you were his little princess. I thought you were just like him. But I learned how far from the truth that was as I got to know you."

There's one question that I need to know, and it's the one I'm terrified of the answer to.

I'm not sure my heart can even take it.

I roll my lips together, tasting the salt tears wetting them as I gather all the courage inside of me to ask.

"So you had sex with me as part of your *revenge*? That's why you took my virginity?"

He closes the distance between us before I can even finish speaking, sliding his hand along my jaw. His thumb stroking my face so tenderly, so reverently, that it only makes the ache in my heart intensify. "No. *No*, Lennon. I abandoned the revenge way before we ever got there. I tried to tell you… that night. I was going to tell you before, but you were so set on it being your decision, and I didn't want to tell you because it didn't even matter anymore. It's not how I felt and hadn't been how I felt for a while. I didn't want to hurt you for no reason. I swear to you, nothing that's happened between us was about my stupid plan. *Nothing*, I promise." His throat works as he swallows, his eyes shining with sincerity. He drops his forehead against mine and inhales, as if he's savoring every breath. Like he's afraid that I'm going to slip away.

My eyes flutter closed as we stand together, neither of us moving.

"I'm sorry. I'm so fucking sorry, baby. I'm sorry that I didn't tell you before now. I just didn't know *how*," he whispers, keeping his head pressed to me. My tears are probably wetting his cheeks as much as they are mine. "How do I tell the girl I've fallen in love with that I fucked up, that I made the most stupid mistake I could've ever made, and beg her to forgive me? To not leave me. I'm sorry that I was so blinded by my hate that I ever even considered doing it in the first place. I never would've gone through with it. I'm not that guy. I don't want to *be* that guy. The one who hurts people to further my agenda. I'm not my father, and I'm never going to be him. Whatever I have to do to prove it to you, I will. I'll do whatever it takes, Lennon."

I can't say anything because my throat feels tight, clogged with emotions.

I'm hurt and sad, and not just for me... but for *him*.

Because of the years of mental and physical abuse he's endured. Because of the heartbreaking fact that the man who was supposed to love and protect him was responsible for it. His own father. Because Saint has been so hurt and angry that he got to this dark place.

That he's been suffering alone, in silence for so long.

He pulls back slightly, staring down at me as he runs his hand over my hair. "I love you, Lennon. I meant every word I said to your father. There's nothing I wouldn't do for you. No line I wouldn't cross. I'm sorry that I fucked up so badly. I'm sorry that I was so fucking lost. But I'm not lost anymore. Not with you."

I don't push him away because... I *do* understand, even though it hurts me to know he started this with me to hurt me.

But I understand his pain and anger. I get the desire to see someone who hurt you and your loved ones pay for what they've done. He's been through more heartache than most people experience in their lifetime, as a *child*.

As painful as it is to hear all of this... I know how hard this has to be for him, to bare his soul and hope that I stay anyway.

"I'm hurt, Saint," I whisper.

"I know, baby, and I'm so sorry. I wish I could take it back. I wish I never would've been so fucking stupid in the first place, but I'm promising you... I will never lie to you or keep anything from you, ever again. No matter what." His fingers curl around mine, and he lifts my hand, placing it on his chest, over his heart, holding it there. I can feel the steady, strong thrum. "You're in *here*, Lennon. I tried to fight it, I tried to lie to myself that I wasn't falling for you flat on my face, but I can't. You're the only good in here. It's *you*. You make me want to be the man that's worthy of loving you. I want to be the man you deserve, the man that makes you proud. The man who puts your happiness before his own. I want to be strong, and steady, and *good* for you. I want to be the man you run to when it all falls apart because you know I'm going to be here to catch you, baby, every fucking time."

He doesn't realize it yet... but he's *already* that man.

My broken man who's weathered so many storms, so much pain, and still has good inside of him.

The man who doesn't want to show the world who he really is because he's afraid.

But I *see* him.

I see the man beneath it all.

I see all of these jagged pieces that he believes to be too sharp, too broken to ever repair.

I see the man who has every reason to be bitter and jaded by a world that has never shown him any kindness.

The one who just wants to be touched with *love*.

The man who just wants to *be* loved.

The man who just wants someone who's going to choose *him*.

Shaking my head, I grasp his face between my hands, forcing his eyes on mine. "You are already that man, Saint. You don't need to change to be anything other than what you are. The man that I fell in love with."

We've both changed in the last couple of months. I'm not the same girl I was the day I walked into the rink, and I know he isn't the same guy from that day either.

My exhale stutters against his lips. "You're right. You did fuck up. You made a mistake that hurts me. But

Saint... When you love someone, you don't leave. You don't walk away when it's too much. When they make mistakes. I don't need you to prove anything to me, Saint. You already have. And you just proved it again. You defended me, protected me, sacrificed for me. *That's* what you do for the people you love. So no, I'm not going anywhere. Not now and not a year from now. Not ever. We're both probably going to make mistakes, do things wrong sometimes, but what matters is that we don't give up on each other. No matter how hard it gets."

His arms wrap around my waist as he pulls me flush against him, not an inch of space separating us, and it feels like... *home.*

Like I've been wandering for so long and I'm finally right where I belong.

We're just two people clinging to each other when everything in our lives is falling apart.

"I love you." I press my lips against his, holding on as tightly as I can. I'll always be his anchor when the ground beneath us is unsteady. "And I'll *always* be your Golden Girl."

His lip tilts as he looks down at me. "Fuck yeah you will, baby."

"Saint..." I trail off, feeling my stomach twist as my head flits to the biggest piece of all of this fucked-up puzzle., "God, I just... it feels like there's more to this. I know my father, how protective he is of his business and his name. He would have done everything he could to get the outcome he wanted."

It's sad that I didn't even doubt what Saint told me, not

even for a moment, because I actually believe my dad could be capable of something as heinous as this.

If there's anything that the last few months have taught me, it's that my father is nothing like the man I thought I knew.

What I do know is that he would do whatever it takes, hurt whoever is in his path, to get what he wants. I've seen that with my own eyes and experienced it firsthand.

Everyone is a pawn. So I feel like there *has* to be more to this. My father is a master manipulator. He wouldn't just rely on lying about Saint's father; he'd never rely on hearsay alone to protect his brand and his business. "My father can't just get away with what he's done. He can't continue to hurt people. To lie, and cheat, and control people without consequence. You can't just let this go, Saint."

"No," Saint says, shaking his head. "I'm done with it, Lennon. Going after your father means going after *you*, your family, and I'm not letting you get hurt because of his fucked-up decisions. No."

Protecting me. Always.

This big, brooding man that I love so much.

I sweep the pad of my finger along his cheek. "You're not going to hurt me. It just... this is not right. None of it. It feels corrupt."

"Lennon... it's over, baby. I want us to move forward and leave all of this shit behind. Both your father and mine have stolen too much of our lives, and all I want is to be with you and be at peace. Be fucking happy. Be free."

Saint places a chaste kiss to my forehead and pulls me into his arms, holding me close to him.

"We will be. Happy and free. We'll just be *us*. Okay?" I murmur, cuddling closer to him.

He's right, our fathers have stolen so much of our lives. But I can't stop thinking about everything I've learned tonight, the shitty things my father has done.

Saint might be ready to let this go, but I'm not.

chapter forty-nine

LENNON

THE HOUSE I spent my childhood in looks perfect from the outside. A sprawling white, three-story Victorian that sits on the corner of St. Charles Avenue and Bordeaux Street, built during a time that no longer exists.

Despite the fact that it's over a hundred years old, there's not a single piece of peeling paint on the exterior. The garden is flourishing, the grass perfectly manicured, the wraparound porch warm and inviting. A place where you could imagine rocking in old wooden chairs, drinking sweet tea, watching the world breeze past.

Now, it feels cold and staged.

I just never realized how much until now. Until this contrived little bubble I had been living in for so long finally popped, and the veil lifted from my eyes. Now, I'm seeing things for what they truly are.

This house might have been where I grew up, where I got my first pair of skates, where I broke my arm for the first time while rollerblading... but it's not a *home*.

A home is filled with love, laughter, happiness. Memories of times that you never want to forget.

Not the place you never want to return to.

I'm hurt, disgusted... angry at my father, and I know that Saint wants to let it go, to move on, but he deserves to know the truth. He doesn't want me to get hurt or for me to get caught in the crosshairs because my family's name is being dragged through the mud. But I don't even care anymore. I'm honestly not sure I ever really did.

All I know is that it feels like more is happening, something I can't even explain except a gnawing sense of intuition in my gut that I can't ignore.

So that's the reason I'm here today. I saw online that my parents are in Baton Rouge, visiting my father's best friend, who's a coach at LSU, which gives me the perfect opportunity to see what I can find. There has to be something, anything, that will implicate him enough so that we can use it to expose what he's done.

I'm doing this for Saint.

I'm *choosing* him.

Over my own family... and I would do it again in a heartbeat. Without another thought.

After what happened over the weekend at the gala, I haven't once heard from my parents. They never called to check on me, to see if I was okay, to apologize for everything that happened. Not even a text. I didn't expect them to. I think it's pretty obvious at this point that they care about themselves and the Rousseau name more than they ever cared about me.

And that... hurts.

Because at the end of the day, they're still my parents.

The inside of the house is quiet as I walk through the hallway, aside from the sound of the air-conditioning blowing at full blast, toward my father's office.

A room that he's kept locked since I was a kid. I've always known where the spare key is, but until today, I never really had a reason to use it. I stop at the large cabinet at the end of the hallway, where he keeps his scotch on display, and slide the antique door open gently, reaching to the very back, beneath the cheapest bottle. I feel the cool metal of the key beneath my fingers, and a smile flits to my lips.

Obviously, some things never change.

After shutting the cabinet, I walk to the office door and blow out a breath.

I don't even know what I'm hoping to find. I have no plan, no clue where to even start. I know there's a chance that I might not even find anything at all. My dad might not have done anything illegal—maybe it's just something shitty—but I haven't been able to stop thinking about it.

It's been churning inside of me, and I just... had to see for myself.

I have to try.

My hand trembles as I slip the old, worn skeleton key into the lock and turn it. There's a soft click, and then the heavy wooden door creaks open, pulling a relieved sigh with it.

His office hasn't changed much since I was a kid. Dark, heavy oak furniture, walls lined with shelves of books that are accumulating dust from never being used. A large desk sits in the middle of the room, with my father's desktop in the center, completely clean of any papers or clutter.

I round the desk in a hurry, starting with the drawers, wrenching one open at a time and sifting through the contents inside. One is full of pens and office supplies. Paper clips, stapler. A checkbook with Rousseau Enterprises stamped along the top. The next, a stack of old-school ledgers, the pages worn with faded ink that I can hardly make out.

I scan the pages, but God, I don't even really know what I'm looking for.

I drop the book back into the drawer and move on to the next, going through them all and coming up empty. There's nothing here.

Jesus, Lennon, what did you expect? Him to leave some kind of bullet-point manifesto just lying around on his desk?

Get a grip.

My gaze flicks around to the computer and the black screen staring back at me.

Realization dawns on me as I toss the last stack of papers back into the drawer.

Why *would* he leave a paper trail? He wouldn't just leave evidence of his wrongdoings lying around.

Duh. That would be stupid, reckless. And my father may be shady, but he's certainly not stupid.

I yank the office chair out and drop down into it as I reach for the mouse, shaking it to wake the computer up.

Completely unsurprisingly, his screen saver is a photo of his most prized possession: his boat.

Rolling my eyes, I click on the password box, my fingers hovering over the keys.

I tap out my mom's name.

Wrong.

Okay... I try *Rousseau Enterprises*.

Wrong.

Surely, it's not...

The computer unlocks as soon as I type in *Lagniappe Lady*, and I can only shake my head.

His fucking boat name.

Of course.

There's no way he made it *that* easy. Either there's nothing on here that's going to incriminate him, or maybe... he has the hubris to *truly* never think that anyone would ever dig into what he's doing.

I start with the desktop, clicking through folders and random documents that I can't even begin to wrap my head around. It's a bunch of gibberish that runs together, but nothing about what happened with Saint's father or anything really about his company.

God, there's really nothing here. Or maybe my father just locked it up someplace safer than his desktop computer.

I'm searching through every single item on here, but there's not much more on the desktop outside of the few documents that I've already gone through.

A frustrated sigh slips past my lips as I comb through some of the files that I've already gone through, once again coming up empty.

There *has* to be something.

I click on the computer's storage system, and then I see that his cloud storage is almost full. Quickly, I click it open and scroll through the folder names.

And that's when I see it.

My heart thrashes in my chest, a sinking feeling careening in my stomach.

DEVEREAUX

It could be nothing. He was an employee at Rousseau Enterprises for years—it could simply be his payment information, certifications. Legal records. It *could* be anything.

But the gnawing, heavy-as-lead feeling in my stomach has me hoping that it's... *something.*

That once I click on this folder, everything is going to change.

Not just with my life but with Saint's too.

My mother, his mother.

With everyone who's involved with my father.

I'm terrified of what may be inside. My hands are shaking so hard that the mouse is clinking against the mousepad, and my pulse is thrumming so loudly I can hear it in my ears, drowning out everything around me.

Saint.

You're doing this for Saint. He deserves closure. He deserves the truth. Even if the truth hurts.

Slowly, I click the folder, and at least a dozen documents are inside, popping up one by one. I click the first one, scanning the document, and at first, I'm not sure what I'm reading.

But then, the pieces begin to align, and suddenly, the

chair beneath me sways, my hand flying to my mouth when I realize what I'm seeing.

Holy shit.

chapter fifty
SAINT

I WOKE up alone this morning, not wrapped around my girl's soft, warm body, and that was surprising as fuck, considering I was in *her* bed, at her apartment.

When I rolled over, one eye cracked open, I saw a piece of pink paper sticking out from beneath my phone that she must have plugged in for me last night after I passed out.

In my defense, that was after spending the majority of the night in a jail cell and giving her *three* orgasms.

Not my finest moment. Getting arrested, I mean.

But fuck, it was so worth it.

The relief I feel is palpable after coming clean to her last night. My shoulders feel lighter without the weight of everything I had been holding in. I hated that Lennon had to hear about how badly I fucked up, but she needed to know the truth. I couldn't tell her that I loved her without being honest about everything.

I guess the truth really does set you free because for the first time in months, I feel like I can finally take a full breath without waiting for the other shoe to drop. I put everything in the open, even though I was terrified she'd leave.

The note she left this morning said she was going to be taking care of something and to lock up when I left. And that she loved me with a cute-as-fuck little heart that had me grinning like an idiot for the next ten minutes.

Never gonna get tired of hearing her say that.

I'm so fucking gone for her. Fully, completely, and don't give a shit about who knows it.

"Saint." Looking up from my economics textbook, I see my mom standing in the doorway to my room, pulling her sweater tighter around her small frame. "There's someone here to see you."

My brows cinch together in confusion. I don't even think anyone knows *where* I live.

Who the fu—

Suddenly, Lennon steps from behind her, a soft smile on her lips as her green eyes capture mine.

"Hi," she says quietly. "You didn't answer my texts or calls, so I just… came here." The way she says it is hesitant, like she's worried maybe I wouldn't want her to.

"Oh shit," I say, grabbing my phone and looking at the screen. There are at least a dozen calls and messages from her. "I was studying, and my phone was on silent. I'm sorry, baby."

"It's okay." She turns to my mom and extends her hand. "Hi, Mrs. Devereaux. I'm sorry I didn't introduce myself when I got here. I'm Lennon, Saint's girlfriend."

That's new… Yeah, I like that way too fucking much.

My girlfriend. *My Golden Girl.*

Mom's face immediately softens, her wide brown eyes crinkling in the corners as she smiles at Lennon. "Hi. I'm Stephanie. It's nice to meet you, Lennon. I guess you're the one that has been keeping my son smiling like that?"

I hadn't even realized I was smiling as I watched their exchange until she said that.

Lennon's cheeks twinge pink.

"I'll leave you two be, but... thank you for making him so happy, Lennon. He deserves some happiness in his life." With one last look, she leaves us, shutting the door behind her.

Her words hit me directly in the chest, the feeling of something foreign unexpectedly pulling at my heart.

We both do, I wanted to say.

But I know that when my mom's ready, she'll let me know. She's just... not yet. Not ready to talk, not ready to admit my dad's no good for her. Not ready to figure out what happens next. Right now, I think we're just taking it day by day. That's all we really can do.

"I'm sorry to just barge in like this. I just ne—" I cross the room in two short strides and cut her off with my lips, kissing her like I didn't just see her eight hours ago. Fuck, I love how she tastes.

How she melts for me.

When I pull back, her eyes are glassy and her mouth swollen from my kiss. I reach up, dragging a thumb along her bottom lip, smirking when she parts for me.

"You don't ever need to apologize, baby. I'm glad

you're here. I wanted you to meet my mom, so it's perfect."

"I... I actually am here because of something important, Saint, and I'm worried that you might be upset at me, but..." She trails off, lifting the laptop in her hands. "I have to show you something."

A sense of dread fills my gut. Shit. What's going on now?

I watch as she carries her laptop over to my desk, then sets it down and opens it before turning back to me. "I know that you said that you wanted to let this stuff with my dad go, but Saint... I couldn't just let it go. I understand why you want to move on. I do too. I just couldn't let it go after finding all of this out, and ever since, there's been this nagging feeling in my stomach that something's not right. My intuition telling me to listen." She presses a few keys on the computer and brings up what looks like the local news station. Her gaze darts to mine. "I think you should probably just watch this first."

I have no fucking clue what's going on as she presses Play.

On the screen is what looks like a press conference. A large wooden podium with a flurry of microphones, the camera panned directly at it. Behind it is a tall, burly Black man with a thick mustache wearing an NOPD uniform.

"Hello, everyone, thank you for being here tonight. My name is Detective Marshall Robbins, and I am a detective with the Financial Crimes unit. I'm here today to release a statement involving an arrest that took place at approximately 5:30 p.m. at a private residence on St. Charles

Avenue. We have taken a Mr. Edward Rousseau into custody on the following charges: bribery of a public official, obstruction of justice, criminal contempt of court, perjury, and fraud. The New Orleans Police Department takes these allegations very seriously, and we will be investigating to the best of our ability. Due to the high-profile nature of this case, we are releasing this statement to keep the public informed and to prevent the spread of false information. We will be working closely with the New Orleans District Attorney's Office and will release further information when available."

Lennon stops the video and turns to me, unshed tears pooling in her eyes.

I think I might be in shock because I'm frozen in place while trying to wrap my head around what the fuck I just heard, what the hell is even happening.

Blinking, I croak, "Baby… what did you do?"

"I *chose* you, Saint." She crosses my room and slides her hands along my jaw, holding me tightly in her small palms. "I went to my parents' house this morning while they were still in Baton Rouge, and I went through my father's computer. I didn't even know what I was going to find, if there would *be* anything, but Saint, I… I found it all. Documents showing that he had been paying off a judge to turn cases in his favor. Evidence that proves he's been falsifying information in cases of negligence brought against the company. Cases like your father's. I'm not sure why… maybe in case he ever needed to use it for blackmail, or he's just really fucking stupid and never thought anyone would look into it."

I laugh, the sound rough and strained from emotion, shaking my head. "I definitely think it's the latter."

"Me too." She grins. "But Saint, it wasn't *just* your father. There's half a dozen more instances of Rousseau Enterprises employees being injured and my father doing criminal shit to keep it under wraps. All so he wouldn't have to admit negligence. To save face. And to save money. All of these poor families who have suffered at his hand. It's sickening."

Holy fuck.

My expression probably reads exactly as shocked as I am because she nods, drawing her lip between her teeth and chewing the corner anxiously. I use my thumb to free it. "I took everything I could find, and I brought it straight to the police department. That's where I've been all day. I told the detectives that I'd be willing to testify about what I found if they need me for their case. You and your mom and all of these people who have been wronged are going to get the justice they deserve."

My girl.

God, I love her so fucking much.

"Lennon, your mom... what about you and your family?" My throat currently feels like I've swallowed sandpaper.

I don't want this shit to touch her. I don't want any of it to ever hurt her again.

Her shoulder lifts. "I don't care what people think of me. If they assume I'm guilty because of him, then that's their problem. My mom will figure it out. These innocent people finally having justice and closure is more important than the Rousseau reputation. Honestly, I'd like to change my name if I could."

"Yeah? One day, you will. It'll be Devereaux."

She giggles as her cheeks flame.

She probably thinks I'm joking, but I guess she's just going to have to stick around and find out.

"It was the right thing to do. I needed you to know that someone would fight for you. I will *always* fight for you. And now we know the truth. We can truly be free, Saint."

My arms swallow her as I drag her against my chest and press my lips to her hair, breathing her in and savoring the fact that she's mine.

I would've been happy and at peace with the fact that she finally knew the truth, but she made sure the world knew.

And when I thought I couldn't love her more, she steals my fucking breath.

chapter fifty-one
LENNON

"LEN, YOUR MAN IS HERE!" Maisie yells from the front door as I straighten the silverware on the dining room table.

I'm pretty positive that I've moved this exact fork like three times, but every time I look at it again, it feels slightly askew, so I attempt to fix it. Again.

A few seconds later, Saint walks into the dining room, his tattooed arms full of paper grocery bags.

Per usual, the sight of him distracts me, my gaze trailing over the dark ink on his skin and veiny forearms.

God, since when did veins start being so stupidly hot?

Probably because the man is literally the hottest thing to exist, and somehow, I ended up lucky enough to have him.

"Stop looking at me like that, Golden Girl, before I have to bend you over and fuck you on this dining room table. Then, you'll be upset because I ruined your Thanksgiving plans," he rasps, his voice doing that thing where it goes all gravelly and deep, sending a shiver racing down my spine. "And you know how much I hate making you upset, baby."

I'm shamelessly pressing my thighs together, and *of course* he notices because my man notices everything.

His mouth tilts into my favorite cocky, sexy smirk as he slowly licks his lips and his eyes travel down my body, pausing on the skirt I wore today. His tongue runs across his teeth. "You also know how much I fucking love these."

I am so obscenely, out of my mind obsessed with him it's ridiculous. Only fair since he's even more obsessed with me.

"Saint," I warn, despite the fact that I want to drag him to my bedroom and spend the rest of the night having him do filthy, dirty things to me. I take a step back, noticing his wolfish gaze, trying to ignore how the space between my thighs throbs. "No. You stay over there, and I'll stay over here."

He chuckles darkly. "That sounds familiar, doesn't it, Golden Girl?"

Okay, you know what? Maybe we could just cancel Thanksgiving.

I mean, it's *just* dinner. Who cares? We can order pizza or something.

Saint carefully sets the bags on the table without disrupting anything, which I'm thankful for since I did just spend the last hour working on this tablescape. Then he saunters toward me wearing a pair of dark jeans that are molded to his thick, powerful thighs and a black, long-sleeve henley that he's got pushed up to his elbows.

He looks good enough to eat.

But judging by the dark, predatory look in his eyes as he closes the space between us, Thanksgiving dinner is *not* what he's hungry for.

I lift my hands between us as I step backward. "Saint, stop it right now."

Another step closer.

"I'm serious!"

Not serious at all.

Okay, maybe a little bit because I'm really excited to host my own Thanksgiving for the first time.

He collides against me, his big, rough hands sliding along my jaw and cradling me not so tenderly in his palms, and Jesus, I love it.

I love when he's like this.

All growly, and dark, and *hungry*. When he doesn't hold me as if I'm going to break.

His lips hover over mine, a breath away, but not kissing me. Yet.

"What do you expect out of me, baby? You wear that little skirt that shows off your legs, making me fucking crazy, and then you look at me like you want me to fuck your pretty little cunt. Like you want me to fill you up. That would be crazy, though, because then you'd be sitting through Thanksgiving dinner with me dripping out of you." He pauses, gaze dropping to my parted lips. His tongue traces along my bottom lip slowly until I'm sure I'm *actually* going to lose my mind. "You'd love that though. My dirty girl loves it when I give her my cum."

I have no idea how I still have rational thought when

I'm currently being touched by a man who knows my body inside and out. And he is *absolutely* doing his best work right now.

"Saint, your mother is going to be here in thirty minutes."

He groans, the deep sound vibrating through me as his head drops to my shoulder. "Baby, for fuck's sake, please do not mention my mom right now."

"Well... it's true. So, *behave.*"

When he lifts his head from my shoulder, I press a quick kiss to the corner of his lips. "It's your mom's first time here. And it's our first Thanksgiving together. I want it to be perfect. I want her to feel comfortable."

It's been just over two weeks since my father was arrested, and Saint and I have been together pretty much every day since.

The only time we've been apart is when he's had hockey or a shift at Tommy's or when either of us has class. I got to experience my very first game last week, and it was... incredible. Not just watching my man in his element, but the atmosphere, the sport itself.

And yeah, it was *insanely* sexy to watch him checking guys against the boards and being all intense and intimidating. When they put him in the penalty box for a two-minute penalty, he looked right at me and lifted his stick, shooting me a cocky, completely Saint-like wink. As if I wasn't *already* blushing so hard I thought I would catch fire after thinking about the last time we were in there... together.

Then, after the game, there was all of that pent-up

aggression and adrenaline coursing through him, and he spent the entire night between my thighs, taking it out on me.

In the best way.

Can't wait for the next game day.

"She's going to be comfortable, baby. I told you not to stress about it," he says with a smile, pushing off the wall behind me.

"I hope you two know how thin these walls are and how *not* quiet you are," Maisie calls through said thin wall between the kitchen and dining room. "Len, no wonder you're looking so tired lately. Saint, give my girl a break, 'kay?"

My God.

"I'm going to die of embarrassment," I mutter as I push past Saint toward the table, attempting to busy myself and not think about the fact that my best friend has absolutely heard all of the filthy things Saint says—and does—to me.

He laughs. "I'm pretty sure she knows we're not playing Go Fish in there."

I pin him with a look, lifting a brow. "Obviously, I'm more of an Uno kind of girl."

"I promise I'll be on my best behavior until *after* dinner." He lifts his hands in surrender, even though he's wearing a smile that tells me he's probably not going to make it through dinner at all. "Oh, did your mom respond?"

My heart squeezes painfully at the question, and I shake my head. "Nope. She… hasn't responded to any of my messages."

Saint slips a strong arm around my waist and leans in, pressing a lingering kiss to my forehead that I lean into, sighing. "Just give her some time, baby. She'll come around."

I'm not even sure why I tried to reach out to her, but there's just some part of me that feels like I had to. I guess at the end of the day, I thought that we might be able to fix whatever had broken between us because of my father.

But... she believes it's my fault that all of this has happened. At least that's what she said during the one and only time I've spoken to her since he was arrested. She blames me for "betraying" our family, for the fact that all of their accounts and assets have been frozen because of the ongoing investigation.

Regardless of what's happened between us, there's a part of me that's still the little girl who just wants her mom, who hopes that we can repair what's broken. But I guess only time will tell.

"Yeah, so it's just going to be us, Maisie, Tommy, and your mom," I say.

It's the first time I've ever celebrated a holiday without my parents, and even though there's still a twinge of sadness that remains, I'm comforted by the fact that I'm surrounded by the family that I chose.

The ones that chose me.

And it really doesn't feel like I'm missing anything at all.

Saint walks over to where I'm standing at the dining table and reaches for my hands, threading our fingers together. "It's going to be great, and I can tell that you're anxious, but it's going to be the best Thanksgiving either of us have ever had. Especially because Tommy's bringing his fried turkey."

I roll my eyes with a laugh. The man is always thinking about one of three things. Food, hockey, or sex.

"I know. You know, Thanksgiving is my favorite holiday." Untangling our hands, I reach for the thin chain around his neck that still holds my ring, and I curl my fingers around it, gently pulling him to me. "And I'm thankful for a lot of things today, but it's *you* that I'm the most thankful for. Thankful that you crossed that line every single time that I told you to stay on your side, that you pushed my buttons and drove me insane. That you didn't let me quit when I wanted to give up. I'm thankful that I get to love you, Saint. And that I get to be loved *by* you."

He shakes his head. "You have no idea how crazy I am about you. How obsessed I am with every single part of you. How much I love you. You're the most pure, good thing I've ever known. *My Golden Girl.*"

Saint swipes away my tears. Undoubtedly, the happiest ones I've ever cried.

"You know, before all this started, Maisie and I made a rule. Never fall for the bad boy…"

His lips curve into my favorite cocky smirk. "Then break the rules for me, baby."

epilogue
SAINT

5 MONTHS LATER

"THINK you might be my lucky charm, Golden Girl." I press a kiss to that sensitive space behind her ear that always makes her go soft in my hands. "And you know how superstitious us hockey players are. Guess that means I'm going to have to keep you forever."

Her giggle is soft and sweet next to my ear, almost as sweet as she tastes on my tongue. "You would've won the Frozen Four with *or* without me."

She's vastly underestimating how much I need her, like usual. I plan to spend the rest of the night showing her.

"God, you were so hot out there," she murmurs, fingers tangling into my necklace and tugging me to her mouth, hovering her lips beneath mine. When I lean forward for the kiss, her lips curve into a sexy little grin, and she pulls back, just enough to where I feel her breath dusting my lips but not close enough to where I can take her mouth. Teasing me. Driving me fucking insane. But I love it. I fucking love that in the time we've been together, she's grown more confident and playful and that she doesn't hesitate to tell me what she needs or wants. "It made me *so* wet watching you score that goal."

"Yeah? Why don't you show me, baby?"

She traces her tongue across her full bottom lip, and my dick feels like it might bust through my sweatpants at any moment. "Well, I *would*... but I only have an hour of ice time."

A deep groan rumbles out of me. "Fucking killing me."

Without a kiss, she drops my necklace and takes a step back. As if that's going to stop her pretty little pussy from throbbing for me.

"Sorry, but you know I have to focus. You are *very* distracting." Bending, she pulls off the guards on her blades, setting them on the boards, and moves to the rink door, pushing it open.

My lip quirks as I follow her out onto the ice. "That would be you in those fucking skirts." Today, it's bright yellow. Short, falling just below her ass. Her leotard is nearly the same shade, and together, they make her look like sunshine. *Literally* my Golden Girl.

"Are skirt kinks a thing? Because I am pretty positive you have one."

I skate up behind her and slap her ass, causing her giggle to echo around the rink.

"I see right through you, baby." My palms curve

around her hip as I haul her backward, flush against my front, and dip my head to her neck, nipping at the place where it meets her shoulder. "You provoke me because you *want* me to chase you around the rink. I remember how much you loved the day that I taped you up and made you squirt on my face in the penalty box. It's right over there…"

My words trail off as I reach up, gripping her chin between my fingers and turning her head toward mine. Her breath is coming quicker, in shallow pants, as she pushes her ass against me.

Yeah, she's remembering every filthy thing I did that day. Pretty sure she came even harder knowing that someone could've walked in. It was our ice time, but that didn't mean that the rink was closed.

My dirty girl.

Suddenly, I drop my hand and skate backward, putting distance between us, and she whips around, those lush green eyes blazing, lips parted.

"Forgot how you needed to focus. Sorry, baby." I smirk.

For a second, she simply pins me with her narrowed gaze, and I have to bite back a chuckle because she's getting a taste of her own medicine. Her hand flies to her hip, and she cocks a brow. "Fine. You stay on your side of the ice, and I'll stay on mine."

"Oh yeah?"

"Yep."

She's feigning like she's not affected by me, just the

way she did when we met here all those months ago. I knew better then, and I sure as fuck know better now.

Everything has changed in the last almost six months. In both of our lives.

We've changed.

But the one thing that's remained the same is how crazy I am about her.

How much I love her.

How she's the best thing that's ever happened to me, and I never take a single day for granted.

How we spend every night wrapped up together in our bed. Well, not officially *ours*. But I spend the majority of my time at her apartment, and it's starting to feel like a home to me.

We're not in a rush, just taking every day as it comes and enjoying getting to be together in fucking peace without looking over our shoulders and waiting for the other shoe to drop.

And I'm not ready to leave Mom just yet. It's been a huge adjustment for her since my father's been sentenced. He's only doing a year in the state prison for battery, which is far too fucking short for the hell that he's put her through. Put us both through.

But my mom filed for a protective order against him for when he is out, and I swear I have never been so proud. I've wished for this for most of my life, that one day she could be free. Could have peace. Could be happy. Every day is a step toward that for her.

She started therapy a couple of months ago, and after she told me how much she felt like it was helping her and healing her, I finally started going to a few sessions with her and now on my own.

I was one of those people who would've scoffed at the idea of sitting on a leather couch and talking to a fucking therapist who could never understand the shit that I've been through.

But now I know that's not true. It's not been an easy process, but it's... helped.

All of our trauma isn't just going to heal itself overnight, and I know that, but at least we're taking steps in the right direction.

Toward a future that we both deserve.

"You know how bad we are at following the rules, Golden Girl. Or have you forgotten?" My voice is low and rough as I watch her eyes go wide. "Do you need me to remind you?"

"Saint..." she warns.

Cat and mouse.

Our favorite game to play. At the rink... at home... wherever I can chase her down and fuck her until she screams.

Lennon has come into herself right before my eyes, and it's been the best fucking thing I've ever experienced.

She's happy and finally discovering the things that she's never allowed herself to experience because of her piece-of-shit, controlling father.

Who is now serving the next ten years at Dixon Correctional for the laundry list of charges he was convicted of just last month. The court process took a while, but finally, the asshole got what he deserved. And now, all of those families, including mine, have justice.

Knowing he's going to spend at least the next five years in prison for what he's done is good enough for me.

Lennon doesn't mention him much, if at all, and I think she tries her best to push it out of her head, to not give him any more space than he already has stolen from her.

The only thing that truly bothers her, I think, is her mom.

She hasn't reached out to her at all, and I know that hurts her. My girl is soft when it comes to her mother. But hopefully, one day, she can have at least some closure. She deserves that.

She deserves the entire fucking world, and I'm never going to stop trying to give it to her.

"I don't even know why we bother coming here together," she mumbles, rolling her eyes with a soft laugh.

Actually, I do.

Because we love this. My favorite thing about our relationship is the fact that we still give each other the same shit we did when we first met... only now, it's out of love and not spite.

I still love to provoke her and rile her up. Now, just so I can fuck the shit out of her.

She's still as mouthy as ever, and I hope like hell it never changes.

She's the other half of me, matching me toe to toe, never letting me be anything other than the best version of myself.

When the ground feels unsteady, she just holds on tighter.

"We come together because you love when I break the rules, baby. You always have."

The smile she flashes me hits me directly in the chest. "I guess you'll always be the bad boy. Just… *my* bad boy."

"And you'll always be *my* Golden Girl."

Need *more* of Saint & Lennon?
CLICK HERE to read an exclusive bonus scene of our favorite bad boy and his golden girl!

Red Card, the first in series of my college rugby book, will be releasing with Forever on August 12th! Want a sneak peek?
Turn the page to read Chapter One!

red card sneak peek

Chapter One
Cillian

"Welcome to Prescott University, *asshole*." The bloke wearing a Prescott Rugby Football Club jumper snickers, checking my shoulder roughly as he walks past me. I recognize him from the team roster I memorized on the plane ride from London.

I wasn't expecting a warm welcome from my new teammates. I knew better. I'd learned early on in life to set the bar low and that way you'll never be disappointed. And judging from the interactions I'd had so far, these wankers clearly don't want me here almost as much as I don't want to be here. Pretty fucking unfortunate for us all since we're going to be playing together for the next two years whether any of us like it or not.

"Yeah? Thanks for that. There a problem you want to

discuss, mate?" I say, turning to face him. "Wanna have a talk about it?"

The laughter from his friends standing beside him dies down before he whips around. "Yeah, *mate*, let's talk about it. Let's talk about how you're the fucking *charity* case that walked on to this team while everyone else earned a spot because no one else would take your fucked-up ass."

"Seems like you're *threatened* or something. Worried I'll take the spot your mummy bought for you?" I smirk tauntingly and step forward, now toe to toe with the arsehole who's running his mouth.

Even though I know this is exactly what this wanker wants—to rile me up and make me react, to get me off the team before I even have a chance to prove what I'm capable of—hot tendrils of anger lash through my body, my temper rising by the second. My hands fist at my sides as I try to tamp it down. Lock it away. Stay in control of the situation so I can stay in control of my *future*.

Before he can respond, the door to the athletic building flies open and a tall, burly man with salt-and-pepper hair busts through.

"Cairney...my office. *Now*. You're late," he spits out before turning and disappearing back inside the building.

Goddamn it. Of course, my new coach would see this shit.

Less than twenty-four hours in this shithole, and I'm already regretting stepping foot on campus.

"Toss off," I mutter, my shoulder hitting his roughly as I brush past him toward my new coach's office.

I can't afford to start off on the wrong foot with Brody

St. James. I can't afford any missteps, which means I can't let this happen again.

Not when my old coach, Coach Thomas, pulled so many strings to make this happen. Not when my shot in America is riding on me being a model player and staying the fuck out of trouble. If I don't, I'll be on a one-way ticket back to London, and my last chance at playing rugby professionally is gone. I can kiss my dream of playing professional rugby goodbye. Forever.

No more chances.

Simple as that. It's the same thing I've been repeating to myself over and over since I stepped off the plane. I've run out of chances, and playing at Prescott is a last-ditch effort to hold on to my rugby career.

I can't fuck this up. I won't. If not for myself then for Aisling and her future. My sister's all I have left, and I can't let her down.

All of this is in my hands. My responsibility.

The doors of the athletic building are painted a deep, rich burgundy, and the heavy wood creaks when I swing it open to step inside. It doesn't take me long to find the coach's office at the end of the trophy-lined hallway, with a bronze plaque outside the door inscribed with the name BRODY ST. JAMES.

My knuckles rapt against the heavy wooden door twice before the voice on the other side calls me in. When I step inside, my new coach is sitting behind a large mahogany desk with a tight scowl on this face. I'll admit, he's pretty fucking intimidating.

Or maybe that's simply because this is the man who

holds the strings to my future in his hands. Either way, it's a feeling I'm not accustomed to experiencing. I'm the player who the sports reports have deemed intimidating because of my aggression on and off the pitch.

And now...the tables have turned.

"Coach." I walk to the front of his desk and extend my hand. He looks down at it for a moment, his eyes dragging over the dark ink on the top that trails up and disappears into the sleeve of my jumper, before shaking it. "I'm sorry about that out ther—"

He drops my hand, cutting me off. "Sit. I've got ten minutes before practice starts."

Without hesitating, I drop down into the worn leather armchair across from him.

Coach leans forward and rests his forearms on the desk. "I'm not going to lie and say I'm particularly happy to have you here. I'm not going to bullshit for the sake of feelings. It's not how I run my program. Stay long enough and you'll see that. You messed up in London, and you're here because I owed a favor. *You* are now that favor, Cairney."

I grit my teeth together so hard that a deep ache forms in the muscle of my jaw. The old Cillian, the one who fucked up and landed us here in the first place, would've told him to fuck off and walked out of his office without a backward glance. Maybe thrown out a few more choice words. But I can't be that guy anymore. Or at least I'm trying not to be.

The guy who acts before he thinks. Who lets his temper, and grief, control him.

I've just got to keep it together, put my head down, and focus until I graduate and get the hell out of here. Until I can get back to London and play rugby. Really start my life.

Coach doesn't give me the chance to respond before he continues. "First and foremost, understand that whatever the hell just happened out there with Banes, it's not happening again. I don't give second chances. Being *here* is your second chance. The only chance you get. I don't baby my players, I'm not hand-holding, and I run a tight program. I know you've had a problem with aggression off the pitch. Fighting."

My shoulder dips. "Here and there."

Not exactly the full truth, but he's got the file in front of him, and I know he's read it.

We both know exactly what put me here. And it wasn't just my aggression.

"If you want to stay on this team, you walk the straight and narrow. No fighting. No drugs. No illegal activities. No fucking your way through the cheerleading team. No creating tension with your teammates. You're not the only one with something at stake here. This program operates on private funding. Boosters who expect a championship win this year, which means that we can't afford a fuckup. Of any nature."

"Understood," I retort, my jaw hardening again as we stare off over the desk.

He nods. "Good. We're on the same page then. Look, I've reviewed your tapes, Cairney…You're a damn good player. Naturally talented in ways that some guys work their entire life to be and never achieve. Don't waste it."

It's not the first time I've heard this. From my coach back in London, from scouts, from my teammates, my sister. From the voice in my head telling me not to end up like my father, who's never been anything but an alcoholic fuckup with a temper that puts mine to shame.

Truthfully, it's been a long time since I've felt like myself. The guy I used to be before Mum died. I've spent the last two years fighting to make it back to that person, and I've got the scars to show it. On every inch of me, inside and out. I spiraled so far down that sometimes I feel like I'll never make it out alive.

What I want more than anything is to leave the mess I made in London behind and start over. To take the opportunity I've been given even if it means moving to a new country and playing for a team of blokes who don't want me here. I can deal with it if it means that I'll have a chance at playing professionally and making sure that Aisling is taken care of.

"I have no plans to," I respond in a clipped tone. "I'm here to play rugby. That's it. I'm not going to cause any trouble. I know that doesn't mean much right now, and I get it—I haven't exactly shown anyone that my word means much, but I want to change that. Starting here. Starting now."

"All right then." Lifting his wrist, Coach glances down at his watch before looking back at me. "I've got to head to practice, but we can talk a bit more later. There's one thing I want to say before I go. You're walking on halfway through a season, Cairney. There's inevitably going to be some challenges. These guys have been playing together for years. There's a dynamic in place, and I know that it's going to take some time for everyone to adjust. And not only that... these guys have a lot on the line, and they know it. Doesn't help that they're feeling the pressure of expectation. I just need your assurance that you're going to give fitting in and becoming a member of this team everything you've got." His voice is low and solemn as he says exactly what I've been thinking since I got the transfer confirmation.

I already have a fairly good grasp on what it is I'm walking into, especially after the confrontation that happened a few minutes ago, but if anything, it's only making me more determined. To show not only Coach that I'm going to follow through, but also the arseholes who think they'll get rid of me as easily as I came here.

I nod, raking a hand through my hair. "I understand. You're not going to have any issues out of me. I'll make an effort."

"Good. Let's head down to the pitch and you can observe for a bit and meet Matthews, our assistant coach." Standing, he rounds the desk toward his door, and I rise, following behind him. "You'll officially meet the team tomorrow, before practice."

The pitch is a short walk from Coach's office and when we arrive, the team has already started their training session. He doesn't attempt to bring me out there to introduce me to everyone, and honestly I'm thankful for it. I'd rather observe from the touchlines and see how they operate as a team from the outside.

Coach St. James introduces me to a short, lean guy with red hair that's so bright it looks unnatural, and I almost wonder if the bloke dyes it.

"Cairney, this is Assistant Coach Matthews. I need to get out there, but I'll leave you two to it and I'll see you tomorrow before practice." He brushes past us onto the pitch, leaving us alone.

Coach Matthews turns to me and offers his hand. "Good to have you, Cairney. I've seen you on the pitch, and I'm impressed. I wanna see you adapt and do the same thing here," he says as he drops my hand, then shoves his back into his pocket.

"I plan on it."

"Got a good team this year," he says, nodding toward the pitch as they run a phase of play. "Powerful. A solid defense, disciplined. And that makes it hard to break through the line. Some fast guys that focus on moving the ball and exploiting gaps in defense."

I nod along but keep my eyes trained on the pitch, watching as they go for a try. He's not wrong; they're bloody good. Their bond is evident in the way they work together and execute plays. These guys are powerful and skilled playmakers. That's the best you could ask for in a team, and it's not just about being talented. It's all about communication and how it plays out on the pitch.

"And I think you'll be the perfect addition to the team if you can keep your head on straight." He adds, "Conditioning at least once a week, two sessions on the pitch until spring games start. I expect you at all of them, putting in the work just like everyone else."

I shove my hands into the pockets of my trousers and nod. "I'll be there."

A long, hard whistle blows down the touchlines, and we both turn to see a girl stomping out onto the pitch over to one of the blokes, her long espresso braid swishing behind her. From our position, I can make out the delicate slope of her nose, the high cheekbones, plump pink lips, pale, creamy skin and a blazing fire in her eyes.

She's *pissed*. And proper fit. But who the hell is she?

When she makes it to the pitch she stops in front of the tallest bloke on the team and shakes her head while sporting a fierce scowl. "Soccer tryouts are in two weeks. If you're not gonna commit to a tackle maybe you should try out."

"But I—" he sputters.

"But I? But I? Drive with your legs and make the damn tackle, *Williams*. Jesus, are we playing rugby or ballet out here?" She does a mock twirl, which would be rather comical if she didn't *actually* look a little scary taking on a guy who's at least a foot taller and outweighs her by at least a hundred pounds.

Holy shit.

Coach Matthews chuckles next to me. "And that…is Rory St. James."

My gaze bounces to him, and then back to the tiny spitfire on the pitch who's now giving someone else a verbal lashing. Most guys wouldn't take a girl like this seriously, but these guys are looking at her with a mixture of fear and awe in their gazes.

"*That's* Coach's... *daughter*?" I mutter, my eyes still widened in shock.

"Yep. She's our equipment manager, but that girl knows more about rugby than half these guys do. You'll meet her when you meet the rest of the team. Look, all I'd worry about, Cairney, is putting in your time and making rugby your top priority. We're not asking for perfection. We're asking you to show up, do your job, and stay out of trouble. Earn your spot on this team. Earn their trust."

I nod. "I know. And I know that I'm an asset. If you give me time, I'll prove it not to just you and Coach St. James, but to them."

Silence hangs between us for a beat, both of us still watching what's unfolding on the pitch.

"You wanna know the *real* secret to getting in with those guys?" He jerks his head toward the feisty brunette on the pitch. "It's *her*."

Fall in love with rugby and Cillian's thighs on August 12th when **Red Card** releases everywhere.
Click here to PREORDER your copy!

need moore?

Want instant access to bonus scenes, exclusive giveaways, and content you can't find ANYWHERE else?

Sign up for my newsletter here and get all of the goods!

In your audiobook era? Find all of my audiobooks here!

Want to chat with me about life, get exclusive giveaways and see behind the scenes content? Join my reader group Give Me Moore

also by maren moore

Totally Pucked

Change on the Fly

Sincerely, The Puck Bunny

The Scorecard

The Final Score

The Penalty Shot

Playboy Playmaker

Orleans U

Homerun Proposal

Catching Feelings

Walkoff Wedding

Standalone

The Enemy Trap

The Newspaper Nanny

Strawberry Hollow

The Mistletoe Bet

A Festive Feud

The Christmas List

Orleans U

Homerun Proposal

Catching Feelings

Walkoff Wedding

Rookie Mistake

Prescott University

Red Card

about the author

Maren Moore is an Amazon Top 20 Best-selling sports romance author. Her books are packed full of heat and all the feels that will always come with a happily ever after. She resides in southern Louisiana with her husband, two little boys and their fur babies. When she isn't on a deadline, she's probably reading yet another Dramione fan fic, rewatching cult classic horror movies, or daydreaming about the 90's.

You can connect with her on social media or find information on her books here ➡ here.

www.ingramcontent.com/pod-product-compliance
Lightning Source LLC
LaVergne TN
LVHW041738060526
838201LV00046B/853